Dark Moon

Dark Moon

The Spirit Wild Series

KATE DOUGLAS

APHRODISIA

KENSINGTON PUBLISHING CORP.

www.kensingtonbooks.com

APHRODISIA BOOKS are published by

Kensington Publishing Corp.
119 West 40th Street
New York, NY 10018

All Kensington titles, imprints, and distributed lines are available at special quantity discounts for bulk purchases for sales promotion, premiums, fund-raising, educational, or institutional use.

Special book excerpts or customized printings can also be created to fit specific needs. For details, write or phone the office of the Kensington Special Sales Manager: Kensington Publishing Corp., 119 West 40th Street, New York, NY 10018. Attn. Special Sales Department. Phone: 1-800-221-2647.

Aphrodisia and the A logo Reg. U.S. Pat. & TM Off.

ISBN-13: 978-1-61773-474-8
ISBN-10: 1-61773-474-8
First Kensington Trade Paperback Printing: February 2014

eISBN-13: 978-1-4201-2810-9
eISBN-10: 1-4201-2810-8
First Kensington Electronic Edition: February 2014

10 9 8 7 6 5 4 3 2 1

Printed in the United States of America

This book is dedicated with a very sincere and heartfelt thank you to my editors—Audrey LaFehr, who read my first Wolf Tales manuscript nine years ago, took that online serial of short stories, and helped me turn it into a series of twelve novels and nine novellas. Audrey gave me the freedom to write my stories without restraint, which is a gift beyond measure. And to her amazing assistant, Martin Biro, who is my new editor, now faced with the difficult task of making me look as if I know what I'm doing. I wish you much luck, Martin! I extend the same gratitude to the entire crew at Kensington Publishing: marketing, publicity, editorial, art, production, digital, and management. You're an amazing team, and you've made this journey way too much fun. Thank you all.

Acknowledgments

Many thanks and much appreciation to my terrific beta readers: Lynne Thomas, Kerry Parker, Jan Takane, Lynn Sicoli, Rose Toubbeh, Rhonda Wilson, Ann Jacobs, Karen Woods, and Nicole Passante. I don't even want to admit some of the things you folks caught in this manuscript, thus preventing me from looking like an absolute idiot. For what it's worth, I really do know which way the earth spins, and that it can't be late morning in Montana when it's barely dawn in Connecticut. Really. I know this.

1

Igmutaka, spirit guide, puma shapeshifter, and currently a very nervous man, stood at the foot of the birthing bed, hands raised in supplication to his gods and the woman's goddess. Tala Temple-Fuentes squatted amid the tangled sheets with her mate, Miguel Fuentes—a man who had long been Igmutaka's charge—supporting her gravid frame.

Her other mate clung to her hand, gazing at her with such love and so much intensity, it was almost as if AJ Temple planned to push the babes out himself.

There were two. The male—the one created from the seed of the white man—would be a strong boy. AJ was a good man, and his son would grow to be a powerful warrior, an ideal sibling for the child Igmutaka waited to meet.

The one who mattered to him most.

The girl child, the one born of Miguel's seed, was to be the first female ever in Igmutaka's charge. Her father, like AJ, was a powerful Chanku shapeshifter, a good, strong man. Called Mik, he was the latest in the long line of Lakota Sioux warriors who had looked to Igmutaka as their spiritual guide.

Always, Igmutaka had watched over the male progeny, but this child was different—not merely because of her gender.

He felt her strength, her power—the feminine power so different from that of the males he had guided. He'd been aware of this babe almost from the moment of conception. He'd known she was special, though he still didn't understand how or why.

He glanced up. He'd been unaware of the bedroom filling so quickly. Other females—shapeshifters all—coming to share the pain and the joy of the one who labored, using their minds and bodies to ease Tala as she pushed the babies from her womb. Men arrived, ready to share in the celebration of new members joining their pack, but also generously taking on Tala's pain.

It was all good. All as it should be.

Igmutaka focused once again on the mother.

She grunted and strained. He had no time to think, no time to question why he should be the one who slipped his hands beneath her straining body and caught the babe amid a wash of fluids and blood, caught her in his big hands and stared into eyes that saw him in a way no one else had ever seen him before.

He held the squirming bundle of new life as his own impossibly long years flashed before him. Hers so new and fresh, his beginning so long ago that most of his childhood was lost to memory. He knew he must have started in a time long past, though not as a babe like this. No, he'd not been a helpless child, born of woman into an ancient world.

He knew he'd been a puma cub. Born one amid a litter of siblings, though he had no memory of that life.

He'd been spirit far too long.

He'd taken on a physical body again only in the past few years, running as a wild puma so that he could interact with the Chanku shapeshifters who had called him from the spirit world.

Then, mere weeks ago, he'd manifested as a human male for the first time, the same male who stood here now, holding Tala and Mik's newborn daughter. A beautiful, dark-haired girl who would one day grow to be a strong and beautiful woman.

Adam, one of their healers, cut the umbilical cord, separating the newborn from her mother. One of the women quickly wiped away the blood and afterbirth on the child he held as Tala delivered the second babe. Twins. A boy and a girl. Both strong, healthy young.

Igmutaka bowed his head as he placed the newborn against her mother's breast. Bowed to the babe and to fate, to the woman this child would grow to be.

A woman Igmutaka knew would change his life for all time.

New Haven, Connecticut, thirty years later

Star Fuentes heard the soft tone that signaled her mother's call, checked the time, and realized she still had a few minutes before her date was due to arrive.

She took a sip of her wine, flipped on the phone, and smiled at her mom, a sixty-two-year-old woman who appeared to be in her late twenties. That was one of the wonderful things about being Chanku—aging slowed and practically stopped at the prime of life.

Tala's mates looked just as young—early thirties at most—both of them so damned good looking it was hard for Star to think of them as her two dads. In reality, Mik was sixty-eight and AJ already seventy-two. As with all Chanku, each faced an unlimited lifespan with those same youthful bodies and minds.

Star quit woolgathering as Tala's broad grin and sparkling amber eyes chased away the discontent that had followed her like a cloud over the past weeks. "Hey, Mom. What's up?"

"You mean other than your fathers?"

Star slapped her hand over her mouth to keep from spewing wine on the small screen. "Too much information, ya know?"

Tala's laughter sent a shaft of homesickness through Star. She hadn't been home to Montana for much too long. She missed Mik, her biological father, and her other dad, AJ, her mom's second mate. Hell, she even missed her damned spirit guide, but that was the last thing she'd ever admit.

"I just wondered when you were planning to come home." Tala's smile slipped. "I miss you, honey. You've been gone so long."

"I visited last Christmas." A short visit—not nearly enough time to reconnect with her mountain home. With her family. Her pack.

"You know that visit was much too brief, and you only let us talk you into it because it was your thirtieth birthday." Her mom sighed. "Don't you think it's time to come back? You're a pack animal at heart, Star." Tala laughed, but Star felt the sting of tears in her eyes. "You can only stay away for just so long, honey. Even Jack misses you."

"Jack said that?" Star rolled her eyes. "Now that's hard to believe."

"You're not kidding. For your twin to admit something like that, well, it's downright scary." Then the smile slipped from Tala's lips and she softly added, "It's been almost fourteen years, sweetheart."

Scrambling for yet another excuse, Star glanced at the stack of papers lying beside her computer. "I don't know, Mom. I'm thinking of applying for another doctoral program. I'll need to make the decision this week."

"Star, don't you think you have enough letters after your name? Don't you miss the pack? Miss your family?"

So much it hurt even to think about it, but she wasn't ready. Not yet. A brisk knock on the door caught her attention.

"Gotta go, Mom. My date's here, but I promise to think about it. I love you."

"I love you, too. The dads send their love. Sunny said to tell you hi."

"Thanks. Give her a big hug for me, and the dads, too. Bye, Mom."

"Star? Before you go, one last thing."

"What's that?"

"You can't hide from him forever, sweetheart. Some things are stronger than we are, and he's one of them. I love you."

A shiver raced along Star's spine as the screen went dark. In all the years she'd been away, her mother had never asked her to come home to stay, had never mentioned the real reason she'd chosen to live so far from the pack. Why now?

Besides, she wasn't hiding. Not really.

He knew where to find her.

Another knock brought Star to her feet, and her womb clenched in what she knew was probably futile anticipation.

That was the problem with living among humans. Her Chanku libido ran circles around that of the average male. Fourteen years of less than satisfactory sex was probably reason enough to call it quits and head home, but damn it all, the risk was too great.

She'd gotten her spirit guide's promise to let her live life on her own terms while she was away at school. Of course, he probably hadn't figured she'd make a career out of getting an education, but she knew that once she returned, he'd be right back in her life.

Taking over her life.

She'd grown up with two fathers, a concerned mother, an overprotective twin brother, and a pack full of uncles and aunties watching out for her. None of them had threatened her independence the way Igmutaka managed with nothing more than a soft suggestion, a raised eyebrow, or the turn of a phrase.

Talk about frustrating. He protected her and guarded her against harm, which also meant protecting her from life in general. He'd also managed to keep all the eligible boys away at the same time, but that wasn't the worst part.

No, it was the fact he was absolutely beautiful, and she'd loved him. Loved him as only a young girl could love. Deeply, with all of her heart and soul. Tall and lean with smooth, bronzed skin, gorgeous green eyes and long, thick dark hair, he had an androgynous beauty that would make him look as striking if he'd been a woman, yet there was no doubting the masculinity of the man. Nope. No doubt at all.

Star practically whimpered as she drew his image close. So beautiful as a cougar, with a sinewy grace that carried over to his human form. He'd rarely shown himself to her as a man, yet his was the face that filled her dreams, her fantasies, and her lonely nights.

Unfortunately, he didn't feel the same way. Igmutaka was her spirit guide, fated to protect her, not to bed her. She'd loved him without reservation from the time she could remember— first as a father figure, and then when she'd realized he was still young and sexy and she was definitely growing older and interested, as a potential mate.

He'd treated her as something fragile. Untouchable. And while she knew he wasn't celibate, he'd certainly kept his charge—the one he called Mikaela Star—that way. She'd not lost her virginity to a man until she finally left home for college.

She still didn't know what the big deal was.

She knew other Chanku women managed to have wonderful sex with humans, though they all eventually mated with Chanku, but she'd never once found satisfaction with a human male.

Not that she didn't keep trying, but since she'd rarely had the chance to have sex with another Chanku, and only on the rare occasions when one of the guys visited her in New Haven, she really had very little for comparison, goddess be damned.

She pushed Igmutaka and a lifetime of sexual frustration out of her mind and opened the door. Her date stood there, poised to knock a third time. He was tall and handsome, his smile as perfect as modern technology could make it.

And for the life of her, she couldn't remember his name.

"Are you ready?" he asked.

"As ready as I'll ever be." She flashed him a bright smile as she grabbed her bag and a soft wrap. At least as ready as she'd be with a man she hardly knew, but who, at least, wasn't her insufferable, sensual, pain-in-the-ass spirit guide.

Sunny Daye sprawled , limp and sated, over the long, lean body of her lover. He was gorgeous, absolutely spectacular in bed, and it just about broke her heart knowing he'd never satisfy that empty spot in her soul, the part of her crying out for a mate.

His long fingers stroked her left breast, and then he playfully tapped her nipple. It tightened immediately, and she felt the touch between her legs as her womb rippled in response.

Supporting her upper body on her elbows, she raised her head and glared at him. Why in the hell couldn't he be the one? She'd known, though. Since the very first time he'd made love to her—the night he gently took her virginity so many years ago—that as much as she loved him, she couldn't love him *that way*. Still, the man could make magic when they came together. She sighed, flopped back on the mattress, and arched into his touch. "I hope you're planning to follow through with that."

Igmutaka gave her a long, lazy smile, reached down, and stroked his sizeable erection with one hand. "Have you ever known me not to follow through?"

She felt her anger sliding away. It wasn't his fault he was absolutely perfect, and at the same time perfectly wrong. For her, at least. She knew the one he loved. Knew that, so far, anyway, that love wasn't being returned. "Star's an idiot."

He grinned as he stroked a line from her throat to her pubes. "Mikaela Star is young. She has yet to discover her path. It will, of course, lead directly to me."

"You sound so sure." She laughed softly as his hands slid up her body and he stroked the sensitive skin beneath her breasts. "What if you're wrong? What if she chooses another?"

Lying beside her, he teased the nipple he'd tapped earlier, working it gently with teeth and tongue for a moment before lifting his head. His lips were shiny—as slick and shiny as her nipple—and they parted on a soft smile. "Then I will kill the bastard."

Sunny laughed. Ig was not really a killer . . . was he?

He grinned at her. "I've not told this to many, but it was foretold when she was still in Tala's womb. I knew Mikaela Star was special when Tala carried her and we actually communicated before her birth. When Tala pushed her forth and she fell into my hands, I knew she was mine." He gazed at Sunny over the dark red nipple he'd so skillfully aroused. "One does not question a gift from the gods."

"I see." She moaned as he lowered his head and began working on the other breast. After only a moment of pure bliss, Ig raised his head again.

"You are a gift as well, Sunny. Not for me, though. Your man is out there. I sense him drawing close. You will know him soon." He tilted his head and frowned. "Very soon."

My man? Soon? Sunny shoved herself up on her elbows so quickly she knocked Igmutaka aside. "Where is he? Who is he? How do you know?"

Laughing, Ig rolled to his back. "I don't know the details. I just know he's coming." He sat up and his look grew pensive as he shrugged those wide shoulders. "Just as I know that tonight Mikaela Star is with yet another young man, another lover who will disappoint her. Before long, she will accept that I am the one who loves her, that I am the only one who can make her happy."

The yearning in his voice was almost her undoing. Sunny ran her fingers through the thick hair tumbled across his forehead. "I know you're not my mate, Ig, but you've never disappointed me, and you always make me smile."

He leaned close and kissed her. Covered her small body once again with his much larger one. She arched beneath him, finding the broad head of his penis already pressing against her labia. With a slight tilt to her hips, she opened to him, felt the slick burn as he filled her, sliding that thick length all the way to the end of her vaginal sheath.

He was big and hard and fit her perfectly. He was funny and sweet, brave and powerful, and so beautiful he made her ache.

A perfect man.

Just not a perfect mate.

At least not for Sunny Daye.

After a really nice dinner, they'd ended up back at his apartment, which was a good thing, especially since Star still hadn't recalled her date's name. She finally spotted it on a framed diploma on the wall. Haydon. His name was Haydon Smith—she finally recalled meeting him in one of the libraries on campus.

Another good thing about ending up at Haydon's apartment was that it was his place, not hers. She hated having to ask a man to leave after sex, but she had sex with a lot of guys and she didn't want them hanging around afterward, especially when they never managed to leave her satisfied.

This guy hadn't even tried very hard, but he'd certainly managed to find his own satisfaction. More than once. Now he slept soundly, so she carefully lifted his arm off of her breasts and slid out from beneath him. As she turned away to get out of the bed, that same arm snaked around her waist.

"Leaving, Star?"

Well, crap. "Uh, yeah. I need to get home." She glanced over her shoulder and realized he was wide awake, glaring at her for whatever reason.

"What if I don't want you to go yet?"

She shrugged her shoulders. "It's late. I had a good time, but I really have to leave."

His grasp around her waist tightened. He was a lot bigger than her, and he pulled her back across the bed and roughly nuzzled her neck. "Mmmmm. You smell good." He bit her earlobe hard enough for it to hurt, but she refused to react.

He was really starting to piss her off.

"You know what the guys call you?" He tightened his hold around her waist. "The Ballbuster. Word is you can go all night and then walk away like it was nothing." His voice dropped to a low, threatening growl. "I haven't had all night yet, Star. You can walk away when I say you can walk. Not before."

Now this was a first. She tried to break free of his grasp, but he merely held on tighter. His breath was hot as he spoke directly into her ear. "I think you owe me the rest of the night, don't you, Star? That was a really expensive dinner."

She'd managed almost fourteen years of world travel, college, and grad school without guys acting anything but grateful after a night of sex. Plus, not a single man had ever guessed she wasn't human. Though the world knew shapeshifters existed among them, she'd chosen to guard her Chanku origins and keep her abilities secret from all but a select few on campus.

Maybe this jerk was a sign. Maybe Mom was right—it was time to go home. And she wasn't thinking of merely going back to her apartment.

She shifted. Even though the wolf came most naturally, she chose her cougar form, twisting her strong, sinuous body out of his grasp as her date suddenly screamed like a little girl and scrambled across the bed so fast he fell off the other side.

Star merely stretched out over the bed, hooked her claws deep into the mattress until the fabric ripped, hung her head over the edge, and stared at him. Eyes wide, he stared back at her. She stretched one broad paw toward him and further unsheathed her long, curved nails.

Babbling, he scrambled backward on all four until he hit the wall, so she crouched on the edge of the mattress and raised her hindquarters as if to leap. Snarling, she let a bit of saliva drip from her open jaws and flexed her muscles.

An acrid stench filled her sensitive nostrils as a pool of urine stained the carpet between his legs. Star chuffed, which was the closest her puma could get to laughter, spun about on the bed, and shifted once more.

She didn't even look his way as she snagged her clothes off the floor and quickly dressed. Grabbing the door handle, she glanced over her shoulder. He was still sitting in a soggy, stinking heap on the floor across the room. She gave him her most disdainful look. "Don't ever pull that stunt on a woman again, or I will hunt you down."

Then she walked out of his room and headed back to her apartment.

Not quite the way she'd expected her night to end, but at least it hadn't been boring. And, if nothing else, it had helped make up her mind about the doctoral program.

Her mom was right. She had enough letters after her name, and she'd played the coward long enough. It was time to return to the pack, even if it meant finally having it out with her spirit guide. Igmutaka had been running her life for far too long—the fact she'd not felt comfortable returning home was proof she'd given him more control over her life than he deserved.

The fact he didn't love her was on him, and it was his loss, not hers. It was time for Star to move forward.

It was early morning when she finally reached her own apartment—still much too early to call Montana. She showered, grabbed something to eat, and gave her folks until six before she finally called home. Her father answered, and she almost broke down and cried when his beautiful face flashed on the screen. There was something so elemental about him with his dark skin and strong Lakota Sioux and Hispanic features, an innate power that few men wore as well. Only Igmutaka came close. She missed her dad. Missed her mom and missed her other dad, AJ, just as much.

"What's up, sweetie? Mom said she talked to you last night. Is everything okay?"

She thought about that, and realized that, yes, it was absolutely wonderful. Finally. "Everything's good, Dad. I've decided to come home, though not right away. I'm hoping for a chance to spend some time alone once I leave Connecticut. Is the cabin at Lassen free? I thought I'd go there for a week or so."

"We'll make sure it's available. When do you need it?"

She loved that about her parents. No questions. They just did what they could to make her life easier. "It's going to take me at least a week to get my stuff packed up and shipped, and probably another week to make the drive. If I can't get out of my lease, I'll have to sublet the apartment, but that shouldn't be a problem. It's a great location."

"It's going to be cold at the cabin. No one's been there for a while. I'll have it stocked for you. Will you be flying to California or driving?"

"Driving. And Dad? Thank you. I love you."

"I love you, too, Mikaela Star. I've missed you. We've all missed you. Be safe. Come home to us as quickly as you can."

Mik grabbed his coffee and walked out onto the deck. AJ and Tala still slept, but he'd had a feeling his daughter might call this morning. The connection between them had always been strong, but lately he'd felt her yearning for something she wasn't finding in her stuffy, academic world of New Haven, Connecticut.

Of course, anyone with half a brain would realize that what she really wanted, what she needed, was right here in Montana. In fact, it appeared that his daughter's fate was strolling up the path to the house on four huge paws at this very moment.

Mik stepped back inside the house and poured another cup of coffee. It was waiting when the huge puma leapt up on the deck and shifted. Mik handed the cup to Igmutaka, who took it without a word and sat in the Adirondack chair beside Mik's.

The two men sipped their coffee in silence, and Mik couldn't help but think of his grandfather and the council meetings among the elders, when the old men would sit around the fire at night and make decisions concerning the tribe.

The man beside him—though definitely Native American—didn't look like an elder. No, he was a beautiful man who appeared to be in his early thirties, even though he was technically older than any living thing, as far as Mik knew.

Right now, Ig merely looked conflicted.

Mik knew exactly what was bothering him, but he wasn't about to make this easy. Not for any man interested in courting his daughter, and certainly not for the spirit guide whose job it was to protect Mikaela Star, not bed her.

Igmutaka sighed and sat quietly for a few minutes. Then he set the mug aside and faced Mik. "You know why I'm here," he said.

Mik nodded. "Tell me."

Ig raised one dark eyebrow. "I should have known you'd give me a hard time."

Shaking his head, Mik chuckled softly. "It's too important to make it easy. A decision such as yours, the prize you seek, is not something to take lightly. Tell me what it is you want."

Nodding slowly, Ig agreed. "As you know, I have watched over your line for time beyond memory, always serving the firstborn male until the next generation is conceived. I guided your grandfather's grandfather and his father, and all the men before him. I watched over your grandfather, and when his only issue was a daughter, I waited for the next male. Her son. That was you."

Mik nodded. He remembered a time when he'd doubted his spirit guide's existence, when he'd languished in prison and wondered if the presence he'd felt beside him truly existed, and if he did, why he'd allowed Mik to end up in a prison cell.

But that cell was the place where he had met AJ and had fallen in love. Where Ulrich Mason had found both men and helped them find their true heritage as Chanku shapeshifters. Had Igmutaka had a part in that? Mik had never asked.

He glanced up and realized Ig was smiling at him. "I did," he said. "At least as much as I was able. So did your goddess. Years later, when you called me to help your packmates and I once again felt the warmth of living flesh, I found it impossible to remain a creature of spirit."

Mik chuckled. "So you're going to blame me for all of your problems?"

This time Igmutaka laughed out loud. "If I was going to blame anyone, it would have to be Mei and Oliver. It was their inability to mate because they couldn't shift into compatible creatures that called me forth in the first place. I like them both, and I like my life as a man too much to complain. No, I'm merely stating the facts, that I was content as spirit until you and your people reminded me what joy could be had in a living, breathing body. But I still watched over you. And I was prepared to watch over your firstborn."

"Even though you knew my firstborn would be female?"

Shrugging, Ig leaned back in his chair. "That threw me off at first. What did I know about watching over a female child? But the gods and your goddess decreed, and I obeyed. And then she spoke to me. Still in the womb, as yet unformed, and she spoke in my mind. Do you have any idea how amazing your daughter is, Miguel? How perfect?"

Mik turned and gazed out across the big meadow and remembered Star as a mere toddler, shifting into a wolf cub and then later that same day becoming a cougar. She truly was amazing. Brilliant, beautiful, and right now terribly unhappy.

If Igmutaka could make her happy, Mik wouldn't stand in the man's way. "Mikaela Star is special. She's always been special."

Igmutaka sighed—the sound of a frustrated male. "But why did she leave? I don't understand everything of modern ways. Why did she force me out of her life?"

At least this was a question Mik could answer. He had, after all, mated his own very independent woman. "You watched over her too closely, my friend. Star has a mind of her own—a brilliant mind. She is an independent woman. A strong woman. You didn't allow her to test herself. To take risks."

Ig bowed his head. "I was so afraid for her. Afraid she'd be hurt, afraid she would be unhappy. . . ."

"Afraid of losing her?"

"That, too, and yet that is exactly what happened. I pushed her away, and I lost her." He raised his head and faced Mik, green eyes sparkling with tears. Mik's heart went out to him—never before had he seen Igmutaka show vulnerability. The man could be stoic and strong, fun loving, even silly if the occasion called for it.

But not this. Never had he looked so completely lost.

Igmutaka nodded, silently admitting the power Mik's daughter held over him. "I want the chance to try to win her back. To win her love. When she was young, I fought against that need, the need of a man for a woman. She was my charge, just a young girl, not a woman to warm my bed, and yet it took her leaving me to realize that was exactly what I wanted. What I need.

"A partner. A lover. A mate. One who can not only stand up to me but stand beside me. This could be my only chance. I sense that she has chosen to return, and I would like your permission to court her. To show her that I've learned, that I can stand beside her, not expect her to follow me, but to be my partner."

Igmutaka was a strong, proud man. Mik wondered how much it cost him to speak the words in his heart. "You don't need my permission, Ig, though I'm honored you would ask. Mikaela Star is her own woman."

The spirit guide laughed. "You're wrong, my friend. I want your permission, so that if I am successful and she chooses me as her mate, you will not have cause to disapprove."

Mik had known this day was coming since Tala pushed his daughter out of her womb directly into the spirit guide's capable hands, but he'd never imagined what it would feel like, to sit here and sense the desperation in the man's voice, to realize how important this moment was to all of them.

Not merely to his daughter, to Mik, AJ, and Tala, but to everyone. They were more than family. They were pack.

He reached for Igmutaka's right arm and grasped him about the forearm. Ig's fingers closed tightly around his arm, and Mik stared at the link they made. Finally, he nodded and raised his head. "I've believed since the beginning that you were destined for my daughter. You have my permission to court her. You do not have my permission to hurt her, to use your powers as her spirit guide to force her feelings or her decision, or to do anything at all that goes against her free will."

Ig let out a huge breath of air. "Thank you. I would never hurt Mikaela Star. She was my charge, the one I watched over."

Mik chuckled. "Except when she told you to get lost."

Suddenly agitated, Ig shoved both hands through his hair. Then he tilted his head and stared directly at Mik. "She did more than that. I haven't been entirely honest with you, Miguel. When she sent me away, she severed our spiritual tie. I don't think she understood the power of her words, but my destined role as her spirit guide ended at that moment. I still watch over her from afar, but I am no longer truly her guide." Again, he sighed. "I've not admitted that to anyone, and hardly to myself. I didn't want to accept the truth."

But it explained so many things. "Ig, that changes nothing. Spirit guide or not, you've watched out for her, haven't you?"

Ig nodded. "I have. I could take no other course."

No, Ig would never give up on his charge, even one as head-strong as Mikaela Star. Softly Mik added, "She'll be at the cabin in Lassen in about two weeks. She plans to stay there for a while. Said she needs time alone before returning to the pack."

Igmutaka raised his head and grinned. "It's been a long time since I traveled near Mount Lassen. It's quite beautiful in the fall." He stood, his naked body glistening in the early morning light, his beauty almost blinding. Mik was reminded of a conversation with his other mate.

AJ, a man who, until Tala, had always preferred the company of men, had said he found it fascinating that Igmutaka, the most beautiful and sensual man among them, had never appealed sexually to either Mik or himself. Now Mik fully understood why.

He'd always figured it was because Igmutaka had been his grandfather's spirit guide, and then his own. Now he realized it was probably because Igmutaka was meant to be their son-in-law.

AJ would certainly appreciate the irony.

Igmutaka stepped away, but before he shifted, he glanced over his shoulder. "Please, do not tell Mikaela Star of my intentions. Somehow, I have to make her fall in love with me. I think my chances are better if she has no warning."

Mik struggled not to smile. "Works for me, Ig. Good luck."

The spirit guide disappeared and a huge cougar stood in his place. Rising slowly to his feet, Mik leaned against the deck railing and watched as Igmutaka bounded from the deck, trotted across the meadow, and disappeared into the forest.

Tala joined Mik a few minutes later, hair still mussed from sleep, lips swollen from AJ's kisses. "Come back to bed, sweetheart." She stretched up on her toes to kiss him, and, tiny little thing that she was, he still had to bend to meet her lips.

"I heard the conversation. I hope he succeeds. Star has loved him since she was a child."

"What?" Mik wrapped his arms around his mate. "If she loves him, why did she leave?"

"Because she wanted her independence more than she wanted a bossy lover. She has her pride. If you'll recall, Igmutaka pushed her away. She had a horrible crush on him, and he kept her at arm's length."

"She was just a kid!"

"She was seventeen. A young woman who, in many cultures, would have already been wed. The power of a woman's love isn't any less because of her age, but it's a moot point now. She's no longer a child, and I think Ig has learned a little bit more about women from Sunny. The timing is much better now."

"I guess." Mik wrapped his arm around her waist. He guided Tala back inside and down the hall to their bedroom. "I think your timing is excellent, by the way."

She merely grinned, grabbed his hand, and tugged him toward the big bed where AJ waited. The day was early, and Mik figured he'd done his part to help his daughter's love life along.

Now it was time to concentrate on his own.

2

Ig trotted away from Mik, fully aware he didn't have any idea
where he was headed or what he was going to do next. It was
too soon to go after Mikaela Star. He had no home of his own
where he could retreat. Generally, unless he was existing purely
as spirit and didn't require a bed, or sharing a bed with one or
more members of the pack, he slept as a cougar, nestled deep
within one of the many caverns that wound beneath the huge
Montana holdings belonging to Anton Cheval.

For whatever reason, he really didn't want to be alone today.
It should have been no surprise when, a few minutes later, he
found himself sitting on Sunny Daye's back deck, wondering
when she'd be home.

The sun was warm, and he stretched out on the hot cedar
planks, measuring a good nine feet of mountain lion from his
nose to the tip of his tail. Dozing beneath the morning sun, he
waited patiently, his thoughts drifting to the time when Sunny
had first come to Montana.

She'd been such a tiny thing, entirely mute, her body terribly crippled and deformed, trapped in her wheelchair. At first,

they'd all thought she was about eleven or twelve, but she'd merely been a badly stunted nineteen-year-old with a quick wit, a surprising sense of humor, and a bone-deep courage that impressed every one of them. It hadn't taken their healers long to figure out she was a Chanku child who had been caught mid-shift at a very young age.

Growing with her bones locked in their unnatural position had left her paralyzed and in constant pain, but it hadn't affected her spirit—or her optimistic outlook on life.

Once she'd been able to shift, her bones had realigned themselves perfectly. She would always be smaller than most of the other women, though what Sunny lacked in size she made up for in pure grit and determination. Nothing stopped her. Nothing kept her from doing what she wanted to do, or what she felt needed to be done.

Ig might not love her as his mate, but he admired and respected her. He loved her as his friend, as his lover and in so many ways, as the only one who seemed to understand why he would never give up his goal to make Mikaela Star his mate.

Sunny honored him with her friendship, but today when he left her bed, he knew that their relationship would be forever changed.

He hadn't lied when he'd said there was a man for her. Ig sensed him coming closer, sensed the strength in him, the power of the wolf—and something more.

Something that had not yet been revealed.

Sunlight warmed his thick pelt. The heat felt good against his long, lean muscles. Thankfully, the buzz of adrenaline from his talk with Mik was finally beginning to fade, and with it the niggling worry about the stranger he sensed. It was not up to Ig to figure out his story. That was for the newcomer to reveal to Sunny when it was time. Igmutaka accepted the fact he was merely the messenger. Sunny was smart and brave and ready for a challenge. Any challenge.

There was no need for him to worry, so he put that concern aside. As the heat of the morning sun seeped into his muscles and his mind drifted, he decided not to worry about Mikaela Star, either.

All would work out as it was meant to.

He would not have been told so many years ago that she was fated for him if it weren't the truth. He would trust in his gods and the Chanku goddess to get it right.

He blinked slowly. Finally, he closed his eyes and allowed his big cat to relax. He was safe here. Among friends. It was a good life. A good place to be.

He'd damned well better enjoy it while he could. Going after Mikaela Star Fuentes did not bode well for a peaceful future. She'd challenged him from the moment she was born and he'd loved every minute following her childhood as her spirit guide.

He missed her. Missed her more than he imagined he could miss anyone, even knowing that she was going to fight him every step of the way. He could hardly wait, but he had no choice. All would happen as it was meant to, only when it was meant to be.

He stretched his big paws out, unsheathed his claws, and marked Sunny's soft cedar deck. He was going to miss her, but Sunny wasn't all that peaceful, either.

Settling into sleep, Ig figured he'd better enjoy the quiet while he could.

Sunny left Lily, Mei, and Liana after their run. The three women shifted and returned to their mates, while Sunny kept her wolf form and trotted across the meadow to her cabin.

Like an idiot, she'd turned down invitations from all three to join them for sex after their run. There was no reason to pass, and it was really stupid, considering the fact her libido was in fine form and she was practically screaming with pent-up arousal.

Part of it could be that her season was due, and the PMS of a premenstrual woman had nothing on a wolf bitch coming into her heat. And then there'd been the dream. A vivid dream that made no sense but had kept her wound to a fever's pitch.

Sunny reached her cabin and trotted up the front steps to the deck, irritated and angry with herself for feeling so bitchy. She was never like this. The anxious shivers fluttering over her skin, the tension in her muscles, and the buzz of frustration in her womb made her feel like a ticking bomb.

An interesting analogy, considering it had been a ticking bomb—literally—that not only brought her to the attention of the Chanku but outed the secretive shapeshifters to the entire world.

And why was she even thinking about that? It had happened almost thirty years ago. Damn. All of this was making her crazy.

This frantic, anxiety-ridden feeling was much more than PMS. What the hell was the matter with her?

Again she thought of the dream she'd had last night and wished she could get it out of her head. A really hot guy she'd never seen before, and a jade amulet. What the hell did it mean?

Growling, she shifted. Mumbling to herself, she headed around to the back of the deck so she could go directly to her bedroom and the shower that sounded almost better than sex about now. No. Rethink that. Nothing sounded better than sex. "Goddess knows," she muttered. "I probably just need to get laid."

Good, because I do, too.

She almost tripped over the big puma stretched out at her feet. Igmutaka sprawled across her deck, his long, lithe body glowing in the morning light.

"Goddess, Ig, you scared me half to death." She glared at the cat. "I thought you'd already gone after Star."

Ig shifted, and Sunny glared at her gorgeous friend sitting on her deck. He shrugged his broad shoulders. "I would never leave without telling you. That would be rude." Unwinding his big body, he stood and took her hand.

Sunny glanced at their clasped hands and smiled. "You're right. It would be rude." She opened the door to her bedroom and dragged Ig in behind her. "So, where's this guy I'm supposed to meet?"

Ig gave her a cocky grin. "Very close, but he's not here yet." He wrapped his fist around his cock and stroked. It was already hard and rising against his belly. "I, however, am convenient."

She looked at him and his image wavered as her eyes filled with tears. "That's what we've been for each other, for all these years, Ig. Convenient. Is it wrong to want more?"

He shook his head. "No. And we both deserve more. That's why I'm leaving. Mikaela Star's going to be at the cabin near Lassen. I've spoken with her father. Mik has given me his permission to court her."

She didn't even try not to laugh. "You actually asked him? Wow . . . I would give anything to have heard that conversation."

Igmutaka looked miffed. "It was a good talk. Not anything for you to laugh at."

"Okay," she said. "I'll have to believe you. I guess. Does Star know you're coming?"

"No." He sighed and gazed out the window. "I'm afraid to warn her. I need to take things slowly, but I don't want her to have time to build stronger defenses against me. Against what the two of us can be. I hope I have the patience to show her."

Sunny stood beside him, gazing out at the mountains towering over their meadow. It was such a beautiful place to call home that she wondered how Star had managed to stay away for so many years. "She's almost thirty-one, Ig. You've known she was yours since her birth. You've been awfully patient, don't you think?"

His soft laughter made her sad. He sounded so depressed. Unsure of himself, which was not something she ever associated with the man. Igmutaka was, almost literally, older than dirt. He had told her his vague memories of being part of a litter of prehistoric cats—before cougars had evolved. Then, at some point, he'd been tapped as a spirit guide by the gods—not the Chanku goddess—and that had been his role ever since.

He tilted his head and gazed at Sunny out of those gorgeous cat eyes of his. "I drove her away. I didn't appreciate the intensity of her feelings, the fact that even a young girl can love with all her heart. I hurt her. I angered her, too."

Sunny grabbed his hand to take the sting out of her words. "Oh, I know you did that, and yes, she was really pissed off. But Ig, she's not staying away to punish you. That's not why she's been gone so long. You realize that, don't you?"

Lightly squeezing her fingers, he nodded slowly and said, "I know. She's staying away because she is strong and proud. She doesn't want to come to me. I will have to go to her. I need to apologize, to convince her my feelings are true."

"You can do it, but that won't be enough. There's more."

"More what?" He cocked his head, and that thick fall of dark hair slid over his forehead, lay across his chin.

Sunny thought how much simpler it would be if Igmutaka was the one for her. If she were right for him. "She's afraid," she said, knowing that Ig didn't have a clue.

"Afraid? Of what? Not of me!"

Sunny laughed. "Oh, yes, Mr. Spirit Guide. Of you. Of the control you've had over her life. All her life. She loves you, but she's afraid of giving you the kind of control that a mating bond gives one mate over another. She needs her independence."

He nodded slowly. "I know that. Now. So much has changed

in this world from the one I remember. I can change with it, but I will have to convince Mikaela Star my goal is to love her, not control her. Even if I succeed, I have a feeling she's going to make me work very hard for her hand."

"Don't you think it'll be worth it?"

"I do. Which is why I intend to leave today. I want to be at the cabin when she arrives, but as the cat, not the man." He looped his long fingers around Sunny's neck and pulled her close. "Make love with me, Sunny. Send me off with the taste of your kisses."

Grumbling, she muttered, "You make me feel like a fluffer in a porn movie." But she was grinning as she said it, and when he frowned, she laughed. Obviously, the man didn't have a clue what she was talking about. Ig could be so in tune with the modern world, sometimes absolutely brilliant with his understanding of things, and then she'd realize he was so totally out of touch that she had to remind herself he was essentially a very primitive man.

Primitive, smart, and so sexy. Star was a lucky woman. Sunny took Ig's hand and tugged him toward the bed. If he was leaving today, this would be their last time together until he worked everything out with Star. Which could take a long time, knowing her friend.

Star was not going to go down easy. Even so, Sunny sure as hell hoped Ig was right about that guy he'd said was coming for her. It was time. She really needed a man of her own.

Life would be so much easier if Sunny were the mate destined for him, but there was no fighting fate. He had always followed the wishes of the gods, and of the goddess when she asked, and they had let him know in no uncertain terms that Mikaela Star would be his. Eventually.

It had been a long, lonely wait, but now that he was ready to actively pursue her love, he was almost afraid to set his courtship in motion. So much hinged on the success of his pursuit. What if he failed? What if she truly didn't want him?

Today, though, he had Sunny, and she would have the best of him. As Igmutaka followed her to the bed, he thought of that time so long ago when they'd first made love beneath the stars. She'd been a virgin, still growing used to a body she could feel, to limbs that moved, to a voice that worked, and yet she'd been absolutely fearless. She'd gone on to show that same sense of fearlessness, that willingness to embrace what life had to offer without reservation, every day since.

Sunny had, in many ways, taught Igmutaka how to get the most out of life—a life that had been so foreign to him, no matter the many thousands of years he had interacted with mankind. She still taught him. She'd made him a better man.

"Ig? Are you okay?" Sunny knelt on her bed, frowning as she stared at him. "You look like you're a million miles away."

He put one knee on the bed and reached for her. "No, Sunny. I'm with you, but you could say I'm years away. My thoughts are on that first night when we made love. I was remembering."

She actually blushed. "I was so shameless." Then she laughed and sat back on her butt. "I wanted to learn about sex so much, and everyone was treating me like I was fragile as crystal, like I was going to break the minute they touched me. Thank goodness you didn't let anyone stop you."

He shrugged and crawled across the bed on all fours. She lay back, grinning at him, looking like a beautiful, little blond elf. He stopped with his hands on either side of her sleek thighs. "I was nervous, though. Afraid I might be too much for you. Many women would be afraid of my size, but you let nothing stop you."

He sat back on his heels and she reached for him, wrapped her fingers around his thick shaft and squeezed. "That's only because I didn't know any better. The only naked men I'd ever seen were on the porn sites I saw on my computer. Those guys were pretty big, but I figured that was just creative filming." She laughed, but he was burning with each soft squeeze of those small fingers around his heavy cock.

She rubbed her thumb across his sensitive crown, spreading a small drop of white fluid over the smooth skin. Gods, but she had him shivering while she chattered away. "At least I got the joke," she said. "It didn't take me long to see why Adam called this thing of yours the Louisville Slugger."

She cocked her head, studying him with a pensive smile on her face. "I was always a big fan of baseball." Then she ran her fingers down the full length to his testicles and cupped him briefly with both small hands. His sac tightened and drew up between his legs, but her torture didn't end there. She used both hands to gently knead his balls before sliding back to his swollen shaft, stroking slowly, almost absentmindedly, tracing the thick veins as she worked her way back to the tip.

He groaned as all the muscles across his belly clenched.

She flashed a gamine smile at him and shrugged. "It was a long time before I realized that most men aren't anywhere close to your size."

Ig laughed, but it was a rather strangled sound, even to his own ears. "Don't let Adam or Oliver hear you say that." His breath caught in his throat. "Dear gods, woman. What are you doing to me?" He leaned forward and kissed her. She wrapped her arms around his neck and clung to him, crawling up his body like a little monkey as he sat back on his heels again. She tightened her legs around his hips, sighing when his glans brushed her damp entrance.

"Whatcha waiting for, big boy?" She thrust her hips forward. Her pussy stretched to take him. Groaning softly, he entered her. She was slick and so hot, clasping him with tight, rippling muscles as he slowly eased deeper inside her.

It always surprised him that he actually fit. He was so much bigger compared to her—well over a foot taller and more than twice as broad as Sunny—and his cock was large even for a man his size. She was so tiny, but as long as he was careful, he could slide in deep, so deep that her soft nether lips touched his groin.

He paused a moment, gave them both time to adjust to the connection that never grew old, the sense that they would always have this amazing friendship no matter who their mates turned out to be. In that, he felt blessed by the gods, though he figured it was the goddess Eve who'd put them together.

Eve had been the one to lead the Chanku to Sunny in the first place. Ig had to believe she'd also led the two of them to find one another. He'd been Sunny's initiation into the sensual world of the pack, teaching her what it meant to be Chanku, and she'd been his anchor, the one who kept him returning to the world of men, even as the call to remain in his spirit form had grown with his conflicted feelings over his charge.

Mikaela Star had been his to protect, and yet he'd known from the beginning that he would one day love her. He'd fought the powerful attraction, even knowing their love was fated.

It wasn't easy to challenge fate, especially when his heart wouldn't let him.

Sunny whimpered, and the catch in her throat, the shiver that told him she was close to coming, sent his need higher, his blood rushing hotter until he forgot how fragile she appeared, how tiny she was. He rose up on his knees, cupped her bottom with his hands, and thrust hard and fast. His fingertips dug into her firm muscles. Her nails scraped over his shoulders. The sharp bite made him want her even more.

"More," she cried, echoing his thoughts, arching her back and driving herself down hard on his cock. He thrust forward, slamming into her.

"More," she said again. Then she bit him, sinking her teeth into the sensitive point where his throat and shoulder met. He answered with a grunt, a curse, and a flurry of short, fast strokes that slid the top of his thick cock over the taut little bud of her clit. Her heels dug into his butt. Her inner muscles held him in a tight clench, and her body spasmed with the first hard rush of climax.

His mind opened, connecting tightly to Sunny's even as his body shuddered in release. He felt each hot inch of his penis deep inside her body, felt how he stretched her, how her womb throbbed with the taut clench and release of climax. Her skin—his skin—shivered in reaction to the wash of sensation, and yet their bodies were so slick with sweat it was difficult to hold her.

But hold her he did. Tightly against his chest until her trembling eased and her spasming muscles relaxed. Carefully, Ig laid her back down on the bed, where she sprawled in wanton abandon. Her legs slipped from around his hips and her bent knees parted. He stared at the picture they made—her sleek muscles now lax with her release, the blond curls between her legs matted with her fluids and his, the thick root of his cock still full and hard with blood, much darker than her fair skin, stretching her flushed and swollen pussy, disappearing inside her body.

Their bodies and minds connected as lovers, but without that soul-searing link of truly bonded mates. Yes, it would have been nice if Sunny'd been the one, but he had no regrets.

And, as tightly linked as they'd been, he knew she had none, either. Instead, they had something special, something that made both of them better people. He slipped out a bit and she whimpered. Grinning, he slowly slid back in and she shivered. In. Out. In again, scraping across overly sensitized flesh until her whimpers became soft cries, until those cries were audible pleas for more. He found his rhythm once again. Deeper. Harder.

Again.

Only this time he took her supine. Lying beneath him, she grasped his shoulders and gazed up at him through half-lidded eyes as he stretched over her slight frame. Her legs sprawled to either side of his thighs, and he supported his much larger body with both hands planted beside her shoulders.

So rarely did he love her in this age-old position, and yet, of them all, this was his favorite. Familiar, and yet different each time, depending on the thoughts flowing through that active mind of hers. He loved watching her face, following the myriad expressions that flickered through her eyes and over her lips.

This time, there were tears. Sparkling at first in her amber eyes, trailing slowly from the corners as she came again, a slow, gentle climax that pulled Igmutaka along with her. As her tremors eased, Sunny lay softly weeping. Supported on his forearms now, Ig kissed the salty tears from her temples, kissed her lips, the line of her jaw, and the sensitive spot behind her ear.

"I will always love you, Sunny."

She opened her eyes and smiled at him. "And I will always love you, Igmutaka . . . spirit guide extraordinaire." She touched the bridge of his nose with her finger and stroked to the tip. Both of them were smiling when she moved to follow the line of his lips. "But the longer you stay with me, the longer I put off finding that one man who is right for me. And Ig, as much as I wish it were so, you are not the one. Why is that?"

He laughed and nuzzled her breasts, kissing first one taut nipple and then the other. "If Eve were in full control, maybe we would be mated, but the gods have a wicked and often cruel sense of humor." He sighed. "Think about it—Eve is only one goddess against a pantheon of egotistical male deities. She's been outnumbered, though I think she's done her best."

Sunny sighed. Then she cupped his face in her small hands, and he felt her focus as an almost physical sensation. "You weren't kidding when you said there was someone out there for me, were you?"

He shook his head. Concentrated on that vague sense of *other* he'd been growing more and more aware of. The male was closer. Much closer. He sensed physical strength and determination, but that was all. "I would never tease you about something as serious as a mate. He's out there, Sunny. Not far, though I don't have a strong-enough sense of him yet to place where he is. When or how he will enter your life."

She ran her hand across her eyes, wiping away the tears. "I've dreamed, Ig. A big, beautiful, dark-haired man wearing an amulet, a wolf carved in jade. I dreamed him last night."

"Dreams are important, Sunny. Sometimes they're visions from the gods, other times our own premonitions. What was he doing?"

"Watching me. Sort of like he was waiting for something. I wonder if it was him or just my wishful thinking?" She shrugged. "I guess that's going to have to hold me—your vision and my dreams. Be safe, Ig. Are you traveling as the cat or as spirit?"

"As a cat. My puma likes to travel, and he's fast. It should take me about a week, hunting along the way."

"I'm going to worry. I hope you appreciate that." She pulled his face close and kissed him. "Contact me when you can. I'm going to worry until I know you're there with Star. And then I'm going to worry that it doesn't work between you. It has to, Ig. You need to know what real love is like just as much as I do."

He sat on the edge of the bed, pulled Sunny into his arms, and then settled her across his lap. "We will both find love, Sunny. And don't ever think that what we have isn't real. We have loved one another truly. Just because we're not bonded, one to the other, doesn't make the love we share any less. I will always love you, and you will always be special to me."

Then he kissed her gently and said, "Thank you for worrying." His emotions were all over the map, sitting here, holding this strong and loving woman in his arms. He felt honored to know her. To know she cared so much. "I've never had anyone worry about me before. It feels good to know you care that I am safe, that everything works between Mikaela Star and me. I will accept only success." Smiling, he added, "I promise to be safe."

He kissed her, tasted tears. "I ask the same of you. Be safe and take care. I wish I had a better sense of what was coming, but I know you can handle whatever the fates throw your way. I hope they throw someone who loves you as much as I do. Someone who will be your mate for all time."

"You're going now, aren't you?"

He nodded. "I am. I'm ready. Because of you. Because of your sweet love and your generous friendship, I'm ready." He kissed her again and set her beside him on the bed. Standing, he walked through Sunny's open door as a man, but it was a sleek and powerful panther that leapt from the deck and trotted into the woods.

Star watched impatiently as the movers quickly loaded the last of the few belongings she planned to ship home and closed the big doors on the back of the van. A hired crew was cleaning her apartment, her bags for the trip were loaded, the batteries that powered her vehicle fully charged. She'd left her keys with her landlord, who'd quickly signed off on her lease. Rent in the area had gone up and he could make more with a new tenant. He'd promised to lock up as soon as the cleaners left.

She'd never imagined how easy it would be to cut her ties to the town where she'd lived and worked for almost fourteen years.

She watched as the van pulled out of the apartment complex and began the long journey to Montana. Her things would arrive ahead of her, but they'd go into storage in Kalispell until she made her final decision where to settle.

Mom and the dads wanted her in Montana, working as part of the Pack Dynamics team. Their search and rescue operations took them all over the western United States, and they'd mentioned more than once that Star, with all her years of training in the psychology of trauma and interspecies dynamics, would be a strong addition to their team.

But Lily Cheval—now Xenakis—wanted her as well, and that would eventually mean settling in San Francisco, working with Cheval International where Lily was CEO. Of course, that could change now with Alex running the business for Lily while she and her new mate, Sebastian Xenakis, settled into married life.

They'd chosen to do that in Montana, since Sebastian was still learning what it meant to be part of a pack, but from everything Star had heard from her parents and from Lily, the man was proving to be not only amazingly adaptable but extremely popular.

It had all happened so quickly. Lily'd met Sebastian, fallen in love with him, and become his mate over the course of about a week. She'd become his wife in a small ceremony barely a month later. Star shivered, but not from the cold. What did that say about her chances with Igmutaka? She'd known him all her life, but nothing had happened. How the hell was she going to deal with the spirit guide in her life once she got home? If he didn't love her, how was she going to handle it, seeing him day after day? She'd have to insist he go off and guide someone else.

Forever.

She couldn't leave things the way they were. Somehow, she'd have to force the issue; pin him down and make him say he didn't want her. Maybe if she knew for certain there was no chance for the two of them, she could get on with her life. Staying away hadn't accomplished a damned thing, other than getting to have sex with any man she chose. Unfortunately, there wasn't a single instance that stood out in her mind as worth the time and effort it took to get naked with a guy.

Her mom said it was all about the connection, the way two

people felt when they made love, which was a whole lot different than having sex.

Star couldn't argue the point one way or the other, since all she'd ever done was have sex. Her mom had openly admitted that she'd been a whore before she met the dads. Mik and AJ had rescued her from an abusive pimp, and they'd been together ever since. Sometimes that's what Star felt like—nothing more than a whore. She had sex, the guys went away satisfied, and after they left she pulled out her toys and made sure she got off as well.

It was a good thing she rarely had a chance to shift and run, because that all-consuming arousal following a shift probably would have killed her. She'd kept her identity secret from all but a few administrators on campus. All that had accomplished was adding so much anxiety, it seriously screwed her sense of well-being. If nothing else, it was time to reconnect with her wolf.

Time to find out if there was a chance for love in her life or if Igmutaka had destroyed whatever hope she had of finding a mate. One who loved her for the woman she was, not because he imagined her as someone different, as the serious academic she had tried to be for so long.

She wanted a mate she could love just as deeply, one who, when they learned everything about each other during the mating bond, was even more beloved. She was so screwed. When she thought of her behavior over the past fourteen years, she knew there might be a problem with that part of the equation.

Sighing, Star went back inside her apartment to take one last look at the place she'd called home for so long when a flash of green caught her eye. "Oh, crap." Muttering, she grabbed the necklace she'd left hanging on a hook by the kitchen window. She didn't wear it all that much, but Igmutaka had given it to her when she was small. He'd told her to wear it when she was afraid because it would keep her safe, but after she'd left Montana, it hadn't felt right wearing it. Maybe now that she was going home she could wear it again.

She tucked it into her purse and checked out the rest of the place. The two men doing the cleaning were almost done, so she tipped them well, made sure she hadn't forgotten anything else, and then turned and walked away.

She felt absolutely no need to look back, though she paused beside her car and checked her phone. No calls, but she sent a text to her mom to let Tala know she was starting the long drive across the country.

Then, leaning against the side of her car and acting purely on impulse, Star called Sunny Daye.

Sunny's adorable face popped up on her screen. "Hey, Star. I've been thinking about you! Your dad said you're moving back. Are you headed home yet?"

Interesting question. For the past fourteen years, she'd thought of that empty apartment as her home. "Yeah. I'm just getting ready to leave now. I'm going to the cabin in Lassen for a few days. I should be there in about a week. If you get a chance, you ought to come down."

Star wasn't sure why she'd offered the invite—it felt like the right thing to do. But Sunny's reaction wasn't what she'd expected.

She actually looked a little flustered. "Uh, if I can get away. I'd love to see you. Call me when you get there. I've got a couple of things going on, but I might be able to make it by next week. You're sure that's when you plan to arrive?"

"It is. I'm looking forward to shifting." Grinning, she added, "I'm definitely ready for some wolf time. It's been ages since I've had the chance to shift and run. I'm ready for some girl time, too. Way too many nerdy men here, all of them with one thing on their collective male mind."

Sunny's laughter shot a wave of homesickness through Star.

"Tell me about it. Sometimes I feel as if I'm drowning in a

sea of testosterone. I don't know how your mom does it with two guys in her life."

Now this was familiar ground. "I don't know, either, but she's definitely the alpha bitch. The dads defer to her on everything. I hope I inherited whatever alpha genes she's got."

"Don't we all. Drive safely, Star. I'll do my best to get to Lassen next week. Check in with me along the way, okay?"

"Will do. G'bye." She ended the connection, thinking how important her friendship with Sunny had been. In spite of the fifteen-year age difference, they'd clicked from the beginning. Sunny had been her babysitter first, and then her friend.

She'd also been Igmutaka's primary sexual partner since Star was little. Sunny had always insisted that she and the spirit guide were the best of friends but not meant to mate. Star wasn't sure how anyone could just know whom their mate was supposed to be, but Sunny said she'd know when it was time.

Star had to believe her. She'd asked Sunny what Ig was like as a lover, but that was one place Sunny wouldn't go. Over the years, he'd simply become something they didn't discuss, other than Star's continual bitching about how controlling he could be, how horribly overprotective.

Sunny had been less than sympathetic, but they were still close friends. One of her few real friends. Star had told the people she'd worked with here in New Haven that she was leaving, more as a courtesy than anything else. She'd been surprised by how many of them seemed to care that she'd chosen to leave academia and return to Montana. They sounded like they were actually going to miss her, which made her feel really guilty when she realized there was absolutely no one she intended to keep in touch with.

What did that say about her personality?

"Good Goddess. I really am a bitch!" Laughing, she put Sunny and Igmutaka out of her mind, quit worrying about the ties she was so easily cutting, and got into her car. She started the engine and pulled away from the curb, heading west. The plan was to take a full week to reach the cabin near Mount Lassen, going slow and stopping to enjoy the sights along the way.

A week before she'd have the freedom to shift when she wanted, to run through the forest without care.

Once she arrived, she'd stay at the cabin for at least another week. Possibly even longer, because she'd probably need even more time than that before she was ready to face Igmutaka.

How could anyone know how long it would take to decide the entire course of their life? She'd had a lifetime already, and she was nowhere close to figuring out what the hell she was going to do about her convoluted feelings for a very stubborn spirit guide.

A man who, in spite of all her bitching, still had a solid hold on her heart, whether he wanted the damned thing or not.

3

"G'night Adam. Liana. Thanks. You guys are truly amazing." Sunny's legs still felt rubbery from one too many orgasms as she crawled out of the couple's big bed and headed toward the door.

Adam raised his head, hair tousled and eyes sleepy. "You don't have to leave, Sunny. You're more than welcome to stay."

"Thanks, but I've got some work to do in the morning. I should get home."

"M'kay." Adam's eyes were already closed.

Sunny figured he wouldn't even remember her leaving, but she was glad she'd come home with them. Everything felt so empty with Ig gone. It hadn't even been a week without him, and she was already going stir-crazy.

Damn but she hoped Star would get her head straight about the poor man. Igmutaka loved her and she loved him.

People could be so stupid sometimes. What was really sad was that if they'd just mate, they'd know exactly what was in the other's head and realize they loved each other. Sort of a conundrum when Star wasn't willing to admit what she felt in her heart, which meant there was no way she'd consider mating.

Sunny closed the door behind her and shifted as soon as she stepped outside. She glanced up and all her worries faded as she lost herself in the beauty of the nighttime sky. She'd forgotten there'd be no moon tonight. Forgotten it would be anything but dark outside, not with a bazillion stars overhead sparkling like diamonds on black velvet.

The night was practically balmy, considering it was already October and the air ripe with the scents of fall. The sweet tang of apples on the big tree near Adam and Liana's cottage, the fresh scent of rain-washed grasses after this afternoon's brief shower, and in the distance the faint yet pungent reek of skunk.

Instead of heading to her own little cabin, Sunny trotted across the dark meadow. Maybe another short run would clear her head, help her sleep better tonight. She was really hoping for a night without dreams. Whoever the guy was, he was persistent, showing up nightly now, and that jade wolf had to mean something.

They'd never had sex in her dreams, though she'd awakened really aroused a couple of times, which was weird. Of course, the guy was pretty hot, but if it was her dream, if she'd been in control, he'd be doing a lot more than just staring at her.

Tonight, with the dreams on her mind and in spite of the great sex with Adam and Liana, she was too buzzed to sleep. She picked up speed and raced through the darkness. A shadow among shadows, she followed the familiar trail that made a big, lazy loop around the huge meadow. Not all that far from the pack, but far enough to relish the freedom of the night, to think about her life and where she was going, what she wanted to do with herself.

Ig had said there was a mate out there for her, but damn it all, she was tired of waiting. She'd waited and wasted too many years already—the whole first half of her life she'd spent trapped in a wheelchair, essentially waiting for death.

Instead, she'd been given a life unlike anything in her wildest dreams, and she'd be damned if she wasted a minute now. Now, when she could fly like the wind, race through the night on four strong legs, and raise her wolven voice to the heavens. She was an alpha bitch, and Sunny wanted—no, needed—to run.

She had no choice. She had to burn off this surge of energy that had her keyed to a fever's pitch. Veering away from the well-packed trail, she headed into the deep woods, running as if her very life depended on it.

Fen Ahlberg crept to the edge of the stone outcropping and stared down at the horrifying proof of what could only be called a massacre. Lord, but he wanted to vomit. He choked the sensation back and pulled out his camera instead.

He needed the evidence. His photos wouldn't help the ones who'd already died, but they would help him bring judgment and stop this disgusting slaughter. Carefully, he focused on the three men working beside a small campfire where they'd strung a dead wolf by its back legs from a stout branch. Laughing and cursing, they skinned the poor beast. Furry bodies were stacked in a pile like cordwood next to the fire.

Poachers, working on private Chanku land. This sure as hell wasn't in his job description. No, all he was supposed to do was check on the health of the wolf population in and around Glacier National Park.

He hadn't expected to find anything like this, though he should have guessed. Should have known when he first began to suspect problems with the local wolf population, which was protected by both federal and state law.

Questions had arisen immediately. Why were the numbers so low when the animals were protected? Between federal park laws and Chanku shapeshifter Anton Cheval's huge holdings where no hunting was allowed, Fen had expected packs to be large, the animals healthy.

Instead he'd found few wolves, and many of the ones he'd been able to photograph and catalog had injuries consistent with illegal snares and gunshot wounds. It didn't make any sense, but he'd started paying more attention to the people in the area, watching for anything that set his senses to humming.

It hadn't taken him long to discover that all was not as it should be, but getting answers out of the folks around here hadn't been easy. Damn, but he wished he could shift. Wished he could get out there among the wild wolves and ask them what was going on. He'd thought of contacting the local Chanku pack, but he had no proof to show them. Besides, he had no idea what good it would do.

Cheval's pack was an autonomous holding within the state of Montana, similar to the reservations for Native Americans. The Chanku lived by their own laws while paying enough money into the local economy that no one bothered them. Sort of a law unto themselves, if what he'd heard was true. Fen hadn't expected much help to come from the shifters, even if he'd been able to reach Cheval.

He'd been given permission to follow the wild packs onto Chanku land for observation, but that had come directly through the sheriff's office. He didn't know if the original permission came from Cheval or merely from the local authorities.

Fen had been working solo, following up on his hunch that something was wrong. What he was witnessing right now was proof enough he'd been a damned fool to come here alone.

Three heavily armed men with enough dead wolves to put them in prison for a long, long time versus one federal parks employee, unarmed except for a cell phone with a camera. He'd better hope like hell no one saw him.

He was focusing for another shot when he heard a whimper and glanced toward the pile of bodies still waiting to be skinned. One of them was alive. The wolf raised its head and tried to get free of the heavy bodies holding it down.

One of the men noticed. He had a sharp skinning knife in his fist. "I'll take care of it."

"Don't damage the pelt. She's a beaut."

"Gotcha."

A female. Fen's vision narrowed on the burly poacher walking across the open area toward the struggling wolf. He felt the animal's panic and pain, and his anger grew, the anger he'd struggled all his life to control, but if there was ever a time to set his inner beast free, it was now.

He dropped the hard-won controls over his rage and freely gave up the final shreds of civilization. It took him barely a heartbeat, but here, now, for the first time in his adult life, he turned his beast loose.

Red filled his vision. Blood rushed through his veins and pounded in his temples. His muscles clenched as, like a silent wraith from hell, he leapt from his perch above the campfire. Leapt out over the two men still skinning the dead wolf and reached for the man headed toward the one surviving animal.

Sunny paused on a high ridge near the point where Anton Cheval's property intersected with the acreage that belonged to his new son-in-law, Sebastian Xenakis. Seb and Lily had been together only since June, and while they lived in the home on Seb's property, they'd hardly had time to explore the huge tract of land that Seb had inherited from his father and generously donated to the pack's holdings.

Sunny'd run farther than she'd planned, but the night was beautiful and she'd needed this time on her own, running free rather than going back to her empty cottage. Still, it was growing late, and she paused before turning to head back.

She'd half expected to run into the wild wolf pack that

roamed these mountains, but there'd been no sign of them. She raised her head and sniffed the air.

An errant breeze brought the smell of death, of fresh, coppery blood and the stench of torn intestines. It hit her like a toxic cloud, and she rubbed her face in the dirt, instinctively trying to remove the horrible smell from her sensitive nostrils. Spinning away from her unprotected spot on the ridge, she ducked down into the brush. The smell wasn't as strong here, but the wind was light, coming out of the north, and she ran that way with her senses wide open.

She thought of calling on the pack but decided to see what the problem was first. Sometimes bison wandered out of the park, and if one had been taken down by wolves, that might explain the stench.

Maybe. But somehow, she didn't think that was it. The scent of wolf was strong, as was the stink of unwashed humans. And there was something else. Something almost familiar, but not quite. Nose to the ground and ears open for any sound, she raced toward the source of the smell, keeping to the shadows and placing her feet carefully to avoid any sound.

She noticed the flicker of a campfire up ahead—a fire where none should be. This was private property and there was no hunting allowed, but the smell was growing stronger and she had to believe it was connected to that fire.

Circling around, she came to a point where she guessed that if she could reach the rock outcropping visible in the flickering light, she'd be able to look down on the campsite.

There was no sound beyond the crackle of burning wood, but the stench of blood and offal hung like a thick fog. Pausing in thick brush behind the rock, Sunny reached for Anton.

Sunny? Are you okay?

Yes, but I'm on that stretch of Sebastian's property that runs beneath the ridgeline. There's a campfire here and the smell of death. I thought I should contact you before I go closer to see what's happened, but I think you need to get up here. Something bad has happened. I'm almost positive.

Be careful, Sunny. I'm putting out a call to the others now. It will take half an hour or more for us to get there. You're a long way out. I want you to wait until we arrive.

She heard a soft groan and a whimper of pain. Wolf! *There's a wolf hurt. I'll be careful, but I'm going to check and see what's happened.*

I'm on my way. Be careful. Keep in contact.

She crawled on her belly along the outcropping until she could hang her head over the edge. Heartsick, she stared at the carnage below. The partially skinned body hanging from a tree and at least half a dozen dead wolves in a bloody pile near the fire had her hackles rising, but it was the violently shredded, eviscerated bodies of three human men that had her backing along the outcropping, shifting and falling to her knees to vomit.

They'd been gutted and their throats ripped out. Torn entrails hanging out of the bodies explained the stench. She shifted as soon as her stomach was under control, knowing that the shift would cleanse her mouth of the foul taste.

Silently, she crept around the rock wall and hid not far from the bodies. *Anton? How far are you?*

At least half an hour. You're farther away than I realized.

Hurry. I've found at least half a dozen dead wolves, one of them partially skinned. Three dead poachers. They've been disemboweled and their throats were torn out. More damage than a wolf could do. They're big men and they were armed. Something horrible got them.

Get out of there. Meet us up on the ridge. Hurry. My senses are firing in all directions.

Mine too. Headed there now. But hurry. I think one of the wolves is still alive, but I'm afraid to go check.

We're on our way.

She backed out of the brush and slipped through a thick patch of willows. It was dark, so damned dark here in the deep forest where even the pale starlight couldn't penetrate, and her eyes hadn't yet adjusted after the glow of the fire.

She didn't hear anything unusual. No more whimpering, and she felt terrible for not checking, but Sunny figured she was no hero. She wanted to get as far away from whatever killed those men as she could. And fast.

Brambles snatched at her thick fur. She pulled free and crept beneath the thick branches. Finally, she found an opening and broke out onto the trail. Pausing, she sniffed the air and took a moment to get her bearings. She needed to head south, back the way she'd come, and then west to the top of the ridge to meet Anton and the others.

One thing she loved about being Chanku was the inborn sense of direction that grew stronger in her wolven form. Now it was a simple thing to swing around a huge cedar and head in the right direction.

She'd run no more than a quarter mile from the carnage when a low rumble coming out of the darkness stopped her in her tracks. She sniffed the air, but the wind had shifted and she couldn't pick up any clear scent beyond the fading stench of death. Ears forward, senses alert, she gazed all about. She tried, but she couldn't pinpoint the source of the sound.

She took a few steps, placing her feet carefully. Dry grass whispered beneath her paws. It was dark here—darker than it had been earlier. Clouds must have blown in and covered the pale starlight. She could still see enough to pick her way along the forest floor, but everything around her lay in shadow.

Heart pounding in her chest and all senses on high alert, Sunny took a few more steps. A sudden flash of insight reminded her she'd not yet ended her heat, that her scent would leave a clear trail right to her for any predator in the forest.

It didn't usually attract the wild wolves, but sometimes they got curious, and a few in the past had been overly aggressive. But she'd never run alone when she was in season, and damn, she should have thought of that.

Too late now.

With that thought came the scent of blood and wolf. She swung her head in a wide arc but didn't see anything. A sudden shift in the air pressure had her spinning to her right as a massive wolf, larger than any she'd ever seen, exploded out of the forest and bowled her over.

She yelped and scrambled out from under him, digging her claws into the thick humus, praying for purchase, but the loose earth flew and she felt the harsh bite of powerful jaws when the beast caught her by the back of the neck.

Snarling, she twisted free and turned to face the creature with her back against a thick pine. The wolf glared at her, eyes shimmering, jaws dripping saliva and blood, but his thick penis was engorged and hanging beneath his belly—proof enough what was on his mind. She spun in a futile attempt to escape as the beast lunged and caught her once again.

She didn't panic. He was huge, but he was still a wolf, and right now it was obvious he wanted to fuck her, not kill her.

His teeth clamped down on the thick roll of skin at the back of her neck, and he shook her as if she were nothing more than a toy. Then he lifted her in his massive jaws and spun away. Carrying Sunny the way a bitch would carry her pup, the beast ran in the opposite direction.

Away from the fire, away from the bodies.

Away from Anton and the rest of her pack. The chokehold he had on her neck cut off her air. She knew she should call out to Anton, but the mechanics of mindtalking escaped her. Branches whipped against her skin, slapping her tender nose and ears as the huge animal raced through the thick underbrush. She felt his teeth biting into her throat, and the darkness grew darker as she struggled to breathe. Then pain faded. Sight faded. Her body went limp and all sense of being carted along like a rag doll slipped away.

Along with any semblance of consciousness.

Reality crept in slowly, and it took him a few minutes to realize where he was, what he was. Fen glanced at the big paws beneath him and wanted to weep.

Memories slammed into him. Memories he'd tried to forget for the past thirty years. He'd been born a wolf. Birthed in a dark cave deep in the forests of Finland, but he'd been little more than a pup when the hunter had killed his mother. At least, when the man realized the bitch he'd shot had been nursing young, he'd searched for her litter and found her only pup.

He took the pup home, raised it as a pet until the day the pup awoke as a young boy, a human boy with no idea how to turn back into a wolf. Fenris the wolf had become Fenris Ahlberg, adopted son of the man who'd shot his mother and then spent a lifetime atoning for the deed.

Fen had grown to love the man, but he'd never figured out how to shift back.

He still didn't know.

But somehow he was once again a wolf, and he'd dragged a young female deep into the woods. When he regained his sense enough to turn her loose, she'd flopped limply to the ground. He'd been terrified that he might have killed her, but she'd quickly regained consciousness.

Now she crouched low in front of him, her eyes narrow slits, hackles up and teeth bared. He didn't blame her for being angry, though he admired the beast's bravery. He was more than twice her size, but she didn't back down.

She turned to run, and her musky scent slammed into his sensitive receptors like a kick to the balls, reminding him why he'd taken her in the first place. All thoughts of admiration fled the second his wolf remembered this was more than just any wolf. She was a bitch in heat, receptive at this time in her cycle, and she was his. Humanity winked out once again as he grabbed her, held her down with his front paw, and sniffed beneath her tail. She growled and twisted beneath him, but he'd backed her up against a fallen tree and she couldn't escape.

Her scent enflamed him. What little sentient clarity he'd retained was gone. All he saw was the female. All he wanted was the female. He'd caught her. He'd brought her here to this secluded meadow, and she was his.

He raked her shoulders with his big paw, but he was so much bigger than she that he almost knocked her over. He did it again, grabbing the thick ruff at the back of her neck in his teeth and holding on.

She broke loose and scrambled away, going low beneath his belly and leaving him with a mouthful of fur, but he spun around quickly and caught her once again. This time, he left nothing to chance. He grappled with her, locked her body between his front legs, clamped his jaws down on her neck, and thrust forward before she realized what he was doing.

He felt her slick heat the moment his cock breached her entrance, felt her helpless struggle against his greater strength, and wanted to howl for the joy of his dominance.

It was fast and bestial, and he reveled in his power over the smaller wolf. He'd never done this before. Never fucked in his wolf form, and it was amazing.

Intense.

Powerful.

Unexpectedly frightening.

He'd not expected the thick, hard swelling that formed at the base of his penis, but it was filling the bitch's vaginal channel, knotting inside her, tying them together.

He knew wolves tied during breeding, much as dogs did, but he'd not realized it would happen to him.

He wasn't really a wolf, was he?

The bitch yipped and then she whimpered. Breathing hard and fast, she collapsed beneath his greater weight and went down on her belly. With his dick still knotted inside her, he followed, lying beside her but still connected.

How long before he could pull loose?

The red haze slowly peeled away from his mind. Reality slammed him in the gut. What the fuck had he done? His first emotion, that he felt ridiculous lying here in the deep forest, knotted to a female wolf like a damned beast, faded now that the mating rage was over. What about the female, lying beside him? Staring at him out of intelligent amber eyes.

Good gods, he'd fucked a wolf. That was wrong. Dead wrong. He wasn't into bestiality.

Except, he was a beast, wasn't he? He stared at the amber eyes glaring at him and felt a moment's regret. She might be only a beast, but he wondered what she was thinking.

And then, without warning, he knew.

She wasn't quite sure if she was pissed off, embarrassed, or scared shitless, but in her entire life as a wolf, Sunny had never once feared rape, and certainly not by a wild wolf. Of course, she'd never seen one quite as big as this guy, either, but how the hell was she going to explain this to the pack?

She never should have run alone, knowing she was in heat, but she'd honestly forgotten about it. Of course, that explained why Adam had been such an attentive lover tonight. Goddess, she felt like a damned fool.

The pack would never let her live it down, though she hoped they wouldn't kill the beast. Maybe she just wouldn't tell them. Now that he'd gotten what he wanted, he seemed calm and perfectly relaxed. He was a beautiful animal, though she'd never seen a wolf quite as large. She wondered what he was thinking as he stared at her with intelligent-looking amber eyes.

She knew some of the pack could communicate with the

wild wolves, though she'd never had much luck. Curious, she opened her mind.

A man's curious thoughts slammed into her. *Holy crap. You're not a wild wolf.* She took a deep breath. Shouting, mentally or otherwise, would get her nowhere. *Who the hell are you? What are you? Are you Chanku?* Sort of an odd question to ask when his dick was stuck in her pussy, but Sunny'd never let things bother her when she wanted answers.

You can speak? In my mind? Oh, fuck. What have I done? His body jerked as he tried to pull away.

Her butt went with him. She yipped. *Hold on, bud. You're not going anywhere. You've just fucked a Chanku shapeshifter. Are you Chanku?*

I don't know! I have no idea if I am Chanku. I was born a wolf, but was raised by a human. I shifted when I was little and I was a human boy. I've never been able to shift back. Not until tonight. I am sorry. So sorry.

You're the one who killed the poachers?

You saw them. He closed his eyes and looked away. Then he faced her and nodded. *I am. I think. I'm not sure. My mind is so confused. I'm a federal game warden. I was watching them skin one of the wolves. Then I heard a whimper—one of the animals was still alive, and I couldn't let them kill her. I was so angry. Frustrated because I couldn't do anything. I don't remember much beyond a sense of blinding rage. Maybe that's what made me shift.*

Could be. Extreme emotion can bring on a shift among Chanku, but I'm glad you killed them. They deserved it. My packmates will be looking for me. Anton will know what to do.

Will he kill me? I murdered three men.

I hope not. You also just raped one of his packmates. It might be a good idea if we separate before he finds us.

I think I can, now. Will you ever forgive me?

She stared at him for a minute, thinking that laughter probably wasn't appropriate, but there was something inherently ridiculous about the situation, as horrible as it was. She couldn't blame him entirely. He was male and, if he was telling the truth, unused to his wolven form. She was in heat. Not the best time to meet strange wolves in the forest.

Or maybe it was. *Yeah. You're forgiven.*

Thank you. I don't know what to say, except that I am so sorry. That's not how I am, at least not as a man. He slipped free, and when he stood, he towered over her, standing almost twice the height of the other males in the pack. Even Tinker McClintock would have to look up to this guy.

Sunny thought he looked embarrassed, but she stood as well. *Link with me,* she said. *Maybe you can see how I do this.* She shifted to her human form, waited a moment, and then shifted back to her wolf. That would help get rid of the evidence that they'd had sex—the scent and his semen. She really wasn't ready to share that bit of news with the pack. Thank goodness she had control of her breeding or that could have been an even bigger problem.

At least he wasn't a wild wolf, but if this was the man Ig had told her about, she needed to have a long heart-to-heart with the spirit guide. Later. *Did you see how I did that?*

I did, but nothing seems to be happening.

You probably need the nutrients. When he stared at her in blank confusion, she added, *There are certain grasses our bodies need in order to complete the shift. I'll make sure you get them.*

He stared at her for a moment and then blinked and gazed back in the direction they'd come. *There's still a wounded wolf by the campsite.*

Let's go. I'll tell Anton where to meet us.

He'd never seen so many wolves in one place, but the pack arrived en masse, as silent as wraiths, drifting out of the forest to stand quietly while the one who was obviously their alpha approached him.

Thank goodness for Sunny. She stood beside him and bared her teeth when the alpha's hackles went up. They obviously communicated, but Fen had no idea what they were saying. Tonight was the first time he recalled using telepathy. He and Sunny had understood one another, but he wasn't quite sure how it worked.

Maybe, when he'd still been a pup . . .

Sunny directed one of the wolves to the wounded female. The wolf shifted and was suddenly a tall, lean man with shoulder-length dark blond hair. Another wolf shifted, a woman this time with long, pale blond hair, and the two of them knelt beside the female, placed their hands on her body, and went very still.

Fascinated, he watched them for a moment, until he couldn't stand it anymore. *What are they doing?* He glanced at the alpha and then at Sunny.

The alpha answered, and this time he understood. *They're healers. Adam Wolf and his mate, Liana. They use their minds to go inside the wolf. They'll heal her injuries, if they can.* He gazed at the carnage and then stared at Fen. *You've left quite a mess for us to clean up. Can you tell me what happened?*

Fen nodded, though it felt odd to do it as a wolf, but he introduced himself and explained as much as he could. So much of what must have happened had a dreamlike quality as he tried to recall, but he did his best. He hung his head in shame once he finished his recitation.

The alpha seemed satisfied. For now. He turned away and shifted. Fen was surprised by his human appearance. The man was tall and lean with dark hair falling to his shoulders. He looked more like a young artist than the powerful leader of what was essentially the Chanku nation.

There was no doubt in Fen's mind that he was looking at

Anton Cheval, a man who was almost legend among the cadre of federal wardens Fen was part of.

As soon as Cheval shifted, the others did as well. There were at least twenty people here—men and woman, all of them about the same age. All of them naked. In fact, Fen felt like the old guy in the crowd. Sunny couldn't be more than twenty, and none of the women looked much older. Cheval might be in his thirties, but it was hard to tell.

At that moment, Cheval turned and grinned at Fen. "Actually, Fen, I'm eighty-four and Sunny is forty-five. Chanku don't age. Once you've had the nutrients, your age will probably begin to reverse itself. I was in my fifties and looked it when I first shifted, but over the years I've returned to what was probably my prime."

Before Fen could fully assimilate what the man had said—and ask how Cheval had known what he was thinking—another man who looked as if he could be Cheval's brother interrupted. "We've got seven dead wolves, Anton. I think they're most of the pack we've seen up here the last few times we've run. It makes me sick, what those bastards did."

The blond who'd been working on the female turned toward them. "She's gonna make it, Anton, but she's got a litter nearby. I've sent a search party out to find them."

Cheval nodded. He glanced over his shoulder. "Sunny? Why don't you take Fen back to the main house. Give him one of the pills and find a place for him to sleep. He can have any of the guest rooms, but make sure the door is open so he can get out if he wants to. I need to call the authorities up here, and I'd just as soon not have that monster wolf in plain sight." He shrugged and looked at Fen. "We'll get this all figured out in the morning. In the meantime, we've got three dead men on our property and proof they've been poaching. At this point, I can't be positive how they died, other than the fact it appears to have been an animal attack. I'm guessing it was the female our guys are healing."

You would do this for me? I'm guilty of murder.

"Not in my eyes you're not. Go. We'll talk in the morning."

Fen turned and stared at Sunny.

"C'mon, big guy," she said. "It's been a long night." She shifted, and her ripe scent teased his nostrils.

He followed her into the forest, fully in control of himself this time, but he'd never felt so confused, or so certain that his life had changed forever.

This certainly wasn't what he'd expected. Anton Cheval watched the two wolves trot away—tiny little Sunny Daye followed by the biggest wolf he'd ever seen. It made the Berserkers that Aldo Xenakis had controlled look like puppies, but there was still a similar sense to the creature. A wildness he recognized.

Slowly Anton turned his head and met his packmate's steady gaze. Stefan nodded.

"Berserker," Anton said.

"I know. It appears they're not all dead. Is Sunny safe with him?"

Anton chuckled and slung his arm over Stefan's shoulders. "The question should be, is he safe with Sunny?"

4

It felt almost surrealistic, trotting back to the compound with the huge wolf on her heels. The same wolf that had scared the crap out of her not an hour ago. What was he like as a man? And he'd said he was born a wolf. Did that make him a Berserker?

He certainly didn't act like one. They'd fought that ferocious and heretofore unfamiliar species of Chanku just a few months back when Sebastian Xenakis had joined the pack. His father—a truly nasty piece of work—had his own pack of killers. They were huge shapeshifting beasts—Berserkers—the legendary wolven warriors of Scandinavian myth.

Except they were no myth. Berserkers were the warrior class of the Chanku, bred to kill. Born as wolves, they could shift and become men, but when they died, they died as wolves. Their primary shape was the beast, not human.

Their primary thought process was more bestial than human.

Was that what Fen was? One of the uncontrollable killers of

the Chanku? If so, what in the hell was he doing trotting along behind her like a loyal pup? Why was he so gentle?

True, he had killed three men, but they were three who deserved what they got. Any one of the pack would have doled out the same justice, had they been in Fen's shoes.

Physically, he was massive, a good four feet at the shoulder. Tinker, the largest wolf in their pack, wasn't even close. Lisa had measured him one time, and everyone had been impressed that he was almost thirty-six inches, so matching Fen up with the rest of the pack was sort of like comparing Igmutaka's cougar to a bobcat.

Still, it wouldn't hurt to check. She sent a quick call to Anton. *Is he a Berserker?*

He answered immediately. *I believe so. Is he bothering you?*

No, but he wants to know who and what he is. Is it okay to tell him?

Of course. He has a right to know. We'll talk in the morning. Be careful, Sunny. Do you feel any threat from him?

She bit back a laugh. *No. He's a perfect gentleman. A very large and furry gentleman.*

She wasn't lying. The wolf following close on her heels wasn't threatening. Not now. Even earlier when he'd attacked her, he'd not actually harmed her. No, he'd behaved exactly the way any wild wolf would act around an unattached bitch in heat.

A voice in her head, the one that generally was the voice of reason, muttered, *You're justifying bad behavior, Sunny.*

Was that what she was doing? So be it. She'd had to justify a lot of things when she was trapped in that damned wheelchair for the first half of her life. It had all worked out in the end.

So she'd put that really poor first impression, that *how we met* crap, aside for now and move on. Starting at square one, that he was a beautiful and thoughtful wolf. A very large beautiful and thoughtful wolf—but what about the man inside?

Was he the stranger from her dreams, the one with the jade

amulet around his neck? No way to know, since the necklace would have ended up somewhere on the forest floor when he shifted.

Was he a killer? He'd proved himself capable of killing, but she knew he had a conscience. If she hadn't been so terrified when he fucked her, she might have actually found him attractive.

She refused to call it rape, even though she'd not been willing and had tried to fight him off, and when she told Anton what happened, which she would, she wasn't going to try to paint it as anything it wasn't. It was sex, pure and simple. It was obvious he'd been totally lost in his beast. In his mind, she'd been an available female wolf in season. That was the way things happened in the wild. She tried to imagine sex with him when they were both aware and willing, but he'd have to shift first.

No more sex as wolves. Not unless the two of them managed to fall madly, irrevocably in love, because every Chanku knew that when they mated as wolves, they were Mated, with a capital M.

Thank goodness they hadn't linked when they had sex, or she'd be stuck with Fen Ahlberg for life, permanently mated to the man with no idea what he was really like.

Of course, she'd find out during the mating link, but if she didn't like what she learned, it would be too damned late. She wondered just how much Igmutaka had known about this guy when he'd told Sunny her mate was "out there." She almost laughed, but damn it all, unless that blasted spirit guide had a really good explanation for what had happened tonight, he had a bit of explaining to do.

Fen trotted along behind the bitch, but it wasn't easy with her ripe scent teasing his sensitive nose and the glorious swish of that beautiful cream-colored tail inviting him close. Her markings were unusual for a wolf—cream all over with black tips on her ears and tail. She rippled like quicksilver as she ran, visible even in the thick darkness of a moonless night.

He followed at Sunny's steady pace, struggling to keep his mental and emotional balance. It wasn't easy. What in the hell had he gotten himself into? He was a fucking federal game warden, and a naturalized United States citizen, but his wallet and all his ID had been in his pants pocket. Pants that were probably in tatters after making the shift.

His phone with the camera and all his photos were lost as well. He pondered that for a moment and then felt like an idiot. Why the hell was he even worried about all that crap?

He was a fucking wolf, with no idea how he'd shifted into one and not a clue how to turn back. He liked being human. For that matter, he really loved how it felt to be a wolf again, but it would be nice to have a little control over the process.

That was important. That and the bitch trotting along ahead of him. She was beautiful. He'd caught a brief glimpse of her when she shifted, and her human form was even prettier. Stunning, actually. Way beyond mere pretty.

His wolf liked her wolf. His human side couldn't get her womanly image out of his mind, but right now the wolf was struggling for control. It really wanted to mate again.

He tightened down on his animal instincts. The thinking man needed to stay in charge, which wasn't easy when the wolf body had other ideas. He'd been a child the last time he was a wolf, and he'd forgotten the power in these wolven muscles, the amazing senses, the ability to see and smell and hear so much more than he could as a human. But his mind was spinning in and out of what mattered and what didn't.

The fact he had no clothes was minor. Controlling the animalistic urges of his wolf was more important, but so far he was doing okay. Knowing he had absolutely no control over when and how he might shift again was absolutely terrifying.

What if he couldn't shift again? What if he was stuck as a wolf? He'd been born a wolf. Had his human life been a mere anomaly?

He'd ask Sunny. She and all the others shifted without any problem at all. She'd mentioned something about nutrients, some kind of pills. Maybe that's all he needed. He sure as hell hoped so. Hoped Sunny would have answers.

They'd been moving at a steady pace for over half an hour. He wasn't sure how much distance they'd covered, but he noticed a glow over the next ridge. When he and Sunny reached the crest, she paused at the top. Fen stared out over the valley below.

It was like looking down at a magical little village. No streets, really, but what looked like meadows and parkland, a few small ponds and a creek. There was a large house off in the distance and a number of smaller cottages and cabins scattered about amid the trees.

Lights twinkled through the branches, though he didn't see any set pattern along straight lines or anything formal, but it gave the appearance of old-fashioned gaslights along the trails that ran between the cottages.

In the distance he thought he saw a lighted runway and a large building that could have been an airplane hangar. Here? In what was basically wilderness? If he'd been human, his jaw would have dropped. *Is that a jet helicopter on the pad?*

Sunny turned to him, tongue lolling, amber eyes sparkling. *It is. Tinker McClintock, one of my packmates, insists on the latest model. It's mostly used for search and rescue. Pack Dynamics—one of the Chanku businesses—is headquartered here.*

I've heard of them. They operate search and rescue worldwide, don't they?

They do, though most of the work is in the western U.S. She turned away and started down the hill. *Let's go. I want to get you started on the pills so you can shift as soon as possible. Unless you prefer to stay as a wolf?*

No, thank you. He trotted along behind, feeling much lighter than he had. Sunny didn't seem to think there'd be a problem. If she wasn't going to worry, neither was he.

And so far, he was keeping his horny wolf under control.

Star's car rolled to a stop in front of the cabin. She turned off the engine and rested her forearms on the steering wheel. Then she laid her head down on her arms and groaned. So much for taking it slow. She'd driven from New Haven, Connecticut, to the pack's cabin near Mount Lassen, California, in a little under three days.

It had taken her just under a week, not two as she'd planned, since making her decision to leave Connecticut, but damn it felt good to be surrounded by real mountains. She hoped her folks had had time to get the place stocked, but when she'd called last night, she'd been more than halfway here.

Her dad hadn't sounded at all surprised when she told him the change in plans. He'd just chuckled, as if he'd known all along that, once her decision was made, she'd act as quickly as she could.

Star raised her head and slowly opened the door, wondering if her legs would hold her. Crawling out, she arched her back and stretched, gazing overhead at the star-studded sky.

The air at this elevation was crystal clear. The Milky Way stretched across the heavens, and the endless dome overhead was scattered with pinpoints of light—stars so brilliant they lit up the night. She'd forgotten how many stars filled the sky once you got away from city lights, but every damned one of them must be visible tonight.

Star stared for a long, long time. She didn't glance away until she felt the tears rolling down her face and dripping off her chin. Damn. What the hell was wrong with her?

Impatiently she brushed them away and leaned back inside the car to grab her overnight bag off the passenger seat. Moving slowly, muscles stiff and legs trembling, she climbed the steps to the front porch and fumbled under the Adirondack chair cushion for the key her dad had said would be there.

It was. "Thanks, Dad," she said, sticking the key into the lock on the front door. It turned easily. She opened the door and flipped on the lights. They'd gone solar years ago, which meant the refrigerator worked all the time and there was light without having to hunt for matches and lanterns, though she sort of missed the way it had been when she was small.

It had been so exciting for the little kids when they'd come here and had to rough it. Not that it was all that rough, even before solar.

She stood in the main room and gazed about at the familiar knickknacks and odds and ends. Pretty rocks and a few arrowheads they'd found as kids, a toy car sitting on top of a bookshelf, and coloring books and crayons stacked in the corner where Luc and Tinker had set up a play area for the kids.

There were drawings tacked to the log walls, pictures of trees and wolves and lots of stick figures that were, at one time, recognizable.

At least to the artists.

The cabin still smelled the same. And it felt the same. Comfortable and rustic downstairs with a couple of bedrooms, and a big loft upstairs. She glanced up, smiling with the memories. That floor was covered in mattresses. When they were little, all the kids had camped up there together. They'd had some pretty wild parties in that loft.

Then there were her parents' stories. Of course, they'd only told the G-rated version when the kids were small, but Star had learned to read between the lines. Both generations had a lot of good memories of that loft, though the parents' were definitely X-rated.

Lots of stories—a few that even made her mother blush, and it took a lot to get a blush out of Tala. Chuckling, Star opened the refrigerator. Her last meal had been over four hundred miles ago, somewhere near Elko, Nevada. "Dad. I love you. You are the best." Laughing, Star reached in and pulled out a huge tray of sliced rib roast and a bowl of potato salad. There were sliced tomatoes and cheeses, and all kinds of fruit and fresh veggies.

Obviously her mom must have had a say in the menu, considering the array of healthy stuff along with the not-so-healthy, but it all looked delicious. Star loaded her arms and carried the dishes to the bar that separated the main room from the kitchen. It took her three trips to find everything she wanted, including a bottle of chilled Pinot Gris.

Everything was fresh, which meant one of the delis in the closest town had handled the menu and delivered the food. It was special, knowing her parents had arranged this for her.

Then she realized how long it had been since her last shower. Leaving the food on the counter, Starr took a quick shower and wrapped herself in a robe that had been left hanging on the bathroom door.

By the time she'd eaten, it was all she could do to keep her eyes open long enough to put the food away and wash her dishes.

Of course, the two glasses of wine might have helped in the relaxing process. Smiling at the thought of a comfortable bed and nowhere to be tomorrow rather than right here, Star locked the door—living in the city for fourteen years had established habits not easily broken—and took the first bedroom downstairs.

It was the one her parents usually stayed in when they were here. She crawled between the clean sheets, thinking of her mom and both her dads; of her twin brother, Jack; and kid sister, Andrea. Andy was already married—she and Connor, Jake and Shannon Trent's son—had been boyfriend and girlfriend from the time Andy was old enough to walk.

Their mating had been such a natural segue of friendship into love that Star had worried Andy might have missed too much before tying herself to one guy.

Leave it to Andy to nail what Star had been missing. *When you know it's right, what's the point of looking further?*

Was that her problem? Had she been looking too far when what she really wanted had been right there all along?

A coyote howled in the distance. Another answered, and then another until the valley was filled with their voices. Their music made her smile. It had been too long. She closed her eyes, drifting in that half-awake, half-asleep space before sleep finally won, listening to the yips and the howls.

A primal scream sliced through the night, jolting her awake and raising the hairs on the back of her neck. The coyotes went quiet. *Puma*, she thought, and that made her smile, too.

She wondered where Igmutaka was on this glorious, star-studded night. Wondered if he ever even gave her a thought.

She certainly thought of him often enough. Her fingers crept between her legs, parted her soft folds, and went unerringly for her clit. Ig's image floated in her mind with his beautiful green eyes focused on her fingers, his full lips slightly damp as if he'd had his mouth where her fingers were so busy stroking.

What would his mouth feel like between her legs? What if he used that long, rough cat's tongue of his? She shivered. Fluids bathed her fingers and she thrust deeper, wishing for more of him than just his tongue.

She'd heard all about the way Igmutaka was hung, including Adam's reference to Ig's cock as the Louisville Slugger. The parents thought it was hysterical, but she'd had to look it up.

She'd giggled for an hour after finding out that Louisville

Sluggers were baseball bats, but she'd only been about twelve at the time, and she'd always loved baseball.

After discovering what they were talking about? Not so much.

At thirty, she appreciated the analogy.

She picked up the pace, circling her clit and then sliding three fingers deep inside her pussy, imagining Ig and his huge cock filling her, stretching her as she hung there, right on the edge, so close to coming that her body trembled.

More! She needed more. She pictured his face—his beautiful face—hovering just above hers as he pumped into her. She felt his hips thrusting, sensed the muscles in his chest and shoulders flexing and rippling, but it was seeing that gorgeous face and those emerald green eyes staring into hers that took her over the edge. She almost reached for him before she realized he was fantasy. Nothing more than fantasy, but so real in her mind.

Her body trembled and her vaginal muscles clenched around her fingers, but it was Igmutaka who'd given her yet another orgasm. It certainly wasn't the first she'd had with his image in mind—no, he'd given her countless orgasms over the years, but always in fantasy. In real life, he'd never even kissed her.

Never so much as hinted at any interest in her other than as his charge.

Damn it all! She didn't want to be thinking of him. Not now, with her heart still racing from her climax, her sucking breaths a harsh rasp in her ears. She punched her pillow a couple of times and flopped back down. Willing herself to think of nothing more than the stars overhead, Star finally drifted off to sleep.

She was close. So very close. Mik said Mikaela Star wasn't due to arrive for at least a week, but Igmutaka had sensed her drawing near earlier in the evening. So well had his tawny pelt blended with the dry grasses, she'd had no idea he watched her from the meadow in front of the cabin. No idea he'd raised his head in the darkness and inhaled her intoxicating scent.

She couldn't know—would never know—how terribly he missed her, how much he'd wanted to touch her. So great was his need when he thought of the long years without her, he wanted to weep.

Instead, Igmutaka snarled softly. He'd not scream again. That had been a foolish mistake on his part, a cry borne of frustration. There was no need to warn her he was nearby. He dare not give her time to strengthen her defenses against him.

She'd been so angry the last time he saw her. Almost eighteen, furious with him for interfering with her life. He'd never told her father or Sunny the terrible things she'd said, the threats she'd made. He hadn't understood them then.

Hadn't understood her. He had to thank the goddess for sending Sunny to him. She'd taught him so much about the way women thought, what they wanted. What they meant when they didn't say the words. That was the hardest part—understanding how women could say one thing and mean something entirely different, though he doubted he'd ever figure it out. Not completely.

Sunny said that was part of the mystery. He'd have to take her word on that. What Sunny hadn't been able to explain was how he was going to make Mikaela Star understand they were fated. That she would love him whether she wanted to or not.

His job was to make her want to love him, or it would never work. But how did a man who was, as Sunny often teased him, older than dirt, woo a beautiful, young, thoroughly modern woman?

His thoughts suddenly clicked into place. Maybe that was the problem. Mikaela Star hated being told what to do. Was it the fact they were fated to mate that kept her from accepting him?

He'd have to think about that for a while. He'd give her time to get settled, maybe time to get a little bored, and then he'd approach her. But not as a man. He would meet her as the puma, maybe even visit her dreams as her spirit guide.

Except he wasn't her spirit guide. Not anymore.

Okay, so he wasn't going to push things, but he wasn't above subterfuge if it would help him win the woman he loved.

He'd let this relationship move on Mikaela Star's terms.

Assuming she cared enough to have terms.

If she didn't care, if he was totally wrong hoping she might have feelings for him, what then? He knew he couldn't go on as he was, existing as spirit, as animal, as only a fraction of a man.

Without Mikaela Star in his life, he'd felt as if he had no life, but he'd still had hope. If she were to mate another and bear a son, could he possibly go on and guide her child?

No. He would end himself before that happened. The goddess couldn't possibly ask anything so cruel, though he wouldn't put it above the gods. They were, after all, male. More capricious in many ways than the Chanku goddess would ever be. Sometimes he was convinced that where the goddess Eve acted out of love, the gods merely acted to entertain themselves. He hated feeling like their pawn, but for so many eons, that's all he'd been.

Enough. He was ready to choose life on his terms. And those terms had damned well better include Mikaela Star Fuentes.

He turned from his vantage point on the outcropping above the meadow. Turned away from the view of the cabin lying in shadow. He knew what room she'd chosen. What bed she slept in.

Alone.

Moving like another shadow within the darkness, Ig found the small cave where he could rest. He'd eaten well—a fat buck that hadn't moved fast enough to escape his cougar—and now the coyotes dined on the rest of the carcass.

Their music would entertain him tonight.

With luck, in a few more days he'd be sitting inside at the table with Star, dining on the food that had been delivered just this morning. He tried to imagine sharing a meal with her, and need washed over him like a flowing wave.

What if she didn't love him? What if Sunny had been wrong? No. Not tonight. He was much too adept at creating imaginary scenarios that had as great a chance of being wrong as right.

Tonight he would think as a cougar. It was all about now. About his own needs and nothing more. A warm place to sleep, a full belly, and no worries. At least, not at this moment.

A lot safer, being a cat, and definitely more conducive to a good night's sleep.

Fen followed Sunny off the mountain along a well-traveled path. He picked up the scent of so many different creatures that he quickly lost track of what animals had come this way—though he recognized the varied scents were all those of predators.

Sunny paused and glanced over her shoulder. *You're smelling Chanku, along with whatever creature they've become. We can shift into all kinds of animals, but all are predatory. Eagles, huge snakes, pumas, wolves. Even coyotes and foxes, though most of us go for the larger, stronger animals. Mei Chen prefers her snow leopard, as does her mate. Most of us choose the wolf.*

Why the wolf?

It's a pack animal, a good fit with our tightly structured society. Wolves are highly intelligent, good parents, loyal to the pack, and very brave. They do well with a single alpha leader, which we have in Anton Cheval. She made a soft chuffing noise that almost sounded like laughter. *Truth? The real boss is Anton's mate, his wife, Keisha. The men accept the fact that this is a matriarchal society. Final decisions rest with the women, though the men will take the lead when protection is needed.*

The women don't fight? After what little he was beginning to know about Sunny, he'd pegged her as a fighter.

The women are deadly fighters, but the hierarchy of the men fighting for us evolved because the women are often watching over children—they protect their young and the men protect everyone.

I've read about the Chanku. Often wondered if that's what I might be, but you start out looking like human babies. I began as a wolf.

You're sure of that?

I am. I remember my mother. Not human. If she shifted, I never saw it. When I awoke as a boy child, I was terrified, though my adopted father seemed to have expected it.

Did you know English?

He would have laughed if he'd had the ability. *No, but I had no trouble speaking Finnish. I was born a wolf in the southeastern forests of Finland. I grew up and went away to school in Helsinki. When I returned to my father, he was dead. I found his frozen body and I buried him, settled his affairs, and came to America to study wolves.*

Obviously, you had a reason to be interested.

I did. And I had heard of the Chanku shapeshifters, but I was fascinated by my studies of wild wolves. Since I knew that you were born human, I didn't think there would be a connection.

We've kept information of your kind from the general population.

My kind? He stopped and stared at her. What the hell was she talking about?

C'mon. She turned away and raced down the hill. *We can talk about it after we get home.*

Home? He'd not had a home since leaving Finland, but what choice did he have? He ran after her, wondering just where they were headed.

*   *   *

Sunny paused on the pathway that could lead them either to Anton's large home with the guest rooms or to her own small cabin. She knew what she wanted, and he could always let her know if he didn't like the idea.

She turned toward her place. Fen followed. Of course, he had no idea where they were going, though he paused at the bottom step when she trotted up the stairs to the deck.

Is this your home?

It is. I thought you might be more comfortable here, instead of one of the guest rooms at Anton's. She sat and gazed at him. *I didn't want you to be alone in a strange place. I have the pills here, so you can take the nutrients and be close to someone who at least knows you a little bit.*

He didn't answer, but he followed her up the stairs. Sunny shifted and opened the door. She held it wide; Fen walked in. He sniffed around the room, followed his nose to the bed, and inhaled deeply. Growling softly, he turned and glared at her.

Sunny grabbed a pale yellow sarong off a chair by the door. Carefully, she wrapped it around herself and knotted it between her breasts. For some reason, his penetrating stare made her more feel more naked than she'd ever felt with her packmates.

Fen visibly relaxed once she was covered. *Do you have a mate? Your bed is ripe with the scent of a male.*

So that was what put the bee up his butt. "You smell Igmutaka. He was here a few days ago. He's sort of a packmate, though Ig's different. He's an ancient spirit guide—also a shapeshifter. I assume he's Chanku. I've never asked. He's definitely a different branch off the family tree, so to speak. Just as you are."

You've fucked him.

She planted her palms on her hips and smiled at him, but she refused to let him bait her. "A crude way of putting what Ig and

I share, but yes. We've had sex. A lot of sex. Except with us, it was consensual, unlike when you fucked me."

He jerked as if she'd hit him. Then he hung his head. *I'm sorry. I don't know what I was thinking. I have no right to question you.*

"No, you don't, but no harm. You'll learn." Sunny shrugged, and then ran her hand over the thick ruff of fur at his neck. "I'm not sure how it affects your kind, but as Chanku, our libido is really powerful, especially after a shift. We need sex. If we don't find relief with another of our kind, it makes us crazy. If you were in your human form right now, I'd be all over you."

He tilted his head and she could have sworn he was frowning. Laughing, she said, "Fen, don't look at me like that! We're very open about our needs. It's a big part of who and what we are. Sex is as important as eating and sleeping, though I don't know about you, about your kind. Maybe you're different."

You keep referring to "my kind." What kind is that? Tell me what you do know. I have to know what I am.

"First, take one of these." She grabbed a pill bottle off her dresser, dumped one of the grassy capsules into her palm, and held it out for Fen. He sniffed it, glanced at her face, and then used his tongue to lift it out of her hand. She watched him swallow it, and nodded. "Good. Once your body makes the physical changes, you won't need to take them every day, but for now make sure you get at least one of these daily, more if you feel as if you need or want them. We all take them. Sometimes our bodies crave the nutrients they contain."

She flashed him a saucy wink. "Mostly, we just crave each other. C'mon. I'll answer any questions I can."

She stood beside her bed, figuring he'd be more comfortable sitting on the mattress beside her. At least they'd be at eye level, and she wanted to watch him with her human perception.

He followed, docile as a house pet, and when she patted the

bed covers, he easily jumped up on the bed and lay down with his front paws crossed. The frame groaned beneath his weight, and she laughed. "You're definitely bigger than most of the company I've had in this thing. Get comfortable, and I hope you don't mind, but I'm going to get a glass of wine."

If I were human, I'd ask for a beer. As a wolf, it doesn't even sound good.

Sunny was still grinning when she returned with a glass of Chardonnay in one hand and the open bottle in the other. She set both on the table behind the bed, pulled the pillows up against the headboard, and then made herself comfortable. Fen watched her, his amber eyes bright with intelligence and awareness. From what she could tell, there was nothing of the Berserker beast in this guy, but size and history didn't lie.

"Okay, here's some background. I am Chanku. I didn't find out until I was nineteen, and that was after spending almost my entire life in a wheelchair as a crippled mute. When the pack rescued me, they determined that I'd made a partial shift as a child, probably when I was being hurt by an abusive parent. It's a natural reaction if you've got Chanku blood in your veins to attempt to shift to escape danger. Probably what forced your shift, the frustration of what you observed. Once I had the nutrients and shifted completely, my bones were able to properly realign themselves as a wolf, and when I shifted back to my human form, I ended up looking pretty much the way I do now."

Until your first shift, you had no idea you were a shapeshifter?

"None, though I'd dreamed of running through the forest at night on four legs, dreams that were so vivid I would awaken with the smell of cedar and pine in my nose." She stared at Fen, remembering. "Those dreams kept me sane, but my real life didn't begin until my first shift."

As a boy, I dreamed of being a wolf, but I don't recall ever dreaming of being human when I was a wolf. I knew I was smarter than the man thought I was. I understood what he said after only a few weeks living with him. Then, a few months after he took me in, I woke up as a human boy. There was no warning.

"From your size and the fact you were born a wolf, I'm almost positive you're one of the Chanku warrior class. Do you know your Scandinavian mythology?"

Some. I was homeschooled until I went away to university in Helsinki.

"Have you heard of Berserkers?"

His eyes widened. *The fierce warriors who became wolves in battle. You're not saying that . . .*

"Actually, I am. The Berserkers are a warrior class of Chanku who came to this world with the original refugees from a dying planet."

Whoa. He lurched to a sitting position and his ears perked forward. *You're saying we're aliens?*

Laughing, Sunny rose up on her knees and threw her arms around his neck. He groaned and leaned against her, almost knocking her over. "It's okay. It's hard to call us aliens when the first Chanku landed on Earth so long ago, even before humans had evolved. We've been here longer than anyone. The Berserkers are a subspecies of Chanku. Bigger, stronger, very fierce. They were the soldiers, the ones who protected the rest of the population. We didn't know there were any of you left, but the mythology is based on fact."

I didn't protect you tonight, Sunny. His chin rested heavily on her shoulder. Sunny stroked the coarse fur between his ears. It was obvious he liked it when she touched him.

"What happened is over, Fen. I'm not hurt and I understand why it happened. When people first shift, they don't always know how to control their wolf."

She ran her fingers through his thick coat, openly admiring the beautiful colors. He was mostly gray with dark tips to his fur, but there was a dark rust color in his coat, too, so that his markings were almost like a fox.

A massive, absolutely beautiful fox.

Sitting up, he towered over her. Big, beautiful, and so powerful he could crush her with a single snap of those jaws, but he moved carefully, rubbing his head against the side of her face. Then he lay back down and rolled over on his side. *I think my day is catching up to me. I need to find a place to sleep.*

Sunny patted the bed beside her. "Right here is fine with me. I'll leave the back door open in case you want to go out, but stay with me, Fen. Please?"

He didn't answer, beyond a low groan. Sunny heard the soft sigh of his breath, and an even softer snore. She ran her fingers through his thick fur. Then she grabbed her wineglass, refilled it, and headed for the bathroom. She hoped a shower would relax her enough to sleep, no matter who was beside her in the bed.

Even a massive Berserker who had fucked her in the forest tonight.

5

Sunny wiped the fog off the bathroom mirror and stared at her tangled mass of blond hair. Short would be so much easier, but she'd sworn never to cut it short again, the way her keepers had wanted it. Back when she was still disabled and unable to care for herself, they'd wanted easy, so that's what she got.

She'd had no say in her appearance at all, but since she'd not been able to walk or talk or even feed herself, the ones who watched over her did as they pleased.

Now Sunny did as she pleased, which meant carefully combing out the tangles and then shifting to dry her waist-length hair. She made the quick transition from woman to wolf and back again so as not to wake the big wolf sleeping so soundly in her bedroom. The hair dryer was loud.

She turned off the lights and walked quietly into her bedroom. Pausing to leave the sliding-glass door open for Fen, Sunny glanced out into the darkness and let the peace and stillness flow over her. What a night this had been!

She glanced over her shoulder at the bed and smiled, wondering if this huge creature might hide the man of her dreams.

Yawning, she walked across the room and crawled quietly in beside the big wolf. He slept soundly on top of the covers, his huge body sprawled full length along the right side of the bed.

She didn't disturb him, even though her fingers itched to tangle in that beautiful, thick coat of his, but it was nice having him here. She'd always felt safe in this cabin, surrounded as she was by her packmates, but never safer than right now with such a massive beast guarding her.

She wondered what he looked like as a man. Was he the one she'd dreamed of? And what significance did the jade amulet have? She was already feeling comfortable with him, but was he someone she might someday love? Was he the one fated for her?

And did Igmutaka have any idea what he was talking about when he'd said her mate was near? That was a question only time—or the spirit guide himself—could answer. Yawning, Sunny pulled the blankets up over her naked body and fell asleep.

The dream began slowly, almost like a movie that faded from darkness into a frame of muted color. She was lying on her back in a field of soft grass, and while she didn't see anyone nearby, she sensed she wasn't alone.

Rising up on her elbows, she watched a dark figure coming toward her. The closer he got, the more familiar the man seemed, until he drew close enough for her to recognize him. It was the man from her dreams, only now she knew it was Fen.

And he'd been looking for her. His thick, dark hair was tousled, long enough to curl around his ears and fall in loose waves over his brow. He was a huge man, but there wasn't an ounce of fat on his solid frame. Muscles rippled across his bare chest, his shoulders were broad, his arms thickly muscled and powerful. Worn jeans hung low on his lean hips.

She stroked her bottom lip with the tip of her tongue, wanting nothing more than to follow that narrow trail of dark hair that began at his navel and disappeared beneath the frayed waistband, just to see where it led.

She glanced up and gazed into those beautiful amber eyes. The jade amulet was right where it belonged, hanging by a leather thong around his neck. The beauty of the carved stone emphasized the masculinity, the power of the man.

She'd always thought Tinker was a big man. Fen was even larger, but Sunny knew he was absolutely perfect for her, and she told him so in her dream. He knelt beside her, brushed a hand over her long hair, and kissed her. His lips moved over hers with practiced skill, and she welcomed the thrust of his tongue as he slowly eased her back to the ground.

He didn't speak, but she heard his voice in her head, clear and gently commanding.

Lie back, he said. *Close your eyes. Let me love you.*

This was new. He'd never made love to her before, but she smiled, closed her eyes, and lay there, waiting.

I want you to spread your legs. Reach behind you and grab the headboard. Don't let go.

The soft grass of her dream had disappeared. She didn't find it at all unusual that she now lay on her bed, so she did as he commanded. Sunny felt the bed dip and someone—it must have been Fen—pulled the blanket off of her legs. She heard her own heart thudding in her ears, felt her arousal growing with each second that passed. Moisture spilled from her pussy and dampened her inner thighs. The cool night air brushed her feverish skin as she spread her legs apart. She shivered. Then, remembering his orders, she grabbed the rails on the headboard.

The bed dipped as he moved closer, but he was such a big man. Her fingers tightened on the rails and she arched her back.

Hold still, he said, and then he pressed her thighs into the mattress with his front paws. The big claws would leave marks on her skin, but she didn't care. She hadn't realized he'd shifted, but she loved him like this, loved the wolf as much as the man, and she wanted him, no matter what form he took.

She felt his hot breath on her pussy, the cold touch of a wet nose, and the sharp, prickly bristles as the short whiskers along his muzzle rasped over her inner thighs. She heard him draw in a breath of air and felt the soft brush against her thighs as he exhaled. He moved closer and his hot breath ruffled the small thatch of blond hair between her legs.

Whimpering, she twisted her body, tried to lift closer to him, silently begging for more. She needed more now, but he was waiting, teasing her with his warmth and the knowledge of what he could do to her.

For her.

Have I told you how beautiful you are, Sunny? How much I want you? I've never seen any woman as lovely as you. As brave.

Great. All wonderful, but . . . *Now, Fen! Don't make me wait. Please.* She'd beg. She'd grovel, do whatever it took, if only he'd . . .

A warm, wet tongue stroked her inner thigh. Not even close to her clit, and yet it almost threw her over the edge. She trembled from head to toe, and the muscles in her buttocks clenched. Anticipation was killing her, slowly, by degrees.

He stroked her again with that long, warm tongue, but this time he went for the backs of her legs, licking the crease between her buttocks, following the line to her clit, and then snaking deep inside where her moisture had become a steady flow.

He lapped at her then, licking up the drops of her fluids, taking them with his tongue when she really wanted his cock inside her. His very human cock.

Not tonight, sweetheart. Tonight I want to taste you. I want to breathe you, all of you, until you fill my senses, until I can't think or see or smell anything but you. I want you imprinted on my heart and brain so that all I need to do to have you is re-member. I will remember what this night is like, and you'll be there. In my heart. In my mouth with your sweet flavors; your scent will be embedded in my skin, an aphrodisiac luring me. Calling to my senses. Let me love you, Sunny. If only for tonight.

That didn't make any sense. Fen was hers. He would always be hers. Hadn't Igmutaka promised him to her? No need to tell him, though. He'd understand soon enough.

But now . . . now she'd enjoy every touch, every lick, every nip. His tongue speared her deep. She whimpered as the tip curled against the inner walls of her vagina and then slowly re-treated until it swept over her clit. His heavy paws held her im-mobile, but she didn't fight him. No, she arched her back to give him greater access, whimpered when he touched her in just the right spot, writhed as her climax grew closer, as her body shuddered and trembled and his tongue drove deeper inside. He nibbled at her damp folds with those sharp, wolven teeth and flicked her clitoris with his velvety rough tongue.

Her climax hit hard and fast, lightning streaking from womb to clit and back again. Enough power to convulse her muscles, to stop the air in her lungs as orgasm consumed her.

Like a wild thing, it grabbed her in its clutches and threw her into the abyss. Keening a long, high-pitched cry, arching against Fen's powerful jaws, Sunny let herself go, a free fall into sensation unlike anything she'd ever experienced, an orgasm that seemed to go on forever and ever, yet ended much too soon.

Sobbing uncontrollably, crying in great, broken gasps for air, she let go of the headboard, curled her body forward, and wrapped herself around the wolf. He groaned and nuzzled close against her, offering comfort as best he could.

She'd never felt like this, never known a connection with

any lover that had left her shivering and helpless, her body sated and her heart crying out for more.

Yet they'd not linked. There'd been no mating link, though she felt the need for it, felt the emptiness deep inside where his thoughts should have filled her. Her body was sated, her heart and mind bereft.

Was this what love felt like? Was this the horrible pain Igmutaka had lived with for the past fourteen years, while Star had been off finding herself?

It was awful. It was the worst pain Sunny had ever known and the most beautiful experience she'd had in her life. Even that first time walking as a wolf couldn't compare. Still holding tightly to Fen, she tried to tell him what this had been like for her, but her disconnected thoughts didn't even make sense to her.

How could Fen possibly understand if she couldn't figure it out? She gave up. Her body relaxed and she knew the dream had ended. That's all it was. A dream. She had no idea what he looked like, so she'd imagined a perfect man—the one who had haunted her dreams for the past week—but her body was sated, her limbs as relaxed as they could be, and she was safe in her own bed.

Curling herself around her huge wolf, Sunny relaxed as sleep claimed her. But as she floated in that dark area between wakefulness and sleep, she wondered if, when she finally saw Fen as a man, would he look anything at all like the gorgeous man of her dreams? Would he be as kind? Make love with as much skill?

With those questions teasing her thoughts, Sunny finally drifted off.

Star awoke to the chatter of squirrels outside the cabin and the loud squawk of a raven. She lay there in her warm bed and smiled, listening to sounds she'd not really heard for the past fourteen years. Goddess, how she'd missed the songs of the forest. The music of her childhood.

Finally she crawled out of bed. Coffee sounded really good, but her wild side was impatient after a good night's sleep, and it had been so long since the last time she'd run.

Naked, she walked out on the front porch and stood there shivering in the early morning chill. Dew sparkled in the dry grass and the sky shimmered in shades of peach and amber. The sun wasn't up yet, but the brilliant glow along the mountainous ridge to the east hinted it would be mere moments before sunlight flashed across the meadow.

She shifted, but for some reason Star chose the cougar. She didn't intend to go far this first day, and mountain lions weren't known for their love of running. Her wolf would want to run far and hard, but she didn't feel up to that yet. Still, it wouldn't hurt to get out and stretch her muscles, and maybe find the cougar she'd heard last night.

She bounded off the deck, moving with the sinuous grace of the cat, slipping through the tall grass in the meadow surrounding the cabin, heading toward the rocky outcroppings on the far side.

She stopped about twenty yards out and sniffed a flattened area in the thick grass. A cougar had crouched here, recently from the freshness of his scent, and it was definitely male. She raised her head and searched for his scent on the air. Nothing. Deliberately she squatted and peed, marking the spot as hers.

There was no sign of him this morning, but the last thing she needed was a territorial cougar moving in on her quiet time here at the cabin. She really didn't want to have to worry about sharing space with another predator.

Light streaked across the meadow as the sun finally burst over the eastern mountains. Star trotted along a game trail that followed a meandering creek. She'd not come this way for so many long years, though obviously someone had been here.

She noticed a few discarded beer cans and other trash along the creek, and farther along the trail the remnants of a campfire.

She stopped to sniff and saw spent shell casings lying in the dirt. Not wannabe archeologists looking for Native American souvenirs as she'd first suspected. This showed all the signs of poachers. There was no hunting or fishing allowed on Chanku land, which meant she'd have to notify the pack they'd had trespassers.

This property wasn't used as much now that most of the pack lived on the Montana holdings, though the Chanku who lived and worked in San Francisco sometimes came up here for their vacations. They'd need to be warned to keep an eye out for strangers on the land. As isolated as it was here, and with human sentiments not always in favor of the long-lived Chanku, any confrontation had the potential of becoming dangerous.

She knew pack members weren't responsible for the trash or the shell casings. They were all taught from childhood to treat the land and its natural inhabitants with respect, and while they did occasionally take game, it was never with a gun.

The hunt was a way of life for creatures who were predators by nature, especially in their chosen animal forms. Just as Star knew that, should she come across a rabbit along the way, she might be able to skip fixing a bowl of cereal for breakfast.

She moved on, still watching for any sign of trouble but well aware that her cougar's senses would warn her in plenty of time to hide. It was a beautiful morning, and the scents of strangers were faint enough that she began to relax again as she followed the trail, slowly reacquainting herself with the area. So many years had passed since she'd been here, and yet, as an almost immortal Chanku shapeshifter, she was still young.

How did one gauge their age and maturity level when they were nearly immortal? She thought of Igmutaka. He'd been alive for thousands of years, living most of his life as a spirit destined to guide and protect her familial line.

How many customs and cultures had he watched come and go through the millennia? How many times and in how many ways had he been forced to adjust the way he watched over and guided those he was destined to protect? He'd had to learn new ways, new patterns of speech, even new concepts of morality.

Dear Goddess. Star came to a dead stop in the middle of the trail as the truth slammed into her. She'd been such a bitch to the poor man. If she honestly looked at herself as Ig might have seen her, she realized just how petty and small-minded she'd been. Not once during all the years she'd complained about him, cursed at him, and begged him to leave her alone had she tried to see through Igmutaka's eyes, through his experience.

How often had she misjudged his motives by comparing him to men of the modern era? Not only had she judged him by unfair standards, she'd done it from the undeniably self-centered platform of a thoroughly modern and extremely spoiled and selfish young woman.

And here she'd been wondering if he might possibly ever love her. Hell and damnation, she'd be lucky if he didn't outright hate her. She moved on along the trail but hadn't gone far when she realized the joy of her morning walk had fled. Instead of reuniting with the beauty of the wilderness, her head was filled with things her parents had said.

Things Star had totally misunderstood.

Her mother had told her she was judging Igmutaka with unfair comparisons, that she wasn't seeing the fact that he wasn't like anyone else she knew. He was unique—a good man with a view of the pack unlike anyone else's because of his vast experience.

Her father hadn't even tried to be diplomatic. He'd told her that Igmutaka had been spirit guide to generations of his line, that he knew what he was doing, had only her best interests at heart, and she'd damned well better get used to it.

Of course, that was about the time she'd chosen to go clear across the country to college. Without Igmutaka.

But AJ had said it best, standing out on the deck the night before she'd left for Yale with his arm looped around her waist and her head tucked against his shoulder. Damn how she missed her other dad. Missed his soft voice and the quiet words that were often so wise.

Words she only now was beginning to understand. *Igmutaka's sole purpose in life is to keep you safe and give you a chance to grow up as you're meant to. When you fight him, you don't hurt anyone but yourself and an innocent man whose only care is for your well-being. You're hurting him even more than you're hurting yourself by going to Yale without him.*

She'd told AJ he didn't understand what it was like, and he'd agreed, because he was a grown man and she was still a young woman. That their life experiences were totally different.

She knew that, but now, for the first time, she saw his words from another point of view—AJ's. When he said their lives had been different, it wasn't merely their age difference. He'd been reminding her that she'd grown up with nothing but love from three parents and an entire pack who wanted to keep her safe.

Something AJ hadn't experienced.

He'd found his mother dead of suicide when he was barely more than a toddler. He'd been raised in foster homes, lived on the streets, and eventually ended up in Folsom Prison for a crime he hadn't committed. Unfortunately, he'd been carrying a loaded gun when he was apprehended, which added even more time to his sentence.

If not for his cellmate Mik Fuentes loving him, and Ulrich Mason who had recognized their Chanku heritage and gotten both AJ and Mik out of prison, AJ might have died there.

He had said so much more to her than merely admonishing

her to grow up, and she'd not understood. He'd been reminding her that everything anyone had ever done for her had been done out of love. Why in the hell had it taken her almost fourteen years to figure that out?

Because she'd been too damned selfish and cowardly even to think about what they'd all tried to tell her. She'd been so caught up in her own drama, in what she thought of as her great love for a man who didn't want her, that she'd been unwilling to tell him why his words hurt her, what she'd really wanted.

She'd chosen to hurt Igmutaka rather than open her heart and tell him the truth. She'd taken her hurt feelings out on him, and then like a coward she'd run away. Not only that, she'd stayed away. What an idiot.

Disgusted with herself, Star turned and headed back to the cabin. She needed to call her folks and talk to them. Maybe ask why they'd let her get away with being such a spoiled brat.

No. It's not their fault you screwed up. Own it. It's your behavior that was wrong. Now you need to fix it.

Goddess, how she hated it when her inner grown-up reared her ugly head. The one she needed to talk to was Igmutaka. First she had to apologize, and then she'd tell him how she really felt—that she was more angry with herself for wanting what wasn't his to give, than with the man himself, but she'd been too much a coward almost fourteen years ago.

He'd been charged with protecting her. Even if he'd wanted to, he couldn't be her lover, though considering the way she'd acted, he'd have been nuts to see her as anything but a spoiled brat.

Hell, she was still a coward, but at least she was finally facing the real issue that had sent her running away from her family and friends, away from everything she loved.

Because the thing she loved the most had been the one thing

she couldn't have—the love of an immortal spirit guide who was here only to watch over her, not to make love to her.

It wasn't the fact he wouldn't let her have a life like all the other young Chanku females that had sent her running. No. It was because she'd fallen in love with every manifestation of the man, the big cat, even the insufferable spirit himself.

She'd fallen in love with someone she couldn't have, and so she'd run.

Star cut along a different route on her way back to the cabin, and it wasn't until she caught the faint whiff of sulfur in the air that she realized she'd circled around by the hot spring they'd bathed in as kids. The trail was overgrown and tangled with willows and brambles, but she found a narrow passage and managed to slip through the belt of greenery around the pond.

Steam rose in the cool morning air, and the smell of minerals and sulfur was stronger here. She raised her head and sniffed the air. No scent of any other animals—or men. She'd have to remember to stay alert. The campfire hadn't been all that old, though the scent was essentially gone, washed away by the early fall rains.

Too bad their trash didn't go away as easily. She'd have to come out with a bag and pick all of it up before she left.

Grumbling to herself, Star reached the soft grass at the edge of the pond and shifted. Kneeling, she cautiously dipped her fingers in the water, and immediately felt her tension ease. The temperature was perfect—not too hot, not too cold—but it was always good to check. Some springs went cold over time, and others reached levels that would burn skin when minor shifts in the ground changed the natural plumbing.

Anxious to soak muscles still sore and stiff from the long drive, she lifted her hair and wound it in a knot on top of her head. After a moment's search, she found a couple of dry twigs that she stabbed into the knot to hold it in place.

Carefully, she waded out into the pond, and then swam across it to the far side and the stone shelf they'd played on as kids. After a moment she found it and eased herself onto the smooth bench. Water lapped against her chin. Consciously slowing her breathing, Star let go of her worries.

A jay squawked nearby, and a red-tailed hawk screamed overhead. There was no wind to speak of, so the trees were quiet, but the spring bubbled up and water trickled over a natural stone dam before falling into the creek below. Soft, natural sounds. Sounds that eased her soul, calmed her spirit, and made her wonder once again why she'd stayed away so long.

How long had it been since she'd really been alone? Since she'd run as a creature of nature? She needed this.

Needed the time to reflect, to figure out what she was going to do with her life. For the first time since she'd left home, Star let her thoughts dwell on the man who'd unintentionally driven her away. What would she say to him now, beyond a serious apology? She definitely had to apologize. Would she have the chance when she went back to Montana? For all she knew, he might have moved on, found another more grateful soul to protect.

Sunny hadn't mentioned him for quite some time.

In fact, now that she thought of it, no one had said anything at all about Igmutaka in the last few years. Only her mother's oblique comment that Star couldn't hide from him forever. There'd been no need to mention which *him* she meant.

Closing her eyes, Star allowed herself the unusual luxury of thinking about the one man on Earth who still had the power to drive her absolutely crazy.

Igmutaka had sensed Mikaela Star's presence the moment she shifted this morning. When she chose the puma instead of her wolf, his heart had actually ached with the powerful surge of love that washed over him.

Now his cat perched on the trunk of a fallen Jeffrey pine lodged in the branches of its neighbor. High enough to watch Star but not close enough for her to notice him.

He hoped.

He watched as she shifted and stood, so proud and perfect beside the pond. She wound her beautiful hair up on top of her head and secured it with a willow twig. Then she slowly swam across the pond and found the smooth ledge that humans had used for thousands of years.

He had a personal code against listening in on private thoughts for those he watched over, but Ig realized he was no longer Mikaela Star's spirit guide. Not since she'd sent him away, though he doubted if she had realized the seriousness of her words at the time.

No. Now he was the man who would court her. Who would do whatever it took to make her his own. With that thought in mind, and only a tiny bit of guilt, he connected with her thoughts, and discovered he was the main topic in Mikaela Star's busy mind.

How does one apologize to a spirit guide? Sincerely, obviously, but if I got on my knees to beg forgiveness, I'd want to take him in my mouth and taste what's always been forbidden.

Her silent laughter filled his head even as her thoughts shocked him. Had she wanted him enough as a seventeen-year-old girl that she still wanted him now, all these years later?

He was glad he was close enough to see her smile, though the image of her kneeling before him and wrapping those beautiful lips around his erect cock was almost more than he could take.

Hadn't he fantasized about just such a thing over the years she'd been gone? Her thoughts stilled a moment, and he forced that purely sexual image out of his head. It had been wrong for such a long time that he still couldn't let himself believe it was okay.

Years ago, when he'd first realized he was seeing her not as his charge but as a woman he wanted, he'd forced himself not to think of her in such a manner. She was his to protect. His feelings were wrong, and he couldn't allow himself to want her.

But after she'd gone, after she'd told him she no longer wanted him in her life and he was no longer watching over her, he'd thought of her any way he wanted. At first with anger—an anger he realized eventually had been nothing more than his injured pride.

Now, after so many years, he realized that those first thoughts he'd had of her kneeling before him had fulfilled his need to dominate, to show her exactly what he had to offer. He would never force himself on her—that wasn't his way even in his fantasies, but those images had changed over the years, until he often thought of her lying beneath him just as he'd lain with Sunny last week. He visualized Mikaela Star smiling up at him, wanting him as much as he wanted her, or looking down on him, her thighs spread to encompass his hips, and his cock buried deep inside her sweet body.

Only in the past couple of years had he imagined her standing beside him, walking next to him as his equal, as his partner. His mate for all time, no matter how hopeless it felt.

Had Sunny been right? Had the two of them been nothing more than star-crossed lovers for so terribly long, or was this a time both of them had needed, a time for each of them to grow from one type of relationship into another?

He watched Mikaela Star, paying close attention now with his own thoughts churning. She looked so relaxed, lying there in the pool of warm, bubbling water. Her head was tilted back against the smooth bank, her eyes closed. The sticks holding her long hair had come loose, and the thick strands lay in midnight swirls about her shoulders.

He heard his name and opened his thoughts, reaching once again for Mikaela Star's words.

Ig, you always used to tell me that if I ever needed you, all I'd have to do was call you. Is that true? I've not called on you for almost fourteen years, and the last time we spoke it was just me, hurling curses at you. Will you still answer my call? Her lips curved up in a smile. *Probably not, if you know what's good for you. I'm going to do it. I'm calling you. Hoping you'll hear me. That maybe you're somehow listening in.*

Igmutaka? This is Star. Remember me? If you can hear me, if you're there at all, I really do want a chance to talk to you. I promise not to keep you for too long, but there are things I need to say. Things I should have said a long, long time ago.

She opened her eyes and gazed all around. Then she shook her head and her face crumpled, as if she wanted to cry. He almost laughed, and he wanted to shout at her and say, *Hey, Star! Give me a minute. I'm good, but even I can't move that fast.*

She'd always been so impatient.

Glancing at the ground a good twenty feet below, Ig's muscles bunched, his long body stretched out, and he jumped. Landing quietly, he slipped through the undergrowth, and with great dignity walked toward the pool.

He sat on the far side from Mikaela Star and waited. She'd closed her eyes, and he sensed her sadness, the unhappiness that seemed to cloak her like a dark shroud.

Would his presence make it worse or better? There was only one way to find out. He lay down with his front paws crossed, and waited for Mikaela Star to notice he'd come in answer to her summons.

Star realized she must have slept because the pond was no longer in shadow. Sunlight filtered through the trees, so bright it made her squint. Warm and relaxed and probably getting pruny from sitting in the hot, mineral-laden water for so long, she slung her soggy hair over her shoulders and pushed herself away from the ledge. She was halfway across the pond before she realized she wasn't alone.

A puma lay in the soft grass right where she'd planned to climb out. She stopped, treading water because she was over the deepest part, and wondered how to get past the big cat. It watched her, green eyes unblinking, ears forward. Curious more than anything.

And familiar. As she stared at the cat, she thought of her call to Igmutaka. "Is that you, Igmutaka? I called you, but I didn't really think you'd come."

I told you that, should you ever call me, I would be there. You called. I am here.

Oh, crap. She swam closer. Her feet touched bottom and she waded toward him. Naked. Why, when nudity was never an issue among Chanku, did she feel so totally naked as she drew closer to the big cat?

Because this was Igmutaka and she had to speak to him. She had to apologize for her behavior so long ago, and explain to him why she'd been so angry. Now, if she could only remember.

Except all she could think of was how beautiful his cougar was. And how she really wanted to see him as a man, to speak to him, woman to man. She reached the shore and shifted, taking the form of the cougar once again.

He blinked, and she realized he hadn't expected that. Good. If she was going to feel so uneasy, it was nice knowing he was a bit unsettled as well.

Please come back to the cabin with me. I want to talk to you, but as a woman to a man. Will you do that?

The big cat rose to his feet and stretched, but he waited patiently without comment. He wasn't going to make this easy for her, was he? Turning away, she settled into an easy lope along the most direct route. Igmutaka followed close behind, but he'd still not said a word. She'd never been able to read him when he didn't want to share, and she had no idea what he was thinking.

She made sure her shields were every bit as high and tight as his. If Ig wasn't going to say anything, neither was she.

And wasn't that a mature way to begin the conversation.

6

Is Fen with you?

Anton's soft question woke Sunny out of a sound sleep. Blinking, she glanced around the morning-bright bedroom and saw Fen lying in the sun on the deck just outside the door. *Good morning, Anton. Yes. He's out on the deck.*

I take it he's still a wolf?

Unfortunately, yes. He tried shifting last night, but couldn't. He's had one of the pills.

Do you feel any threat from him?

She wanted to say, *Only to my heart.* But she didn't. *No. He's been a perfect gentleman. I found out he's Finnish. He'll have to tell you his story.*

I would like that. Would you mind joining us for breakfast?

Half an hour okay? I was asleep.

His laughter was a bit apologetic, as much as she could expect from the man. *I figured as much, but I'm anxious to know more about him.*

Aren't we all? We'll be there as soon as we can.

It wasn't until she went in to use the bathroom that Sunny

spotted the bruises on her thighs and saw the marks of Fen's sharp toenails where they'd pressed into her skin.

She ran her fingers over the bruises, remembering and somehow relieved to know her dream hadn't been merely a dream after all. Her body heated, reacting to the sensual memory, the knowledge that he had indeed been a thoughtful and attentive lover, even as a wolf. Smiling and hoping she wouldn't have to explain the blush that heated her cheeks and the flush across her chest, she slipped into a comfortable pair of yoga pants and an old sweatshirt she'd left hanging on the hook behind the door.

When she stepped out of the bathroom, Fen waited beside the bed. Sunny walked straight to the huge wolf, leaned close, and wrapped her arms around his neck. She kissed the top of his head and whispered, "Thank you for last night. You were the best sexy dream I've ever had."

I wasn't certain if you knew it was really me. Then I was afraid you might be angry. I may have been born a wolf, but this form, the way this mind works, is still so foreign to me.

"I think you're doing great. You certainly did last night."

He hung his big head. *I felt it was the least I could do, after the way I'd . . .* He leaned away and sighed. *I am still very sorry.*

She stepped back from him. Folding her arms across her chest, she let out a frustrated sigh. "Look, Fen. I already said this: It happened, it's over, and I'm not holding a grudge. Don't play the martyr with me. It won't work."

His eyes went wide and then he seemed to think about what she'd said. After a moment of close study through those beautiful amber eyes, he appeared to accept her word. Standing, he faced her. *Your alpha wants to talk to me?*

"He does. After he feeds us breakfast. Please don't worry. Anton's a good man. A fair man."

She had a feeling he wasn't totally accepting her word, but within fifteen minutes she and Fen were walking along the pathway to the big house. Fen stuck close to her side, such a large wolf that his shoulders reached almost as high as hers as a woman.

"Hey, Sunny! Wait up. Are you guys headed for Mom and Dad's?"

Sunny paused with her hand on Fen's back. "G'morning, Lily. Sebastian. Yeah, your dad invited us down. He wants to talk to Fen." She smiled at the wolf, wondering how he felt being introduced by his human name while standing beside her on four feet. "Fen Ahlberg, these two are Lily and Sebastian Xenakis. Lily is our alpha's daughter."

Lily tugged Sebastian closer as she nodded to the wolf. "It's good to meet you, Fen. Sebastian and I were there last night, though I don't think you saw us. We ended up going out with Mei and Oliver to hunt for the missing litter."

Is the female okay? I was so afraid they would kill her.

"She is. Thanks to you." Sebastian had an arm draped loosely over Lily's shoulders, but his love for her was an almost palpable bond between them. Sunny wondered what that kind of connection would feel like. If she'd ever experience it.

"We ended up rescuing four pups," Lily said. "They're so cute, only about three weeks old. Adam, our healer, has put them with the mother in a small cave below the ridge. It's close enough so he can check on them and the pack can protect them, so she shouldn't be afraid. She's very intelligent and knew she'd been rescued by an exceptionally large shapeshifter. You are definitely a big one, Fen."

"You're a Berserker, aren't you?" Sebastian glanced at Lily, and Sunny was sure he was thinking of the fierce wolves who'd been his father's hired killers.

That's what Sunny and the alpha think. I was born a wolf, shifted to human as a child, and never shifted again. Not until last night.

"Well, if you were going to pick a time to shift, I'd say last night was just about perfect." Sebastian shared another private look with Lily. "We're headed to breakfast, too. If you don't mind, we'll walk with you."

Fen lay on the sun-warmed cedar planks with Sunny leaning against him as she sipped her coffee. He loved coffee, but the odd thing was, as a wolf it held no appeal. Now Sunny, whether human or wolf, appealed.

With that thought floating through his mind, he gazed at the gathering out on the back deck of the big house and decided this was definitely bizarre. He still felt terribly unsettled, but Anton Cheval was a gracious host and his wife an absolutely wonderful woman. Besides Fen, Sunny, Sebastian, and Lily, Adam Wolf and his mate, Liana, the healers from last night, were here. Keisha, Anton's wife, had set up a buffet under an awning, and they all sat out on the deck to eat, some on chairs, and others, like Sunny, on the sun-warmed deck. It was a casual gathering and surprisingly comfortable, considering he was the only wolf here.

He'd been offered cooked fare as well as meat, but the slices of raw venison had appealed to his carnivorous side. Now, with appetites sated and everyone relaxing in the morning sun, Anton rapped his spoon against the side of his coffee mug until he had their attention.

"I wanted to update all of you on last night's event. I'll inform the entire pack this evening, once we've gotten the official report from the sheriff's office. They were still trying to nail down the identities of the poachers this morning, and had a few more facts to check, but they said they'd have it sent before the end of the business day. I'm sorry to confirm we lost seven adult wolves, all young males. Thanks to Fen, the lone female was protected and Liana and Adam were able to heal her injuries. Sebastian and Lily found her pups, and they've been reunited with their mother, but this incident is a powerful warning. We need to step up our surveillance of even the most remote regions on our holdings."

Sebastian interrupted. "I have to take blame for this one, Anton. Lily and I spent half the night tracing the hunters' tracks, and it appears that not only did they enter through a gate I didn't even know existed, but most of the animals were shot on what was my father's land. I haven't surveyed that property at all since his death." He let out a disgusted sigh. "Lily and I are committed to going over all of it before the winter snows so we can figure out just what the wolf population is and how to better protect the wild packs."

Anton shook his head. "You're talking several square miles, Seb. You can't take the blame for what happened. The point is, those men broke the law. All the property is well marked, and the more public areas are fenced to deter trespassing. No Hunting signs are posted around the entire perimeter, and that includes your land. When I spoke with the deputies who were on the scene last night, they agreed that we've done everything in our power to discourage both trespassing and hunting, especially since it's legally declared Chanku land."

Keisha broke in. "What infuriates me is that it's public knowledge this land is held by shapeshifters. The law gave us sovereign rights equal to those of Native Americans, and we are free to set up whatever rules and regulations we want within the property boundaries. No trespassing and no hunting on Chanku land are common knowledge among the human population. Those bastards could have shot any one of us. They could have killed one of our children running in their animal form. The casual observer can't tell a wild wolf or mountain lion or any other predator from a Chanku shapeshifter."

She glanced at Fen, frowning, and he almost admitted that he'd made the same mistake last night when he thought Sunny was a wild wolf bitch in heat, but Sunny beat him to it.

She burst out laughing. Then she smiled at Fen, and there

was such tenderness in her eyes that he was confused. What was she thinking?

"That's how Fen and I met," she said, and he thought maybe he'd just slink away while he had a chance. Then she wrapped her arms around his neck and held on. "He'd just shifted and killed those three poachers. He was confused and still wound up in the adrenalin rush of his unexpected shift and bloodlust, when I came trotting through the scene."

She smiled at him, shaking her head. "Picture this—wolf bitch in heat comes across very large, extremely overstimulated male."

Anton choked back a laugh. "Oh, Fen. You didn't . . ."

Nodding, Sunny didn't even try not to laugh. "He did. Luckily, I thought he was a wild wolf and he thought the same of me, so we didn't even try to link, or the poor guy might have ended up permanently mated to me."

Fen gazed directly into Sunny's sparkling eyes. *It would not have been a bad thing,* he said. *At least not for me.*

I'm beginning to think I wouldn't mind, either, Fen, but there's no need to rush. First we have to help you shift back to yourself.

Anton steepled his fingers and studied both of them. "We also need to figure out why Fen, who in spite of the fact he's obviously a Berserker, appears to be a fairly decent fellow."

Fen shot to his feet with Sunny still hanging on around his neck, and as much as he tried to remain calm, he knew his hackles were bristling. *What are you implying, Cheval?*

Sunny squeezed him tightly, as if she might actually think she was strong enough to hold him in place, but her soft words in his mind had a definite calming effect.

It's okay, Fen. Calm down. He didn't mean to insult you.

Glancing at Lily and Sebastian, Anton shrugged. "Sunny's right. I didn't mean to insult you, but you have no reason to know what I meant. We've had a little contact with Berserkers,

Fen. All of them were killers, dangerous as wolves, and vicious as humans. You don't appear at all like them, and yet I have no doubt you are of the same breed. Still Chanku, but born of the warrior class, a group of wolves more closely aligned to their feral side. We had no idea there were any of your kind left, and I'm hoping Eve can give us some answers."

He relaxed enough to sit back down. *Eve? Who is Eve?*

"She's our goddess." Sunny smiled at him as if it wasn't anything unusual to expect answers from a deity.

"It's not," Anton said, proving once again that he could see or hear whatever Fen thought, whether he was blocking or not. There had to be a trick to this mental telepathy crap that he just didn't get.

"No trick, Fen." Anton chuckled. "Keisha says I have an insufferable sense of entitlement, but I think it's mostly that I'm insatiably curious. And determined."

Keisha muttered, "Hardheaded," and everyone laughed. Even Anton.

"Point being, very few people can block me." He glanced at his daughter. "Well, except for Lily, but she's had a lifetime of practice, and probably more than sufficient reason."

"I had no choice. It was either learn to block his snooping or murder him in his sleep." Even Anton laughed at that, which told Fen a lot about this bizarre yet fascinating group.

"And to answer your question," Lily said, "Eve is a spirit who was once a living human. Adam's mate, in fact. She now exists on the astral plane and watches over us."

"A lot better than I ever did," Liana added. She leaned against Adam and smiled at Fen as if she had a secret to share. Except, what she shared was difficult to believe. "For millennia, I was the goddess charged with protecting and watching over the Chanku. I failed miserably, and because of my failure, the Chanku population scattered and lost touch with their heritage. Then Eve died before her time. Again, my fault. My punishment from the Mother was to live as a corporeal creature, to suffer real life with a flesh-and-bone body. To experience pain."

She shrugged, and Adam planted a kiss on her temple. "It didn't quite work that way—it's been a blessing, not a curse. I've had three wonderful children and I have a good life." She reached behind her and cupped Adam's cheek in her palm. "I found love with Adam. Eve is a much better goddess than I ever was."

"Liana proved to be better suited to birthing babies and healing the sick." Adam kissed her cheek. "And putting up with me. That's a full-time job."

Liana chuckled. "That's the truth. You are definitely a trial, m'dear, but it's good to hear you admit it."

Fen realized how much he'd missed by not having a family, or, as Sunny had said, by not being part of a pack. Everyone laughed together and supported one another. From what Sunny told him, they loved together as well. He found it fascinating.

"What do you suggest, Dad? Should we take Fen to Eve?" Lily stood and began clearing dishes from the buffet table. Sebastian helped, carrying things into the house, while Sunny gathered up everyone's plates.

Anton glanced at Sunny. "It's really up to Fen. Sunny? What do you think? You know Fen best. Eve, or maybe Igmutaka?"

Sunny paused with her arms loaded with dishes. "Igmutaka sensed Fen was coming days ago. In fact, the night before Ig left, he told me . . ." She glanced at Fen and blushed, but then she sort of straightened her spine and swallowed back whatever was bothering her. "He said my mate was near, that I would know him when I saw him."

She looked straight at Fen, as if daring him to argue with her, but all he wanted to do was cheer. *Who is Igmutaka? Isn't he the one whose scent was on your sheets?*

Yes. He's also the one who told me to expect you.

Fen didn't even try to block their conversation. What was

the point? *Then maybe he's the one we should speak to. Possibly he can tell more about me. Who I am, where I'm from.*

I thought you said you were from Finland. Sunny shot him a grin and carried the dishes through the open door into the house.

Fen turned and stared at Anton and caught him grinning like an idiot. *You think this is funny?*

"Actually, Fen, I do. I'm guessing that, in your human form, you are a very strong man, both physically and mentally, and also extremely intelligent. Those qualities are evident in your wolf, so I doubt you've rarely met your match with either a man or a woman. Until now."

Fen turned and stared at the door through which Sunny had disappeared, and sighed. *Unfortunately, I believe you're right, that I have met my match.* He glanced over his shoulder at Anton. *Why, I wonder, does that appeal to me so much?*

Like I said, you're an intelligent man. Smart enough to know that it takes a woman who's even smarter to keep you on your toes. Anton glanced at his mate with a pensive smile on his lips. There was no doubt in Fen's mind that the alpha had chosen Keisha for exactly those qualities.

Star had thought of shifting into a wolf for the short journey to the cabin, but her inner feline wanted to tease the spirit guide with a feral beauty he'd not be able to ignore. Her cougar was long and lithe and, she hoped, absolutely tantalizing to Igmutaka's big cat.

She didn't even look his way when she started down the trail, but it was impossible not to be aware of him following closely on her heels.

His scent was an aphrodisiac all on its own, so potent that she wanted to stop and roll in the grass where he walked, to rub up against him and leave her own scent on his thick fur.

But that would defeat this entire program, wouldn't it?

Goddess, she hated playing games, but how else would she ever find out what Igmutaka thought of her?

Maybe you could just ask him?

Sometimes the damned voice in her head really pissed her off, except Lily had told her once that she was almost positive the voice they heard wasn't their own conscience speaking—it was Eve. But what if, instead of asking him, Star offered?

When she shifted, she'd be naked. There'd always been an unspoken rule between her and Ig, even when he was actively watching over Star as her spirit guide, that when she was nude, she quickly covered herself. When she was unclothed after a shift, he always averted his eyes.

The few times she'd seen him naked, it had been an accident, and a rare one at that. He rarely allowed her to see him as a man. Not her. Others in the pack, but never Star.

She still didn't know why, though the few glimpses she'd gotten had fueled her dreams and her fantasies for years.

Well, she was a grown-up now, and instead of letting Igmutaka call the shots, maybe it was her turn. So aware of him that she could barely think, she wondered if she'd be able to keep her head in the game, if game it was.

But it could be the only chance she'd ever have, and there was no way she was going to waste it. The cabin came into view. Star leapt over the few steps in front and landed on the deck. Ig paused on the dirt path in front of the cabin.

He cocked his head to one side and studied her. She tried to link with him, but there was absolutely no access. She made sure her own shields were just as tight before she spoke.

Please come in, Igmutaka. I've not had breakfast yet, but there's plenty of food. If you like, I'll make breakfast for you.

I would be honored.

You, Ig. Not the cat.

Then she turned away from him and shifted. She paused just long enough for him to get a good look before she opened the door and stepped inside. Leaving the door open, Star walked past the dark jade sarong hanging on its hook and went directly to the kitchen to make coffee.

Her naked back—hopefully a back that would catch Ig's interest and hold it—was to the door, her thoughts were blocked, and her nipples so tight from arousal that they ached.

It was a sweet ache, one she rarely felt with her human lovers. She and Igmutaka might have a long and convoluted history, but he'd never been her lover.

She'd never really allowed herself to ache for him. Not even when her childish crush morphed into the love of a young woman.

With any luck, she hoped to change that, and the ache she felt now was proof, of a sort, it might be working.

She reached for a hair clip left on a small shelf, stared at it a moment, and then set it back. Instead, she lifted the heavy weight of her dark hair, leaned over to finger comb it and shake out the tangles, and then she straightened. Her thick hair fell in smooth curls down her back and over her breasts. She hoped it emphasized her nudity.

It certainly made her feel more naked. She decided that it felt decidedly primitive, standing here in a modern kitchen, entirely nude with her long hair swirling over her shoulders.

Apologize for the hateful things she'd said, the anger she'd felt so many years ago? No. At least not right away. She'd changed her mind between the front door and the kitchen. With a silent apology to Eve, Star admitted she fully intended to fight with whatever weapons she could think of for Igmutaka's love.

Ig paused at the open doorway, took one look at Mikaela Star, and hung his head. She expected him to enter the cabin as a man. Naked, just as she was. Goddess, she was beyond beautiful with all that long dark hair falling in soft waves over her shoulders. It emphasized the dark honeyed glow of her smooth skin, the sleek line of her lean, muscular frame. He sensed her arousal, smelled the rich sweetness of the moisture that would soon spill between her thighs if she didn't control her need.

Did he really want her to control it? He took a step over the threshold.

It wasn't her need he was worried about. It was his own. There was no way he could hide his feelings from her as a man.

No way at all.

She didn't turn around. "The man is welcome, not the cat."

He snarled and backed out of the cabin. In the past, when she'd given him ultimatums, he'd merely refused and waited her out. It had always worked.

It didn't appear to be working now. He sat in the doorway and stared.

She ignored him.

He snarled again, a little bit louder.

No reaction.

She continued with her chore, pulling the bag of coffee beans out of the refrigerator, filling the small grinder. He heard the thing whir, and then the scent of freshly ground coffee tickled his nostrils.

Without thinking, he raised his head and sniffed.

The rich scent of coffee, the even richer scent of Star.

She was trying to kill him. He sighed. And waited.

She continued what she was doing, pouring the ground coffee into the filter, filling the coffeemaker with fresh water. Her back was long and lean, the muscles gently rippling over her shoulders, along her narrow spine. She stretched her right arm overhead to return the grinder to a top shelf, and he wanted to lick the smooth bunch and flow of muscles running from shoulder to waist, from waist to buttock to thigh.

It had always been wrong to see her this way, to appreciate her feminine beauty, to inhale her scent and allow the sweet power she wielded wrap around his heart and soul. Now . . . now he had her father's approval. He appeared to have Mikaela Star's approval as well, if her seductive movements were any clue.

He was no longer her spirit guide. Almost fourteen years ago, she'd denied him in front of her goddess and his gods, and while she might not have realized the import of her words at the time, it had effectively severed the ties that had bound him to her since her conception.

So why did he wait? His muscles bunched and the tip of his tail twitched in feverish display. She had no idea what she did to him. Or maybe she did. Maybe this was all on purpose: Star flaunting her beauty until he couldn't fight it any longer. Until he was forced to shift, forced to take her in his arms.

Forced to love her.

He'd told her father he wanted to court Star, and that required more than a man grabbing a woman, throwing her over his shoulder, and hauling her off to the nearest bed. He was almost certain that wasn't the kind of courtship Mik had in mind.

But for some reason, he was getting the feeling that might be exactly what Mikaela Star wanted.

He was so damned confused. The longer he stared at her, the harder his heart pounded, the more the air rushed in and out of his lungs—great, uneven gasps for air that left him lightheaded and his thoughts spinning.

She waited while the machine did its job, while the rich scent of coffee filled the air. He waited, watching Mikaela Star until she turned again and reached for two ceramic mugs. She poured one cup of coffee. Poured another and set it beside the first one on the counter. He stared at the cups, at the steam rising, at the woman glancing over her shoulder, smiling at him as if she knew exactly what thoughts were screwing with his head.

He felt as if time slowed. Each soft sound echoed, drumbeats in his head. She turned again, reached for both cups.

Time sped up.

His nails dug into the threshold, scarring the soft wood, and he felt his composure—whatever fragments that were left—snap.

Igmutaka shifted.

Standing tall, he used both hands to shove his long hair back over his shoulders. Then he took a slow, deep breath to calm his raging libido and did his best to ignore the rampant erection swelling hard and high against his belly. He stepped through the open door, moving stiffly on legs that wanted to leap across the room and grab the woman. Fighting for control, he held the beast at bay.

Praise the gods, but he reached the bar separating the kitchen from the main room before Mikaela Star turned with the mugs in her hands. He sat on one of the tall stools, slipping beneath the counter before she had a chance to see just how hard his damned cock was.

How much he wanted her.

She finally turned, not acting at all surprised to see the man in her cabin. She set one heavy mug on the counter in front of him. Then she took a seat on a stool across from Ig, on the opposite side of the bar. He sighed his relief.

With any luck, his erection might actually subside before she saw him. "Thank you," he said. Then he picked up the mug in both hands and took a swallow. It burned his tongue, but he didn't let on. Mainly, he hoped she wouldn't notice that his fingers trembled.

Mikaela Star sat quietly, staring at him with a bemused expression on her face. "I'm trying to remember the last time I saw you as a man. You've not changed a bit, while I'm totally different."

He raised his head, both hands still grasping the heavy mug, and pressed his lips together. Then he spoke what was in his heart. "You've only grown more beautiful. I knew, when you finally matured, you would be breathtaking. I was right." He took another, more cautious sip of coffee. "How are you, Mikaela Star? It's been much too long."

She hung her head. Her hair flowed over her shoulder and he clutched both sides of the mug to keep from reaching across the counter to run his fingers through the dark silk.

"I know. And for that I want to apologize. I said some terrible things to you the last time I saw you. Things I regret now, because I didn't mean them. I wish I could take them back."

"I deserved every word." He glanced toward the big picture window that looked out over the meadow. He couldn't look at her while he admitted failure. Mikaela Star was obviously stronger than he could ever hope to be. "I tried my best to keep you unaware of my terrible truth, that I had become obsessed with you, with protecting you from everything and everyone, including myself. You were still so young, but so bright. So beautiful. And yet, I watched over you as if you couldn't be trusted."

He shook his head, finally admitting a truth he'd tried to hide from himself for so many years. "It was me who couldn't be trusted. Because I wanted you for myself, I was unwilling to let you grow and experience life. I was so stupid, Mikaela Star."

He sighed and then turned to look into her dark amber eyes. Hoping for absolution? He didn't deserve it, any more than he deserved this woman's love. He loosened his grip on the mug and set it aside, fully aware he'd been holding on to it to keep from reaching for the woman. He had to remind himself, she was no longer an innocent girl but a woman grown. It was time to show some backbone. To prove he was worthy of her.

"I didn't realize that by holding such a tight rein on you I drove you away, but in the end, I'm glad you left. I couldn't be trusted to protect you from the greatest threat, and that came directly from me, the one whose job it was to guide you. To watch over you."

He chuckled, but it was a rueful sound that haunted him, just as the memories he'd tried to forget for so long haunted him. "I can only assume you've stayed away all these years rather than have to deal with me again. For that, I should be thankful rather than blame you."

She reached across the bar and grabbed his left hand. Her touch sent a flash of awareness along his fingers, up his arm. She raised her eyes and he knew she'd felt it, knew it confused her even as it thrilled him, but she shook her head, denying it.

"I'm the one who has to apologize. Yes, you made me angry, but I had no right to lash out. AJ nailed it when he told me everything you said or did was done out of love. I was judging you through the eyes of a selfish and spoiled girl. I like to think I've finally grown up."

She smiled at him, but she was still holding his hand, and that was all he could think about, the way her fingers wrapped around his, the warmth of her grasp, the connection. Then she tilted her head, and all that beautiful hair fell to one side. He fought every instinct he had that wanted him to reach out and wrap those silken strands in his fist.

"I had no idea you were even interested in me," she said. "Much less obsessed. I think I like that."

"What?" Frowning, he tried to see what she was thinking, but her shields were so tight he practically bounced off her mind. "Why? I don't understand."

This time she laughed out loud. "Because it makes this so much easier. I need to know what it is between us that's been driving me nuts for almost fourteen years. More, if you count the years when I was still home and you were making me crazy. You might have been obsessed, but I was no better. What I didn't realize is how that would make you feel, knowing that your purpose as my spirit guide was to keep me safe—probably from guys just like you. For that, I do owe you an apology."

Ignoring her apology—one she didn't owe him—he asked,

"How do you intend to find out?" Then he shrugged, hoping like hell she wouldn't realize he was tied in knots sitting so close to her, their fingers intertwined. "This thing you say is between us?"

His heart practically pounded out of his chest. An unwelcome bead of sweat threatened to trickle down his right temple.

"It's simple, really. I think you need to follow me into that bedroom." She glanced over his shoulder. "And since we're both already naked, all we have to do is follow through with what both of us obviously want."

He tried to swallow, but his mouth had gone dry. Was she really asking what he thought?

"I think you need to be more specific," he said. Then he grabbed his cup with his free hand and took a deep swallow. Thank goodness it was cool enough now that he didn't burn his tongue.

"Oh, Ig." She laughed again and wrapped both hands around the one she'd been holding. "You can't be that thick." She squeezed his fingers and then let go of his hand, stood, and walked around the bar. Without any warning at all, she slid onto his lap and rested her arms on his shoulders.

She'd not even glanced at his cock, but there was no way she could miss that monster, pressed as it was between her thigh and his belly. "We're going to finish our coffee, get off this stool, and go into that bedroom. There, you and I are going to get into that nice big bed and take care of exactly what it was that drove us both crazy so many years ago."

"Are you saying . . . ?"

"We're going to fuck, Ig. You and me."

He was still trying to wrap his mind around the words he was sure she'd said when Mikaela Star slid off his lap. She paused a moment, gazing at the rampant erection standing between his legs.

"Bring that and follow me."

Then she turned away and, hips swaying in time with her hair, sashayed down the hallway to the first bedroom.

Ig stared at his erection, and it almost felt like the damned one-eyed beast was staring back at him. "I'm not so sure this is quite what I was planning," he said, to no one in particular. He gazed down the now-empty hallway, took a last sip of his coffee, and, feeling like a man on the way to the gallows, followed Star.

7

Fen had another of the nutrient capsules after his meal and waited outside while Sunny helped Liana and Adam clean the kitchen. Lily and Sebastian remained on the deck, telling him some of the history of their pack and how so many of them ended up living on Anton—and now Sebastian's—huge holdings in Montana.

I vaguely recall my father talking about how the Chanku went public. He kept my existence as a shapeshifter quiet, and I've continued to live my life closeted. Of course, I couldn't shift, so it wasn't an issue.

Lily sat close to Seb, holding his hand but focusing entirely on Fen. "Legally, being a shapeshifter is not an issue, but we still face discrimination, and we have to be careful traveling alone. There will always be those who want us gone."

"My father didn't help the situation, either." Sebastian glanced briefly at Lily. "There was a series of grisly rapes and murders—young women raped by a human and torn apart by wolves. Of course, suspicion rested firmly on the Chanku communities, here and in San Francisco where the crimes were committed, and he did his best to foster that belief. Even I was a suspect for a period of time, but it turned out to be a psychotic plan of my father's. The killers were Berserkers, which is why we were all so surprised to meet you and discover you're a decent guy. They were vicious killers, not very smart, very little sense of humanity, even in their human forms."

"They were thugs," Lily said, gazing at her mate. "But so was your father, in his own way."

Sebastian nodded. Fen figured he'd have to get the details from Sunny. *Were they raised as wolves or as humans? That might account for their feral natures as humans.*

"We'll never know," Lily said. "They're all dead." She stared at Fen for a moment and then frowned. "Fen, I know you said you preferred to meet with Igmutaka rather than Eve, but I have a feeling . . . Oh!" she said, and smiled. "C'mon. Dad's office. Get the others, Sebastian. She's coming here."

Here? Your goddess? Curious, Fen followed Lily into the house, trotting after her as she ran quickly down a broad hallway. Sebastian headed in the opposite direction, presumably going after the others.

They walked into a large room, and at first he couldn't figure out what was so different about it, until he realized it was shaped like a pentagram with five walls. A long granite bar ran the length of one of the walls, and there was a huge video screen on the wall opposite. Anton sat at a massive oak desk in one corner. He appeared to be working on a computer.

Lily went straight to him and parked one hip on his desk. He raised his head, obviously surprised. "Lily! I didn't hear you."

"Eve just contacted me. She wants to meet Fen and suggested your office. I think she loves the fact it's a pentagram."

Anton glanced at Fen and winked. Then he rose and pulled the shades on the large windows, darkening the room. "It's easier for Eve if she doesn't have to take an entirely solid form. This way we can see her better."

Adam, Liana, and Sunny walked into the room with Sebastian. Sunny went directly to Fen and hugged him. "Looks like we were overruled. You'll love Eve. She's amazing."

Fen leaned against her. He wished he could shift so he could hold her in his arms, though having her arms around him wasn't bad at all.

Everyone found a place to sit. Sunny, Adam, and Liana ended up together on the big leather couch with Fen sitting upright on the floor at Sunny's feet. Anton and Sebastian sat in a couple of leather recliners, while Lily perched on the arm of Seb's chair.

Lily glanced at Fen, and then at a spot in front of the video screen. "We're here, Eve, and anxious to hear from you."

A pale glow filled with tiny sparkling lights began to coalesce out of nothing at all. As Fen watched, it swirled, grew brighter, and began to take form. Within seconds, the form became recognizable as a female figure. The figure stepped away from the glow, still gaining her physical shape as the sparkles spun and then merged to create the translucent image of a human figure.

The hairs along Fen's spine stood on end as the shape grew more distinct. A beautiful woman in a flowing white gown with long blond hair reaching almost to the ground smiled and gazed about the room. She focused on each of them in turn, pausing only when she saw Adam and Liana. "I didn't realize you two were here. It's so good to see both of you." Her voice was low pitched with a soft echo, and Fen realized he heard her inside his skull as well as with his ears. She nodded in his direction.

"And Fenris. I had hoped you would one day find your way here." She walked toward him. He sat very still. His wolf wanted to leap for her like a house dog after a treat, but his adult male knew better. Even so, it was a struggle to remain in place.

She knelt in front of him, reached up, and placed her hands on either side of his skull. He whined but quickly stopped, embarrassed by the sound he'd made, but it was such an amazing feeling when she touched him. Almost as if she was inside him and around him all at once.

He stared into her eyes, and the oddest thing happened. Though his color vision as a wolf was mostly shades of gray, he saw all the colors swirling in her eyes—amber and blue, gray and green. He felt his mind begin to swirl with them, and he blinked to stay connected to the here and now.

After a moment, she nodded, ran her fingers over his head, and then, to his surprise, planted a kiss on his wet nose. "Did you know you are named for Fenrisúlfr, the mythical wolf of Norse fame? The one who slew Odin? Please realize, this goddess wishes you no harm." Laughing, she stood and, with her fingers tangled in the thick fur at his neck, looked at the others.

"Fen is indeed a Berserker. There is much in his history that won't be revealed until he chooses a mate." She glanced at Sunny, and Fen wanted to cheer. "When he does, during the mating bond, he will need someone strong and level standing beside him."

Sunny's eyes instantly focused on his.

He couldn't have looked away if he'd wanted. *You're the only one I would want beside me,* he said. *But only if it is your wish.*

I will be the one, she said. *Just try and stop me.*

While the others were probably eavesdropping, it felt as if he and Sunny were the only two in the room.

At least, until Eve spoke again. "Fen, in one more day, maybe even tonight, you should be able to shift to your human form. You are much closer to your wolven side than the average Chanku. The nutrients you've had will merely aid your natural ability. Once you have your human form, there is much of the mundane that must be done. You'll have to notify your employer that you're taking a leave of absence from your work. When you explain your role in stopping the poachers on this property, they will understand. As a Chanku male, one with your training and education, you will be more valuable to them should you wish to return to your line of work."

I should tell them I killed men?

She nodded. "You should. Truth is always best, and if you hide it, the act will weigh heavily on your conscience. Once you've reported to the local authorities and your superiors, you and Sunny will go south, to the cabin in Lassen. Why will be made clear once you arrive. I wish I could say more, but I don't know the reason behind the instructions I'm giving to you, only that I've been asked to send you."

"Is the Mother involving herself in Chanku–human politics again?" Lily was standing now, and she glanced at Sebastian as if this were something of grave concern to both of them.

Eve merely laughed. "It appears so, Lily. I hadn't planned to come here until I realized I had no choice. I am merely her messenger. Remember, the Mother has only your best interests in mind, but beyond that, I've learned not to try to understand her thoughts. It's merely best to follow her instructions and hope for the best."

Sunny's arms went around Fen's neck. "Thank you, Eve. We really do appreciate your help."

"You're more than welcome. Now, I must return to my own *where* and my own *when*. It is difficult to remain in a world where I no longer belong, though please know that I watch over all of you with all my love." She turned to Anton with her hands held out. "Thank you, Anton, for your lovely pentagram. It anchors me when I need to visit. The Mother's blessings on all of you, and all of yours."

She raised her hands as if in supplication, but then her eyes flashed and she gazed at Fen. "You must find the jade wolf," she said. Slowly she dissolved until only a small cloud of sparkles remained, and then even those disappeared.

Fen shook his shaggy head. *I find it difficult to believe what I've just witnessed.* Adam's short bark of laughter startled him. Fen swung his head around and stared at the man.

"Tell me about it, Fen. At one time, Eve was my mate. The woman I loved. I will always love her, but she's much happier in the life she has now, and the woman beside me holds my heart." He turned and kissed Liana's lips, just a quick little taste that left her smiling.

Anton walked over to the windows and opened the shades. "Our road has been convoluted and sometimes painful, Fen, but knowing that the goddess and the Mother watch over us gives all of us strength. We lost Eve as a member of our pack, but we gained Liana. Somehow, there is always balance."

"Anton? Do you need Fen and me for anything else?" Sunny stood with her fingers still tangled in the fur at the back of his neck. "I'd like to take Fen for a run, show him around."

"Good idea," he said. "But before you go, do you have any idea what she meant by the jade wolf?"

Sunny glanced at Fen. "In my dreams, I saw a man who wore a jade amulet, a carved wolf. I think the man is Fen. I won't know for sure until he shifts."

Anton nodded. "Go, then, but keep an eye out for poachers, for any sign of them. We have no way of knowing if those three were the only ones." He looked at the others. "That goes for all of you. Warn the others to be aware and alert. Keep the little ones close, at least for the time being."

He walked over to his desk. "Sunny? Would you carry this for Fen? It's his wallet. Oliver and Mei found it. Oh, and your cell phone, Fen. I imagine the sheriff will be interested in whatever photos you've got when you go down and give your statement."

* * *

Sunny led Fen back to her cabin so she could drop off his wallet and phone. She thought about peeking at his driver's license to see what he looked like.

You're welcome to look, you know. Though if you see my face and decide you don't want me after all . . .

He looked so disconsolate, she laughed. "I think I know what you look like. The man I saw in my dream last night? Did you give me that image?"

No. Open the wallet, Sunny. I need to know if you approve.

"I already approve, but it would be nice to know who to expect when you shift." Holding the wallet in her hands, she studied him. "Since you're Finnish, I should probably picture a big, blond Viking type, but I don't. I'll go with the guy in my dream—dark hair, worn a bit long, dark amber eyes, skin more a coppery shade than fair. In many ways, I picture a man with coloring more suited to a Native American than a Viking."

He didn't say a word, but he stared at the wallet so intently that she finally gave in and opened it. When she pulled his photo identification free of the plastic holder, her fingers were shaking so hard she could barely hold on to it.

Once she had it free, she couldn't stop staring. "It's you."

Of course it is.

She laughed. "No. You're the same one from my dream last night, from my dreams all week. And you're wearing the amulet on a leather thong around your neck." She raised her head and stared at him, a beautiful wolf watching her so intently. "How did I know what you looked like? I've dreamed about this man for days."

I don't know, but it makes me believe our meeting must be fated. I wish I'd not lost the amulet. My father gave it to me when I was very young, but I think it was my mother's.

"Then let's go back to where you shifted. Eve says we need to find it, and that's the logical place to look." She stuck the wallet and phone in her desk drawer and quickly undressed.

Fen waited patiently, watching her every move as she stripped off her clothing, opened the door, and then shifted.

His wolf reacted to the bitch beside him. He sniffed her face and lightly pawed her shoulder before quickly backing off. *I'm sorry. I need to learn to control the wolf better.*

Your wolf is only thinking exactly what I've got in mind. C'mon. She wrapped her tongue over his muzzle in a sloppy kiss, and then the two of them leapt off the deck together and headed toward the forest.

Knowing Fen was the same man who had come to her repeatedly in her dreams left Sunny feeling strangely unsettled in so many ways and yet at the same time more certain than ever that Igmutaka had been right.

Fen was the one destined to be her mate. There were secrets to be revealed, things he would learn that he didn't know now. She was anxious to move forward, if only she knew for certain that he felt the same. That he wasn't just caught up in the newness of his shift and the change in his own slice of the world. Sunny wanted a mate who would love her always.

And Goddess but she hoped it was Fen.

Igmutaka paused in the doorway and stared at Mikaela Star. She stood on the opposite side of the big bed, looking down as she straightened the covers. Somehow, seeing her doing something so domestic relaxed him as nothing else could.

Oh, he was still hard as a post and so damned horny he ached, but he wasn't afraid anymore. He never should have been. This was little Mikaela Star all grown up, but she was still the same person, the same amazing soul that she'd always been.

She was just as beautiful. As smart and funny and caring as he remembered. And she wanted him.

At least for tonight. Somehow, he had to make her want him for all time. He stepped into the room, grabbed the heavy blanket she'd just pulled flat, and tugged it out of her hands.

She raised her head and stared at him, and he realized she was every bit as terrified as he was. Afraid that this wouldn't work, that they wouldn't find the link each of them hoped was there. A gentle wave of relief washed over him as Igmutaka realized he had no reason for doubt. He loved her. He'd loved her all her life, but that love had grown and morphed into something unbelievably powerful, maturing now, as Mikaela Star had matured from child to adult.

And for the first time, he fully believed that she loved him just as much. She wouldn't be this conflicted, this determined to have him in her bed if she didn't. A beautiful woman didn't carry feelings for a man for so many years unless there was something powerful holding them close.

Now, seeing her as she was, a woman grown with a sharp mind, a quick wit, and a powerful sense of who she was and what she wanted, he was almost positive his days as an unmated male were shortly numbered. Jerking the blankets free of the bed, he tossed them over the footboard and let them tumble to the floor.

Then he folded his arms across his chest and, fighting a stupid grin that threatened to destroy any semblance of the ferocious male he wanted to present, gazed at her. "If we're going to make love, I want nothing in the way. Nothing that will hide your beauty from me or cover even an inch of your lovely skin. If anything covers you, it will be me. Only me."

She nodded. A short, sharp jerk of her chin. Where was the woman who'd said she wanted to fuck? Now he grinned and shook his head. "Ah, sweetheart. You didn't think I'd follow you in here, did you?"

Her chin lifted and her answer came much too quickly. "I did, too."

"Ah. My mistake, then." He planted one knee on the firm mattress and reached for Mikaela Star. She stared at his open hand for more than a few heartbeats. Then she took a deep breath and wrapped her fingers around his.

He tugged. She fell against him and he quickly rolled her beneath his body so that her slim hips were trapped between his thighs. His elbows rested at either side of her face, and he thrust his fingers deep into the dark silk of her tousled hair.

It was every bit as soft as he'd imagined. He leaned close and inhaled her scent, filling his lungs.

His eyes filled with tears that didn't spill. It had been so long, and he'd been afraid this day would never come. He'd never kissed her before. Never held her like this. He bent close, touched her lips with his, tasted her sigh, inhaled her soft breath and made it his own. Small, innocent kisses that barely brushed her lips, the line of her jaw, the soft shell of her ear.

She lay still beneath him, eyes open, lips slightly parted. He lowered himself against her so that they touched along their full lengths, from legs and knees to their bellies. Her breasts to his chest, with nothing but the thundering beat of their hearts between them. His erection was a hot brand riding high on his belly, cushioned by the softness of hers, and his balls nestled in the V of her thighs. Close, so very close to heaven. He held his full weight off of her but covered her. Warmed her with his body, breathed with the rise and fall of her chest.

"What are you doing?"

She sounded breathless. He liked that. He nuzzled her neck, breathing in her scent, absorbing the feel of her. "Something I've dreamed of for years," he said, nibbling along the edge of her ear. She squirmed beneath him, but he tightened his hold on her hair and used his body to hold her down, lying over her full length. "I've wanted to be your blanket. Wanted to cover you with all of me, hold you so close that we'd not be able to tell where you ended and I began. Indulge me in this, Mikaela Star. Please?"

She blinked slowly and then her smile spread across her face. "Whatever you want, Ig. However you want. I'm yours, and tonight I'm open to absolutely anything."

"Only tonight?" He kissed her fully, then. It was their first real kiss, and he put a lifetime of skill into the gentle touch of his lips to hers. A lifetime of want and need in the slight contact of his tongue searching and then tangling with hers, before mating her mouth in a slow series of thrusts.

He wound his fingers deeper in her hair, cupping the curve of her skull in his palms, and held her exactly the way he wanted, controlling this strong-minded woman with the touch of his lips and tongue, with the gentle massage of his fingertips over her scalp.

She arched her back, pressing her pubes hard up against the underside of his cock, but he did his best to ignore that part of her—and him—for now.

He moved his kisses away from her mouth, followed the line of her jaw, the taut cords of her throat to her collarbone and beyond. It took him longer than it should have, finally to arrive at her nipple, but he wasn't about to rush what he'd wanted for so long. He went for the taut peak over her heart, pressed his lips around the rosy flesh, and applied as much pressure as he could with lips and tongue.

Crying out, she arched her back and thrust her breast closer to his mouth. He worried that nipple until she was sobbing in frustration, and then turned his attention to the other.

By the time both were thoroughly wet with his saliva and dark red from his teeth and lips, she was writhing against him, her body twisting beneath his as she searched fruitlessly for relief. A steady litany of curses echoed in his mind, almost lost in the whimpers and moans she made as he loved her.

Lifting away, he nibbled and kissed his way to her belly, nuzzled the tiny thatch of dark curls covering her mons and then pushed her legs apart so he could kneel between them. His cock was hard and flush with blood, a dark brand against his own coppery skin. From this position, he knew he looked huge to her.

That was good. He didn't worry about the fit—she was Chanku and he knew she could take all of him. What he worried about was making this good for her. She would climax easily—after a run, after shifting, Chanku bodies were primed for sex—but he wanted this to be perfect for Mikaela Star.

He wanted to satisfy the woman, not merely the need sizzling in her veins. He'd sensed her frustration over the years.

He hoped to make up for as much of that as he could, today and every day for the rest of their lives. He slipped his big hands beneath her buttocks and lifted her as he sat back on his heels, looped her long legs over his shoulders and spread her thighs until he could gaze at her, at the slick petals of her sex and the dark slit he wanted to fill. Her eyes went wide—she'd obviously not expected this from him.

Instead of smiling, he gazed at her as if she were the feast and he a man dying of starvation, but wasn't that exactly how he felt? "Do you have any idea how long I've wanted to do this? How long I've waited to taste you?"

He didn't wait for her answer. Instead, he dipped his head as he lifted her close, stroking her labia with the flat of his tongue, licking and nipping at her until she cursed him and twisted beneath him. He took his time working his way to her clit, but when he found it, he easily shoved her prepuce down with his tongue and drew that entire bundle of nerves between his lips. Her clitoris was hard and rubbery, distended by her arousal into a perfect nipple for him to suck. Gently, he pulled her sensitive bud into his mouth as he slipped three fingers inside her pussy, plunging deep, stretching her to the point of pain.

Mikaela Star's legs tightened against his head. She arched her back and screamed, and her body thrashed in the throes of her climax. Her inner muscles clutched at his fingers and rippled around them as he continued pumping in and out of her wet sheath.

Her body continued to tremble and jerk as, still licking and sucking, Ig slowly eased her down from her orgasm. She lay there, spent, sweating and shivering, her eyes closed and lips parted.

He gave her no respite. Instead, he grabbed hold of his thick shaft and slowly parted the wet folds of her sex with his sensitive glans.

The crown was broad and smooth, and he'd never been so fascinated by his own cock, watching as he slipped between her flushed labia and slowly entered. He watched her face, too, to make sure he wasn't hurting her, but if her expression of bliss was any indication, she wasn't in pain.

He had dreamed of this moment for so long. Dreamed of it but never expected it to become reality. He entered her inch by slow inch with a sense of reverence, stretching her so much, watching the dark pink petals of her sex spreading so wide to give him access that it looked as if it hurt.

But she was smiling and lifting her hips to help him, pressing forward along his thick shaft as he slowly thrust deeper. He felt every ripple of her inner muscles clenching and squeezing him. Felt the heat and the slick moisture easing his way, and it was almost too much to try to hang on. He'd wanted to come inside Mikaela Star since the first moment he saw her last night, and it was taking a strength he wasn't sure he had to hold himself back now.

Finally he felt the hard mouth of her womb, the slight indentation that told him he'd bumped against her cervix. Her muscles, still spasming from her climax, clasped him tightly, but he couldn't hold still any longer.

With a soft groan, he began to move, thrusting slowly, going as deep as her body would allow. His balls slapped gently against the curve of her buttocks with every forward push. Ig closed his eyes, breathed slowly and deeply, and experienced his first taste of the woman he'd loved for far too long to be appropriate.

And then, when he knew it was time, he opened his mind to Mikaela Star Fuentes. Opened his mind, and bared his very soul.

Star's first thought, when Ig slowly crawled across the bed to take her was that Adam's joke about Igmutaka's Louisville Slugger had been right on target. She'd never seen a man so well endowed, but if Sunny could take the best of him and love every inch, Star figured she could handle it, too.

When he grabbed her and so smoothly laid her beneath him on the bed, she knew she'd had her first taste of what her mother had tried to explain. That sex with any guy was just sex, but sex with one you loved was special. From the heated look in Igmutaka's eyes to the rigid set of his jaw and the tension in his sleek muscles, Star knew she was the woman he loved. Knew he was the man she'd wanted all her life.

Love? She still wasn't sure, but there had to be something to this amazing sense of homecoming, the feeling this was where she belonged, here, beneath this beautiful, gentle, and yet powerful creature. She wanted to dissect the sensation, but after he kissed her, from the moment his lips lightly touched the corner of her mouth, conscious thought slipped away.

She lost track of time, of what he did and how he did it. Her world narrowed to the man covering her body, to the touch of lips to lips and tongue to tongue, of teeth and fingertips and thick, thrusting fingers, hard kisses and warm, sweet breath, the press of his body to hers and the heat of them combined. There was a rhythm to their loving. A rhythm of life, set to the metronome that was the beating of their hearts, the sound of them thundering in sync, one with the other.

Each new touch took her higher, further from reality. Further from what now felt like over a decade of wasted years.

When he brought her gently down from the most overwhelming orgasm she'd ever experienced, Star couldn't recall why she'd ever left him. And when he filled her, slowly forcing that huge beast of his into a sheath that had never taken anything remotely this large, she knew she'd never leave him again.

She felt every fraction of every inch as he entered her, and both of them were drawing deep, ragged breaths when he bottomed out against her cervix.

Gazing into eyes that glittered with emerald fire, she gasped when he withdrew and whimpered when he thrust deep again, faster this time, and again. Her body adjusted, taking him easily now, and the sound of him pulling out, the soft suction as he left her, the slap of flesh to flesh when he went deep again, was as much an aphrodisiac as the sight of the man naked had been.

Naked . . . dressed. Panther or human—it didn't matter. The only thing that mattered was that he was here in her bed, making love to her after so many years of fantasy. Gazing at her as if she mattered more than anyone else, as if he needed her as much as she needed him.

Closing her eyes, fighting tears that threatened to tear her apart, Star instead opened her mind. Lowering the shields she'd held in place since she first saw him by the hot spring, she tried something she'd not been able to do with all her human lovers; something she had never attempted with the few Chanku who had visited her over the years.

Knowing she was baring her soul to the man, Star opened her thoughts and welcomed him inside.

She'd expected a tentative link—a testing of the waters, so to speak—but the moment she opened to Ig, he flooded her with sensation. The tightness of her vaginal walls squeezing his thick cock, the silky slide of her hair now hopelessly tangled in his fingers, the press of her taut nipples against his chest when he lay full length along her slim body.

He gave her everything—every sensation, every emotion, all of him as it was now, entirely immersed in his Mikaela Star.

She felt it all. The heat in his balls, the way his buttocks clenched with each powerful drive. There was nothing tender about their joining from his point of view. Nothing gentle or sweet.

His was a claiming, and he wanted her to know it. Her body was his, and his was hers. He wanted her to feel what he felt, to want what he wanted.

To need every bit as powerfully as he needed.

He wanted Star in every way possible, and for her, and her alone, he would take the form of the wolf, he would give up his beloved puma and become the wolf so that they might one day mate beneath the moon and pledge themselves, one to the other, as mates for all time.

He loved her. He'd always loved her, and when she left he'd known it was the right thing to do. His feelings for the girl he'd helped raise were not merely inappropriate, they were wrong. He and she had needed that time apart for her to grow, to know what she really wanted in a mate, and he thanked the goddess that Mikaela Star had been strong enough, brave enough, to make the decision to leave, because Ig couldn't have done it.

He'd feared losing her too much. If she had chosen another, if she had chosen not to return, not to search for him, not to call him . . .

There was nothing beyond that thought for a long, silent period of darkness. And when she saw the depth of his love, felt the passion, the despair and then the hope, the need in the man she'd run away from, Star finally admitted to herself why she'd never found love with another. Why she'd never even looked.

It was here, with Igmutaka. Knowing that, knowing how he

truly felt about her, gave her the courage, finally, to open herself completely.

To share her own feelings, her fears, the love she'd tried to deny for so long. She clutched his shoulders with both hands, fully aware her nails were leaving bloody half moons in his back.

Sobbing uncontrollably even as she lifted her hips to each powerful thrust, she finally freed herself and shared the truth and the depth of her love with Igmutaka, spirit guide.

Stunned as Mikaela Star's heartfelt passion, her love for him—so unexpected, and yet so unbelievably pure—and her enduring and overwhelming need for a man she'd thought forever out of her reach slammed into his mind, Ig faltered in his tireless rhythm.

He reached between them, touched her gently where their bodies came together, and silently asked her to come for him, to let herself go so that he, too, could find release.

She cried out, and her body arched beneath his. Wrapping his hands around her, he pulled her close and sat back on his heels, his hips still thrusting, meeting hers in that age-old rhythm of man and woman. She held him tightly, her face pressed against his shoulder while her tears fell.

He wondered if she felt his. He, a man who never cried, wept with relief. She loved him. Mikaela Star loved him.

And gods, but he hoped she realized that what he wanted from her could last, quite literally, forever.

8

Fen followed Sunny along the same trail they'd taken last night. Her scent was still rich and ripe in his nostrils, though she'd said her heat was ending. Try telling that to his wolf! He wanted her more with each moment that passed—wanted her to want him with the same urgency, the same sense of destiny that grew more powerful with every minute spent beside her.

She paused by a small stream and he stood close, absorbing her scent and the mere fact she stood beside him while drinking the cool, clear water. He took a moment to appreciate his surroundings, surprised at how easy it was to relax with Sunny close to him, as if she belonged there. There was something about her—something that seemed to feed the empty places in his soul.

Just as this beautiful, pristine forest provided a sensual feast for his feral mind and a virtual paradise for creatures of the wild. Their presence filled his senses, the scent of elk and deer, squirrels and rabbits, and myriad other creatures of the deep, dark woods. Of course, once they'd registered on his wolven mind, he'd found it easy to dismiss their existence altogether.

All he really wanted was Sunny. The hunt and the needs of the wolf whispered in the background of his mind, but right now all of that was overwhelmed by thoughts of hunting Sunny. Capturing her as he had last night, but loving her as he wished he'd done, not forcing her. Never again would he force her.

Sunny raised her head from the creek. Small droplets of water glistened along the stiff hairs at her muzzle. He leaned close and licked them off. She blinked in surprise, and then he was positive he felt her smile in his mind.

Her wolf merely stared at him out of those gorgeous amber eyes. Then she turned and gazed up the trail. *We should be there in about ten minutes.*

As if nothing had happened? He wished he knew what she was thinking. *I thought I recognized the creek. We crossed it last night.*

We did. She raised her head and sniffed the air. *The stench of blood and death is gone. That's how I found you last night. I smelled the blood.*

He didn't want to think about last night. The image of the carnage still nauseated him. The memory of what he'd done to Sunny disgusted him. No matter that she excused him, it would forever be a stain on his honor.

He leapt over the creek and headed up the trail. Sunny followed close behind—a vast improvement, because her scent no longer surrounded him. Even so, he was still much too aware of the beautiful cream-colored bitch following on his heels; he could barely concentrate on his surroundings.

Anton had cautioned them both to watch for anything that seemed unusual. Fen decided that covered just about everything he saw or felt or smelled. He'd not been a wolf for so long that he'd forgotten the scents and the sounds of the forest, even the feel of pine needles and dried leaves beneath his paws.

Now, with Sunny trailing behind rather than leading him, he realized he could concentrate more on the world around him.

His hearing was absolutely amazing—the raucous cries of jays overhead and the soft rustle of mice in the grass along the trail. A small snake slithered out of their way, a sound his feral mind immediately identified. A bull elk bugled in the distance, and his nostrils flared in an instinctive search for game. Air currents rippled over his thick coat. His muscles were powerful, his strength as the wolf—especially a wolf of such massive size— almost without limit.

He noticed nothing that seemed unusual, but who was to say what was normal? What was typical? He was treading new ground with every step, and they covered ground quickly, running at a steady pace that would have exhausted him as a man.

Before long, Fen began to recognize a few landmarks.

His hackles rose with the faint miasma of death.

Just ahead he saw the outcropping of rock where he'd hidden as a man and watched the poachers. Where he'd taken pictures.

Sunny paused just outside the area where so much evil had occurred. She seemed terribly businesslike as she scanned the area and then turned to him. *Did you shift down here, near the fire, or were you up there on the rocks?*

He struggled to recall, but it was all a whirl of anger and frustration, and then blood. So much blood. *I don't remember. I was a man, lying on my belly on that slab of granite, when I heard the female wolf whimper. One of the men went for her with a skinning knife, prepared to cut her throat. That's when I lost it. I think I jumped as a man and shifted midway, or I might have shifted before I jumped. It's all pretty confusing.*

Let's look up there first.

Sunny trotted around behind the rocky ledge and went up the back side. Fen waited below, keeping an eye out for any danger. She was gone only a few moments. *Nothing there. I was hoping to avoid going close to where it all happened.*

Sorry. No such luck.

Show me again where the men were, where you think you landed. I was so terrified last night when I found this place that it's not clear in my mind. I would imagine whatever you were wearing shredded when you shifted, as big as you are. She was back down and beside him now, and she looked up at him, measuring, he guessed.

I'm curious. Just how large a man are you?

Six foot six, about two thirty.

He actually sensed her relief. *Large, then, but not as oversized as your wolf.*

He hoped she sensed his laughter. *I've been told I have presence, whatever that means.*

It means you're a big sucker, and probably scary. Let's find that amulet.

He stepped carefully near the campfire. The smell of blood and death lingered, but most of the evidence of what had happened here just hours ago had been removed. He wondered if Anton had dealt with it, or maybe the sheriff's deputies.

Or wild animals. He picked up the scent of porcupines and skunks, even coyotes. The scavengers of the forest. Following his nose, he sniffed the area where the bodies of the wolves had been stacked, while Sunny hunted around the base of the cliff.

He wished he'd asked Eve what happened to the souls of the dead beasts. Did they just die, or was there an afterlife for creatures of the wild? Maybe Sunny would know.

Add it to the list of questions that kept popping into his head.

Fen! I see it. It's here.

He spun away from his musings and trotted over to the base of the rocky cliff. Sunny stood on her hind legs with her front paws planted on the granite wall. She stared at a small, dead tree sticking out of a crevice in the otherwise sheer rock. It was at least fifteen feet above their heads.

His amulet dangled from the leather strap that appeared to

be tangled in a cluster of branches. He glanced at Sunny. *We'll have to come back with a ladder or climbing gear.*

No, we won't. Give me a minute. I haven't done this one in a while.

He was still trying to figure out what Sunny was talking about when she shifted.

Shocked, Fen yipped and jumped back. A large golden eagle sat where the beautiful cream-colored wolf had been standing. Sunny didn't say a word, but she leapt into the air with powerful downbeats of her wings and circled up and out of the campsite.

As Fen watched, mesmerized by the fluid grace of the bird, Sunny dropped down toward the dead tree and landed on a stout branch. The tree creaked and shuddered, and loose pebbles bounced down the face of the cliff. He held his breath and hoped the snag wouldn't pull free, that the branch wouldn't break, but Sunny didn't seem at all concerned.

Using her beak, she plucked the amulet by its leather cord, twisting and tugging until it came free. Then she fell forward with wings spread wide and drifted in a lazy half circle to the ground. Setting the amulet on a flat rock, she glanced up at Fen and shifted again.

This time it was Sunny, a naked nymph standing in the sunlight, laughing at what Fen was certain was a shocked expression on his face. She leaned over, picked up the amulet, and held it in her palm.

"It's beautiful, Fen. It's definitely a wolf, carved out of jade, and for what it's worth, it's the same amulet I saw in my dreams. I can tie it around your neck—I think the leather thong is long enough. It's not broken, see?" She held up the two ends. "It looks like it just came untied."

First, tell me how you did what you just did.

"The eagle? Most of us can take more than one form. I don't know about Berserkers, since you start out as wolves, but most of us can take our pick of predators. Once you're able to shift back to human, we'll give it a try. You never know what you might have in you, ya know? Now let me tie this on you."

He dipped his head and she held the cord around his neck as she tied it. "I used a square knot so it'll be easy to get it undone, but it shouldn't come loose on its own. Did you lose anything else?"

Other than my humanity? No. Let's get away from here. This place will always smell of death, I think.

I agree.

He'd been looking away and didn't see her shift, but Sunny's cream-colored wolf stood beside him. *There's a beautiful spot I want to show you*, she said. *It's not that far from the compound, but it's really special. A good place to talk.* She stared at him a moment before adding, *I want to know you better. Follow me.*

They needed to talk, preferably somewhere private that didn't have a bed, because Sunny realized that the only thing she'd been able to think about while trotting along the trail on their search for Fen's amulet was getting naked and having sex.

If there was a bed, they'd never get around to talking. At some point, they needed uninterrupted quiet, a chance to learn more about each other, to find out if this connection she felt so strongly was more than mere sexual attraction.

More than her Chanku libido in search of gratification. She was going to have to figure out how to control that part of her personality, because she was perfectly comfortable with the idea of the same kind of sex they'd done last night. Pretty self-ish on her part—obviously it hadn't given Fen any relief at all.

Rather than beating herself up over it, she led him to the only place that she could think of—a place with a sense of magic so powerful, it might actually take her mind off getting laid.

And wasn't that a crass way of describing what intimacy with Fen was like? Just that one time last night, and she knew he would be an amazing lover. Even as a wolf in what was essentially forced sex, he hadn't hurt her.

But last night, when her dream had segued into that deliciously talented tongue and those heavy paws holding her immobile, Sunny knew she'd never had a lover like him. Not even Ig, with all his skill, or Adam or Doc Logan or any of the other men in the pack.

They were good, but she'd not responded to any of them the way she had with Fen. She glanced behind her, at the big wolf following so close, and realized he was as trapped by her scent as she was in her memory of last night.

Maybe this wasn't such a good idea.

But they'd reached one of the access points to the system of caverns that ran beneath the property, so good or not, it was the idea she was going with. She jumped to the small ledge opening into one of the many tunnels that linked to a most amazing grotto. A couple of her packmates had shown her how to find it, and she'd been back many times since. It was secluded and quiet. Not once had anyone else intruded.

Fen landed gently beside her and followed as Sunny slipped through the narrow opening. It wasn't as easy for him, big as he was, but he scrambled through and stood beside her within the dark cavern.

I had no idea there were caves up here.

Not many people know about them. This actually leads to a series of tunnels and caverns that will eventually take you to a staircase that goes right into Anton and Keisha's kitchen. But that's not where we're going today. Follow me.

The first part was a squeeze for Fen, but he managed to get through the small tunnel that opened out into a medium-sized cavern with a large pool of fresh water.

They both got drinks, and then Sunny followed a larger tunnel that wound down and around so far that she knew Fen had to be hopelessly lost.

But he never questioned her. That took trust. She remembered the first time Igmutaka had brought her into this system of caves and tunnels so many years ago. It was frightening to recall that terrifying race for their lives with a wildfire raging, blocking all other paths to safety—and yet special because it was her first night as a wolf.

It was also the night she'd lost her virginity.

She hadn't questioned Ig then, either. Not about hiding out in the caves to escape the fire. As far as her first sexual experience? She'd demanded that. At nineteen, after spending almost her entire life in a wheelchair, hearing about but never experiencing sex, she wasn't going to let Igmutaka tell her no, even though he'd done his best to discourage her.

A lot of good that had done the poor guy. She might not be very big or physically strong, but one thing folks around here learned quickly—when Sunny Daye set her mind on something, she generally got her way.

Which led her back to thoughts of Fen, and whether or not they would make a good match. She'd known him less than twenty-four hours, and yet she felt as if she'd known him all her life.

The dreams had helped, but she wondered how he felt about her. Could he love her?

Where does the light come from in here? It should be much darker, but I can still see enough not to run into the walls.

Typical guy. She almost snorted. Here she was, worrying about their future together, or even if they had a future together, and Fen wanted to know what made light where none should exist. Sometimes she wondered if males and females were more than just an opposite sex.

They often felt like a totally separate species.

She hoped he didn't hear the laughter in her voice when she replied. *The walls are covered with a type of lichen that glows. It's not all that bright, but better than nothing.*

That explains it. Fascinating stuff. Now, are you going to tell me where we're going?

She wished she could read him better. Was he laughing at her? *It's not far, but it's magical. Can you trust me?*

With my life.

No laughter in that comment at all, and the sincerity in his mental voice made her heart leap with joy. How could she already feel this way about Fen? They hardly knew each other.

And yet she knew him better than any other man, including Igmutaka, and she and Ig had been lovers for more than a quarter of a century. At some point, she hoped that made more sense than it did now. *This way. We'll go about fifty yards and then meet up with a wider tunnel. You'll see light at the end.*

Light at the end of the tunnel? Why does that sound so apropos for my situation?

This time she did hear the laughter. She didn't answer, but as they turned into the wider tunnel and the soft glow ahead grew brighter, Sunny picked up speed until the two of them were racing toward the light.

She halted in a wide opening that led to a grotto she still thought of as a place that should be home to fairies. It was a huge, natural bowl curving over the top where a relatively small break in the stone ceiling let in light and air. The sides of the bowl looked almost smooth. A couple of the more scientific minded in the pack had decided it wasn't carved by wind and water but was instead the remnant of a massive air bubble of molten rock that must have burst during volcanic action eons ago.

Fen stood behind Sunny, both of them gazing upward at the small patch of blue, blue sky overhead. Ferns grew from every tiny crevice and each nook and cranny, and a thin stream of water fell at least a hundred feet from one side of the opening at the top, before splashing into a beautiful, crystal clear pool below.

The entire setting was absolutely magic—the shimmering pool, mirroring the sky, and dark walls curving above that small patch of blue. Sunlight filled the grotto and reflected off the surface of the water here at the bottom, at least for now, but as the sun shifted, the grotto would fill with shadows.

Sunny knew the water wasn't all that deep until you reached the center, but the depth was hard to judge simply because the water was so clear. Add that clarity to the bands of rock beneath the surface that exploded with color, and as beautiful as it was to look at, it really messed with her perspective.

In the spring, birds nested in the clumps of ferns growing in whatever small crevices they could find on the walls, but now it was fairly quiet here in this curved bowl, in spite of acoustics as effective as any amphitheater.

A narrow ledge stretched along one side of the pool. Water spilled over a low spot at the center and drained into the caverns below. Sunny sometimes wondered if she was the only one who sensed the magic here. Everyone in the pack knew of it, but very few took the time to come here, which suited her perfectly. She loved the quiet and the timeless beauty, almost as if peace and eternity were stored here, just for Sunny to hold.

She figured that she and Fen could use a bit of peace right now. The past few hours had truly been life changing.

She glanced at Fen. He'd been so quiet since they arrived, and since he wasn't broadcasting his thoughts, she felt uncomfortable snooping. She shifted and walked over to the edge of the pool, went down on one knee, and ran her fingers through the water.

"It's not real cold, but it's no hot spring." Smiling, she glanced over her shoulder and caught Fen watching her instead of the water. "We have a number of hot springs on the property, but nothing as magical as this."

You're the magic, Sunny. You look like a woodland nymph, kneeling at the water's edge. Did you know the sunlight is shining so brightly off your hair, it looks like polished gold?

Laughing, she stood and stared at him with her hands planted firmly on her hips. "Polished gold, Fen? Sweet words from a wolf who sees in black and white and shades of gray."

Not entirely. I can't explain it, but I saw the colors in Eve's eyes this morning, too. Amber, blue, gray, and green, swirling and spinning and so hypnotic they almost sucked me in. I've never believed in magic, Sunny. I do now. Since last night, I've seen magic. Felt it and lived it. You, Sunny, are magic. And yes, I really do see the golden light in your hair.

He stared at her for a long moment. She could think of absolutely nothing to say. No one had ever moved her the way Fen did. She wanted to wrap her arms around him as a man. Hold him and make love with him. And hopefully, if he wanted it, mate with him—two wolves in full agreement this time. By choice with hearts and minds in sync. Not once, of all the Chanku men she'd met, had she coveted one as her mate.

Now she wanted with a need that almost brought her to her knees. Eve had said he'd be able to shift by tomorrow. Could she even wait that long?

I don't think you'll have to.

Dear Goddess. She'd been broadcasting. Then what he said sunk in. Sunny cocked her head to one side and stared at him. "What do you mean?"

He didn't answer. No, he just wavered from sight for an instant, and in place of the massive wolf was the man—the same man from her dreams. Tall and broad and so beautiful he made her ache. Bigger than any of the Chanku she knew, his body could have been sculpted in bronze. She took a step toward him. He reached out, caught her hand, and pulled her close.

Without any hesitation at all, Sunny wrapped her arms around his waist and buried her head against his chest. He smelled wonderful, like green forest and clear nights, a fresh breeze over a sun-swept meadow.

He felt like home, like the end of a long journey.

"Oh, Fen." Two words, and then she burst into tears.

"Sunny? Don't cry, sweetheart. Please. You'll have me crying, too."

She cried for a moment longer. Then she sniffed and pulled away. He let her go, but he stood there, holding his hands out as if to grab her back. She knelt beside the pool, scooped water into her hands, and splashed her face. "The biggest problem with being naked when you shift is no pockets."

He smiled broadly, and then gazed down at the huge erection arcing up between his legs. "For you, maybe, but right now I'd say it's not my biggest problem."

Sunny burst into laughter as he said, "I know what you mean, though. If I were dressed, I would have been a gentleman and offered you a handkerchief."

Still laughing, she scrubbed her face with her hands. Then she raised her head and stared at him. What she saw made no sense to her at all. "The amulet is still around your neck."

"What?" He reached for the carved wolf at his throat. "I didn't even think about it. I was wearing it before I shifted. Why are you so surprised?"

"Anything foreign to the body generally falls away during a shift. Tattoos, piercings, earrings, wristwatches, barrettes in our hair—whatever we've got on our bodies that's not a natural part of us. The amulet should have fallen off."

He shrugged as if it was no big deal. "I wish I knew its significance, why Eve said I had to find it. Maybe it's part of me. Maybe Berserkers are different. Who knows." He stepped closer, frowning. "Are you okay now? I didn't expect tears."

"Me neither. I'm generally not a crier." She stood, shoved her hair out of her eyes, and gave Fen a critical once-over.

"You're definitely a big boy. And you have an accent! I don't hear an accent in my head, but your Finnish is showing."

He stepped close and ran his palm over her hair. "My accent is worse when I'm nervous."

Frowning, she gazed up at him. "Do I make you nervous?"

"A little."

"But, why?"

"Because I'm going to kiss you, and I'm not sure how you'll react. We hardly know each other, after all."

She folded her arms across her chest, hiding her breasts. "Well?"

"Well, what?"

"Are you going to man up and give it a try, or do I have to take the lead?"

Smiling broadly, he stood straighter. "You've challenged my masculinity. I have no other option." Then he pulled her into his arms and she realized that, in spite of their difference in size, she fit perfectly. He leaned over, she tilted her head, and their lips met just the way they should.

Met and might have fused for all she knew, because there was no way she ever wanted this kiss to end.

She was so tiny. He'd always been such a big man that he generally dated large women—women who were tall and big boned, strong enough to handle a man his weight and size. But what Sunny lacked in physical size, she made up for in sheer grit.

She met him kiss for kiss, her mouth moving over his as if she wanted to eat him alive. And damn, but he was so willing. There was no place soft, not a single blade of grass or even a bed of moss where he could lay her down, but Sunny didn't let that stop her.

She wrapped her legs around his waist and, still kissing him, managed to slide down on his raging erection as if he wasn't big enough to split her in two.

Except, he obviously wasn't hurting her at all, and she took him fully, deeply, until the soft lips of her sex kissed his groin at the root of his cock.

He stood there, legs braced, holding this tiny wisp of a woman as she settled herself over his cock and then moaned in pure carnal satisfaction. Fen took a few steps to the side of the grotto until he could lean against the stone wall. Then slowly, carefully, he began to thrust.

She was hot and slick, and her inner muscles rippled the full length of his cock, holding him tightly when he bottomed out deep inside, and then shivering along his full length as he withdrew.

Sex had never been like this for him, not this mindless joining of two souls totally immersed in the pleasure, the pure physicality of the act.

Then it slipped into another level altogether. He felt her questing mind and opened to her thoughts, something he'd never done as a human. Sensation filled him—what he did to her, how she felt, what she thought—all of it exploding into his mind as if he were Sunny, experiencing this great lug of a man making love to her. He would have said fucking, but she didn't see him that way.

No, she loved the way he moved, loved his strength and his size and the way he held her. And she shared exactly what she felt when he drove deep, how her body reacted when he pulled out almost all the way, paused, and left her hanging with arousal and need until he went deep again.

He'd never experienced anything remotely close, this unending loop of sensation—his reality and hers, blending into a single seething coil of arousal that wound itself around Fen, around Sunny, tightening and drawing them together, two souls so totally in sync that it was impossible to say where he began and she ended, what was Sunny's reality and what was his.

They came together on more levels than Fen knew existed. His body was a machine with limitless power, with perfect knowledge of Sunny's body, with an ability to continue stroking in, sliding out, knowing exactly what Sunny wanted, what he needed. Her strong arms were around his neck, her legs clamped tightly around his hips and he knew he could do this forever, for the rest of his life if need be.

But the precipice was there, waiting, calling to him to make that leap of faith, a leap he'd not take alone. Holding Sunny close, loving her, he kissed her lips and murmured words of love, words he'd never expected to speak to any woman.

Words of forever, of now, of children, and holding one another for all time. Promises of commitment that came from some previously unknown place so deep in his soul he'd never touched them before.

He wanted her. Not just for this moment but forever. He begged her to accept him, to promise herself to him for all time, and when she sighed against his lips and promised forever, he wanted to weep with the joy, the relief, the love he'd never felt for any other until now.

He broke the kiss and stared into Sunny's amber eyes, into eyes of a soul older than time. "I want you forever, Sunny Daye. I want you as my mate. Will you take me? Will you be mine?"

Her eyes filled with tears, and he knew she trembled on the same precipice as he did. She didn't speak. She nodded and whimpered as the first tremors of climax washed through her body, tremors Fen experienced in this amazing link.

And then there was no room for thought, for questions or answers. There was only sensation and fulfillment of so many needs, of so many desires neither one had known even existed.

Long, long moments later, with legs trembling and breath still rushing in and out of tortured lungs, with the thunder of two heartbeats pounding out a syncopated cadence, Fen leaned his forehead against Sunny's.

"So, dear one. Tell me. Is that the mating link you speak of?"

She looked at him wide-eyed and then started to laugh. And she kept laughing until she was sobbing in his arms. He walked with her to the pool and kept on going into the cool water, his cock still firmly planted deep inside her body.

When the water hit his balls and her butt, she started laughing again. He dunked both of them, squatting low enough that the water washed over their heads, and then he came up, both of them sputtering and laughing.

"Thank you," she gasped. Shoving her hair out of her twinkling eyes, she grinned at him. "No, Fen. That wasn't the mating link. That wasn't even close. You know what that means?"

He nodded slowly, grinning as he said, "I do. It means when we mate and link as you've described, it's going to kill us."

She cupped his face in her palms and planted a quick kiss on his lips. "I don't think so. But I have to tell you, that was absolutely magnificent. I love you, Fen. I don't know how or why it can happen so fast, but there's no doubt in my mind."

Fen took a moment to look at her. To really see her as the beautiful woman she was. She looked about twenty, with a gamine grin and an almost constant twinkle in her amber eyes. She was smart and funny, strong and brave, and she had a sense of honor, of honesty, that was as much a part of her as the flowing blond hair that floated in golden ripples in the water around them.

He kissed her, slowly parting her lips with the pressure of his, tangling with her tongue, branding her as his once again. "There's no doubt in mine, either. Though I don't think it happened all that fast. I think I've loved you all my life, Sunny Daye. I just hadn't met you in person until now. You're the woman I've fantasized, the one I've dreamed about, the one I've prayed for. You are mine, now and for always."

"As you are mine, Fenris Ahlberg." She cupped his face in her palms, connecting with eyes and hands, with a soul-searing sense of destiny. He felt it surrounding them, holding them together when she softly whispered, "As you will always be mine."

"When, Sunny? I want us mated. I feel a powerful drive to make you mine, almost as if the goddess is asking us to hurry. Does that ever happen?"

She shook her head. "I've never heard of it, though I know she's taken an interest in you. I'm ready whenever you are. I hardly know you, and yet somehow I do. I accept, without any fears or doubts, that I love you."

He kissed her quickly. "As I love you." He thought a moment, wondering if there was any reason at all not to do this thing that would change both of them forever. Only one question came to mind. "Do we need permission from your alpha?"

Her smile was so infectious that he realized he was grinning right back at her. "No," she said. "Anton's not like that. We're all pretty autonomous as far as personal decisions. He's met you. It's not like I'm bringing a stranger into the pack, but I'll tell him you asked. He'll like that, the fact we're actually talking about practical things and not acting purely on passion."

He laughed. "Passion works. In fact, it seems to work really well."

"That it does." She glanced at the sky overhead. Clouds had formed and the temperature felt cooler. "It looks like the weather might be in for a change. Most of the matings I've heard of were in the forest." She glanced about the grotto, and smiled seductively at him. "Do you have any problem with doing it here?"

Slowly he shook his head. Already this magical place had the feeling of a sanctuary to him, as if making love with Sunny had somehow blessed the space. "Here is absolutely perfect. I feel as if we're in our own cathedral."

She gazed around them again, slower this time. He was in her mind, seeing the sleek stone walls, the beautiful ferns, the water falling steadily into the pool below just as Sunny saw it, discovering just how deeply she agreed. Standing here in water past his waist, Fen acknowledged something he'd never really considered before—that maybe their lives had been fated for them to reach this moment together, this place in time.

Sunny's lover, the spirit guide Igmutaka, had alerted Sunny to his coming. She had dreamed of him for days before they met. Fen had long held an idealized vision of the woman he would love—never a physical image, but always an idea of the personality, the sense of humor and intelligence that would forever entertain him. Just as he was the man Sunny had seen in her dreams, she was the woman he'd longed for in his heart. Sunny was the ideal, the fantasy woman he'd created in his imagination but had never expected to find.

Not only had he found her, she'd just agreed to be his mate.

9

Hours passed before Ig and his Mikaela Star crawled out of bed long enough to eat, and even then he had to fight the desire to drag her back. To make love with her once again. She was so perfect—more perfect than even his fantasies had made her.

He had wanted this woman for so terribly long.

But he managed to let her go, though she was still within sight. They worked together in the kitchen, the two of them splitting up the chores—Mikaela Star got the food together while Ig set places at the breakfast bar.

She set out plates of roast and salads. Igmutaka grabbed a bottle of red wine and held it up for her inspection.

Mikaela Star shook her head and tried to look formidable. "It's barely three in the afternoon."

"True," he said, turning the bottle to better inspect the label. "But I want to celebrate."

"Oh?" She slanted a flirtatious smile in his direction. "And what event would that be?"

He leaned over and kissed her. "Event? I celebrate you,

Mikaela Star. I celebrate my mate to be, even as I bid farewell to eternity as a spirit guide."

Frowning, she stared at him a moment. "What do you mean? Won't you be a spirit guide anymore?"

"No." He shrugged. It was a difficult choice in only one respect—he knew how to be a spirit guide. He didn't have any idea at all how to be mated to a woman like his Mikaela Star.

But he was willing to learn. Anxious, in fact, but he didn't want her to feel rushed. "Once we mate," he said, "I'll lose my ability to exist as pure spirit. I will essentially be returning to my corporeal Chanku roots. Mating will change both of us, me probably more than you. As a spirit guide, my primary form is spirit. As your mate, my primary form will be the man you see now, or a wolf or puma, whatever we choose together. I'll have to maintain some form of corporeal body to survive."

She stared at him, wide-eyed. Then she shook her head and looked absolutely stricken. "Ig, I had no idea. I guess I haven't thought this through. I give up nothing and yet I gain everything by mating with you. Your sacrifice seems unfair."

He lifted her chin with his fingertips. "I gain you, Mikaela Star. You are more important than anything else. Already, knowing I have your love, I am fulfilled in ways I never imagined." He smiled at her and then nodded in the direction of the plates of food. "Though I could use another kind of filling. You've worn me out. I need to eat so I can keep up my strength."

"Oh." She glanced about as if she'd not even been aware she'd been standing, sat down, grabbed a plate, and proceeded to fill it. "We can't let you grow too weak," she said. Ig didn't move. He could fill himself on her beauty, the sound of her voice, the myriad expressions that flitted across her face.

After a moment, she glared at him. "Eat. Now. I want you well fed and ready for whatever comes."

"Yes, dear." He almost laughed aloud. He was not the subservient type. No wonder she stopped and stared at him. Then she seemed to drag her gaze away and concentrated once again on her meal. He filled his plate with something of everything she'd set out. Then he poured a glass of wine for each of them.

He wanted his strength for tonight, because tonight, beneath the dark moon, Igmutaka fully intended to take this amazing woman as his mate.

He wondered if she realized how quickly he hoped to claim her, so afraid was he that something could come between them now that he was so close. He had trouble taking his eyes off of her, and whether watching Mikaela Star or not, he was unable to entirely relax.

Everything was going so well—almost too well—and it was hard to accept that he was actually afraid she'd turn on him and say she'd changed her mind. Doubt was generally not a part of who or what he was, and yet he glanced her way more than once after they finished their meal, watching closely as she put the leftovers back in the refrigerator and wiped down the counter.

Still very aware of every move she made, every word she said, Ig cleared their dishes off the table, carried them to the sink, and carefully rinsed and placed them in the dishwasher. As he quickly lined the plates and silverware up in the rack, the almost comfortable routine of doing the dishes made him think of that first morning so many years ago when he'd first manifested in this physical body.

He'd chosen a decidedly androgynous look, assuming he would be less threatening to Chanku who had only known him as spirit or cougar. He knew that, as a man, he would be taller than average with broad shoulders and a powerful build. Unable to do anything about his size, he'd at least had control of his appearance.

He'd chosen with care so others wouldn't notice his size or strength when they looked at him. What they saw was a man who was unbelievably fair of face, with emerald green eyes framed in dense, black lashes, his dark hair falling in thick waves about his face and shoulders, all the way to his waist.

His appearance had worked so he'd kept it, more out of relief than vanity, but he still remembered his trepidation that very first morning when he'd introduced his new human form simply by joining the pack alpha, Anton Cheval, for coffee. He'd chosen an hour early enough that no one else had yet risen.

The guise of a nonthreatening human male, so beautiful he could have been a woman, had worked. Anton had known him immediately, and his only reaction had been to pour Igmutaka a cup of coffee and invite him to sit at the table. His almost feminine beauty had hidden his inborn power and physical strength from everyone but Anton, and he'd quickly been accepted as a member of the pack.

What had not happened as quickly was his ability to act as one of the pack. Disdaining manual labor as something beneath him, he'd been rather forcefully reminded that even the pack's alpha took out the garbage and helped in the kitchen.

Now, as he neatly stacked the dishes in the dishwasher to run the machine later when there was a full load, Igmutaka thought of how far he'd come. How much he had changed.

But was it enough change to satisfy the woman he loved?

Raising his head, he caught Mikaela Star smiling at him. "I'm broadcasting, aren't I?" He shook his head. "I must be slipping. I'm never so open with my thoughts."

"Actually, I love this insight into the spirit guide who made my life a living hell." She rose up on her toes and kissed him. "I'd heard that you had a hard time adjusting to the fact you had to do simple chores, and yes, you do appear to be making an effort. The woman who loves you appreciates it very much, but I have to say, Igmutaka, you really were a disdainful bastard."

He ducked his head to hide the blush staining his skin. No one had made him blush. Not ever. No one but this saucy wench who still pushed all his buttons, both good and bad. "Even Anton said it took me longer than he'd expected." He shrugged. "I had no idea how to be part of the pack. I loved the sex with everyone, not so much the rules and simple courtesies. Those were not easy to learn—so many rules when one takes a human form."

"But learn them you did."

"With everyone but you." He brushed his palm over her hair, twining the long strands around his fingers. "I was so caught up in protecting you, in doing my job, that I forgot you were still a young girl. And then you were a young girl I began to dream of, to build fantasies around, and that was wrong. I was furious with myself but taking that anger out on you. I was unfair to you."

She nodded, her eyes dark with memory, with emotions he couldn't define. "Always with more rules," she said. "With more criticism. I couldn't please you."

Her voice cracked on the last word as her misery flowed over him in a soft, dark wave of sadness. He tightened his fingers in her thick hair, holding on to her. Holding her close. Did she realize how she broke his heart with every word she spoke? Every reminder of the many mistakes he'd made, the things he should have done differently, should have said differently? If only he'd known, but he'd been such an idiot. So certain he had all the answers, and so terribly stupid and selfish where her feelings were concerned.

He cupped her skull in his palms and gently forced her to look at him. "My sweet, innocent Mikaela Star. You had no idea. No way of knowing that everything you did, every move you made, every word you said—they pleased me too much. You pleased me too much. You were smart and outspoken, self-confident and self-assured. As for me? I couldn't see beyond the fact you were the ultimate temptation. I thought the gods had sent you to test me."

She laughed and laid her cheek against his chest. "And I blamed Eve for sending you to drive me nuts. I wanted you. I used to lie in bed with my fingers between my legs, wishing they were you. Your lips. Your hands." She raised her head and grinned at him. "Your Louisville Slugger."

He burst out laughing. "Please tell me you didn't know about that when you were a kid. You didn't, did you?"

This time, she was the one to blush, which made him laugh even more, especially considering what the two of them had been doing over the past few hours.

"Of course I did!" She covered her eyes with one hand for a moment, but her cheeks were still flushed when she raised her head. "Think about it, Ig. There are no secrets in the pack. Can you recall any time ever that Adam has kept his mouth shut over something he thinks is funny? All the kids used to joke about it. We were constantly trying to catch a look at you when you shifted so we could see if it was really as big as Adam said."

He slanted a glance at her, seeing her now as a teenaged girl playing with the other kids, all of them a constant presence in one form or another. "And did you?" he asked. His voice sounded unusually deep, sort of rough, and he realized he was growing aroused once again. Imagining her seeing him naked so many years ago had a profound effect on him. "Did you ever see me naked?"

"Only once, that I can recall, which is strange now that I think about it. We're all so open about our bodies. But I saw you shift one night on our deck. You'd gone running with both my dads and Mom, too. Sunny was there as well, before we were such good friends, and I think Adam and Liana. Everyone was aroused after the run, and you left with Sunny, Adam, and Liana after a few minutes, but I remember looking at you and wondering how any woman could fit that big thing inside her.

Then I realized I was already taller than Sunny. I knew the two of you were lovers."

She laughed and hugged him. "Believe me, my fantasies took on an entirely new quality after just a glimpse of you that night!"

He wrapped his arms tightly around her, kissed her, and then leaned away. "I have to ask. Does the reality come close to the fantasy?"

She grabbed the back of his head in both hands, pulled him close enough to reach his lips. "The reality has totally changed my fantasies." She nipped his bottom lip, ran her tongue over the sting to sooth it. "They're going to be even more exciting now that I have a current visual of the real thing in my head. But why should I need fantasy when I can have that part of you in my body? Reality is so much better than pretend."

He growled. It was definitely a growl, but Ig didn't care. He picked her up, and they were both laughing when he threw her over his shoulder and headed back to the bedroom.

Sunny gazed at Fen as he smiled at her. Such a big man, and yet he'd treated her with nothing but gentleness. This wasn't what she'd expected from one of the feared Berserkers, but there was nothing vicious or cruel about the man.

Raindrops spattered the pond and shimmered in the changing light. The clouds were growing dark, the temperature beginning to fall. "Come," he said. He took Sunny's hand and led her to a sheltered spot beneath the curved wall of the grotto where he found a smooth chunk of rock to sit on. Then he gently pulled Sunny onto his lap.

"I want to know more about you. Who you are, where you come from. What your childhood was like. Your life before you knew who and what you are."

She wrapped her arms around his neck. "You don't really want to hear all of that."

"But I do. You know my story. I need to know more of yours, what made you so brave, so sure of your place in the world."

What? She almost laughed, but he wasn't kidding. "Fen, I must be better at my act than I think. I'm not like that at all. My childhood was a disaster. I was abused when I was small, hurt badly enough to scare me into a shift, but I was too young. I changed just enough to cripple myself and spent the next eighteen years in a wheelchair, living in foster care. When I was nineteen, I was in Washington, DC, at a special luncheon given to honor a group of young people when one of the secret service men guarding the president's daughters recognized me as Chanku.

"He and his mate got me out of there as fast as they could and brought me to Montana. The healers here realized I was caught midshift, gave me the nutrients, and helped me through my first shift. I wasn't paralyzed as a wolf, and when I shifted back to my human self, my bones and muscles realigned the way they were meant to. I've been here ever since, and other than being more grateful than you can imagine to the ones who rescued me and the pack that holds me close, I've never felt all that confident."

He hugged her close. "I will continue to admire you for all the things you say you're not. For now, let me hold you. I want to relish this time, and think about how it will be when we join as mates. What it will feel like to have someone of my very own to love."

She wrapped her arms around his waist and squeezed. "I want that same thing, that sense of someone to care for, someone who cares for me. Who loves me as much as I love him. Is that too much to ask? Are we looking for a Shangri-La that might not really exist?"

"It exists because we will it to be." He kissed the top of her head. Her cheek was pressed against his broad chest, the steady beat of his heart a soothing rhythm against her ear.

Together they watched the silvery raindrops falling into the placid pool. The light took on a golden glow as sunlight filtered through scattered clouds. For a brief moment a rainbow arched across the grotto and then, ephemeral as spirit, melted away.

Even knowing that their mating bond would divulge all these stories, all of their life experiences, one to the other, they talked. Stories about everything and nothing, about the structure of the pack and the college in Helsinki where Fen had studied. About their political beliefs and thoughts on education, and as the afternoon wore on, Sunny realized that the more she knew about this man, the more he fascinated her.

The more she loved him.

He made her laugh with his stories, and a couple of times she found herself weeping when she realized how lonely his life had been. A pack animal at heart without knowing what he lacked that left him so unfulfilled, what he needed to make him whole, he'd wandered for years, always searching for something.

"It wasn't until I found you, Sunny, that I realized what I needed. Such a simple thing, really. It was you."

She was flustered by his declaration. He obviously saw a woman who wasn't real, but she wasn't going to argue. Sunny loved the woman he saw—she wanted to be her, as much for herself as for him. Instead of disagreeing with him, though, she said, "We need to shift, Fen. It's dark and I'm getting cold. My fur coat sounds really good right about now."

He laughed. "I know. I think my butt is numb." He stared at her for a long moment. Then he kissed her. Gently, and yet she felt the passion behind the kiss. Felt his need. "Are you ready?" he asked. "Are you sure?"

Nodding slowly, she said without any doubt at all, "I am."

"You're not afraid, are you?"

She giggled. "It's not like we haven't done this before."

Fen covered his eyes with one hand and groaned. "You're never going to let me forget, are you?"

"It'll be a great story to tell the kids, don't you think?"

He blinked and stared at her. "Kids? You would want children with me?"

Tilting her head, Sunny slowly smiled. She'd had no idea the depth of his pain. How much he needed to hear that she truly loved him, no matter what. "Of course I would. Don't you want babies?"

His beautiful eyes filled with tears. "As much as I want you. But Sunny, I never imagined, never dreamed you would be willing. Knowing . . ." He shrugged and glanced away. "Who I am. What I am."

"Are you always such an idiot?" She pulled away from his arms and stood. Reached out to tug him to his feet.

"Unfortunately, it appears so. Do you still want me?" He stood beside her. Towered over her.

His size and his strength didn't frighten her a bit. She tilted her chin back and stared up at him. Studied him. "Well," she said. "I guess so. You're housebroken, right?" Laughing at his growl, she shifted.

So did Fen. His wolf was every bit as massive as she remembered, and he was already aroused, but instead of the forceful taking she'd experienced last night, he was patient. Gentle. His every move meant to reassure.

He lightly pawed her shoulder, lifted over her, balancing most of his weight on his hind legs to take the pressure off of Sunny. And when he filled her, she sensed his restraint and realized that wasn't what she wanted at all.

Harder, Fen. Fill me. You are the alpha wolf to my alpha bitch. I want every bit of you, all of you, just as you are.

He didn't answer, but his front legs tightened around her

ribs and he filled her completely. His body whipped against hers, back arching, hips thrusting. She braced herself, strong enough to hold this huge beast, to take him into her body, to clasp him tightly when the huge knot in his penis swelled within her sheath.

The power of the beast thrilled her, the sense of danger leashed, of even more power waiting in reserve—it gave her a sense of strength she'd never known before. This man, this beast, had the strength to take her in any manner he wished, and yet he treated her with care, with respect. With love.

She opened her mind to his, expecting that same love, but met only darkness. Searched deeper, knowing he was there, knowing he waited for her, but the maelstrom of thoughts was foreign, so different than she'd expected. So unlike the Chanku she'd grown to love. Then, like a ray of sunlight through clouds, she felt his questing thoughts, the mind of the man so deeply enmeshed within the reality of the beast that at first she wondered if this was truly Fen.

She opened wider, invited him in. Opened and discovered a world as alien to her as Sunny's must be to Fen, a feral existence with the trappings of humanity lightly worn. An existence where the primary force was that of the beast, where the wolf ruled, and the man was but a construct, something to hold the animal's sanity in a world where he'd never truly belonged.

A world where he'd walked alone almost his entire life.

Sunny tread lightly at first, introducing herself as the one who loved him, as the one he loved. She had no road map for this link, no rules to follow other than the rule of love, and she let that love guide her. The path grew easier, the memories more pronounced. Stark, vivid, terrifying memories the man had buried so deeply, neither he nor his wolf had known the full truth.

Memories buried, just as Sunny had buried hers.

So much darkness. Violence unlike anything either of them

truly remembered, and yet it had always been there for each of them, buried in the everyday lives they'd chosen to live. Pain and violence, controlled, forgotten, and yet not gone. Still very much a part of Sunny, of Fen.

Very much part of the link they shared as they came together in a deep and powerful bonding, a mating like no other, the two of them forever bound beneath the dark moon.

Their climax was, in so many ways, anticlimactic. A light rain had begun to fall again. Raindrops sparkled off their rough coats as each of them panted softly, bodies and minds still connected while coming down from what had been as confusing as it had been enlightening.

Fen lay beside Sunny, staring into the eyes of his mate, doing his best to sort out the myriad images swirling within his mind. Images of his own childhood, of Sunny's. Of things he'd never known, of things he wished had remained hidden.

No, Fen. Knowledge is always good. It will strengthen us. Help us understand why we are the way we are. Who we are.

The man who raised me was my real father. Why didn't he want me to know?

Because he would have had to admit that when he killed your mother, he knew exactly who and what she was. He wanted a son, but he didn't want the wolf.

She loved him. I remember lying beside her as she told me of the man who was my father. That someday he would come back for me. He hung his head and sighed. *Well, he did. He came back and killed her and took me away.*

I'm so sorry, Fen.

He gazed at her and felt the wonder, the truth in her. *I know. This mating bond, it's not like anything I ever imagined, but I feel your sorrow. It's real. Heartfelt. Thank you. You're right, though. This is something I needed to know. But what about you? Reliving the beating that caused you to shift? That crippled you for so long?*

She returned his steady gaze, so direct in her manner. So sure of herself. Her eyes were bright and sparkling, not at all sad with the knowledge she'd gained. He was proud of her for her strength, and loved her all the more for her loss.

It's okay, Fen. Now I know it wasn't my mother. It was a drunken boyfriend. I knew she had died. I didn't know how she died, or that she died the day I was beaten. He killed her. My mother died trying to protect me. All my life, I've believed she was the one who hurt me.

Fen licked Sunny's ear and rubbed his muzzle against hers. She was so brave, so strong, and he was terribly proud of the toddler she had been. Of the woman she was now. *No. I saw it through your eyes. She put herself between you and that bastard to protect you. She loved you.*

As your mother loved you. Your father, too, in his own horribly misguided way. What he did was wrong—wrong and awful—but he wanted his son. Wanted you badly enough to kill for you.

Fen thought about that. Thought about the beautiful, dark wolf lying dead in the snow, remembered the terrible pain of loss, the horror of so much crimson blood staining the white ground. *I know you're right, but I can no longer mourn the man. He took too much from me. I can't really hate him, either. There must have been something terribly wrong with him that he could have killed my mother and then talked of the remorse he felt for killing a wolf. He gave me a good life, but he lived a lie and he lied to me. I will never know what could have been.*

Sunny rested her chin on his shoulder. *Can you live with that?*

I can. As long as I have you. I know I can live with you, Sunny. You are the light that guides me, the joy I've never known. You are more than I dreamed. So brave, so good. I hope I can be worthy of your love. Hope I can be worthy of you.

The mating knot had gone down. Fen gently freed himself from Sunny. She stood, eye to eye with the huge wolf while standing on all four legs and he still lay on the ground. *Ah, Fen. Look at us. Two totally mismatched shapeshifters, damaged in so many ways and yet absolutely perfect for each other.*

He licked her muzzle before standing. Once he was up, he shook the raindrops from his coat and then gazed toward the tunnel leading from the grotto. *I think you're right. Are you ready to go back to your cabin? It feels as if the rain has settled in for the night.*

I know. She shook the water off her coarse coat. *At least it's not snowing. It's not unusual to have really cold weather in October. C'mon. We can go all the way to Anton's through the tunnels if you like. It's not late, and I don't think he'll mind if we cut through the kitchen. Besides, I want to tell Anton and Keisha we've mated.*

She paused and sniffed the air and then gazed toward the dark tunnel. *Fen, I don't know about you, but I feel a strong sense there is something we need to do. But not here. Somewhere else, with someone else.*

He stared at her for a moment, amazed to be so totally in sync with another soul. The feeling had been building in him for the past few hours, an unease he'd not been able to pinpoint, a sense he couldn't identify. At least Sunny had been able to put it into words. *I've had the same feeling, a growing sense that something is waiting, that someone needs us. It's tied into the goddess Eve's directions to go to Mount Lassen.* He took a step toward the dark tunnel. *Maybe Anton can help us figure it out.*

Sunny trotted on ahead, her tail waving like a white flag in the darkness. *Good. Besides, he needs to know the pack has just increased by one very large wolf.*

* * *

"You asked my father *what?*"

Ig shrugged, which wasn't all that easy to do while lying on his back in Mikaela Star's big bed with her sprawled over the top of him, his cock still buried deeply inside her rhythmically clenching pussy. She might have had a glorious climax, but he'd been holding out, waiting to give her one more before he allowed himself that same pleasure.

"I asked him for permission to court his daughter."

Laughing, she rolled off of him, lay beside him in the bed, and kept on laughing. He sighed. This had taught him an excellent lesson—do not talk of anything of importance during sex. At least not until he was finished. "Why do you find that so funny?"

"Oh, Ig. No one asks for permission to court a woman anymore. I don't need my father's permission to do anything. I do as I choose. I choose you, with or without his blessing."

"I know that." He scooted back until he was leaning against the headboard. Mikaela Star wrapped her arms around his waist and stared at him. He spread his fingers over her hip and held her close.

"Well, if you knew that, why did you ask him?"

"Because I respect your father. He was my charge, and we have always had an honorable friendship. I did not do it for you, my love. I did it for him. And for me. We are men with a history that goes back to your father's birth. To his grandfather's birth and to all the men before, until the beginning of your line. I owed him the courtesy."

"So . . . what did he say?"

"I thought you said it didn't matter."

She shoved herself up on her hands and glared at him. "Do not tease me. It matters what he said."

He tapped her nose with his finger. "I know, and that is why I asked. He said that he'd always believed you and I were meant to be together, that I did not need his permission to court you because you are your own woman."

"He said that? My dad? I'm amazed. He can be a bit of a chauvinist where I'm concerned. Of course, so can you." She kissed his chin to take away the sting of her words, but he felt it just the same.

"I know I can. I'm working on that, and yes, he did say that. But he also said I could not harm you in any way, nor could I use my powers as a spirit guide to coerce you. I swore to him that I would not."

"So, uh, he didn't say anything about the Louisville Slugger?" She ran her fingers down the full, hard length of him.

Ig growled. "Someday I will make Adam pay for that."

"No, you won't. You love Adam, and he loves you, or he wouldn't tease you the way he does."

"You're very perceptive. Are you ready to run? It's almost dark. We've spent the entire day in bed."

Her laughter tickled over his senses. "You look as if you're prepared to stay a lot longer. Are you certain you don't want to take care of that?" She bent at the waist and kissed the broad tip of his cock.

If anything, her kiss made him even larger. He sighed and tugged her away, wrapped his arm around her, and held her against his side. "If we made love every time I was aroused because of you, we would never leave our bed." He kissed her—a quick, proprietary kiss that left her grinning. "I want to see if I can actually become a wolf. I chose the puma as my primary form eons ago. I'm not sure I can still howl."

She licked the nipple over his heart. "I bet I can make you howl."

Laughing, he tilted her chin up with his fingertips and glared at her. "I know you can. Come. Before I forget that I actually want to leave the bed."

"Are we going to mate tonight?"

"So impatient, after making me wait for so many years?" He sat up, swung his legs off the bed, and stood. "Come, Mikaela Star Fuentes. Come while I run for the very first time as a wolf."

"You've never taken that form?"

"Not since becoming a spirit guide. Not that I recall."

"But why?" She stood beside him, gazing up, and he was reminded once again how much like her mother she was—a powerful force in a fairly petite package. At five six, she was almost a foot shorter than he. When she took her cougar form, she was small beside him. What would she be like as a wolf? He'd not seen her in her wolf form for many years.

What would he be like?

Maybe it was time to find out. And yes, he wanted to mate her, but only on her terms. He'd promised Mik he would never force his daughter.

Looking into Mikaela Star's twinkling amber eyes, Igmutaka had a feeling their desires were exactly the same.

10

Naked and walking on two legs for now, Star followed Igmutaka out onto the front porch. Goddess, but the man was absolutely stunning. His legs long and rippling with lean muscle, his buttocks taut and hollowed at the hip, flaring into strong, muscular thighs. She decided she rather enjoyed walking behind him, though the drawback lay in not seeing his face. Or the chest she'd explored so intimately, or the flat belly ridged with muscle, or his thick cock with the perfect sac beneath.

She wanted all of him, all the time. Would this need ever diminish? Would there come a time when she could look at him, at his naked body, and not want him close to her?

Inside her?

Probably not. Sighing, she forced herself to look away. It was already growing dark—a shimmer of navy blue against the western sky the only remnant of the day's light.

They'd spent almost an entire day in bed. Making love. Talking, and then making love again. After a lifetime of wanting the man, it still felt like a dream, knowing he loved her not as his charge but as a grown woman.

Knowing he finally believed that she loved him.

The air had turned chill. Star wrapped her arms around herself and shivered. Igmutaka glanced over his shoulder and raised an eyebrow. Gently he pulled her into his warm embrace with her cheek tucked against his broad chest. The blatant reminder he'd not lost his desire for her rose high and hard between them, his cock a fiery brand against her belly.

She tilted her head to better see his eyes. They appeared an even darker green in this light—more like the forests in Montana than their usual emerald, but every bit as beautiful. She sighed, knowing she would be happy to stand this way for hours, wrapped in his arms, held close against his powerful frame, but she wanted more.

She wanted all of Igmutaka, spirit guide.

But just in case he'd had second thoughts, she asked again. "You're sure you want to do this, Ig? I don't want to force you. I had no idea you'd have to leave behind such a huge part of who you are. What you are."

"That part of me has survived longer than any creature has a right to live. I'm ready for a rebirth, my beautiful Mikaela Star. Ready to start the next chapter of my life. Are you ready? Or are you the one having second thoughts?"

In answer, she slipped free of his arms and shifted, choosing the wolf this time. She sat on the top step and watched him. Ig raised his hands as if in supplication, and she linked with him to see if he truly needed to call on his gods to shift.

But no, he was asking for Eve's blessing. Thanking her. Thanking Eve and the Mother for standing beside him throughout all his years as a spirit guide. Asking for their blessing as he gave up that life and moved on to another, on to a life with the woman he loved.

Deeply touched by his sincerity and his thoughtfulness in giving thanks to the Chanku deities, Star wondered, as well, at his choice to thank the Chanku goddess and not the Sioux gods she thought he served. Was he switching his allegiance? Turning to Eve but away from his gods? Did his gods even exist? When she'd asked Eve about them, the only answer she got was unsatisfactory, to say the least.

There is much in the universe that will always remain a mystery. Know that I will be there for you, but there could be others as well. Others who care just as much, who interfere as often, who are aware of who and what you are. And then Eve's presence had faded from Star's mind and she'd been left knowing absolutely nothing more than before she asked.

Ig smiled at her, and before she could ask him anything about his prayer of thanks, he shifted.

And then, all she thought of was the wolf. He was beyond gorgeous. Bigger, more powerful than any she'd seen, and 100 percent Chanku wolf. His fur was the tawny gold of the puma, but black tips shadowed his tail and painted a line down his back, the tips of his ears and the thick ruff of fur around his neck, until he looked as if someone had lightly brushed him with India ink. He was larger than usual, just as his cougar was oversized, his shoulders broad, his teeth sharp.

Star nipped his shoulder and leapt from the deck, running for all she was worth. She wanted him as her mate. Wanted that amazing bond that she'd always known was waiting for her with this man and no other. But she wasn't going to give in easily or fast. She fully intended to make Ig work for her love.

That meant he had to catch her first.

His puma had never been fond of running, but the wolf wanted to stretch his long legs and go forever—as long as forever included catching the beautiful bitch running just ahead. She was dark where he was light, with silvery tips to her charcoal gray fur. Her scent was intoxicating, her every move an invitation to take her, to love her.

He'd been so certain they shouldn't mate right away, that

they should give themselves time to be sure. He'd not expected the fire in his blood, the overwhelming need to claim her.

To make her his.

He knew he was crowding her, but it was a struggle to back off, to give her the space to run free. The feral mind of the wolf was different than the cougar, the need to pursue stronger. The bitch easily jumped across a small creek and he followed. She twisted and turned, racing through a stand of brilliant aspen, slipping easily between trees growing so close together he could barely follow.

He sensed her laughter and knew she led him on this chase to prove the wolf's speed, its strength and sure-footedness, and racing like the wind, he laughed with her.

Freedom unlike anything he'd known, this beast so different from his cat. His senses were sharp, his endurance so much more than the puma's. Mikaela Star disappeared through a small hole in a tangle of bare willows. Instead of trying to navigate the narrow trail she'd found, he leapt entirely over the patch and landed just behind her.

She yipped and dashed to the left. He followed, and his blood raged with need. She ducked and tried to go beneath him, but he caught her tail in his strong jaws and clamped down.

Not fair!

All's fair in love and war, right?

Panting, she sat.

He let go of her tail.

She raised her nose and sniffed the air. Stopped and sniffed again. *Do you smell that?*

Inhaling deeply, he checked the air currents. A foreign scent tickled his sensitive nostrils. *Wood smoke? A forest fire?*

No. Not a forest fire. The smell is wrong.

Campers, maybe?

She stood and pointed her nose into the wind, inhaling

again. *If it is, they're trespassing. Over ten square miles of this land is private property. It's all posted, and we're just about in the middle of it. If they're close enough for us to smell a campfire, they're trespassing. Only Chanku are allowed here. I need to see who it is. Why they're here. Then I can tell them to leave.*

Not alone, you don't. Follow me. And shift. I think our cats might be quieter. He watched her, wondering how she would take his giving orders, but she followed his lead without hesitation.

Her puma stared back at him, probably wondering why he was still a wolf. He gazed into those perfect amber eyes and called up his cat, shifting so automatically that he was hardly aware of the change, but as he watched her, Igmutaka realized this was an important step.

When she was younger, she would have questioned his command. Now, she accepted the fact he made sense and did as he asked. Satisfaction left him feeling almost giddy. This was one more sign, one more thing to admire—she didn't worry about power plays. She followed his lead because she knew he was more familiar with the territory. Another alpha bitch might have questioned his taking control, but not Mikaela Star.

She was suddenly all business, no longer the flirtatious female teasing him with coy glances and quick nips. He liked the flirt, but he admired the female in front of him. Admired her and loved her, and he knew that, yes, he was more than ready to mate.

Once they took care of the trespassers.

Still cougars, Igmutaka crouched beside Mikaela Star amid boulders and shrubs on a small rise above the campfire. Ig's arousal had turned to white-hot fury at the scene below.

Four men sat around the fire, passing a bottle he recognized as cheap whisky among them. A large buck, gutted but not skinned, hung from a nearby tree. The entrails had been dragged a short distance from camp, but they'd not even made an effort to bury the bloody mess. The head with its set of trophy antlers rested on a plastic garbage bag on the hood of an older model club cab pickup truck sitting high on big tires. Small, broken trees, flattened plants, and furrows in the damp earth led to the spot where it was parked, evidence of the cross-country route they'd taken to the site.

Trash littered the campsite—takeout food containers and beer cans along with the stench of human waste—evidence they'd been here for a while.

They're pigs. Ig curled his lip in disgust. They'd fouled an otherwise perfect night with their presence.

I agree. Mikaela Star slowly turned and gazed at him out of her cat's eyes. *It explains the trash I saw along the creek.*

We need to go back to the cabin for clothing. Then we should return and force them to leave. It wasn't nearly enough, but he didn't want to unleash his feral side. Not in front of the woman he loved. It felt wrong, especially on this night, of all nights.

I've got a better idea.

There was a definite sound of satisfaction in her mental voice. Ig raised an eyebrow and wondered how effective that was on a cougar's face. *Oh?*

You're a really big cougar and I'm a pretty fair-sized wolf. What say we attack, scare the crap out of them, and then call the sheriff?

They have guns.

We've got teeth. And claws.

And we're smarter than they are.

That's obvious. She shifted, and she'd been right—her wolf was definitely larger than her cat. *Do you want to circle around, come in from behind?*

When you hear my scream, run through their camp. Snarl and growl, and go for the big one who acts like he's in charge.

You sound as if you've done this before.

If she only knew. *You'll have to ask Adam and Oliver about the hunters we've chased off the Montana land. With Mei's help, of course. Her snow leopard is quite effective.*

Go. If I'm laughing like a hyena, I won't sound nearly as scary.

He slipped away and circled the camp, quietly moving close to the four. When he was about six feet behind them, he cut loose with a scream that even Anton had admitted could make the hair stand up along his spine. As the shriek turned into a horrific snarl, Mikaela Star leapt from the cairn of boulders. Growling and snarling, she ran directly at the men.

Ig shot into the clearing from the other side. Tripping all over themselves, the four scattered. One man reached for his rifle, but Ig got to the weapon first and stood over it, snarling while the guy backpedaled, tripped over a rock, and fell backward into the fire.

Screaming and cursing, he flailed about like a turtle on his back, but the others had run for the truck with Mikaela Star biting at their heels. They locked themselves inside the cab.

Ig shifted, pulled the man from the coals, and shifted back, moving so quickly in the darkness, he hoped no one saw him.

He stood over the injured man, snarling for just a moment. Then he turned and kicked dirt over the fire with his hind legs before trotting into the shadows where Mikaela Star waited.

The one he'd saved struggled to his feet. His coat was burned, but he appeared to be unharmed. Ig screamed again, and that ungodly panther's cry sent the hunter racing to the truck.

He jumped in, and the one driving backed up so fast he stuck the wheels in mud beside the creek before throwing it into four-wheel drive and peeling out of the hole the big tires left behind. The buck's head and trophy antlers rolled to the ground.

They left the gutted body and all their gear behind. Disgusted, Ig shifted and began to gather up the guns and sleeping bags. "What should we do with all this crap?"

"Burn it." Mikaela Star had her hands filled with the buck's head and antlers. "This poor guy deserves a funeral pyre. It's damp enough here by the creek that it won't spread."

Working together, they gathered up everything and set it beside the fire. Piece by piece, Ig threw the camping gear into the coals. Once he had it hot enough, he unloaded the guns, tossed the shells into the weeds, and threw the firearms into the flames. The fire was roaring, sparking high in the night sky when Igmutaka and Mikaela Star carefully laid the body, the entrails, and head of the dead buck in the heart of the flames.

They washed their bloody hands in the creek and then stood quietly in a moment of silence. There was honor in the killing of an animal taken for food, one hunted by tooth and claw. Not when the poor creature had been needlessly killed, its life taken for no reason other than to provide a trophy.

Mikaela Star glanced at Ig and grabbed his right hand. He raised his left, holding his palm open to the heavens.

To the Chanku goddess Eve.

Take this creature's spirit, we ask of you. Restore his honor in death, honor that was denied him at the end of his life.

He sensed a ripple of power in the air around them. The fire seemed to draw in upon itself and then flashed with a burst of intense heat. Igmutaka grabbed Mikaela Star against his chest and turned his back on the sudden roar of the flames.

A moment later, the intense heat was gone, along with the body of the buck. There were tears in Mikaela Star's eyes when she raised her head, but she was smiling. "It appears Eve is paying close attention."

"Much closer attention than the gods, it appears." Ig planted a kiss on his woman's soft lips. Then he found a spot out of the smoke and sat on a large, flat rock with Mikaela Star in his lap. "This was not how I intended to spend our night."

She leaned her head against his shoulder. "The night isn't over." She kissed his shoulder. "You sure know how to show a girl a good time." Then she winked at him.

He'd not expected that. "You're not angry?"

"At you?" When he nodded, she laughed. "Of course not. Why would I be angry with you? You're the one who scared the crap out of those jerks. I never would have been brave enough to do that by myself. I just hope they don't come back."

"I got the license number off the truck."

"I didn't even think of that." She laughed and hugged him. "And here I think of you as the primitive one and myself as the modern woman."

"Primitive? How so?" As if he didn't think of himself the same way. Primitive but adjusting.

"You've always seemed closer to your animal side, even when you're in spirit form. As if violence is always there, just beneath the surface."

"You're not afraid of me, are you?" He'd never worried about such a thing, but what did he really know of this grown-up version of the girl he'd watched over so long ago?

"Never. I love you. I truly believe that you love me. I don't fear you. What I fear is ever being without you."

That will never happen. You are mine, and when this fire has burned down a bit more so we can safely leave it, I intend to make you mine forever.

She didn't answer him, but he didn't need words. All he needed was the woman beside him as they watched the fire until there were only ashes. Ashes that they doused with water from the creek, and then covered with soft sand until they were sure it was out.

The twisted remains of the rifles were just about the only solid evidence that hunters had even been here. When the ashes were cold, Ig stood and held his hand out to Mikaela Star.

Smiling, she wrapped her fingers in his and stood beside him when he tugged her to her feet. "The hot spring sounds awfully good about now. I want to wash away the stench."

Knowing she meant more than merely the smoke, Ig shifted. He chose the wolf. When he changed shapes, he also cleansed himself of all the smoke and filth—none of that would have made it through the shift—but bathing in the mineral-laden pool struck him as an important part of the ritual of their mating.

Mikaela Star took her wolf back as well. Together they trotted along the narrow trail that led to the hot spring. Ig had only three things on his mind—soaking away the events of the night, holding his woman close, and claiming her as his mate.

He raised his head and sniffed the air. There was no scent of the hunters, but the scent of the bitch beside him stirred his blood. With Mikaela Star trotting at his shoulder, Ig chose the shortest trail to the hot spring.

"I've learned it's important to follow my hunches." Anton Cheval leaned against his big desk, one hip resting on the smooth surface, his arms folded against his chest. "If you both feel a need to be doing something, don't fight it. Instead, you need to focus on what, exactly, that something is."

Sunny turned and gazed at Fen. All she really wanted to focus on was her mate. The man was amazing, and somehow absolutely perfect for her. He'd pulled on a pair of sweats she'd found hanging by the back door leading to the Chevals' kitchen, and now looked absolutely relaxed, sitting here in Anton Cheval's comfortable study with a glass of the alpha's good cognac in his hand. The borrowed sweatpants clung to his lean hips, his chest was bare, and the jade amulet rested at the base of this throat. His overall demeanor was one of authority. He couldn't look any more self-confident if he'd been wearing a suit, seated in a boardroom conversing with Anton.

Anton Cheval was the undisputed alpha, holding court in his own home, and while Fen showed him nothing but respect, it was obvious that Fen expected that same respect in return. Fascinated, Sunny sat back and observed the quiet drama of two powerful men interacting, knowing full well that Fen was still feeling his way in this reality that had been thrust upon him so unexpectedly.

To discover he was a shapeshifter—not merely an anomaly able to shift once, yet never again—then to kill three men, meet a woman and fall in love, and end up mated to her in less than twenty-four hours? Unbelievable.

Even Sunny, who had always just accepted whatever happened, had to admit that this had been a pretty wild night and day.

Thunder rolled over the house. Lightning streaked across the sky, flashing so close through the big back windows, it was almost blinding. Sunny blinked away the afterimage and then grinned at Fen. "I'm glad we took the tunnels."

Fen laughed softly. "I'd like to say it was a good hunch, but I think the fact we had a very wet mating had a bit to do with the decision."

His arm rested lightly across Sunny's shoulders, and she thought how right that felt. How right Fen felt. She sensed Anton's gaze on her and glanced in his direction. He studied them, and she knew he wondered at their mating, at how quickly they'd jumped into a lifelong commitment. But his lips lifted in a smile, and she almost giggled when he winked.

He tilted his head and stared at Fen for a moment. "Your amulet? It's the jade wolf Eve mentioned, isn't it?"

Fen touched the green wolf nestled at the base of his throat. "It is. I've always had it. According to my father, it belonged to my mother, but I know nothing about it."

Sunny glanced at Fen. Would Anton know? "When Fen shifts, the jade wolf goes with him. Every time. It's around his neck as a wolf, and still there when he's a man."

Frowning, obviously curious, Anton pushed away from the desk and stood in front of Fen. "Do you mind?"

"Not at all. Go ahead."

Anton lifted the jade carving away from Fen's throat, rubbing his thumb over the glossy surface. His eyes narrowed as he studied the amulet. Still staring at the piece, he said, "You know nothing else about it?"

"No. I've always worn it. I feel as if it's a link to my mother. It's all I have of hers."

"What do you know about her?" He let go of the jade wolf. Once again it rested against Fen's throat.

Fen shook his head. "Nothing. I never saw her in her human form. She died a wolf. She was beautiful. She was food and warmth to me, and I was her cub." He squeezed Sunny's hand, and she sensed his curiosity. Why was Anton so fascinated by the amulet?

Anton stepped back and folded his arms across his chest. "There's magic in the carving. I'm not sure why or what kind, though there's no sense of evil about it. More a feeling of extreme age. Nothing came to you during the mating link? No memories of it?"

Sunny gazed at Fen, but he merely shrugged as thunder rumbled overhead. "If it did, I haven't yet made sense of the information. Sunny and I decided there was so much we shared that it might take the rest of our lives to figure everything out."

Anton chuckled and once again leaned against his desk, but his gaze was thoughtful as he studied both Fen and Sunny. Then he frowned, glanced out the window, and said, "I know why you're going to Mount Lassen." Lightning flashed again, right on top of the thunder. It was followed by a loud pop and a brighter flame from one of the power poles behind the house.

The lights went out, flickered for a moment, and then came back on at much lower wattage when the emergency generator kicked on.

Fen glanced at Sunny as she turned to him. Both of them burst out laughing. Fen finally got himself under control and, still obviously fighting the laughter, turned to Anton. "Sunny said you were a powerful wizard, but do you always get that sort of reaction to your pronouncements?"

Sunny giggled. She noticed the corner of Anton's lips twitching. "Only when I'm right," he said.

"And he's always right." Keisha, Anton's mate, stepped into the room carrying a basket filled with sandwiches. "Which can be difficult to live with at times, except he's worth it. Mostly."

She set the basket on the coffee table in front of Sunny and Fen. "You two must be starved. Congratulations, and Fen, welcome to the pack. Anton just told me you and Sunny have mated." She held out her arms and Fen stood to receive her hug and kiss. "You'll do well in this group, Fen." She laughed. "They're all a little afraid of Sunny. I can tell already that you'll provide just the kind of backup she'll need."

It was said with a smile, but then she turned to Anton. "Any idea why Igmutaka will need them? Or when?"

Anton nodded. "Igmutaka and Star. Star arrived earlier than expected. Sunny and Fen will have to be there Thursday, at the very latest. Preferably Wednesday night. I don't know why, or what the problem is, but the feeling they have to go soon has been growing for Fen and Sunny all day. I've felt something as well, but it wasn't until the storm that I realized the discomfort was settling on Igmutaka and Star. Word from Eve just confirmed my suspicions."

"I know." Keisha turned to Sunny. "I wish we had a better sense of what's happening, but Eve doesn't know the details or she would share them with us. Star and Ig are facing danger, but until it happens, you must not interfere. Eve is most specific in that."

"Has she spoken directly to you?" Sunny was clutching Fen's hand without even knowing when she'd grabbed him, but holding on to her mate gave her a powerful sense of courage, of both physical and emotional strength.

Anton shook his head. "No. She connected with Lily. Lily's just shared it with her mother and me."

Fen shot a quick glance at Sunny. "Why would she tell Lily when it affects Sunny?"

Sunny squeezed his hand. "Lily is the only person I know who is best friends with a goddess. The two of them have always had a very special connection, and now Sebastian is included. I think it's pretty neat. Chanku are the only people I know of who communicate on a first-name basis with their deity."

"Adam said she was once his mate." Fen glanced at Anton. "What happened?"

"She was. Eve was killed in a car accident, and we almost lost Adam to his grief, but Liana saved him."

"Liana and Igmutaka. I think the spirit guide was involved as well." Keisha smiled at Sunny. "How do you feel about Ig hoping to claim Star as his mate? The two of you were lovers for so many years."

Sunny glanced at Fen, who knew everything of her long relationship with Igmutaka. After the mating link, there were no secrets left, and the freedom of knowing Fen was fully aware of all the men—and women—she'd been with, and yet held no ill will toward any of them, was something Sunny knew only a Chanku man or woman could appreciate.

"You all knew Ig and Star were fated to mate from the moment of her birth, and he was very upfront with me from the very beginning. Considering that he connected with her while she was still in Tala's womb, and he's waited all these years for her to grow up, I wouldn't have expected anything else. We used to talk about it a lot, and while I will always love Igmutaka, I knew from the very beginning he wasn't for me."

She glanced at Fen. "Of course, I never realized how long I'd have to wait for the one who was destined to be mine."

Fen lifted her fingers to his lips and kissed them. "I hope I was worth the wait. You certainly are for me."

She knew her eyes must be sparkling. "Hell, yeah." And if she tried to say anything else, she'd probably end up crying for joy. None of this felt real. Not yet. Blinking at the quick sting of tears, she turned away and changed the subject. "Is the chopper available? Can Tinker take us to the cabin? We'd have to leave tonight to get there by Thursday if we drive, and I hate that trip if the weather's bad. Besides, Fen still needs to check in with the sheriff's office."

Anton nodded. "You're right. Fen? Do you want me to go with you tomorrow? I want the sheriff to understand why you couldn't come in today, that it wasn't possible until you were able to shift. I know he's going to want to see your pictures and get your statement."

"I would appreciate that. Thank you."

"Good. That's settled. Be here at eight and we'll get it done early. And Sunny, regarding the chopper, that's an excellent idea. Tinker's flying me to San Francisco either Wednesday afternoon or Thursday morning, depending on the weather. We can detour over the Lassen property, make a quick stop, and drop you and Fen off at the cabin. I've got a meeting with Alex Thursday afternoon in the city." He slanted a sexy smile at his wife. "Why don't you come, too? We could ask Stefan and Xandi to join us. Your shopping trips are always a boost to the economy."

Keisha rolled her eyes, but the look she gave Anton was so hot and so full of sensual invitation, it was all the incentive Sunny needed to leave. Times like this reminded her that Keisha and Anton were even more in love than they'd been when she first met them, so many years ago.

She stood and tugged Fen's hand. He rose to stand beside her, towered over her and made her feel loved, protected, and safe. That was a good thing, especially now, with so many questions about their upcoming trip. She wondered what they'd be facing in Lassen; wondered what was going on with Star and Igmutaka.

She hoped everything was working out for them. It was definitely working for her and for Fen, if the look in his eyes was any indication.

"C'mon," she said. "Let's get moving before these lovebirds embarrass us."

"Take the sandwiches," Keisha said. She winked.

Anton chuckled, but he'd already dismissed them. His eyes were on his mate. Sunny glanced at Fen, saw the heat in his eyes, and decided now was definitely a good time to leave.

Fen wasn't sure how to explain it, the way everything felt since they'd mated this afternoon. Sunny was in his mind all the time, but it wasn't at all intrusive. She was merely a presence, just as he imagined being a presence in hers.

For the first time in as long as he could remember, Fen realized he wasn't entirely alone. This funny, loving, bright, and beautiful woman had gone from being a total stranger to someone permanently lodged in his heart and his mind.

He was aware of her on so many levels—the surprise was the power of the sexual draw, the fact that he saw her and wanted her all the time, in all ways. That wasn't how he'd been before—sex had always been a pleasurable, sometimes pressing, need, but it hadn't defined every thought he had. Not the way it seemed so much a part of who and what he was. Of how he saw his mate.

But the best and most wonderful thing about the newness of their link was how right it felt. How perfect. As if they'd been a couple forever, though they'd known each other barely a day.

"It's because of the link, you know." She glanced at him and he realized she'd been right there in his head as he considered all the changes in his life. "Our desire for one another, as well as for other members of the pack, will continue to grow. That active libido is very much part of your Chanku heritage. I don't imagine Berserkers are any different." She laughed. "At least I hope you're not. I don't feel anything different about you. With the link, we know everything there is to know about one another, though there was so much input that it will likely take us days or even weeks to comprehend everything we've learned."

"Like information about the amulet?"

"If we're lucky."

He nodded. "It's fascinating. Tonight when you were talking about Igmutaka, I was aware of your relationship, but without all the details. Then, as you kept speaking, more and more made sense to me, as if I know the man as intimately as you do." He grinned. "Though I am curious about that Louisville Slugger."

"Curious enough to want to find out for yourself?"

He stopped. Stared at Sunny and frowned. Again there was that reference to sex with others besides his mate. He wasn't quite certain what she meant, until images flashed into his head. A visual buffet of sex, of Sunny with Igmutaka, with other couples and their mates, with Adam and his mate. He saw Sunny with Adam, and Adam with Igmutaka, loving each other even as they loved Sunny.

He'd never been with a man. Never even considered it, and yet he found himself growing aroused with the vivid images Sunny shared with him.

His life had definitely changed, and yet he had a feeling the changes were just beginning. His mind was spinning when Fen left the sweatpants on a hook by the back door. Sunny untied her sarong and hung it next to his pants, and the two of them stepped outside, shutting the door behind them.

She leaned close and planted a kiss on his chest, just over his heart, and then she shifted. So did Fen, loving the ease with which he was able to make the change from man to wolf.

He grabbed the basket of sandwiches in his teeth

Lightning flashed and thunder rolled over the valley as they raced through the rain, heading for Sunny's little cottage. There was a big bed waiting for them. A fireplace in the room and a view of the mountains.

Sunny nipped Fen's shoulder as he ran beside her and the two of them reached her steps together, bounded up the stairs, and shifted at the sliding-glass door leading to her bedroom.

Laughing, leaving their wolven shapes and the cold rain behind them and the basket of sandwiches on the dresser, Fen and Sunny tumbled together on the big bed.

He was mated. Mated for a life that suddenly stretched much longer and more wonderful than he'd ever imagined. But as Sunny rolled beneath him, as she lifted her lips for Fen's kiss, he knew forever wouldn't be long enough.

There could never be enough time to tell Sunny Daye just how much he loved her. To thank her for saving him.

"But you don't have to tell me, Fen." She stroked her fingers along his jaw. "I feel it when you look at me. When I hear your voice in my mind and know it's my mate speaking to me. When you make love to me." She giggled. "We've never done this in a bed. Maybe we should give it a try."

Lightning flashed, lighting the room, casting their shadows against the wall. There was no power here in the cabin—the generator ran only Anton and Keisha's house—but Fen didn't need lights to see his mate.

As thunder rolled over the cabin, he made love to her. Sweet, gentle love, promising forever.

11

There was no moon to light the velvet sky, but an endless number of twinkling stars made up for its lack. Steam rose from the thermal spring and hung in the still night air. Igmutaka's strong arms were a comforting band across Star's ribs, lifting her breasts, holding her close. Her back rested against his firm chest and his long, strong thighs encased hers. Warm water bubbled over her skin, the smell of sulfur and other minerals from the underground springs blended with the scent of dried grass and pine, and Star knew she'd never experienced a moment of contentment quite like this.

Ig loved her. Loved her and wanted her for his mate. His scent filled her, all warm male and wood smoke, the scent of the mountains and everything wild. It was the scent of her childhood, of the one who had held her when she was small, had read to her when she couldn't sleep, and though he'd been mostly spirit as she grew older, his voice had been a constant song in her mind. He'd been as real to her then as he was now.

Now, when his heart thundered against her back and his

warmth surrounded her; now, when, if she concentrated, she heard the rush of blood in his veins, the soft inhalations he made with each breath. He was real and he was hers—all strong, solid male.

She'd imagined him loving her for so long, the reality was difficult to accept. Was this merely a dream? Would she awaken from this moment as she'd awakened on so many nights with her fingers lodged between her sweating thighs, her pussy clenching in need?

"Never, my sweet."

Slowly, she tilted her head back to stare into the face of this man she'd loved for her entire life. "I know. My head knows, my heart knows. My body is even convinced, but it's been so long. Even knowing that you love me, knowing that we're together, I find it hard to accept it's all real."

"Then we must make it real. Here. Tonight." He rubbed his jaw across her cheek and kissed the corner of her mouth. "I told myself I wasn't going to rush you, but after what happened tonight, after watching you risk yourself against those foolish men, all I could think of was everything that could have gone wrong. I might have lost you before you were ever truly mine."

"I'm yours, Ig. I've always been yours." She smiled at him, staring into that beautiful and beloved face. "Even before you were ready for me. Mom said you were the one who caught me when I was born. She's always thought you were more surprised than anyone to end up with a slippery newborn in your hands."

He laughed, and she felt the joy in him as much as she heard it. "I did, and she's right. I was terrified I might drop you! I had never even held a newborn, but your mother's labor was fast. I remember her squatting on the bed with your father supporting her and AJ holding her hand, looking for all the world as if he wanted to give birth himself, he was so worried. She grunted and pushed and you dropped into my hands. You were tiny and red and wrinkled and"—his voice went deep and gravelly—"so ugly."

"Gee, thanks."

He grinned and planted a kiss on the top of her head. "I'm lying, you know. You were truly the most beautiful thing I had ever held, and I loved you from the very first moment I saw you." He tightened his grasp. "Not, of course, the way I love you now. You are still the most beautiful thing I've ever held, and I imagine I'll say that until you gift me with a child. Then you might discover you have competition." He frowned. "You do want children, don't you?"

"I've imagined carrying your babies for years, Ig. Only yours." She felt him harden beneath her buttocks. "It's time, don't you think? For mating, not for babies. I want to wait awhile on those."

He grew very still. Then he nodded and pushed away from the ledge, but he kept a tight grasp on her hand as they swam across the small pool. When they reached the shallower side, Star felt the sandy bottom of the pond beneath her feet and shivered with the tickle of hot bubbles flowing out of the sand and between her toes. Water lapped just beneath her breasts, warm and almost fizzy with the natural effervescence of the spring.

Ig paused, still holding her hand. He turned and gazed at her, his eyes filled with love. "You have questions, Mikaela Star. I feel them."

She nodded. "I do. You've always been the puma for me. That beautiful, long, sinuous cougar I used to dream about as a kid. I want to mate as cats. My cougar to yours. Are you willing?"

He chuckled softly. "You've not heard Mei complain about Oliver?"

She laughed. "I know. The barbed penis, right." She leaned close and kissed him. "I'm not looking forward to that, but it certainly hasn't stopped Mei. I do feel that when we mate, I want it to be with the creature I fell in love with. Your puma was the beast of my fantasies." Kissing his cheek she added, "Of course, that was before I learned about the barbs, but I don't care about them. Please? At least for our mating."

He stared at her for a moment. Then his beautiful lips curved into a smile, and he nodded. "Nothing you could ask would please me more. Come."

Tugging her fingers, Ig pulled her along behind him to the shore. He shifted the moment he was out of the water, and his mountain lion was everything Star loved about the man. Strong and long, a sinuous, aloof creature, beautiful beyond imagination. His tail twitched, broadcasting his impatience, and she took her time, walking slowly out of the pond, standing for a moment to fully appreciate the pleasure of Igmutaka watching her.

Then she shifted, taking the shape of the puma. Where Igmutaka was a huge cat, Star felt rather petite in this form, and somehow more feminine than she did as a wolf. She strutted up to Ig and rubbed her face all along his side, but when he pawed her hip, she turned and snarled at him.

There was no need to make this too easy for the man! She walked away and found a soft patch of grass where she stretched out. Ig circled her, sniffing at her back, her face, her paws. When he reached her tail, he lay down behind her and inhaled her scent, stroking the full length of her sex before slipping his long, rough tongue deep inside.

She snarled again, but she didn't move away. She'd never had sex in any form other than human, and the feral response was as fascinating to her cougar's mind as was the amazing sensation of Ig's mobile tongue stroking her intimate flesh.

She opened to him and found a mind even more feral than her

own. He was fully into his cougar. Igmutaka the man had slipped deeply into the creature's subconscious, but Star wanted the man, not just his cat. *Igmutaka? Come to me. Don't lose yourself in the puma. It is our mating as much as it is our cats'.*

Without answering, he raised his head to draw in great draughts of air. Star recognized his behavior as pure cat—he was inhaling her scent, taking in the flood of hormones that would make her more receptive and his cat even more ready.

Impatient now, Star snarled and batted at him with one big paw. She sensed his laughter. *Impatient, are we?* He dipped his head and once again ran his tongue over her sensitive tissues. Then, without warning, he was on her, his body curving over hers, his claws digging into the thick fur at her shoulders.

She felt his penetration, the slick slide of that long penis as he filled her in one, quick thrust. Startled, she snarled and jerked as if to pull away, and the movement set the barbs she'd heard Mei bitch about so much.

Somehow, for whatever reason, the pain was exquisite. Deep inside, not so much holding them together as scraping the lining of her sheath, those tiny, sharp points, each a separate spark of sensation. She screamed her panther's cry, and he roared so close to her ear that she felt his hot breath, sensed the innate dominance of the male.

And then, again without any warning at all, she sensed Igmutaka. The man, the spirit guide, the shapeshifter—a man with memories older than recorded time, entering her thoughts, linking with her, binding her both body and spirit as the mating link snapped powerfully into place.

Memories spilled into her head. Memories of Ig, not as a child among primitives as she'd expected but as a kit in a litter of young cats. Different than the puma he was now—and she sensed his breed was a precursor of the modern wildcat, not quite a saber-toothed tiger but something really close. The setting was lush and game plentiful, but then she saw him as a young man, almost as beautiful as he was now, a shifter among primitive hunter-gatherers, already on the cusp of change.

Far from the grasses of Tibet, they were losing the ability to shift. Descendants of the well-educated people from an alien world, these more primitive offspring had settled in this wild land and were slowly making it their own.

And Igmutaka was one of them, though not. More cat than man, his ability to shift was passing as well, but he was losing the ability to remain human. He was known by a different name then, called Wahkan, which meant sacred.

His people knew he was special, and already they turned to him for guidance. Star watched him grow from child to adult in a kaleidoscope of images, shifting from cat to man, but choosing the cat more often than not as frames flashed, one to the next.

He was tall and strong and very intelligent, but his was a caring nature, and the gods noticed. She was witness to the day when he received the call that he was needed as a spirit guide who would help those of his people who eventually settled in the lands that would one day be the Dakotas. He gave up his physical body then. Gave up the cat as well as the man for life as spirit, and so he remained for thousands of years, always watching over the people he thought of as his charges, his children.

They were the men who were her ancestors, those powerful warriors who, generation after generation, depended on their stalwart spirit guide to keep watch over them. All those years, and all those warriors, culminating in Miguel Fuentes, her father. Ending now with Mikaela Star, who would be Igmutaka's last charge.

He had protected them all. Guarded them, learned to love them, and then had watched as they eventually grew old and died. The shapeshifter genes were still there, but they had lost all knowledge of their heritage. They had lost so very much, including their almost immortal lifespans, but Igmutaka stayed. Stayed and guarded them, waiting, hoping that one day they would rediscover their true birthright.

She saw her own birth through his eyes, and every detail of her childhood until she began to blossom, to become the young woman who had caused him so much grief. She felt his yearning for her younger self, his self-recriminations for loving the one he was charged to protect, until finally, as their bodies and minds were joined as one, she rejoiced in the here and now, in the knowledge that his love for her and hers for him was returned.

She saw him with Sunny on that night so long ago when he took the virginity of the young woman who had never known love, and she listened to the many conversations the two of them had shared, as Sunny tried to explain the way a modern woman thought.

Star decided she truly owed her friend for the things she had managed to teach this primitive lover of hers. And still her mind was filled; bits and pieces of so many memories that even Igmutaka had long ago forgotten their relevance. Now he saw it all just as she did.

Just as he knew everything there was to know about Star. The long, lonely years in Connecticut, the many lovers who had failed to please her, the sense of failure when she finally realized she had to come home and face the man she'd loved for so long.

She might have felt embarrassed, but this was the way of a mating bond—the ability to accept everything about the one who would be her partner for all time, just as she must learn to accept some of the uncomfortable truths about herself.

Neither of them were even close to perfect, and yet those imperfections made them perfect for each other. Star knew that somehow, that was the most important thing she would take from this amazing bond—the fact that she was the right woman for Igmutaka, just as he was the only man for her.

So lost in the montage of memories flashing through her mind, she'd lost track of the actual mating itself—his lion to hers, his rather formidable size covering her, that damned barbed prick of his scratching deep inside as he withdrew after each thrust—and yet it was right.

This was right. They'd had such a prickly relationship for so many years, it seemed only fitting that their mating bond should be between two independent, strong-minded cats. Fitting that the hundreds of tiny barbs on his penis should cause her pain even as it excited and aroused her.

The memories had ended, and yet the connection between them remained so strong that Star realized she was still in his mind, just as he was in hers. She tapped into the sensations of the mating, how it felt to thrust hard and deep as the big cat, and she shared the sharp pain on each withdrawal.

He stopped. His body went stiff and she felt his shock; his dismay was an almost palpable sensation. *Why didn't you tell me? I'm hurting you! Never, my sweet. Never would I want to hurt you.*

Don't you dare stop. She turned and snarled at him, baring her teeth. *Yes, it hurts, but I need this. I want it. And when we finish, I want the wolf. Don't you see? I want it all. All of you, in all ways.*

He lowered his head and rested his broad chin on her back. With a few short, sharp thrusts, he brought her to her peak, and then, just as quickly, followed her over.

Unlike wolves, there was no tie. Igmutaka shifted to his human form to pull free of Star's body, and there was no pain.

But she felt his love. It was strong and true, and she held this new connection close to her heart. Igmutaka was her mate, her one true love.

No longer a spirit guide, he was once again fully Chanku, a member of the pack. And he loved her. Loved her for all time.

Stunned, Igmutaka tried to untangle the unexpected memories, the confusion he felt over a past he'd expected but never really believed. The biggest surprise—he was truly Chanku, and yet not. He wasn't sure if he was actually a Berserker—he'd not begun as a wolf, but even as a puma, he was similar to that warrior breed.

He'd wondered if he was something other than Chanku, if his life as a spirit guide was the life he'd been born to. Not so. He'd been chosen by the gods.

And now he'd given it up. He hoped for their forgiveness. Hoped they understood, and he was glad he'd thanked the goddess and the Mother before mating Mikaela Star.

The biggest surprise was the fact this human body he'd chosen had been just that—a choice. But the young man in his memories had been the same man he was now. He'd not manufactured his appearance. This was the man he was meant to be, and he now understood why the cat had always felt more comfortable to him than any other creature. It was his true self, just as the wolf was his mate's.

What other secrets had their bond uncovered? It could take him days to sort everything out. One thing he was certain of, even though he'd begun as a puma, Igmutaka would never again mate his woman as the cat. He had hurt her.

Connected to her physically, mentally, and emotionally, he'd been appalled by her pain. Their mating, the ultimate goal of every Chanku male, had been sullied by his thoughtless agreement to mate as pumas. He shifted once again, so connected to Mikaela Star that they stared at one another as wolves across the small patch of beaten grass.

I hurt you. He hung his head low. *I am sorry. That was never my intent. It will not happen again.*

I love you. She licked his muzzle and then rested her chin on his broad shoulders. *The pain didn't take from the pleasure. It made the connection feel more . . .* She raised her head and gazed toward the sharp peaks surrounding their valley. *It was more real. It tied me to your past, to the long, long life you've lived. I always knew your story, that you'd started as a cat, but I didn't know you were truly Chanku.*

He licked her muzzle with his long tongue. *I'm as surprised as you are, Mikaela Star. This was unexpected, and as the memories settle into my mind, I hope to understand more. But I do apologize. Please believe I would never intentionally hurt you.*

I know that what you did wasn't on purpose, but it made me feel closer to you. You have experienced much pain in your life. More than I ever imagined.

I have no desire for you to share any of my pain. Only the joy. My dear Mikaela Star, there is much joy with you in my life.

Ah, Ig. Thank you, and I love you for thinking that way, but that's not living. Living is all of it—the pain, the joy, the ups and downs, and those smooth, often dull moments between. You are my mate just as I am yours. There will be pain at times for us. There will be sorrow and joy. We're supposed to share everything.

She nipped his shoulder and took off, moving so quickly she left him standing there, staring at her. A moment later she sensed his laughter, the fact he welcomed the chase, the chance to run, to shake off some of the intensity of their mating.

She raced toward the thickest part of the forest, knowing just how much easier it would be for her leaner, faster wolf to cut through the tangled branches of willows and aspen.

He followed close behind, and she took a different trail, one that led her up the side of the mountain, twisting and turning amid the scattered boulders and loose scree.

She let him catch her in a secluded bowl where pines and firs grew thick and the night fell like a black velvet curtain all around them. He raked her shoulder with one big paw, and this time, when he mounted her, there was no pain.

Instead, a sense of homecoming filled her heart when Igmu-taka entered her mind as well as her body, and shared their joining from his point of view. Shivering with a heady rush of love, of pure joy, she opened to her mate. *I feel you. Your mind and the way your cock fills me.*

She sensed his laughter.

I'm making sure there is no pain.

It must be easier. You're not quite as big in your wolf form as when you're a man, she said, teasing him. *In fact, unless I'm mistaken, though your wolf is massive, parts of him are . . .* She paused and glanced over her shoulder. *Practically average.*

Then I'll have to do something to make this more memorable. You shouldn't be thinking about my size—or lack thereof, woman. You're supposed to be so enthralled with my lovemaking that you know I am the biggest and the best you'll ever have. Laughter spilled into her mind. *You should be thinking of me. Only of me and how wonderful I make you feel.* He arched into her, again and again, clasping her body tightly to his, filling her, thrilling her as his wolf easily dominated hers.

And he was the best and the biggest, and he made her tremble with the power of his loving, but Star really hated giving in so easily. She braced all four legs, better to take his weight. *I will admit you're doing a magnificent job. No pain, my love.*

As if that was all she felt! There was definitely no pain, but there was so much more. He was slick and hot and absolutely huge, his thrusts filling her in a rapid rhythm, stretching her to the point of pain but not beyond. The solid knot of hard flesh at the base of his cock filled her tightly and held them together as once again orgasm washed over the two of them.

This time, the mating link was even more intense, the sense

of mental and emotional joining every bit as powerful as the physical tie holding their bodies together.

Star's legs collapsed beneath her as she rode out her climax, and she went down with Ig still thrusting hard against her. She lay there, panting, as he found his own completion. Her sheath tightened, clasping the mating knot and holding him close as his thrusts gentled and slowed. Finally he lay beside her, his wolven penis still locked tightly inside her sheath.

Her body rippled around his, the mental connection allowing her the chance to share this orgasm from both his and her perspectives. She raised her head and caught him staring at her, his eyes still cat green, even in the face of his wolf.

Let's go back to the cabin. Now.

She would have laughed if she'd been able to. *Not gonna happen, Ig. Not until we can separate.*

I want to make love to you in a warm bed.

That sounds absolutely wonderful, but I don't understand. You're a creature of nature. Where's your sense of adventure?

You, my sweet Mikaela Star, are all the adventure any man could possibly want. And I want you again. She heard the laughter in her mind when he dryly added, *In a bed.*

Ig shifted, and the change pulled him free of her body. He stood as a man, towering above her, looking every inch the primitive native warrior he was. Strong, powerful in both body and bearing, he was truly an alpha male in his prime.

The sky behind him was growing light with the first hint of dawn, outlining his beautiful form as he stood there. Star fought the compulsion to shift, to meet him almost eye to eye. He crossed his arms over his broad chest and stared down his very aristocratic nose at her.

When he spoke, he sounded almost reluctant, as if he would just as soon not have to say anything at all, but apparently that didn't stop him. "If I seem impatient," he said, "it's because I've waited all your life for this to happen. Since I first knew I loved you, I've wanted you. Now that I know you love me, we've had sex as an unmated man to a woman. We've had sex and mated, forging that most enduring link as cougars." He shrugged and glanced away before focusing on her once again. "Not going to do that again—the sex, anyway. I will not purposely hurt you. Never again. We've mated as wolves—we'll definitely repeat that—but we haven't made love in our human forms since mating. And it's too cold out here to do all of the things I want to do with you, especially when there's a warm bed waiting."

Again he shifted, and the wolf stood beside her, every bit as aloof and imperious as the man. Even so, Star had absolutely no desire to disagree with his reasoning. With her ears pricked forward and her tail waving like a flag in the night behind her, she led her mate through the early morning chill, back to the warmth of their cabin.

"I don't recall ever spending an entire day in bed." Fen rested his weight on one elbow as he brushed the tangled hair from Sunny's eyes with his free hand. "I do believe I could learn to enjoy this."

"Well, it wasn't the entire day. Anton had you most of the morning. Should I ask what the two of you actually did together?"

He laughed at her teasing innuendo and planted a very possessive kiss on her swollen lips.

She glowed. Her cheeks were flushed and her eyes sparkled. The reddened patches between her thighs and under her breasts where his beard had scraped her tender skin counted as badges of honor as far as Fen was concerned. He'd certainly marked Sunny as his woman, and he might have felt badly about that if she'd seemed at all bothered.

She wasn't the least bit upset. He knew that because of their link, that amazing bond that made him feel as if he were never alone, as if she was part of him all the time.

And even as she teased him, he thought of how she'd been with him all morning, a silent presence through their bond. "The visit to the sheriff was what, an hour? You know exactly how long it took, because you were there—in my mind—with me."

She reached up and ran her fingers through his tangled hair. "I was worried about you. I didn't want you to feel alone."

"I didn't. Not for a second." He kissed her again. "Anton, by the way, is an amazing man. I hope he realizes how much I appreciate his help. He got us through the questioning in no time at all, and the sheriff was appreciative of the pictures I turned over to him. Then we checked in with my supervisor, settled the work situation—I'm now officially on loan to the Chanku nation, by the way—took a quick swing by my hotel room to grab my stuff and pay the bill, and he brought me back to you."

Fen kissed her again. "Definitely too long to be away from you, but I believe we're making up for it." Nuzzling her breasts, he sucked in a deep breath, filling his lungs with her scent. He licked one dark, red strawberry mark he'd left just above her nipple and had to fight the compulsion to suck on it again, to make it darker, more permanent.

Of course, she had marked him as well. The love bites on his inner thighs and the dark hickeys crossing his throat and chest were going to be around for a while, unless shapeshifters really did heal faster than humans. He hoped her marks stayed with him for a long, long time. He wanted the world to know that Sunny was his. That he was hers.

He nuzzled her breasts again and drew in another deep breath of her scent. Sunny's fingers trailed along his ribs, swept over his hip and encircled his growing erection. He'd lost count of how many times they'd made love, of how many ways. He should be exhausted by now, not feeling this fresh rush of pleasure, the growing need for her as if he'd been celibate for months.

He had a feeling celibacy wasn't going to be an issue anymore. Not with a woman like Sunny in his life. Fen leaned close and ran his tongue over the very tip of her left nipple. Sunny groaned and arched her back, lifting closer to his mouth. He felt the softness of her flaccid nipple give way to taut arousal and his cock answered, swelling hard and hot against her hip. He sucked harder, wrapping his lips around that single point, pulling the hard nub against the roof of his mouth, trapping her with the flat of his tongue.

He didn't touch her anywhere else, even though she writhed against him, begging with her soft moans and whimpers. "If you insist," he said, before returning to her nipple. To please her, he ran his fingers gently over her thigh, across the taut muscles of her belly and through the blond thatch of curls guarding her needy pussy.

Her clitoris rose out of its small hood, already swollen with arousal. He circled her slowly, gently, fully aware he merely teased and tickled when she wanted more. As she pressed closer, he pulled back, barely touching her, teasing her even more until she grabbed his wrist with both her hands and forced his fingers hard against herself.

Laughing, Fen rolled over and covered her with his much larger body. He'd never been with a woman so willing to let him know exactly what she wanted, what her body needed. He used his hand to force his cock down between her legs and then slowly rose and fell against her, rubbing the thick, hard length through her moist folds. He felt her climax rising and pulled away just enough to slip inside. Her legs came up around his hips and he filled her in one, hard thrust.

Then he followed it with another, and yet another until the

bed rattled against the wall. Fen sat back on his heels, pulling Sunny close up against him. She wrapped her arms around his neck, her legs tightened about his waist and that flattened her surprisingly full breasts against his chest. Rising up on his knees with Sunny impaled on his thick length, he rolled his hips, increasing the speed and the power of each deep penetration as he filled her. She met him with her heart and her body, taking him fully, clasping tightly with inner muscles that squeezed him on every thrust. He opened his mind to her, slipped inside Sunny's thoughts as she entered his and the link completed perfectly.

A link Fen realized would sustain him all the days of his life. He was Sunny Daye, taking everything this huge man she loved had to give. He was Fenris Ahlberg, a simple man whose life had changed completely over the past three days. Together they were unstoppable. A mated pair, connected on so many levels that only death could divide them.

Her inner muscles tightened around him and held as her own climax took control. The sweet pressure sent Fen over the top. Sunny cried out, and then, as he filled her with his seed, as his big body shuddered with the power of his climax, the two of them dissolved into laughter.

Tumbling back to the tangled sheets, Fen lay on his back, laughing so hard that tears leaked from the corners of his eyes. Sunny still clutched his body with her arms and legs, but she pushed herself upright, up on her knees. Sitting astride, she flattened her palms on his chest and, still giggling, leaned close and kissed him. Then she did it again, taking longer this time, tasting his lips, tangling her tongue with his, claiming Fen as he had claimed her.

Finally, she collapsed against his chest and lay there gasping deep breaths as Fen's laughter faded into a sigh. After a moment, he felt the tip of her tongue circling one of his nipples.

He cupped her cheeks in his hands and lifted her just enough so that he could look into her eyes. "Enough. I need food. And rest. And more food. You must be trying to kill me."

She laughed and turned her head just far enough to tongue his palm. "Never. It's not going to happen. You're tough and so am I. I love you, Fen. Damn, since I don't think we can kill each other with all the sex, I think I could get used to spending days in bed, too."

Fen? Sunny? Change in plans. Can you be packed and out at the helicopter pad in twenty minutes? There's a cold weather front moving in, and Tinker said if we don't leave now, we might not be able to get out of here in the morning.

Groaning, Fen glanced at Sunny. She merely grinned at him and then answered Anton. *We'll be there. If Keisha's got any leftovers she can send along, it would probably save the life of a starving man.*

I'm sure she does. We'll meet you at the chopper pad.

Fen didn't think they'd be able to make it, but he and Sunny were freshly showered, their bags packed, and they were waiting beside the helicopter when Keisha, Anton, Stefan, and Xandi arrived in Anton's big SUV with Oliver at the wheel.

Dark clouds were rolling in from the west, already obscuring the mountains, and the wind was rising. Tinker and his mate, Lisa, had arrived earlier, and Tinker had the chopper fueled and prepared for takeoff. As all of them piled into the craft and buckled themselves into the comfortable seats, Tinker took the controls with Anton settled in beside him as copilot.

The clouds boiled higher over the mountains while Tinker went through his checklist and then lifted the helicopter off just ahead of the storm. Within a matter of minutes they'd left the weather front behind.

They circled over the long valley, moving quickly in the jet-powered machine. Fen grasped Sunny's hand and realized he'd not even thought ahead to where they were going, what they might be doing.

Two people needed them—people he'd never met. A man who had been Sunny's lover for years, and a woman who had not been part of the pack for almost as long. Two people who were Chanku, just like Sunny.

But not like him. He was a Berserker. Different, and in many ways feared because of the heritage he still didn't fully understand. Was that why he was needed?

Berserkers of history were known as fierce, violent warriors. Creatures as ferocious as anything that had walked the face of the earth.

He wasn't a killer by nature, was he? He had killed, though. He'd killed those poachers without any regret at all, and then Anton had gone with him to the authorities and he'd made his report and walked away. To kill without consequences? That was not something he'd expected, but Anton Cheval was obviously a very powerful man. His word pulled a lot of weight, even among the area's duly-appointed law enforcement officers.

Fen couldn't help but wonder if that's all the pack wanted of him—someone who could kill without remorse.

Because if that was the case, he wasn't sure they had the right guy. He knew, in his gut, that he'd done the right thing when he'd killed those men, but he still felt badly about it. Still felt something, if not actual remorse.

Did it matter if he felt he'd made the right decision? He glanced at Sunny, and the love he felt for her almost shattered him. He'd never known feelings like this, never expected a love like this. It came to him then, so powerfully, so strong and true, that he could kill if needed, to protect Sunny. To protect his pack. Maybe he was that man. He looked at Sunny and saw his future. He saw children and a life filled with laughter and love.

Right now, he was on his way to do something, though he had no idea what it was. Something that was somehow linked to the goddess who guided the Chanku. Linked to the man who had been a spirit guide for so many thousands of years that even he didn't know his age. How had Fen come to be part of this? And what if he failed? What if he wasn't the right one for whatever job waited?

"Fen?"

His name, spilling softly from her lips, pulled him out of his twisted and tangled thoughts. "What, sweetheart?"

She grinned at him and handed him a sandwich, something Keisha must have brought. "Thank you," he said. Grateful, he took a bite, but Sunny wasn't through.

"Stop worrying. Whatever happens will happen in its own time. Whatever you're supposed to do will get done. Worrying won't make it happen better or worse, or sooner or later. It won't change who you are or how you will act. All it will do is take away the joy of this time, this day, these wonderful people we're with. Live for the moment, for this moment. When you live almost forever, it's easy to forget the importance of each moment."

He tipped her chin up and kissed her. "When did you get to be so smart?"

Her smile held more sadness than joy, and it made his heart hurt, to realize there were some things beyond him to fix for her. Like her memories.

"I think when I was trapped in a wheelchair without a voice or a body that worked. I had to find little things to keep me going. I learned then that wishing for something didn't make it happen. That wanting something badly enough didn't make it magically appear. I had to learn to enjoy each day, to find something in every day that I could hold close and remember."

"And when you were out of the chair?"

"I discovered that there truly was joy in every moment. And now that I have you, I feel that more than ever."

Her words seemed to open up a dark spot in his heart. Open him up, and spill light over everything. He changed the subject, but he knew he'd return to this conversation, just to recall the feelings Sunny's words gave him.

"Tell me about Igmutaka, about Mikaela Star. Will they accept me? I'm the same kind of creature that tried to kill Anton's daughter and her mate. Will they hold that against me?"

She shook her head. "Have you felt any animosity at all? From anyone in the pack?"

"No. But that could change."

"It won't. You're my mate. The man I love, the one I've chosen. You're part of the pack because you're part of me. Now sit back, eat your sandwich, and enjoy the trip. We should be there before dark."

Anton turned in his seat and smiled at both of them. "We'd better be. Then we're going to bug out as soon as we drop you guys off. Tinker says there's a storm due to hit San Francisco, and if we hurry, we can slide in just ahead of it."

Smiling, Fen glanced at Sunny. "He doesn't miss a thing, does he?" Sunny had a huge grin on her face as he leaned back in the comfortable seat with her hand clasped tightly in his.

He hadn't realized how exhausted he was. He'd like to blame the changes in his life, but he figured it was more than just the fact that he was shifting from human to wolf. Now it was probably two days without sleep and a whole lot of sex with a wonderful woman who had, most inexplicably, fallen in love with him.

Fen decided to take Sunny's advice. He held her hand, shared his sandwich with her, and enjoyed the moment. And each moment that followed as the chopper swiftly covered the miles between Kalispell and Mount Lassen.

He was still enjoying each moment as he and Sunny watched

the helicopter fly over the hills after dropping them off in front of the small cabin to meet Igmutaka and Star.

At least until a low, blood-curdling snarl raised the hair on the back of his neck, and Sunny's soft gasp had him turning to face the huge golden wolf that suddenly barred the steps leading up to the cabin.

12

"Ig? Is that really you?" Sunny shot a disbelieving glance at Fen, but she was grinning broadly as she marched closer to the vicious-looking wolf. She stopped not a foot away from him with both hands planted firmly on her hips.

"You sure that's a good idea?" Fen was ready to leap to her defense, but the wolf ignored Sunny altogether. No, the damned thing was focused entirely on him.

"Amazing." She laughed.

There was absolutely no fear in his mate at all, though Fen was fighting a powerful urge to shift and face off against the beast. If this wasn't a challenge, he wasn't sure what was.

"I've never seen you as a wolf, Ig. You're gorgeous, of course." She sighed dramatically. "I guess I should have expected that. You somehow missed all the ugly genes. Where's Star?"

The wolf slowly turned his face to Sunny, stared at her for a long moment, snorted in what sounded like disgust, and then shifted. A huge, bare-assed, and outstandingly beautiful Native

American man stood there with arms folded across his broad chest, glaring at Sunny.

She obviously wasn't the least bit intimidated by his glowering appearance; instead, she leapt into his arms. He caught her, and when the man laughed and swung her in a huge circle, Fen finally allowed himself to relax.

Curious. Shouldn't he feel jealous? His mate was in the arms of another man—an absolutely beautiful man without a stitch of clothing covering anything, including his rather sizable package—and yet all Fen felt was a sense of relief that she wasn't in danger. Then he realized that Sunny was in his mind, and the mating bond strong and true. Her love for him was the main thing on her mind—not the fact that she was clinging to another man.

There was obviously a lot he still needed to learn about the dynamics of shapeshifter relationships, but this lack of jealousy was one he'd not expected. Weren't wolves territorial?

And something else, equally unexpected. Interest. Arousal, even, at the sight of another man—a man whose muscles flexed and whose cock was hard beneath Sunny's butt, but instead of jealousy, Fen experienced desire.

For both Sunny and the man.

It shook him. Badly. She'd told him it would be this way, but to actually experience such feelings was something else. Something . . . well, not really unpleasant. Merely strange, though most definitely arousing.

Sunny cupped the man's face in her hands and kissed him. "You did it, didn't you? You and Star mated. I can tell. I can feel it."

A tall, olive-skinned woman stopped in the doorway. Like the man, she was totally nude and even more beautiful, if that was possible. Fen's cock swelled within his jeans before he had a chance even to consider his reaction, much less control it. Her hair was long and wavy, curling over her shoulders and par-

204 / Kate Douglas

tially obscuring her perfect breasts, and the shock of desire surging through his body surprised him as much as it thrilled him.

Sunny definitely had to be kidding, though it was hard not to react to such beauty. He really needed to ask her if there were any ugly Chanku.

So far, every woman had been beautiful, every man tall and powerfully built. This gorgeous woman winked at Fen as she leaned against the open door, but she smiled at Sunny, and he had no doubt the big guy currently hugging Sunny was this woman's mate.

It was obvious by the look on her face that he was the one she loved, and just as obvious she had no problem at all with Sunny clinging to her mate's bare chest.

Then Sunny spotted her. "Star!" She leaned out to her right to look around the man holding on to her. "I knew you were here the minute I saw that cougar-colored wolf. Only you could get him to shift into something besides a damned cat."

Star laughed, ran down the stairs to Sunny, and held out her arms. "Goddess, Sunny, I've missed you. There's a reason he's a wolf, not a cat."

Giggling, Sunny whispered, "Barbed cougar cock?"

"Yes, damn it! Ig, put her down. I want a hug."

Ig let go. Sunny scrambled out of his embrace and rushed to hug Star. After a brief, hard embrace, she pulled out of Star's grasp, turned, and held out her hand to Fen. He grabbed her fingers and she tugged him close.

"Star Fuentes, Igmutaka, this is Fen Ahlberg. Ig? Remember when you said my mate was near? You were right."

Igmutaka shot a dark frown at Fen, but he focused on Sunny. "You've already mated? You and this . . . this . . . damn it all, Sunny. He's a Berserker! I had no idea when I first noticed his presence that . . ."

Fen actually felt Sunny's hackles rising, and he rather liked the fact she was ready to defend him, but these were people who worried only because they loved her. Because they cared about her safety.

"It's okay, sweetheart." He pulled Sunny close and wrapped his arms around her waist, but he met the man eye to eye.

Alpha to alpha. "Igmutaka, I'd prefer that you didn't curse my mate. She knows exactly who and what I am. So does the pack's alpha. His mate, too. If they have accepted me, along with all the others in the pack who have met me, you might at least try to be civil and hold judgment until we get to know each other."

Ig crossed his arms over his chest and stared at Fen. Sunny glanced at Star, who merely grinned at her. A moment later, Ig nodded and a slight smile lifted the corner of his mouth.

"At least it appears you have found a man who will defend your honor." He held out his hand. "My apologies, Fen. Please forgive me, but I will always see Sunny as someone I need to protect, even though I know she's perfectly capable of defending herself. Welcome and congratulations to both of you." He reached for Star and pulled her close. "This is my mate, Mikaela Star Fuentes, a woman who has driven me absolutely crazy for almost three decades."

Fen glanced at Sunny. "Interesting. We've known each other for only three days. Why'd it take him almost thirty years?"

Sunny giggled. "Well, you know how some guys are."

Ig leaned back and glared at Sunny. "No, Sunny. I don't. How are they?"

"How about I ask Star?"

"Works for me." Star slipped close to Ig and wrapped her hands around his left arm. "My man is hardheaded, stubborn, and arrogant." Then she kissed his cheek. "And a pain in the ass, but he's also absolutely perfect. For me, at least."

Ig glanced at Fen and shrugged. "I think that was actually a compliment. Or as much of one as I'm going to get."

Fen nodded sagely. "I'd suggest you take it as such."

Ig clapped him on the shoulder. "Welcome, Fen. Come in. We were just getting ready to go for a run. Why don't you and Sunny stow your things and join us?"

"Is the loft available?" Sunny grabbed her small travel bag in one hand and Fen's hand in the other. He allowed himself to be dragged up the steps and through the front door to the main room of the cabin. "If you guys aren't sleeping up there, I want the loft."

"It's all yours." Star said. She glanced over her shoulder at Fen. "Lots of great memories associated with that loft. If you've mated, I'm sure you'll be able to find a few." Laughing, she turned and headed toward the kitchen. "Let us know when you're ready to go."

Fen followed Sunny up the stairs. When he stepped into the big, open loft, he didn't even try to stop laughing. The room was huge, but almost the entire floor was covered in king-sized mattresses. Clean fitted sheets covered each one, and there were a few blankets folded along one wall, along with a basket filled with things Fen couldn't quite identify.

The purpose of the room was more than obvious.

"This has got to be the Chanku vision of heaven."

"It was certainly a teenager's slice of paradise." Sunny linked an arm through his. "Star's parents' generation was the one that christened this room. They were the first generation in a long time to learn they were Chanku. All of them had grown up sexually frustrated, trapped in a Chanku body with its increased libido and yet governed by human morality. Almost all of them had miserable lives until they finally discovered their ability to shift and, for the women at least, that they could control their fertility. Plus, there wasn't a cure for AIDS yet, so the threat of disease was a huge factor affecting sexual freedom before they knew they were immune to human diseases."

She sighed and leaned closer to him. Fen slipped his arm free of her grasp and wrapped it around her shoulders. "It's hard to even imagine what that was like. It affected me differently. I was in a wheelchair and my sex life was all in my head, so I was mentally frustrated, but without the physical drive. Trying to contain their sexual needs must have been horrible before they knew who and what they were.

"Anyway, once they hit puberty, the kids in Star's generation were raised to embrace their sexuality, and a lot of that embracing happened here. Puberty generally happens older for Chanku—fifteen or sixteen is about average for both girls and boys—but as soon as the boys' voices began to change and the girls had their first heat, they were considered adults and allowed all the sexual freedom they wanted." She grinned at Fen and chuckled. "Of course, a lot of the kids were experimenting much earlier, but we don't talk about that."

Fen thought about the sexual frustration he'd known as a kid. His had been social as well as physical and more due to isolation than rules—there were few people living nearby in the southeastern forests of Finland. He'd been homeschooled before going off to college, where he quickly made up for lost time.

But not once had he experienced the sexual and emotional satisfaction he'd found with Sunny, a satisfaction that seemed to grow each time they made love.

Sunny shook herself. He sensed her withdrawal from old memories, from times she'd rather not recall. Then she tilted her head and smiled at him. "Let's go for a run. It's going to be dark in less than an hour, and I want you to see this country at dusk. On a clear night like tonight, it's breathtaking." She laughed. "Besides, if Star's anything like me, she'd rather hunt down a fat buck for dinner than have to cook."

Sunny held tightly to Fen's hand as they walked out on the front deck. She wore a pale blue sarong in deference to Fen.

The Chanku comfort with nudity was something he was still getting used to, and she'd quickly covered herself the minute Fen slipped on a pair of sweatpants while up in the loft. Then she'd kissed him to let him know she was perfectly okay with taking all these changes one step at a time.

Star and Ig hadn't bothered with clothing. They sat on the top step, staring at the ever-changing colors crossing the sky. It would be dark shortly, but the moments of early evening were always spectacular in these mountains.

"Sorry to take so long," Sunny said. She untied the fabric she'd knotted just over her breasts and draped the sarong over the deck railing. When she glanced over her shoulder, Fen was tossing his sweats into an empty chair. She flashed a smile his way and was relieved when he grinned at her and acted as if he was checking out her body. So far so good. This was his first time to run as a wolf with anyone besides her. His first time naked in front of people who were essentially still strangers to him. She could feel his nervousness. He didn't want to do anything wrong, though she'd done her best to convince him there was no wrong.

Wolves were wolves. Sometimes they acted noble, other times not so much. Just like humans.

Star glanced over her shoulder. "No problem. Ig and I were just trying to figure out which way we wanted to go." She shot a quick look at Igmutaka.

"We had a run-in with a group of poachers last night," he said. "If you don't mind, I'd like to head toward their campsite and make sure they haven't come back."

Fen glanced at Sunny. *I should tell them,* he said.

I agree, but it's your story to tell.

He let out a frustrated breath, and Sunny quickly sent him a mental hug. He immediately looked more relaxed. "We had a problem with poachers on the Montana property," he said.

"On Sebastian's place, next to Anton's. That's how I found out I was a shapeshifter."

"Because of poachers?" Star shot another quick glance at Igmutaka. He kissed her forehead and focused on Fen.

Fen nodded. "They'd trapped and killed seven wolves. In my other life, I'm a forest ranger, and I'd been researching the local wolf population. I trailed the poachers, found their campsite, and was trying to figure out how one unarmed guy—me—was going to stop three armed men, when I heard a wolf whimpering. One of the wolves they'd thought was dead was struggling to get out from under the bodies of her packmates. One of the poachers grabbed a knife and headed toward her."

Sunny felt the tension in him, the way his heart raced as the memories returned, and she tightened her grip on his hand.

"I didn't know I was a shapeshifter, but at that moment, when I realized I had to stop him from killing that injured wolf, something snapped. The next thing I knew, I was wandering in the forest, covered in blood. I found out later that I'd shifted and eviscerated three armed men."

"I am sorry, my brother." At some point, Igmutaka had stood. Now he planted his right hand on Fen's shoulder, and his eyes were troubled. "The first shift should be a time of joy."

Fen shot Sunny a quick grin. "Well, in a way . . ."

She snorted. "To make a long story short, I was running alone, and like an idiot hadn't taken into consideration I was still in heat." She glanced at Fen. "Picture this—traumatized wolf with no idea how he'd gone from two legs to four, sexy little female . . ." She poked Fen with her elbow. "That would be me, of course, trots along under his nose and . . ."

"Is that when you mated?" Wide-eyed, Star stared at Sunny.

"Well, no." Fen hugged Sunny. "That's when the wild wolf and the hot bitch fucked. She didn't have much of a choice. Lucky for me, she's a very forgiving sort."

"Well, we worked things out and mated properly, after we decided that, yes, this might actually work just fine." Sunny stretched up on her toes and met Fen's lips. "It wasn't all that bad, that first time. I was just glad he was a shapeshifter. Can you imagine explaining getting screwed by a wild wolf while running innocently through the woods? The pack would have never let me live it down."

Ig threw his head back and laughed. Star stared at him, and then shook her head in disgust. "Men," she said. She grinned at Fen. "The disgust is aimed at him, not you." Then she shifted and leapt off the deck. Sunny followed, but Fen remained behind.

She sent him a questing thought.

I want to know your lover better, he said. She decided not to ask. Male bonding was something totally out of her league.

And she hadn't run with Star in years.

Fen watched as the two female wolves raced across the big meadow. He wanted to follow, but at the same time he was drawn so powerfully to Igmutaka that he decided to wait until the man was ready to run.

Ig pulled it together and cocked his head as he gazed directly at Fen. "You feel it, don't you?"

Slowly, Fen nodded. He wasn't sure what it was, but it was . . . something. "A connection. You and me." He shrugged. "I don't know what it means, but it's very strong."

"It helps explain why I sensed you before you and Sunny met. The fact there is something between us. Come. Shift, and let's catch up to the women. I worry about them running alone until we know for sure those jackasses haven't returned."

Fen shifted at the same time as Ig. His wolf was bigger than Igmutaka's, though not by as much as the other Chanku he'd seen. He wondered if they shared the same Berserker background.

He ran just behind and to the left of Ig's wolf. This was the first time he'd run with someone other than his mate, and he wasn't sure what the rules were. There had to be rules. Had to be something that would keep so many potentially dangerous creatures from turning on one another.

Good manners, mostly.

What?

Ig continued running, following the scent of the females, but his mental voice was clear in Fen's mind. *When we shift, while our appearance and our senses are totally feral, we usually retain our human sensibilities. Most of the time, anyway. Our ability to reason can be overwhelmed by bloodlust or by the call to mate, but generally we are able to think along the lines of humans. To behave reasonably.*

I certainly wasn't thinking like a human when I raped Sunny.

Do not call it rape. Wolves don't rape—that's a human concept. What you did, while still caught up in the feral bloodlust, was smell a female in heat and do what came naturally to your wolf. The reasoning part of your brain wasn't even engaged, and Sunny certainly doesn't hold it against you. She recognizes it for what it was—a natural act in an unusual situation. When did you realize what had happened?

When I tried to apologize to the wild wolf and Sunny answered.

Once again, Fen knew Ig was laughing. Finally, the wolf slowed and stared over his shoulder at Fen. *I would give anything to have been there, just to see the expression on your face.*

It was not my best moment.

No, I imagine it probably wasn't. He spun away and took off at a full run. *C'mon. They're just up ahead.*

Fen followed, easily keeping up with Igmutaka. He found himself studying the wolf, watching the graceful way the creature ran, the strength in his muscular body, and that made him think of the man he'd seen, the tall, powerful Native American who was so beautiful he would have been lovely even if he'd been a woman.

Such a strange concept, that kind of beauty in a man, but Igmutaka was not someone you could easily ignore. Fen had never really paid attention to the form and attractiveness of other men—not before he shifted. Since then, he'd caught himself watching Anton and Stefan, even feeling a certain attraction toward Sebastian Xenakis.

Sunny had tried to explain that Chanku weren't necessarily heterosexual or homosexual—not even bisexual. They were just flat-out sexual.

Creatures with a powerful sex drive that often dictated physical responses beyond conscious thought, they had to learn to live with a libido well beyond anything human mores dealt with.

Which meant, for now, anyway, pushing all thoughts of Igmutaka and his gorgeous body out of his head. He was a wolf, the night was cool and the breezes gentle, and he needed to concentrate on the moment.

Not on when he'd be having sex with Sunny and whether they'd be joining Star and Igmutaka in bed. Though he couldn't help but wonder, even as they cut through a thick swath of willows and followed a steep trail downhill. Wonder, and realize that he hoped the night progressed in that direction. Desire was something he wore now like a second skin. Whether in his wolf or human form, it didn't seem to matter, so he decided to follow Sunny's advice and go with the moment.

They rounded a tumble of boulders and spotted the women below, drinking from a narrow creek that rushed through the draw. Fen narrowed his focus to his mate.

Sunny raised her head as soon as Fen and Ig appeared on the trail. She yipped at Star, and the two of them joined the men.

There was a certain amount of sniffing and growling, a nip or two as if they'd not seen one another for days instead of minutes, but it all felt totally natural while at the same time out of his control. In this circumstance, Fen's wolf knew what it wanted; the man was merely along for the ride.

Then, as one, they took off, running fast and far. Fen knew he'd never known such exhilaration in his life. To be one of the pack, to feel the world around him as he'd never experienced it before. Not just the sights, sounds, and scents through his powerful wolven senses, but the camaraderie of three others like him. His Berserker lineage made no difference in the way he was treated. He was, for the first time in his life, accepted as an equal by others enough like him that their differences didn't matter.

The night grew darker and his sense of belonging stronger with each mile they covered. They checked out the poachers' campsite, and all was as Ig and Star had left it. That chore accomplished, the four of them raced through the night, exploring the miles of wilderness encompassing Chanku property, checking for trespassers, following trails that might lead to a meal.

It was Star who brought them to a halt not far from the hot springs Sunny had told him about. *Game.*

Fen sniffed the air. The strongest smell was sulfur from the nearby spring, but his feral mind recognized the scents of both deer and rabbits. He cocked an ear and stared at Star.

There, she said, *in the meadow through the brush. At least two, maybe three or more deer.*

How do you want to proceed? Ig's question was directed at Star. She'd scented them first. Though she'd not hunted in the wild in many years, Ig was reminding her that it was her hunt.

She took over immediately. *Fen and Sunny to the left. You can cut off their escape along the creek. Ig and I will go in from this side. Ig, you're bigger. You go for the kill.*

They split up. Fen stuck close to Sunny's heels. This was all new to him, this concept of hunting on four legs. His heart thundered in his chest, his senses were all firing at once, and he would swear that the night lived and breathed all about him.

They crept through the scrubby willows and shrubs growing at the water's edge until the meadow came into view. Darkness had fallen rapidly, and even with his acute feral vision and the tiny sliver of a new moon, Fen had trouble spotting the animals. Then he saw them—five deer standing close together, heads up, ears alert. They stared toward the far side of the small meadow, the direction Star and Ig had taken.

The wind has shifted, Sunny said. *They can smell Ig and Star, but there haven't been wolves here for many years. Since wolves aren't familiar, the deer don't recognize the scent. Instinctively, though, they know we're not a good thing. Be ready. We're downwind. This looks like a well-traveled trail, so if they run, they'll probably come this way.*

Which one do we want?

Watch them a moment. See that buck on the right? He's favoring a back leg, his ribs are showing and one of his antlers is broken. All signs that he's older, probably not in the best health. We usually go for animals that are past their prime, the ones that might not make it through a harsh winter.

Good. As a ranger, he liked that approach, the idea that they consciously culled the weaker animals. As a wolf, he merely wanted a target. Fen crouched low, instinctively preparing to leap when it was time. The human side of his mind stepped back, fascinated by his instinctive responses. Saliva dripped from his jaws, and his whole body felt twitchy.

His feral side ignored the human curiosity. It merely wanted to kill and eat.

A beautiful doe with a half-grown fawn was the first to bolt. She raced straight toward the brushy cover where Fen and Sunny waited, and it took every bit of Fen's human will to hold the wolf back. Two more—a doe and a young buck with spikes rather than a full rack—ran past. Then the older buck was on them.

Fen exploded out of the brush.

His jaws stretched wide as he leapt, and he clamped down hard on the buck's throat, hoping like hell he'd be able to bring the animal down and not make a fool of himself.

He hadn't counted on his Berserker size and weight, which were far beyond that of an average wolf.

He snapped the buck's neck on impact.

Crouching over his kill, Fen snarled at Sunny and then turned and faced off against Ig and Star. They held back, and that moment, that brief slice of time where his feral mind had ruled, simply blinked out.

Fen was back, standing over the buck, feeling slightly embarrassed by his territorial display. Stiff-legged, he backed away from the kill.

It's okay, Fen. Sunny stared at him, ears forward, tail high, and obviously not the least bit concerned about his behavior. *The kill is yours. You have a right to defend it. Of course, then you have to share.*

How could anyone stay uptight in the face of his mate's constant good humor? Fen shook his head, clearing his mind and then taking a deep breath to calm his racing heart. *I cede the kill to you, Sunny. You and Star go first.*

Thank you, she said. *We will.*

He sat back on his haunches, feeling proud of his wolf. Proud of his mate. Feeling good about life in general. He glanced at Ig, sitting calmly beside him. *Is it always like this? This feeling that life is perfect, that it couldn't possibly be better?*

More so when we're in our wolven form. We tend to fall into the natural state of the wolf, of living for the moment. Of not worrying about anything beyond the immediacy of here and now.

Sunny's words made sense now, more than ever. *That's something Sunny told me. She said I should live for the mo-*

ment, for this moment, that when you live almost forever, it's easy to forget the importance of each moment.

She's right. And at this moment, I'm hungry and that buck looks good enough to eat.

Ig went to work on the animal's haunch. Fen had never once, at least in his adult life, imagined himself as a wolf eating from an animal he'd killed with his own jaws. One that was still warm and bloody.

It was even better than he'd expected.

With bellies full, they left the carcass to the coyotes and other scavengers and trotted down the trail to the hot springs. Ig remained alert, sniffing the air, checking for signs along the trail, but there was still no sign of the poachers.

With Sunny and Fen here, he felt even more responsible than when he'd had only Star to worry about. Sunny was such a sweet little thing, but much too trusting as far as he was concerned.

And Fen didn't know a thing about being a wolf, though he obviously adored Sunny. Even so, Igmutaka found it difficult to believe she'd mated a man she hardly knew, much less one who was a Berserker. Granted, Fen hadn't shown anything other than concern and love for his mate, and he appeared to be a decent guy, but Ig couldn't quite bring himself to relax around the man—or the wolf.

Damn but he was big. Igmutaka was a large wolf, larger even than Tinker McClintock, but Fen made him feel like a blasted puppy. In his human form, he was only about an inch taller, but Ig figured Fen outweighed him by a good forty pounds, and none of it was fat. The guy was solid, rock-hard muscle.

And sexy as hell, but asking him to join them for sex was probably pushing things, at least this soon. Fen was so new at this—he'd just rediscovered his shapeshifter heritage. Finding out that both Star and Ig were already looking at him as a potential sex partner might be a bit much.

Before he could take that line of thought any further, they reached the hot spring. Steam rose off the shimmering surface, and the barest sliver of moon hung low in the sky to the east. Ig and Star shifted at the same time as Fen and Sunny.

"Amazing." Fen stood behind Sunny and wrapped his arms around her. Ig wondered if he was shy around people he barely knew. Maybe uncomfortable spending so much time without clothing among people who were still essentially strangers.

"How hot is it?" Fen asked. "How deep?"

Sunny laughed. "Hot enough that we've spent time in it when there was snow all around and we stayed toasty, but it won't burn you. You can wade about halfway across, and then it's over my head, at least. I don't know about Ig."

He smiled at her. She really was a tiny thing. "Well, I'd like to say it's just because you're short, but it's over mine, too. I have to swim the last few yards, but there's a smooth bench on the far side that will seat about six. It's mostly natural, though I think Star's dads built it up somewhat."

Fen caught that. "You have more than one father?"

"Well, my mom is mated to two men. One of them is my biological father, and the other is my twin brother's father." She leaned back against Ig. "I guess I'll just have to make do with one guy."

"You poor thing." Sunny shot a grin at Ig as she moved out of Fen's embrace and grabbed his hand. "C'mon. I'm getting cold." She stepped into the water and he followed, with Star and Ig right behind.

Igmutaka and Fen ended up on the ends with the two women between them. Water lapped at their chins, while Ig and Fen had water bubbling across their chests.

Fen sighed. "Amazing. And so quiet. Nothing but the sound

of the water. This is definitely paradise. Now, tell me why you choose to live in Montana instead of here."

"It's a long way to the grocery store, for one thing." Star leaned back against Ig's shoulder. "Even longer to any of the places where we work."

"Where do you work?"

"Nowhere, right now. I just left Yale. I was a teacher's assistant finishing up my doctorate when I decided I'd rather be with the pack."

"Finishing your what? Third doctorate?" Ig chuckled when she poked him in the ribs.

"Only my second. Behave." She smiled at Fen. "I decided not to go for the third. I figured I had more than enough letters after my name." Then she laughed and winked at Ig. "What if I just choose to be your sex slave? Would you go for that?"

Ig actually thought that sounded pretty good, but he answered her seriously. "I'd love it, though I'm not sure if it would appease your parents. Both your dads want you at Pack Dynamics."

"That's the search and rescue team, right?" Fen glanced at Sunny. "The one you said the chopper was mainly used for."

"It is. I've done a lot of work for them over the years, and so has Ig. It's not one of the moneymakers for the pack, but it's really good PR. We have a lot more successes than failures."

"Lily wants me to work for Cheval International," Star said. "But that would mean living in San Francisco." She turned and gazed at Ig, and he actually felt her love. Felt her deep inside. "And I don't think I could ask Igmutaka to live in the city."

"I will go wherever you choose, Mikaela Star."

"I know." She kissed him. "Which is why I want to choose wisely." She turned to Fen. "I've lived away from the pack by choice for a long time. I think what I really want to do, at least for a while, anyway, is be part of the pack again. Especially now, when I've finally got this guy." She ran her fingers down his arm, across his chest, and then along the line of his ribs. He felt his arousal growing, his need for her something unquenchable. Something he hoped would never ease, would never be sated. She turned to him, oblivious to Sunny and Fen, focusing on Ig. He felt her intensity, her need, and though they'd made love so many times over the past day, he wanted her now. Again, as if he'd not been with her for many days.

This overwhelming desire for his one partner was something new. Something he truly wanted to investigate further. He'd always loved the variety of sexual partners, but while it had been days since he last made love to Sunny, and he'd never been with Fen, right now he wanted Star. Only Star.

Giving in to desire, he grasped her slim waist in both hands and pulled her over him. She wrapped her legs around his middle, and he filled her.

As far as Ig was concerned, they were the only two in the pond. The only two who mattered.

Just Star. His woman, the one he'd never dreamed would want him. The one woman who made him whole.

13

Never before had Fen seen anything as sensual, as beautiful as Igmutaka making love to Star in that hot, mineral-laden water. Pale moonglow reflected off the whorls of steam floating over the surface. Star sat astride Igmutaka's lean hips with her long hair floating in the water behind her and his falling over his shoulders, drifting in the water, tangling with Star's.

Her lips had twisted in a taut rictus of pleasure, and her eyes drifted shut as the big man entered her, and Igmutaka's face—that unbelievably beautiful face—was hollowed and creased with strain in his struggle for control.

Fen and Sunny moved closer—so close that Sunny ended up in Fen's lap and his shoulder pressed against Igmutaka's. So close that he absorbed Ig's tension and Star's, their powerful sexual need through that single touch, that simple expedience of two strong men pressing flesh to flesh.

Filled with Igmutaka's sexual need, his own arousal and the amazing visual of two unbelievably beautiful women, Fen lifted Sunny and pressed his thick cock between her slick folds. The water around them was hot, but she was even hotter as he opened her, entered her. She groaned. He paused for a moment, allowed her to slide his shaft deeper inside at her own speed, and she took him all the way without any hesitation. Engulfed in heat, surrounded by the rhythmic pulse of her sheath, and wrapped in Igmutaka's and Star's need as much as his own, Fen's entire body tensed.

When he opened his mind further, Sunny was there, loving him with everything she had. Then he felt Ig and Star, their connection as close, as sensual as if he made love with the two of them as well as his mate.

He felt the burn and stretch as Ig filled Star and then shared those feelings with Sunny. She connected with Star's mind, and Fen knew exactly what the women felt, what their men did for them. What Igmutaka experienced, and what he wanted.

What Igmutaka wanted took Fen's breath. The graphic visuals he shared startled Fen and then took him higher, hotter, than he'd ever gone.

Ig wanted him. Wanted Fen in his bed, either beneath him or topping him—it didn't matter to Igmutaka. He shared his first time with a man—it had happened the first night he'd taken human form in centuries, when he'd gone to Adam and Liana's bed. He shared his confusion over what he'd expected, his absolute joy in finding a powerful connection with Adam, the healer Fen had met.

The man who had mated a goddess.

With his mind full of visuals, from Sunny, from Star, and the big man beside him, Fen reached his peak long before he'd intended. He tried to hold back, but then he felt Sunny fly free, and the tightening of her internal muscles all along his shaft took him over the edge.

And held him there, caught in a never-ending loop of sensation. This orgasm was an experience unlike anything he'd ever known. His mind and Sunny's, connected through the mating bond, their every feeling shared. Igmutaka and Star joining them, sharing everything through Igmutaka's close link with Sunny as well as the connection that had somehow formed between Fen and Igmutaka. It was amazing, bizarre, and addictive, this sense of communion with three other people, all caught in the sensual overload of their shared climax.

Fen was both Igmutaka and his beloved Mikaela Star. He was Sunny, and he experienced his own joy through Sunny's mind. There was no diminishing the power of their climax, and their peak seemed to grow and expand until he feared he might never come out of this unbelievable, kaleidoscopic experience of pleasure.

Visuals, sensual patterns, and impossible images filled his mind—images that had to be Igmutaka's because they weren't from Fen's past. They couldn't be—he saw things both primitive and foreign, so far in the history of old memories that Fen had trouble explaining what he saw.

There was no description for what he felt, that wash of pleasure drowning him in sensation. He must have lost consciousness for a brief moment, because suddenly it was over and the four of them lay together on the narrow ledge, lungs heaving and lips parted to draw in great draughts of air.

Sunny lay across Fen's chest, her body limp but her lungs and heart still working just fine. Star was stretched across Igmutaka, and Ig had one arm around Fen's shoulders. Fen raised his head and stared into Igmutaka's green eyes.

Ig grinned at him. "Well, that was certainly different."

Fen slowly shook his head. "What the fuck just happened?"

"Do you feel me in your head? The way you feel Sunny?"

Frowning, Fen searched his memories. "I do. But how?"

"I'm not really sure. We didn't have sex, and we're in our human form, not animal, but I think that, somehow, you and I and Mikaela Star and Sunny have linked. Almost like a mating bond. I've never heard of anything like this before."

"What does that mean?" Fen shook his head. It felt as if he had cobwebs in his brain.

I'm not sure, but I can mindspeak with you as easily as I do with Mikaela Star. Is my mental voice clear?

Very. But you're sitting right next to me, and we had no trouble linking when we were wolves.

True, but look beyond the link. I feel your heart beating, the way I do my mate's. I feel your lungs expanding. I am in your thoughts, so close they could be my own.

Fen studied the sensations swimming through his system and discovered that Igmutaka was hooked in on a much deeper level. It was an almost symbiotic sensation—as if they were two parts of the whole. *What do you suggest we do?*

I think we need to fuck. See where this takes us.

Fen bit back laughter. *That seems to be the answer for just about everything for Chanku, doesn't it?*

Only because it works. Let's go back to the cabin.

Star raised her head. "You're such a baby, Ig. You always go for the warm, comfy bed."

"I'm only thinking of you, my sweet." He kissed her nose. Then he gently lifted her away from his cock. Fen noticed that Igmutaka was still hard as a rock.

Just the way he was.

Ig's mind wouldn't stop spinning. Whatever had happened between him and Fenris Ahlberg had never happened to him before, not once in his long, long life. Granted, he'd not had a corporeal form in this millennium until thirty or so years ago, but he'd had a lot of sex, with a lot of different partners.

Why did the link with Fen affect him so deeply? What brought the women into their link? He and Star were newly mated, as were Fen and Sunny, but the link had somehow originated with Fen. He was almost positive.

The man was a mystery in so many ways. He was Berserker, yet not. Born a wolf, and yet he'd lived his life as a man—a very normal human man. Ig had been inside his mind. He'd essentially learned as much about Fen as Sunny had when they mated, but why?

Very little happened in life without reason or purpose, yet nothing was clear to him. Nothing but his growing need for Fen, a need that called to him on so many levels, he'd yet to figure out the ultimate reason behind any of it.

They reached the cabin and he was up the steps to the front porch before he even realized they were home. The past few miles had passed in a fog of questions. Unanswered questions, but Sunny, Star, and Fen were right behind him, and all of them shifted the moment they reached the front door.

Ig stood there with his hand on the door and stared at the other three. The girls were in high spirits, laughing and so glad to be back together after Star's long absence, but Fen stood a couple of feet back, and his focus was entirely on Ig.

When Igmutaka caught his steady gaze, Fen nodded just once. Ig couldn't move, so completely trapped in the man's stare he felt immobilized. Star and Sunny quit laughing, and Star took his hand. Sunny went to Fen and then she shot a knowing look at Star. "I hope you guys don't mind, but Star and I really need some girl time. You're on your own, boys."

Still smiling, she kissed Fen's cheek as Star planted a big kiss on Ig's mouth. He thought he kissed her back. He wasn't really sure, but his focus wasn't on the woman he loved.

No. For whatever reason, it was entirely on Fen. And it was Fen who shook his head and broke away from whatever held the two of them as if caught in some strange stasis.

"The loft?"

Fen asked so quietly, Ig was amazed he actually heard the question through the roaring in his ears. He nodded. In fact, he thought that if he'd tried to speak, nothing would have come out of his mouth, but Fen stepped through the open door and headed straight for the stairs.

He paused at the bottom step with his back to Igmutaka, took a deep breath, and bowed his head. Ig had no idea what he was thinking, but he didn't search Fen's thoughts. He stood in place and waited until Fen turned and held out a hand. Ig wrapped his fingers in Fen's and then he stared at their clasped hands. Fen was Scandinavian, and yet his skin was almost as dark as Igmutaka's.

He raised his head and really looked for the first time at Fen's facial structure. At his high cheekbones and strong nose, the beautiful dark amber eyes—all of it gave him a look more native than European.

Was that the connection? One of blood?

As if he'd been listening, Fen slowly shook his head. "No," he said. "I don't think it's that. Not exactly. Come with me."

Ig followed.

It was dark in the loft, though some light filtered in from lamps in the rooms below. Fen paused in the middle of the room, standing between a couple of mattresses. His and Sunny's bags were against the wall, but other than their things and a couple of baskets of what appeared to be odds and ends, the room was empty.

Drifting up from the other end of the cabin, the sound of Star and Sunny's laughter told Ig the two were in one of the downstairs bedrooms, probably already making love and definitely enjoying their reunion. He could link to his mate and find out, but somehow it didn't matter. She was with Sunny, and he knew they were both safe.

Nothing else mattered except what was happening here. Now.

With Fen. It was quiet up here. Quiet enough that he heard his heart beating. Heard Fen's heart as well, and the rush of blood in their veins, the soft exhalations as each of them breathed, and it was as if they breathed as one, beat as one.

He cocked his head to one side and stared at Fen, and that was when he noticed the amulet. A jade wolf on a leather thong tied about Fen's throat. But he'd just shifted, and Ig knew he hadn't carried it with him. Had it been around his neck as a wolf? It was small enough he might not have noticed it, lost in Fen's thick coat, but it made no sense.

Of course, very little of this night was making sense. He reached out slowly and touched the carved jade. There was life in it, a sense of magic he almost recognized, but the memory was hazy and he couldn't make a connection.

Later. He would wonder about this later. Fen's gaze never left Ig's as he let go of the amulet and pressed his hand against Fen's broad chest. He felt the same sense of magic in the man. The same faint hint of memory.

That, and so much more. So much strength that he bowed to the greater power. It was such a strange thing to acknowledge that, of the two of them, Fen was the more powerful wolf, but there was no doubt in Igmutaka's mind. Fenris Ahlberg was the stronger man. The alpha in the room.

It should have been an uncomfortable feeling, but it wasn't. It was different—as spirit guide, an ageless being of untold strengths—Ig was used to being the ultimate alpha. He'd bowed to no man except Anton Cheval.

A subservience both of them accepted as a courtesy rather than an actual admission of any pack hierarchy. Had mating Star changed him that much? Giving up his spiritual strengths had seemed a small price to pay. Was it more? Would he regret what he'd lost?

Fen smiled at him and shook his head. "No. You've not lost anything. Somehow, I've gained. I hear your every thought as if I spoke the words. I have an understanding of who and what I am, though I'm still trying to make sense of a lot of it. I feel more confident, more sure of myself in this new role as shapeshifter. As a child, I somehow lost the ability to shift, but now that I have it back, it's slowly reawakening parts of me I had either never known or forgotten existed. You, I believe, are one of those parts."

Smiling broadly, he covered Ig's hand with his. "I think you were right, my brother. We need to fuck."

Ig turned his palm away from the warmth of Fen's chest and clasped his hand. Once again he experienced that subtle shock of awareness, as if their bodies recognized one another on a cellular level, far beyond conscious thought.

"First, there's something you need to know," Fen said.

He held Ig's hand tightly but didn't draw him closer. Did nothing but stand there, a big, sensual man with a powerful body and an erection that left no doubt what that body wanted.

Igmutaka nodded, and met Fen's steady gaze.

"Eve came to us, to Sunny and me, at Anton Cheval's home. In front of witnesses, she said that the two of us needed to be at Lassen by tonight, or tomorrow morning at the latest, but she had no idea why. At the time, we didn't realize you and Star were already here. Star wasn't expected for a few more days, and Sunny didn't know if you'd arrived or not."

"When did this happen?"

"The first warning came early in the day Tuesday—yesterday. But last night she sent a more specific message through Lily Xenakis, that Star and Igmutaka were somehow facing danger and we needed to be here."

There was no doubt in his mind. He turned Fen's hand loose and ran both hands through his hair. "It makes sense. Last night we routed the poachers. I've worried about them returning all day. That's the only thing I know of that could be dangerous for me or Star."

"But there was no sign of them tonight?"

"None. But that doesn't mean we don't need to be on guard."

"After we fuck?" Fen's raised eyebrow was like a kick to the solar plexus.

Grinning, Ig nodded. "Yes, my brother. After we fuck."

Fen wasn't sure where this sudden self-confidence came from, but it had to have something to do with the strange link he'd forged with Igmutaka. Whatever the reason, he had no doubts at all about sex with another man—at least with this one—even though he didn't have a clue where to start.

Ig didn't appear to have any problem. He planted both hands on Fen's shoulders and looked at him as if he were memorizing Fen's face.

Fen curled his lip into a grin. "Damn, Ig, but you are just too pretty to be a man."

Ig closed his eyes and bit his lips. Fen knew he was struggling not to laugh, but then Ig snorted. Fen lost it at about the same time, and the two of them ended up hanging onto each other, laughing hysterically for no real reason at all, other than a powerful need to release the tension that had been building since the moment they'd climbed the stairs together.

Gasping for breath, they finally collapsed side by side on top of the closest mattress.

Fen was the first to get himself under control. He rolled to his side and looked at the man who had introduced his beautiful Sunny to sex so long ago, and felt nothing but gratitude. "I owe you my thanks, Igmutaka."

"For what?" Frowning, Ig rolled to a sitting position.

"For everything you gave to Sunny. You introduced her to sex, to her own sensuality, in a beautiful way. What could have been painful or frightening was an amazing experience for her. You've remained her lover, even though both of you knew you were not fated to mate. She will always love you, and I honor that love. Because of our mating bond, I realized very quickly that I love you as well, and I need to say this. I don't want you to think I hold anything against you for all the years the two of you were lovers. I don't want your relationship with my mate to end because of me."

"This is a beginning, Fen. Not an ending." Ig leaned close, wrapped his long fingers around the back of Fen's skull, and held him close. He pressed his mouth to Fen's, and the sensation of a man's lips against his mouth was the most amazing thing Fen could recall. They were both big men, their bodies large and strong. They were aroused to the point of pain, but the kiss was such a tender and fascinating sensation, so unexpected, that Fen didn't want it to end.

Ig shared the sensations as he felt them, acknowledging that he rarely kissed his male lovers, that it was usually all about the down and dirty kind of sex, but there was a different connection with Fen. As if they were mates, not just two guys wanting to get laid. This was far beyond sex for release. This was something much deeper.

Fen agreed. He just wished he knew what the fuck it meant.

His tongue slipped between Ig's lips. He licked the sensitive spot behind his teeth, stroked his tongue against Ig's, sliding in and out of his mouth, finding a rhythm that had him rolling atop the other man, pressing all along his length—thighs to thighs, belly to belly, with their heavily engorged cocks sliding between them.

Fen was easily as large as Igmutaka. His shaft lay alongside Ig's and their balls pressed together beneath. This was his first sexual contact with a man, and it was right. More than right, it affected him on so many levels—not merely physical and emotional.

His rational self responded as well.

There was something important happening here tonight. Something beyond Fen's understanding, beyond Igmutaka's. He felt like a chess piece with no idea who was playing the game, or what the final stakes might be.

And he'd never been so aroused in his life. Ig slid low along his chest, kissing, nipping, finally reaching Fen's cock and taking him deep inside his mouth. He groaned as he was engulfed in Ig's hot, wet mouth, with the slide of teeth along the sides of his shaft and the slick pressure of Ig's tongue teasing the sensitive underside.

He fought for control, fought the powerful need to let go and give his desire full rein. It took a few deep, steadying breaths before he was able to pull it together, to turn about on the mattress, and bring his mouth level with Ig's cock. Ig's mouth continued to work magic on Fen's erection, but he locked the sensations away in his mind until he could concentrate on the beautiful length and breadth of Ig's impressive equipment. He'd never really looked at a man's cock—not even his own—this closely. It was fascinating, from the dark, blood-flushed surface with its pattern of darker veins and the soft cowl of Ig's foreskin rolled back behind the darker, plum-shaped head to the heavy sac beneath.

His fascination drew him close, and he ran his tongue over the dark crown. Hard as iron and yet soft, almost silky at the tip. He swirled his tongue over the soft curve, dipping into the tiny slit at the tip, tasting the bittersweet drop of fluid, inhaling Ig's scent.

He linked with Igmutaka, sharing the taste and scent, the texture and the sense of arousal that had become a strong and steady beat thrumming in his veins. Ig's experience spilled into Fen's mind and he knew his own taste, his own shapes and textures. Such an intimate knowing of himself and his lover. So unique and unexpected. His arousal spiked another notch higher.

Trembling, his muscles tensing more with each passing moment, Fen grabbed Ig's buttocks and held him close, sucking and tonguing his full length, feeling the strong pull of lips and tongue and teeth around his own cock. He continued sharing the sensation, the newness of this experience, until he felt the tension grow, the beat rising as he drew closer to climax.

But Ig pulled away, gasping like the rush of a bellows. "Not this way." Sucking deep draughts of air as if he'd run a far distance, with sweat glistening on his chest and lips shiny from sucking Fen's cock, he still looked almost regal—a native god in the throes of pleasure.

It took Fen a moment to find enough control to pull away from Ig, and when he did, he was breathing just as hard. "How then? I'm new at this, remember?"

Ig exploded in laughter. He rolled to his back and flung his arms wide. "Goddess, help me, I shouldn't laugh, but I was like you the first time Adam Wolf showed me what two men could do." He rolled his head to one side. "You know there's more," he said, and he grinned at Fen. "Top or bottom?"

He hadn't actually considered anything beyond oral sex, but this? Fen let out a deep breath he'd forgotten he was holding. "You mean I have a choice?" Then he sat back on his heels and stared at Ig, really looked at him for the first time as a sexual partner. It wasn't a difficult leap—the man was beautiful. But large. In every respect he was large.

Fen realized he was focused on an erection that was as big as his own. Long and thick, and obviously much larger than any orifice it might be entering. He sat there a moment, working through the logistics in his head.

Ig must have felt sorry for him. "This time, I'll make it easy on you. You can top."

Fen's mouth went dry. It was real, then. They were going to have sex. *Make love.* He refused to call it anything else but what it was. He wanted this. Wanted it more than he thought he could. Wanted the connection with Igmutaka—the physical, mental, and emotional connection he fully expected.

Why did it feel like a mating? "What if we were to do this as wolves? First as men, then as wolves." He shook his head. "I don't know if that's my idea or not. Why do I feel as if I'm being led . . . as if the two of us are following someone else's directions?"

Ig nodded. "I've felt the same way. You're here because the goddess told you to come, though the attraction between us is not something even the gods could have fabricated. It's real, Fen. You are somehow connected to me, and I to you. Let's do this as men, with the rational connection men are capable of forging."

Then he shook his head. "Honestly? I've only been with Mikaela Star in my wolf form. Right now, that connection is special. Sacred to me. I want to keep it that way."

Fen nodded. What Ig said made sense. He realized he felt much the same way about Sunny. Their bond was still fresh, his feelings, while powerful, still too new.

Ig rolled over and reached for one of the baskets sitting against the wall. "Got it," he said, and held up a tube of something. When he rolled back across the mattress, Fen realized it was a new tube of personal lubricant.

His cock twitched. They really were going to do this. He reached for the tube, but Ig held it back. "I'll do the honors." He scooted closer, poured a big dollop of clear gel into his left palm, smiled at Fen, and raised one eyebrow.

Fen sat back on his heels. "I'm all yours." His cock rose in a gentle curve, but when Ig wrapped his right hand around the base and used his left to slowly stroke from base to tip, there was nothing gentle in Fen's response.

Lightning flashed from his cock to his balls. All the muscles across his abdomen clenched painfully tight. "Holy shit." He groaned. It was a struggle to hold still. Watching another man handle his cock was the biggest turn-on imaginable. His legs were trembling by the time Ig stopped stroking him, and his cock was so hard he ached. His balls had drawn up tight between his legs.

Ig lay on his back on the mattress with his knees bent and his feet planted up close to his thighs. He handed the tube to Fen. It was a simple thing for Fen to cover his fingers in the gel and then slowly work his way along the dark crease between Ig's buttocks, to find the taut muscle and slowly press his slick middle finger against it.

Slowly stroking, he linked with Ig. He didn't want to miss any of this, wanted to experience the feelings, the sensations, Igmutaka felt as he rubbed and slowly stretched his sphincter and then entered that dark passage with his middle finger.

Images, feelings flashed into his head, exploding with sensation. He might not know what he was doing, but if Ig's arousal was anything to go by, Fen was getting it right. He added a second finger, scissoring in and out, stretching Ig. Making room for something much larger and longer than mere fingers.

Then he scooted closer, lifted Igmutaka's hips in his big hands, and pressed the broad, slick head of his cock against Ig's perfect ass.

The mental link faded as Ig pulled his thoughts back, and Fen sensed that all his concentration was focused on relaxing his muscles to prevent Fen from doing serious damage to his ass.

But Fen wasn't trying to enter. Not yet.

He moved slowly. Press and retreat, press and retreat, and then pausing with his cock pressed against that small, taut orifice, pressing steadily now until the muscle slowly relaxed. He paused a moment, sensing when Ig was ready.

Wondering if he was ready.

"Now," Ig said. "Now," he repeated, his voice a rough whisper this time as Fen slowly pushed forward.

The sensation was unlike anything Fen had ever known—Ig groaned again as the broad head of Fen's cock compressed as it breached that tiny opening, stretching taut muscles, sliding inside a sheath that was hot and sleek and already contracting around his thick shaft.

For a moment, the rhythmic, muscular constriction along his entire cock brought Fen to a standstill. Sensations so unique, so utterly amazing, that he lost track of the man he was fucking, lost track of the fact that he was making love to another man.

Then he caught himself, remembered why he was here, what he was doing. Wrapping his gel-slick fist around Igmutaka's cock, Fen stroked Ig's hot length from base to tip as he slid deep inside. A deep groan vibrated up out of Ig's chest, and Fen opened his mind, invited Igmutaka to share what he felt, the way he felt.

The link slammed into Fen, filling his mind with a kaleidoscope of images, visuals and feelings, memories and fears, so much more of Igmutaka's long life than he'd expected.

Far, far beyond the mere link of casual lovers sharing a good fuck.

Enthralled by the mind of the man, by the overwhelming wash of experiences dating back to a time before time, Fen lost himself in Igmutaka's mind, in his memories. In his past. Lost himself in the sheer volume of knowledge spilling into his head.

The connection spiraled deeper, and Fen's hips kept up that rhythmic in and out and then in again, while his right hand rose and fell along Igmutaka's thick shaft, almost as if his body worked independently of his mind.

Except nothing was independent. He was connected to Igmutaka, and Ig to him, and the glut of knowledge moved both ways across the link. Two men, sharing lives so totally different and yet so very much alike.

Two ancient souls, both born of wild creatures, nurtured by predators, and yet mating as men. And as realization slammed into Fen and Igmutaka at the same time, the mating bond clicked firmly into place.

Igmutaka to Fenris, and by virtue of their earlier mating bonds, each of the men to both Sunny and Star.

Orgasm flashed over Fen like a lightning strike. It spilled onto Ig, a shock of amazing, overwhelming pleasure, and with it a sense of timelessness, a sense that this mating was fated, that this connection predated any memories either man might have.

Confused, not a little bit frightened, Fen collapsed over Igmutaka's chest, his cock and balls still pulsing with the power of their shared release, his fingers stroking Ig's pulsing cock and his mind spinning as he tried to sort out the meaning behind this amazing new link.

14

Dressed in worn sweatpants and nothing more, Fen sat across from Igmutaka at the kitchen table. Each man had a cold beer—open but untouched—in front of him. Neither of them had spoken since Fen slipped gently out of Ig's body and the two of them had headed into the shower. Shifting would have cleaned away the sweat and semen, but somehow the act of carefully washing one another seemed to strengthen whatever bond they had created.

One they continued to build upon.

Now, clean and dry and his libido sated—at least for the moment—Fen shoved his fingers through his tangled hair and wondered where in the hell to begin.

Ig slowly shook his head. "I know what you're going to ask, but I will tell you right up front—I don't have a fucking clue what we did. Except I think you and I are now mated."

Fen laughed. "I agree, but I think I know how and why it happened." He held up his hand when Ig raised his eyebrows in obvious disbelief. "Just a minute now, and don't laugh. Think of it. . . . Chanku are born of human parents with the ability to shift into animal forms. When they mate, they mate as animals, usually choosing the wolf, since that's their default animal, so to speak. Yet you and I were both born of animals—a wolf for me, a cougar for you. We just had sex as humans—not our primary form. Could that account for the mating bond?"

Ig's look of disbelief slowly changed to one of grudging acceptance. "You might have something, though I've never heard of it. It would certainly explain the odd connection we felt at the hot spring when I was making love with Mikaela Star. I remember the sense of your shoulder touching mine, knew that we somehow connected when that happened. But for what purpose?" He laughed and covered Fen's hand with his. "Not that I don't want you as a mate, sweetheart, but it wasn't something I sought."

Fen chuckled, but then he shrugged, turning his hand beneath Ig's to grasp his fingers. "Maybe it's something we need."

Ig took a minute to respond. "Why would you say that?"

"Because so much of what's happening lately feels as if it's totally out of my control." He shook his head and released Ig's hand. "Not that I'm complaining, mind you."

Ig took a few swallows of his beer, stared off across the room, and then turned to Fen and grinned. "I just checked on Mikaela Star and found Sunny's mind at the same time. They're both asleep."

Fen downed his entire beer in a few swallows and pushed his chair away from the table. "I couldn't sleep now for anything. Do you feel like running? If you shift to your wolf, you might be able to keep up with me."

"Smart-ass." Ig finished his beer. "My cougar could kick your wolf's butt. Probably not tonight, though." Grinning broadly, he nodded. "Let's go. I'll leave a note for the girls."

Fen leaned against the table while Ig hunted for a pad of paper and a pen. "That's odd, don't you think? We both think of them as girls, but why? Sunny's actually nine years older than I am, though she looks younger. Still, they're grown women. Very powerful women, physically and mentally."

"Frightening powerful women." Ig glanced up from the note he'd started. "At least that's something I learned about Mikaela Star through the mating link. She's stronger than I realized. I've always known Sunny had a lot of strengths."

"Sunny looks like a teenager."

Ig shrugged. "I met Sunny when she still was a teenager, and I was there at Mikaela Star's birth. She will always be a girl in my mind, though I accept that she's a woman grown. She was such an amazing child." He shook his head, and the memories spilled into Fen's mind as Ig added, "I still can't believe she's loved me all these years."

Just as Fen couldn't believe Sunny loved him—after only a few days. Lost in thought, he waited while Ig jotted a quick note to say they were out running, and he realized that the biggest question floating around in his head wasn't the mystery of why he and an ancient spirit guide had bonded. No, it was the fact that Sunny truly loved him. The other pieces of this current puzzle would somehow fall together, but Sunny's love was a mystery he would cherish forever.

Ig finished his note with a flourish and a cartoon sketch of a paw print. When he was done, the two of them went outside, stripped down in the chill night air, and shifted. Together, two massive wolves raced off into the darkness.

Fen took the lead, fully aware that, even after his shift, he still wore the small, jade amulet around his neck.

Fen stopped so quickly that Ig almost ran into him. The big wolf raised his head and sniffed the air. The moment Igmutaka followed suit, he smelled the bastards.

They'd come back. *That's them. I recognize their scent—the same men Mikaela Star and I ran off the other night.*

I knew something smelled wrong. Fen lifted his nose into the wind once again. *I think they're back at the same campsite, the one you took us to earlier tonight.*

I agree. We'll need to get the authorities involved. We reported them before but didn't ask the sheriff to come out since we'd already run them off. As much as I'd love to gut the bastards the way you did your poachers, it would cause too many problems for the pack.

Unfortunately, you're right, but before we call it in, I want to check and see what they're up to. At least we'll know what to report. You take the lead, okay? You know the area better than I do.

Ig slipped ahead of Fen, but as he moved past the big wolf, he was reminded once again just how large a beast he was. Igmutaka's wolf was huge, but Fen was still bigger—taller, broader, overall a massive animal.

It wouldn't hurt to let the humans at least see him. They might reconsider any future trespassing on Chanku land.

Star came out of a sound sleep with a sense of unease. Something wasn't quite right, but what? Sunny slept beside her, though she appeared restless. Was that what had awakened her?

She cast out her thoughts for Igmutaka, expecting to find him nearby. When she picked up his thoughts, he felt far away.

She tapped Sunny's shoulder, and Sunny's head came up. "What's wrong?"

Frowning, Star concentrated on Ig, and shook her head. "I dunno. Link with Fen."

"Wouldn't it be just as easy to walk upstairs?" She grinned and then frowned. "Huh? I feel him, but he's not here."

"I know. C'mon." Star grabbed a robe to ward off the chill, tossed an extra one to Sunny, and walked quickly down the hallway with Sunny right behind her. The loft was dark and there was no sense of the guys.

"Ig left a note." Sunny flipped on the kitchen light and

grabbed a sheet of paper off the table. "He said they went for a run." She held it up, laughing. "He even got artistic."

"Ig? I'm learning all kinds of stuff about my man. Cute paw print. Is it a cat or a wolf? More important, where'd they go?" Star walked to the front door, opened it, and peered out into the darkness. The night was quiet, and Ig hadn't written a time down on the note. She had no idea how long they'd been gone. "Maybe they're doing some guy bonding."

"I think they got plenty of bonding done upstairs."

Sunny grabbed a bottle of chocolate milk out of the fridge and held it up. Star glanced over her shoulder. "Can you heat it? I think it's a hot cocoa night."

Sunny grabbed two mugs, filled them with chocolate milk, and nuked them in the microwave. The she added a dollop of whipped cream from a can she'd found in the refrigerator, added a shot of brandy for good measure, and handed a hot mug to Star.

Star pulled out the stool to sit on one side of the small bar and shoved her handbag out of the way. It toppled to the floor, and of course it landed upside down and open.

"Crap. My purse spilled all over the place." She knelt to pick up the lipsticks, her comb, her wallet, and all the other stuff she'd shoved into the bag for her trip.

The jade amulet lay on the floor. It was such a pretty thing, a carved cougar that Ig had given to her when she was about seven or eight. Rather than shove it back in her bag, she slipped it over her head. The cool jade nestled between her breasts, where it lay hidden beneath her robe.

For some reason, it not only felt right to wear it, she felt closer to her mate with it around her neck. After sticking the rest of the stuff back in her bag, Star sat on her stool. Sunny took the one across from her. As the two of them sipped their chocolate, Star kept her mind open, searching for a stronger sense of Ig, but the link felt different.

She concentrated on the mental signals and stared at Sunny over the top of her mug. "I'm picking up Fen almost as strong as I am Igmutaka. What gives?"

"I was going to ask you the same thing. That's really weird. It feels almost like the communication we've had with our mating bond, but I've never felt that before with Ig." She shot a quick grin at Star. "It's terribly intimate, sensing him this way."

"I know. Feels the same way with Fen. At least you and Ig have been lovers for years. I feel as if I'm snooping on a total stranger."

"Well, I doubt he'll be a stranger for long." Sunny took another sip of her chocolate.

Star raised her head and caught Sunny staring at her. "What?"

Grinning, Sunny just shook her head. "Tonight was really special. I've missed you, Star."

"I've missed you, too. After tonight, I realize I can't see living in San Francisco if you're going to be in Montana, and I know Ig doesn't want to be away from the pack. What's Fen want?"

Sunny shrugged. "Hell if I know. You've known Ig all your life, but I've only known Fen for a little over forty-eight hours. We've been mated for almost half that, but I still don't really know him. I know he's a good man. He's strong and brave and he's honorable to a fault, and . . ."

Sunny actually blushed. Then she giggled and slapped her fingers over her mouth. "You know that Louisville Slugger we tease Ig about?"

Star almost spewed her chocolate. "Oh yeah. I'm well aware of that part of Ig's anatomy. At least, I am now."

"Fen's in the same ballpark, pun intended. Goddess, Star, but he's an absolutely terrific lover, so we haven't talked about as much stuff as we should. I have no idea what his dreams are.

The poor man's stuck with me now for the rest of his life, so I figure I'll have plenty of time to discover the details."

Star grabbed Sunny's hands in hers. "I'm so glad you found each other. And I'm really glad to be back." She thought of all those wasted years, except, seeing where she was now and how she'd been when she left Montana, Star realized she hadn't really wasted them. She'd grown up a lot and she'd finally realized the importance of her Chanku heritage, of being part of the pack.

For the first time since she could remember, she couldn't wait to get to Montana. She missed her mom and both her dads. She'd never appreciated what she had when she'd had it all. She'd had to go away to realize what she'd left behind. It had taken leaving to be able to come back to the man she loved.

Fen crept toward the campground, using the thick brush along the creek as cover, while Ig in his puma form worked his way around to the top of a bluff opposite Fen's hiding place.

Settling in a copse of twisted scrub willow, Fen studied the campsite. Four men sat around a blazing fire, but something felt wrong. They were laughing and passing a bottle, but he didn't smell alcohol. He spotted at least four rifles braced against a tree away from the fire, but he was almost certain he detected bulges under coats as if they carried hidden sidearms.

After a few more moments, he contacted Igmutaka. *Something's off here, Ig. It's almost as if they've staged the scene.*

I think you're right. If it was just the two of us, I'd say let's give 'em a scare, but not with our mates so close. We'd better go back to the cabin and call this in. There's a chance they might have seen me shift Tuesday night. If they know it's Chanku they're up against, they could be here looking for trouble. They have to know it's Chanku land.

I'll meet you downstream where we split up. Fen slowly crept back along the bank, moving quietly beneath the masking sound of the creek. He'd gone only a few steps when a brilliant light flashed behind him. The night sky turned to daylight, then the brilliance quickly faded. He spun around to see what had happened. Gunshots split the darkness.

A cougar screamed. Another barrage of gunfire.

Fen's link to Igmutaka disappeared.

He turned and raced back toward the camp. Three of the men stood around Ig's body with handguns trained on the big cat. The fourth had run for the truck and was reaching into the back for what looked like a net of some sort.

Fen killed him first. He didn't remember killing any of those men in Montana, but his thoughts were cold and clear when he charged out of the brush and snapped the bastard's neck with a single, quick bite. His leap had taken him into the bed of the truck. Fen dropped the body and continued on out the far side.

Cursing and shouting, the other three scrambled for their rifles, but he met them at the base of the tree. One died quickly, the other not as fast. Not before firing a shot from what looked like an illegal assault rifle.

The bullet caught Fen in his lower chest. The concussion almost knocked him over, but his sheer size gave him the power to rush the shooter and grab his left arm. Fen bit through flesh and bone. The man screamed and tried to pull free.

He got away, but his arm was left on the ground where Fen dropped it. Still functioning on adrenaline alone, Fen lunged for the man, catching him in the back with his full body weight.

The bastard was dead when he hit the ground.

Rising up, Fen searched for the final hunter. He stood twenty feet away with his gun pointed at the cougar.

His voice trembled as badly as his hands, but the gun he held could easily kill Ig—if the cougar wasn't already dead.

"You come close, I kill the cat. I know he's a shifter, just like you. He's still breathing, and he's gonna be worth a bundle to me when I get him out of here."

His eyes flickered as he glanced at the bodies of each of his three companions. "They're such idiots. Shooting bullets when they coulda used tranqs. This guy's not going anywhere, and it looks like you won't, either. I figure you'll bleed out in another half hour or so. Gut wounds are like that. Hurts like a son of a bitch, doesn't it?"

The man's confidence seemed to grow as Fen's blood flowed across the ground. He felt light-headed, knew he was losing consciousness.

He struggled to stay awake, to link with Sunny. Found both Star and Sunny searching desperately for their men. His legs had started to shake, and his back legs suddenly buckled. Fen went down hard when his front legs folded under him, but he held on to the link.

Ig's badly wounded. I've been shot. One guy here with a high-powered rifle. The others are dead. I'm close to blacking out. Contact Anton. Call the sheriff. We're at the poachers' campsite. Don't come. Too dangerous.

He hoped like hell they'd wait until either Anton or the authorities arrived before coming to search for their men, but he couldn't worry about that. Couldn't worry about anything but that cougar lying in the dirt, bleeding from numerous wounds.

Fen feared that any of the shots could be fatal, but he forced that fear out of his mind, too. He reached for Igmutaka. Opened his mind to a man he'd known for mere hours and yet knew almost as well as he knew himself.

There was darkness where he'd sensed nothing but life. Then he sensed it, touched a mere shadow of thought, and he pushed. Pushed harder until his focus was little more than a pinprick of intensity, a narrow connection all the more powerful for its severe limits. He shut out everything else. The killer standing over Igmutaka's body, the waves of pain that battered him. Forced all of it out of his mind. There was no room for any distraction, for anything that would keep him from connecting to Igmutaka.

Spirit guide.

Mate.

There! Fen sensed the faint beat of the big cat's heart, but it stuttered in his chest as if the next beat could be his last. He tried to strengthen the link, tried to synchronize his heartbeat to Ig's, but that might not help. He was dying. There was no doubt in his mind that his was a mortal wound, but he couldn't die. Not yet.

Somehow, he had to stay alive and keep Igmutaka alive until help arrived, but he was tired. So damned tired. His eyes drifted shut. He struggled to hold them open, and still they closed. He took a few shallow breaths, concentrated on opening his eyes. Once more he raised his lids, but he couldn't see. Everything had grown dark. He knew his heart still beat, but it was pumping his blood out of that big hole in his belly.

Pumping his life's blood all over the ground.

I don't know if you can hear me, Ig, but please hang on. Help's coming. I made contact with the girls. Our girls, Ig. We love you. Sunny and Star. Me. Definitely me. We all love you.

His thoughts drifted, but an image filled his mind. An image of a smiling blond with amber eyes, and then a cream-colored wolf with dramatic black tips to her ears and tail.

His wolf. His Sunny. *Sunny, I love you most of all. Be safe. Remember that I will always love you.*

Stunned, Sunny searched for Fen, but his voice had faded so quickly she knew he must have passed out. She reached for her phone and hit Anton's code. Star was already talking to the local sheriff's office. They didn't know her, but they'd met Igmutaka, and all of them knew Anton Cheval. The Chanku were good neighbors, generous to a fault and popular among the local authorities.

Sunny's conversation with Anton was quick and to the point. He'd already sensed something terrible had happened.

Tinker had the chopper ready, and Tinker, Stefan, and Anton would be in the air within the next fifteen minutes. As Sunny ended the call, Star got off the phone and told her help was on the way.

"Good. I know you heard Fen tell us to stay here. I don't know about you, but I have no intention of waiting for help."

She didn't wait for Star, either. Instead, Sunny raced for the door, stripped off her robe, flung it over the rail, and shifted in midleap. Star was right behind her. They raced across the big meadow, heading in the direction of the campsite.

It hadn't seemed all that far from the cabin to the poachers' camp before, not when she'd been running with her mate beside her, with Ig and Star just ahead. Now it felt as if they ran forever. The night was dark; the tiny sliver of moon had slipped behind the mountains to the west, and clouds obscured the stars. She ran by instinct alone, placing her feet carefully on the rocky trail, leaping over small obstructions, focusing always on Fen.

Searching for his voice in her mind. Searching for the sense of him on the night wind.

She smelled his blood instead. The scent brought her to a sharp halt with Star beside her. Sunny raised her muzzle and sniffed the night breeze. Ig and Fen. Both of them were injured, and not far from here.

There's so much blood. Not just our guys, either. Star's words trembled in Sunny's mind. She nodded, but she couldn't let herself think of what they might find.

Slowly, she and Star crept along the trail, listening. Sniffing the air, the ground, the brush alongside the trail. Fen had come this way, but at one point Ig must have gone in from the opposite side. Sunny couldn't find his trail, and neither could Star, but the smell of their mates' blood grew stronger.

So did the blood of humans. Thick and cloying, but it was so different. The smell of human blood reeked of death. Sunny knew they were close. A moment later, she spotted the glow of a campfire flickering against the rocky bluff.

A man's voice, talking quickly, a one-sided conversation. "Yes, damn it. I have two of them, but if you don't get here quick, they're gonna bleed out. You heard me. The idiots shot them, but you should see this one dude, the wolf. He's as big as a damned horse. Yes, he's a shapeshifter. I'm sure of it. So's the other one. Yeah, the cat. Big fuckin' mountain lion. I've never seen one this big."

Blocking her emotions, tamping down on the bloodlust that had Sunny ready to tear into the bastard, she and Star slipped closer. Fen was closest. He'd fallen flat on his chest with his back legs twisted to one side, his front legs folded beneath him. His muzzle lay in the dirt. There was blood all over his face, but Sunny couldn't tell if it was his or his victims'.

He looked dead, but she knew he wasn't. Her mate bond would tell her that, wouldn't it? She focused on his muzzle, on the dark stains that had to be the blood from the ones he'd killed.

It couldn't be Fen's. She refused to accept it might be his. Ig lay in the dirt on the far side of the campsite. She couldn't tell if he was dead or alive. It was impossible to tell if he was breathing, but right now that wasn't where her focus lay.

No. It was all on the man standing between the two wounded Chanku. He was facing the other direction with his gun hanging loosely from his left hand.

Sunny glanced at Star. *If we both rush him, he won't know who to aim for. I think surprise is our only option.*

Agreed. We need to get rid of him. Now, before the authorities arrive.

Star slipped through the brush until she was about six feet from the man. Sunny had managed to get just as close on his other side. She heard Igmutaka moan, but there was no sign of life from Fen at all.

She ignored Ig. Put thoughts of Fen out of her mind. *Focus on the here and now.* She had to, if there was any chance of saving the guys. *Are you ready?*

Yes. Now!

Star exploded out of the brush and went straight for the man's throat. Sunny clamped her teeth down on his left arm and twisted, using all her weight.

The sound of snapping bone was more than satisfying, but the man probably didn't feel it. Star's attack had broken his neck.

Sunny checked to make sure he was dead and then went to Fen. The dirt beneath his body was soaked in blood, but he was still bleeding, which meant he had to be alive, didn't it? She'd never done any healing of wounded Chanku, though Adam had taught her to help him with wildlife when there were injuries from fires and such. Right now she was Fen's only chance.

She shifted and pressed her hands against his thick coat. Her fingers tangled in the leather thong holding the jade wolf. She wrapped her fingers around the jade, needing an even closer connection to Fen.

The amulet fit in her palm, warm from Fen's body, smooth as glass, but she could have sworn it felt alive. Then she searched for the quiet in her mind, the part that would let her move inside Fen and attempt to repair the damage from what appeared to be a wound from a very large-caliber bullet.

Star shifted about the same time as Sunny. It was almost totally dark without her wolven vision. The campfire threw very little light, but she pressed her ear to the big cat's chest and heard the faint beat of his heart. Then she began exploring his body with her fingertips. She found at least one bullet wound in his upper chest and another in one of his back legs. There was no exit wound for the one in his chest, but the one in his leg had passed completely through.

His head was bleeding, but it looked as if the shot had merely grazed his skull. There could be serious internal injuries from the chest wound, but there was no way for her to know.

She heard a helicopter coming in low over the mountains in the west, with big lights blazing. Not Anton, so it had to be the sheriff's deputies. She quickly threw a log on the fire along with some torn paper. As the flames leapt high, the chopper circled in their direction and landed about fifty yards from the camp. A spotlight lit up the entire area.

"Over here! Hurry, please." She waved and a big man ran across the dark ground. He stopped beside Igmutaka's body.

And pointed a gun in her face. "Back away from him. Now."

Stunned, Star stared at the jerk. "Are you crazy? He's been shot. I'm trying to help him."

The man frowned, and then his eyes lit up. "Jasper!" He waved to a man coming toward them from the chopper. "Bring the restraints. We've got four of 'em! There's two pair here. Two males, two females." He laughed, and she felt sick inside when he added, "We hit a fucking gold mine, Jasper. Their mates are in no shape to protect 'em."

Sunny had no idea where they'd been taken. She'd been sitting beside Fen, but her consciousness was separate from her body, inside her mate, trying to repair his injuries, when she'd been jerked away from him. There'd been a moment of total panic when she feared she'd not be able to return to her physical form, but the link had finally snapped her back.

Stunned and shocky from the rough separation, she'd hardly been conscious when she and Star and their guys were loaded into the chopper, flown somewhere that was not far from where they'd been taken, and locked in a large, dark room without lights.

The floor was cold concrete. It had one door and no windows. A bowl of water sat near the door. A couple of blankets had been thrown in a corner.

Star sat beside Ig, stroking his thick coat. Sunny immediately went back to work on Fen. She'd found the injury and had started repairs before they were moved, and somehow the magic in the amulet appeared to have helped. She'd known exactly what to do to repair injuries unlike anything she'd seen before, even though Adam had only ever taught her the basics of healing.

Fen was still weak from blood loss, but the bleeding had almost stopped. He wasn't conscious yet, but his heartbeat was stronger, his breathing shallow but steady.

It took her only a few minutes, holding on to the jade wolf and sending her consciousness inside her mate, to complete the work she'd started. She was exhausted when she finally sat up and turned to Star, but not ready to quit. "How's Igmutaka?"

Star shook her head. She'd been crying, and Sunny knew the tears had made her furious, but she had no idea how to help her mate, and frustration had to be eating her alive. Sunny wrapped her arms around Star and hugged her.

"As soon as we get the guys out of here, I'm going to show you how to fix injuries from the inside out. Adam taught me a little, but nothing like fixing bullet wounds. I think that . . ." She looked closer at Star. "Where did you get that amulet?"

"Huh? This?" Star grabbed the jade cougar and held it in her hand. "That's really weird. How come I've still got it? It should have come off when I shifted at the cabin." Frowning, Star rubbed her fingers over the carved amulet. "Ig gave it to me when I was little."

"Put it on him, now." Sunny reached for the leather thong and helped Star tug it over her head.

"I'd forgotten all about it." Star carefully slipped the necklace over Ig's head. "I almost left it at my apartment when I moved. It was hanging on a hook by the sink. Why's it important?"

"I don't know, but Fen has one that's identical, except it's a wolf. Anton said Fen's has magic, though he didn't know what kind, but I held on to it when I was healing Fen. I think it helped me know how to fix his injuries, and I have a feeling this one might help Ig now."

She pressed one hand against Ig's shoulder and grasped the amulet in the other. With a quick prayer to the goddess, Sunny made the mental crossing from her own body into Igmutaka's.

15

Drifting. So strange to be drifting in darkness, but he knew he wasn't alone. For the first time in a very, very long life, Igmutaka wasn't alone, and the presence of others who loved him was a most amazing sensation in spite of the pain.

He hurt everywhere, but at the same time he felt as if he could accomplish anything. Strength pulsed through his body. Strength and life, and the affirmation that his mates were close.

Mates? Yes. He had more than one mate. After what amounted to many lifetimes alone, he was surrounded by those who loved him. Those he loved in return.

Then, as he raised his head, the reality of his situation slowly blossomed and unfolded. He was still the cat, but this was not the forest near the Lassen cabin.

What was wrong? He sensed Mikaela Star, Sunny, and Fen nearby. His mate was awake, her fear so strong it felt like a fifth entity in the room, and yet even her fear wasn't as strong as her determination. Or her anger. Sunny lay sound asleep next to Fen, who hung restlessly between sleep and wakefulness.

Ig knew he'd been shot. Knew just as well that his injuries had been healed, but how? And where in the hell were they?

Darkness in here was almost absolute.

Mikaela Star? Answer me, but silently. Don't move. Do you hear me?

He heard the sharp intake of breath and then her arms were around his neck and if he'd been a man, he would have laughed. Why did he assume this wonderful, headstrong mate of his would obey him?

Her sobbing was audible. At least her voice was silent, though the words spilled into his mind so fast it was difficult to understand her.

Oh, Goddess. I thought you were going to die. We've been kidnapped. I don't know who they are, but the ones who shot you had some kind of deal to deliver Chanku to the men who have us now. The four who attacked you are dead. Fen's badly hurt. He took a bullet through his chest or his belly. I'm not sure.

How is he? Will he survive? I sense his spirit fighting to awaken, but he's still unconscious.

I know. He almost bled to death, so he must be terribly weak, but Sunny thinks he'll be okay once he has time to recover. She patched him up as best she could. She healed you, too, the same way Adam and Liana do it, by going inside you.

Sunny did that? But how?

She said the jade cougar helped.

My jade cougar? The one I gave you so many years ago? He'd forgotten all about it, but could that be the connection? At least it explained why Fen's seemed so familiar. The jade wolf and the jade cougar had to have a common denominator.

That's the one. Sunny said that when Anton saw Fen's, he touched it and felt magic. She said Fen's wolf helped her heal him, and then she saw your jade cat around my neck and asked to use it—she said it helped her know how to heal you. The bullet is still in you, but when you shift, it'll come out.

That was something proactive, something he could actually do. Ig shifted, heard a soft *clunk*, and the bullet lay beside him on the floor. Mikaela Star was in his arms, and the jade cat was still hanging around his neck. He'd not realized it would stay on him during a shift.

He'd worn it all his long life, but it had been a spirit totem without solid form, just as he had been spirit. When he'd first taken the puma shape after so many thousands of years, he'd left the amulet in one of the caves on Anton's property to keep it safe.

Then he had given it to Mikaela Star, in the hope that she would always remember him no matter what, and with the wish that, if there was power in the charm, it would keep her safe.

Now he wrapped his fingers around the smooth jade, remembering what he could. There wasn't much.

I've had this so long, I've forgotten what it's for. I never wore it after I took solid, corporeal form. Not as the cat and never as a man. I know it's a charm of some kind, but I don't know its power. We'll figure it out later. He kissed his mate's temple. *How long have we been here?*

I'm not sure. Maybe a couple of hours. I've tried to contact Anton, but haven't had any luck.

She leaned close. He wrapped his arms around her and felt her trembling. It was cold in here. They should probably return to their animal forms. Later. For now, he needed information, and wanted to process it with his human brain. His puma was too pissed off to be entirely rational. *How many doors in this place? Any windows? Any idea how big?*

One door, no windows. No power outlets or wall switches that I could find. Maybe an overhead light, but I can't see well enough to tell. It's too damned dark in here. Floors are concrete, walls are metal. I think it's a storage unit, maybe ten by twenty feet. I paced it off shortly after they left us here. I had to do something while Sunny was healing you. Pace or scream. Pacing sounded like a better idea.

He pictured her walking the perimeter of their prison in darkness, trying to gain information even though she'd been terrified. He still felt her fear, but she was controlling it. Pride for her had him smiling in spite of their situation. Pride, and anger that she was stuck in such a horrible mess.

I'm sorry, Mikaela Star. You should not be involved in this situation. I am your mate. I have failed to protect you.

She sighed softly, and he could feel her head moving against his chest in denial. *No, Ig. Just the opposite. This is my fault. If you were still a spirit guide, you could easily have taken your spirit form and escaped whatever they tried. Bullets wouldn't have harmed you. You would have protected Fen and none of this would have happened. If you hadn't mated with me . . .*

I would be dead.

How can you say that? She pulled away from him, and if he could see better, he'd probably find her glaring daggers at him, but she deserved the truth.

He opened his deepest thoughts. Invited her to see that he was telling the truth. Felt her denial, even as she realized he'd not been lying. *I had already made the choice,* he said. *Should you not want me as your bonded mate, I would return to my spirit form forever. Disperse my consciousness, and end my being.*

No! That's just . . .

Holding her close, he kissed her. *Not going to happen. Now that you're my mate, I have everything to live for. Remember those babies you promised me?*

I do. He sensed the smile in her voice. *But I still want to wait. I want time alone. Time with you, and only you.*

He chuckled softly. *There may be a bit of a problem with that.*

What do you mean?

She pulled entirely out of his embrace. Ig almost laughed at her outrage. *When Fen and I made love? We bonded as mates.*

There was a long, telling silence.

You and Fen? Are you saying you mated as wolves?

She sounded much too calm. *No, my love. We mated as men. Our primary forms are the puma and the wolf. Just as Chanku begin as human babies, we began as feral young. Just as you mate in the opposing form, Fen and I have mated, but as men.*

Did you know this? Did you plan it?

This time he definitely laughed, though he managed to keep his laughter quiet. Still, the situation really was funny, now that he felt the deep bond he and Fen had created—a powerful bond between two men who truly preferred women as lovers and had known one another only for a very short time.

No. I had no idea what we were doing. Not until I found myself mated to a very handsome man, though he's not nearly as attractive as my lovely female mate. There is no one to compare to you, my sweet Mikaela Star.

I'm not all that sweet, so don't expect me to act sweet. She planted a kiss on his chin. *But what you say makes sense. When Sunny and I tried to reach you guys, when we first realized you were in trouble, she sensed you as strongly as she sensed Fen, and I had the same experience.*

We wondered about that.

Exactly. Your mating bond with Fen and his with you appears to have included your women. I think that makes us the first official four-person bonding in modern Chanku history.

He loved the laughter in her mental voice. Loved the fact that even now, trapped as they were and with one of their mates severely injured, she was able to put her fear behind her.

But what next? *Stay here, in case they're watching us. I want to try something.* Ig wrapped his fingers around the jade puma and called on his spirit self. In the past, he'd not needed the amulet—he'd merely needed to think himself spirit, and his corporeal body disappeared. He'd lost that ability, but with luck . . .

It appeared he didn't have any to spare. *It didn't work.*

What?

I'm not really sure, but maybe . . . just a minute. I want to check on Fen. Moving silently in the darkness, he found the big wolf. Fen lay on his side, but his breathing was smooth and even, and his heart rate sounded normal.

Ig pressed his hands to Fen's skull and tried to connect. He found his mate, conscious, but deep in the healing process. *How long before you regain your strength?*

Soon. I'm growing stronger, but I'm not there yet. Are you okay?

Healing. Thanks to Sunny. I have a plan to find out more about our jail as well as our jailors. I need to borrow energy from your jade wolf.

Anything of mine is yours, my brother.

Ig wrapped his left hand around his jade puma and grasped Fen's wolf in his right. Holding on to the two created a charge that felt electrical in nature. Once again, he called on the ability to become spirit.

This time, his body winked out. *Thank you, Eve.* It had to be the Chanku goddess who was helping him. His gods would never respond so quickly. *I'm in my spirit form, Mikaela Star. Our mating hasn't taken all my tricks. Be safe. I'm going to check on our captors.*

And then, with centuries of practice behind him, Igmutaka, spirit guide, disappeared beneath the door of their prison.

Fen lay there, still in his wolf form, taking stock of his injuries. He'd been so close to death—thought he had actually crossed that threshold—but now he was almost back to his normal strength. Sunny lay close beside him, sleeping so soundly he hated to awaken her, but they had to be ready to escape.

Had to be ready for whatever Igmutaka set into motion.

Sunny? Do you hear me? I hate to wake you, sweetheart. I know you're exhausted—you must be, after healing both Igmutaka and me. Did you have any idea how troublesome it would be once you found your mate?

Actually, Mr. Ahlberg, one mate was just fine. But then I awoke and discovered I had three. Her sleepy laughter eased his mind—and his heart—when she added, *And, as much trouble as all of you are, I have never felt so complete. Star? Are you in the link with Fen and me?*

Yep. I'm here. Just didn't want to intrude.

I don't think mates can intrude. They're too connected. Any idea what Igmutaka is up to? I can sense him, but can't tell where he is.

You were asleep, Fen said. *He somehow drew power from my jade wolf and his jade puma to find his spirit form. He disappeared.*

Star! I thought he lost that ability when you mated.

He did. But not anymore. There was outright jubilation—and obvious relief—in her voice. *He's outside now, finding out what we're up against. Wish him luck.*

Igmutaka drifted beneath the door, an invisible mass of energy with neither form nor substance, but his mind was clear and his life force stronger than it had ever been.

Somehow, he was drawing from Fen, and once again he wondered about the story behind their jade amulets, but now was the time for action, not for answering riddles.

He took form in the midst of the storage unit. The other three were wolves, but he took his human shape. "Here's what

I know," he said. He grabbed a blanket and threw it on the ground beside Mikaela Star. She shifted and sat beside him.

Sunny shifted as well, and then Fen. Ig heard the sound of a bullet hitting the floor. So this was Fen's first shift since the attack. Thank the goddess, all of them had survived what could have been a disaster. Now the four of them, somehow, some way now mated, sat together as humans for the very first time since the mating bond with Fen.

Ig looked at them and, though it was difficult to see their faces in the darkness, he couldn't stop grinning. Probably not an apropos reaction at a time like this, but he'd never felt so connected, never once considered himself so clearly part of a family. His family now. The four of them, now essentially able to function as one. He had no doubt they would get out of this mess, because their connection made them truly invincible.

"We're in a storage unit in the town of Burney, so we're not all that far from the cabin—maybe an hour's drive. I connected with Anton, and I'm glad I got ahold of him. After our last contact, he and Stefan and Tinker were headed to Lassen when the chopper developed some mechanical problems and they had to set down in Sacramento.

"Anton got in touch with the Sheriff in Lassen County and they'd found the campsite, the bodies of the poachers, and way too much blood. Anton said they were afraid we'd been killed and our bodies taken somewhere, because he couldn't even sense us. I let him know that we're all okay, and he said they'll be here as soon as they can get the part they need for repair. They tried to rent another helicopter, but there's nothing available, so for now, at least, we're on our own. Tinker's doing his best to get it fixed."

"Why can't we reach Anton from inside this place?"

"I don't think they're purposely blocking us, Sunny, but I think it's the same reason Anton couldn't find us with his mind. There's an alarm on the door that's set to warn the guards if we attempt to escape. Unfortunately, it's sending out some sort of interference that's blocking telepathic signals, incoming as well as outgoing. Pure luck on their part, because Anton's convinced it's not common knowledge that we're able to mindspeak.

"I can get us out of here—it's almost dawn and there are guards out there, but they're half asleep. I'm proposing that I go out as spirit. I'll shift and take care of the guards, and I can turn off the alarm system before I open the door. The thing is, I don't want to leave until we know who's kidnapped us. Any suggestions?"

"I'll stay behind." Fen glanced at the others. "I'm still a federal warden with the authority to arrest poachers."

Sunny leaned against him. "Then how come you keep killing the bastards?"

He kissed the top of her head. "Because they keep pissing me off so damned much."

"Exactly." Sunny threw her arms around him and kissed him soundly. "Which is part of the reason I love you so much. There's nothing as sexy as a really bloodthirsty killer."

Fen rolled his eyes. "I bet you say that to all the boys."

"Only to you. But you are not staying here by yourself."

"C'mon, Sunny. It's the only way to catch the bastards."

Before Sunny could answer, Ig shook his head. He focused on Mikaela Star, but he was talking to all of them. "I don't get it. How can you be joking around? You should be terrified. You're prisoners of a group of killers."

His beautiful mate wrapped her hands around his arm. "Are you terrified?"

What a foolish question. "Of course not."

"Exactly." She flashed him a satisfied grin and looked at him as if he had a clue what she was talking about.

Would he ever understand her?

"Let's all get out of here first," Sunny said. "Then we can figure out how to catch them."

"Makes sense." Ig glanced at Fen. "You'll have your chance to get them, Fen, but first I need to touch your jade wolf."

Fen leaned close, but as Igmutaka wrapped his fingers around the carved wolf, Fen reached for Ig's jade puma.

When Igmutaka took his spirit form, so did Fen.

"Holy shit, Star. Did you see that?"

Star stared at the spot where Ig had been sitting, and then at the place across from him where Fen had been. "Ig's still able to become spirit using the amulets, but how did Fen disappear?"

Sunny shook her head. "I have no clue. He's never once said he could do the spirit thing. It certainly didn't show up when we mated."

"Ig shouldn't be able to, either. When he became my mate he told me that he was giving up his ability to become pure spirit. Now that's twice he's done it. I don't get it."

"I think I do." Sunny wrapped her arms around herself. "It must have something to do with the jade amulets both of them wear. They both touched them, and I felt something when they shifted. Almost like an electric shock. What about you?"

Star nodded. "The same." Like a charge in the air around them. The hairs along her neck were still standing on edge. "What now?"

"They'll be back really fast. I'm sure of it. They won't want to leave us alone in here." Sunny's voice cracked on the words. Then she scooted so close she was almost in Star's lap, which was a huge surprise, given the fact that Sunny'd always been the tough one. Older than Star, more experienced with life in general, but right now she was trembling like a leaf.

She wrapped her arms around Sunny and hugged her tight. "Hon, it'll be okay. We're safe in here for now."

"It's not me I'm afraid for. I've been so scared for Fen," she said. "I finally fall in love, and I almost lost him. I can't believe

Fen's strong enough to go with Ig. I didn't think he was going to make it tonight. He almost bled out. It was terrifying."

Star tightened her arms around Sunny. "Ah, Sun, sweetie. Stop shaking. He's okay. We'll be okay, and whatever you did for him worked." She brushed Sunny's tangled hair out of her eyes. "I can't believe you figured out how to fix that horrible wound. There was so much blood. I thought he was dead, and I was so afraid for Igmutaka. What was it like, going inside him? I wish I could have done that for Ig. Thank the goddess you could."

Sunny's voice still shook. "It was terrifying. I wasn't sure if I could help him or if what I did would make him worse, but I felt a power guiding me. I went straight to the wound, and even though I know this sounds stupid, it was like building something with those little LEGO blocks that kids are always playing with. I kept finding loose cells, and somehow I knew where to put them. I know it sounds nuts, but I'm convinced that damned jade wolf had something to do with it. I just wish I knew what."

There was a soft click, and Star grabbed Sunny's hand. Then Ig slipped through the open door, silhouetted by the lights outside. "Hurry," he whispered. "Shift. Fen's got both guards down, but we need to get out of here. The sun's going to be coming up soon. I want to get as far from this jail and these bastards as we can before someone sees us."

Ig shifted into a wolf as Sunny and Star ran past him. Star led them across the road and down into a nearby creek bed.

The three of them huddled there in the thick undergrowth, much too aware of how quickly it was growing light around them, of the increasing traffic on the road between the creek and the storage units, but it was only a couple of minutes later when Fen's big wolf ran across the road and joined them in their hiding place.

I left them locked in the storage shed, he said. *They're sup-*

posed to turn us over at eight this morning to a couple of men from a syndicate interested in our purchase. It's almost seven, so there's not a lot of time if we're going to do anything.

Star shivered. This was just too close for comfort. *Do you know what they want with us? With Chanku?*

Fen growled. *It's bizarre, if what they say is right. They want a chance to study our DNA. They have scientists who want to develop Chanku longevity among humans.*

Star's ears flattened against her skull. *Don't they realize it's the shifting that makes us live so long?*

Obviously not. Sunny's lip curled, and she glanced at Fen before she spoke. *Everyone thinks there's some huge secret behind our so-called eternal youth. The fact that cells are renewed with every shift just doesn't compute. They can't duplicate that if they're not Chanku.*

Star shared her frustration. *They don't believe it because they don't want to hear it.* She glanced at Ig. He'd not said anything at all.

But then he looked at her, and there was so much love in his eyes that it made her ache. Love, and something else. Something that absolutely terrified her.

They still need to be stopped, he said, and his gaze was focused solely on Star. *We can't live in fear, and we can't allow our children to live in fear. These bastards need to learn not to interfere with our lives.*

And then, he added, *they need to die.*

Fen stared at Igmutaka for a long, solemn moment. Star felt the connection to him, the sense of *mate* when she looked at the big wolf—one she'd never even had sex with and yet they had a mating bond strong enough to feel.

And he was big. More than twice the size of either Sunny or her. Big and deadly, and focused on Igmutaka. After at least a full minute, he sighed.

No, my brother. He shook his massive head. *We do not kill because we are afraid. There are laws in place to protect our kind. We use those laws. We go after these men in a very public venue. We make them pay and we use their laws to stop them. If we kill because we are afraid of them, we become them.*

Ig's hackles went up, and he growled softly. Menacingly. *So much for all your talk of killing.*

As you said earlier, we were being silly. I do not take any man's death lightly. Not even one who wants to do me harm. If I'd had control of my wolf in Montana, I would not have killed the poachers. I would have found another way. Last night, there was no other way. I weighed your life for theirs. Yours won. But killing for the sake of ridding the world of someone you fear is not the answer.

Ig stared at him for a long, tense time. Then he bowed his head. *I know you're right. But how? How can we stop them?*

We need to find out who they are, where they live. Then we get in touch with Anton Cheval, have him contact the authorities. We'll need clothing in order to give our statement, though the authorities should see us first as the animals we are. I want them to make the connection between our predators and our human selves. I want them to know we are rational, intelligent beings, not the killing machines the media describe.

I'll see if I can reach Anton. And on the honor of our goddess, I hope to hell you know what you're talking about.

The sharp call of a flicker might have blended with the bird-song around them, but Fen recognized a good imitation when he heard it. "Stay down," he said. Then he shifted and stood, using the thick brush along the creek for cover.

He spotted two men at the edge of the road above. They had a look he recognized. "We're down here." He waved, and they spotted him and headed down the steep bank.

"Fen Ahlberg?"

"Yes. And I apologize for standing in the bushes, but I just shifted. No clothing." He stuck out his hand.

"Agent Rem Caruthers. FBI." He showed him his ID and shook Fen's hand, and then nodded toward his partner. "This is Josh Fagan." The younger man merely nodded. "Mr. Cheval said you would need something." He glanced at the other man. "Josh, grab the bag and bring it down."

Josh turned and left.

"I'm surprised the FBI's been called in, but thank you."

"It's a kidnapping, and we have intel that says they intended to take you out of the state. Our people are interrogating the ones you left in the storage unit."

"You already suspected we were at risk?"

"No. At least not here, not now. We were following up on some leads after Aldo Xenakis was killed, contacts he had that went beyond the crazies who were part of his cult. They led us, in a roundabout way, to the ones who tried to snatch you." He glanced around. "Are the others here?"

"In their wolf form."

"I see." He focused once again on Fen. "Mr. Cheval suggested one of your group might be able to follow the men coming here to collect their property." He put an emphasis on the word that led Fen to believe he was as disgusted as Fen was right now. "We don't have time to secure a warrant. Can one of you follow and still report?"

Can we do that, Ig?

I think so. Tell him.

"One of our group is a spirit guide. He has abilities that are unique to his kind." He turned and signaled to the others to come out of the brush.

The agent's eyes went wide as the three wolves silently approached and sat in a half circle beside Fen. His partner arrived then and handed the bag to Fen. "Sweats and some athletic shoes. Mr. Cheval said to tell you he got the sizes from his wife."

Fen laughed as he took the bag. "Then they should fit just fine." He pulled out a couple of pairs of warm sweats that would fit the women and took the largest pair for himself. "I'll hang on to Igmutaka's, if you don't mind."

Sunny and Star shifted, and Fen tried to ignore the agents' gasps of surprise—and of appreciation. He couldn't blame them—both women were stunning, and not the least bit self-conscious of their nudity. They dressed quickly.

As Fen slipped the shoes on, he turned to Ig's wolf. "You should probably shift so the agents get a good look at you, Ig. If you shift during any action, I'd hate for anyone to mistake you for one of the bad guys."

Ig shifted, and the response he got was almost as impressive as the way they'd reacted to the women. Fen wondered if his mate even noticed the looks anymore.

Agent Caruthers raised his head and stared toward the street. "Stay back," he said, speaking into a hidden mic. "We'll make certain they're tailed."

He turned to Igmutaka. "There's a white van that just pulled in and parked in front of the unit. They can't know you're following."

"They won't." He turned and kissed Sunny and then Star. Held on to his carved jade puma and grabbed Fen's wolf in his other hand. Then he leaned close, kissed Fen full on the mouth, and disappeared.

"Holy shit." Caruthers looked all around, and then shook his head and stared at Fen and the women. "Can all of you do that?"

Sunny and Star shook their heads, but they both grinned at Fen. He merely shrugged. "I've done it once. This morning. And yeah, it's pretty cool."

"I can't even imagine." Caruthers held his cell phone so all of them could see the screen. One of the other agents was transmitting video, and while they watched, three men ran out of the unit, jumped into their vehicle, and sped away.

They'd left the bound guards behind.

"You're sure he's with them?"

Fen nodded. "He's there."

"Let's go." Caruthers waved for them to follow him up the embankment to the road. "You'll let me know if that guy, Ig, contacts you, right?"

Fen grabbed Sunny and Star's hands and dragged them up the steep bank. "He's in the back of the van now. They're headed northeast on Highway 299. He says they're speaking Ukrainian."

Caruthers cast a quick glance at his partner. "I knew it," he said. Then he turned to Fen. "And no, I don't want to know how you know what your partner is discovering or even how he knows what Ukrainian sounds like—I merely want any info he gives you."

"Good, because I can't give those details."

Caruthers nodded. "I'm glad we're on the same page." He turned and spoke again, directing his agents to pick up the vehicle's trail on Highway 89 north.

"Do you know where they're going?"

"Their local operation is out of McCloud, an old logging community south of Mount Shasta, though their main headquarters is in Seattle. They're part of a group that has been smuggling illegal drugs and arms into the country for the past six years, but we've not been able to pin anything on them. We suspect the drugs and arms are to fund a larger project. One of domestic terrorism."

Caruthers paused at the top of the bank. "Their interest in your kind is a recent development—their leader was a friend and confidant of Aldo Xenakis—but it will give us the reason we need to pick them up. If we can get them by charging them with kidnapping and attempted murder, we can hold them just as long—and probably more effectively—than we can on gun and drug or terrorism charges."

He glanced at his phone again. "How far before you lose contact with your partner?"

Fen shrugged. "I have no idea. I only met him yesterday."

Caruthers stared at Fen for a long time. His lips twitched and he broke into laughter. After a minute, he shook his head and held up one hand. "I'm sorry. It's just . . . never mind." He was still smiling when he added, "Like I said, I really don't want the details."

16

_____

It was almost midnight Thursday when Caruthers parked the big, dark SUV in front of the cabin at Lassen. Sunny, Star, Fen, and Igmutaka climbed out, all of them exhausted beyond belief. Fen leaned in through the open passenger door and studied the agent. "You're sure you won't come in? We can at least offer you a meal—and a place to sleep if you need it. This has been a pretty eventful . . ." He paused a moment. "I was going to say day, but it's been longer, hasn't it?"

"That it has." He grinned at Fen. "No, but thank you. And Igmutaka, thank you as well. I know what you did was not without risk. Your abilities are not only damned fascinating, they've helped us crack a case that's been driving all of us nuts. Obviously, there won't be any charges brought against any of you for the killings last night. It's more than obvious they were made in self-defense. As I told you earlier, our team has already recovered the bodies that were on your land, along with whatever physical evidence they could collect."

He took a deep breath and stared out the windshield before

turning to look once again at Fen. "I'd like to say the case is closed and it won't happen again, but we both know better."

"We prefer to work within the system, Agent Caruthers." Ig shot a quick look at Fen standing beside him. Fen couldn't help but recall the discussion they'd had so early yesterday morning. "It's much easier with someone who doesn't treat us like idiots. You've been more than helpful. We all appreciate your courtesy."

Caruthers shrugged. "I'm sorry that's been your experience, but thank you. I imagine that happens a lot more than it should. I'll be in touch. We'll need your testimony, but I promise to do what I can to keep any intrusion into your lives as minimal as possible. Again, thank you. All of you." He looked off in the distance, frowning.

Then, as if he'd reached a decision that didn't make him very happy, he gazed at Fen once again. "This was much bigger than an attack on a few Chanku. Much bigger and more involved than I'm at liberty to discuss, but we owe you. The whole country owes you. Take care."

He waved, Fen closed the passenger door, and the agent drove away. Fen turned with Ig, Sunny, and Star, and the four of them slowly climbed the steps to the cabin.

"Well, that was interesting," he said.

Ig laughed. "Understated, don't you think? I wonder what he meant."

"I don't know. In fact, I'm probably better off not knowing." Fen followed Sunny inside. "I do have to say I learned more today than I really want to know about Sebastian's father. Aldo Xenakis sounds like he was a real asshole, and the ones who believed in him are flat-out scary."

Sunny linked her arm through Fen's. "They're determined to strip us of our rights as free citizens, or, like the ones who were arrested today, find out what makes us tick so they can steal our so-called secret. It's jealousy and fear. They don't want us here, but they want what we've got."

"I think there's more to it than that," Ig said. "Just a feeling I can't shake, especially after what Caruthers said."

"Thank goodness he's sympathetic to our side." Star said. "Today could have gone so much worse. I avoided all of this when I lived in Connecticut by not telling anyone I was Chanku. I'm not doing that ever again. I refuse to deny who or what I am." She stopped and glared at no one in particular. "I'm proud of who I am. It's about time I acted like it."

Ig wrapped his arms around her. "You did what you did to survive in the world you'd chosen to live in. I'm glad you're home. I'm glad you finally chose me." He kissed her, and she clung to him.

"I've never been faced with discrimination, but I guess I'd better get used to life in the real world." Fen shut the door and sagged against it. He was exhausted. His body felt numb, but at the same time he realized how important this past twenty-four hours had been. "I had put my shapeshifter past behind me, figured it would probably never happen again."

Sunny stood on her toes and wrapped her arms around his neck. "That'll teach ya."

"As long as you're the teacher." He lifted her against him, loving the way she clung to him. Loving Sunny. "I love you," he said, and looking into those beautiful amber eyes, he knew he'd barely scratched the surface of that love. He kissed her again, losing himself in her taste. Her scent was an aphrodisiac; so was the way she felt in his arms.

His exhaustion disappeared when she kissed him back. Then the scent of food hit his sensitive nostrils, and Fen started across the room with Sunny clinging to him, laughing.

Star and Ig had gone straight to the kitchen. Star was already pulling trays of food out of the refrigerator. Igmutaka had a bottle of dark red wine and had attacked the cork with an opener. He raised his head and focused on Fen. "A lot has happened over the past couple of days. We need to celebrate."

Star set the plates of food on the counter and wrapped her arms around Igmutaka. "I agree. Anton said they're planning a reception for all of us when we get back to Kalispell, but we really need our own party here. Tonight." She winked at Sunny.

"After we eat." Fen set Sunny on one of the tall stools at the bar. "What can I do to help?"

"You can tell us about growing up in Finland." Ig finally got the cork out of the bottle and began filling glasses.

"Fine. He can do that." Sunny took a glass of wine and held it up to the light. Then she cocked her head and stared at Ig. "If you'll tell us how come you speak Ukrainian. I thought I knew everything about you. That was a surprise."

"I'm a man of mystery." Ig handed a glass to Fen and then poured one for Star. "To us," he said. His voice had gone deeper, almost gravelly with emotion, and he turned and smiled at Star with so much love in his eyes that it brought tears to Fen's.

"To my beloved Mikaela Star. I knew you were destined to be my mate from the moment of your birth. It may have taken you a while to come around, but you are and always will be well worth the wait." He kissed her and then gazed at Sunny. Again, his eyes sparkled with love and what looked suspiciously like tears.

"Sunny Daye, you have been my most beloved friend since the very first day I met you. Brave and funny and so willing to open your heart. Thank you for your patience and your willingness to teach me all those scary secrets about the way women think. Because of you, maybe Mikaela Star will hesitate before actually murdering me while I sleep." He kissed Sunny as well.

"Don't be so sure of that." Star sent him a dark glance that had all of them laughing.

Then Ig turned toward Fen and held his glass up once more. "To you, Fenris Ahlberg." There was no denying the moisture filling Igmutaka's green eyes now. He blinked rapidly and then slowly shook his head, grinning at Fen.

"What a wonderful surprise you are. I have known you such a short time, and yet I know you almost as well as I know myself. I never expected the mating bond, but it clicked into place so naturally that I look forward to a lifetime of getting to know you even better. Someday, I hope we discover the mystery that connects us. Until then, I call you brother. Friend. Mate."

He clinked his glass against Fen's, against Sunny's, and then with Star's. Fen in turn connected with Sunny and with Star, and the four of them drank to Igmutaka's toast.

Ig's eyes were twinkling when he glanced at Sunny. "As far as the Ukrainian, it's simple, really. As spirit guide, I had knowledge of all languages. I can even understand Fen when he thinks in Finnish. It appears I've retained my linguistics ability, which means the three of you will share it once our mating bond has time to settle in."

He tipped his glass to Fen and handed him a plate filled with food. "Now, I believe our rather large mate needs to eat."

For the first time, the four of them had a chance to sit and talk without the fear of someone trying to kill them or kidnap them, which made for an undeniably relaxing meal.

Fen talked about growing up in Finland. An isolated, lonely kid who always knew he was different, but not why, and his story made Sunny love him even more. In so many ways, their younger years had been alike.

Isolated, lonely, and unfulfilled.

Now? None of the above. Life was good, and Sunny figured

she could get used to this. Star and Igmutaka were absolutely hysterical the way they bounced comments off one another, almost as if they'd been doing a stand-up routine for years—she knew Star could be funny, but she'd never realized what a wonderful sense of humor Ig had. Now that he had his women tied to him, it appeared he could relax and be the man he'd always been—at least the man he'd been when he wasn't trying to keep Star under lock and key.

"I'm so glad those days are past." Star leaned against Ig and gazed at him with a little half smile curving her lips that spoke volumes.

"Me too," Sunny said. "All those years listening to you gripe about the poor man when I knew you loved him and he loved you, and you were both too hardheaded to say anything. Thank the goddess you two finally figured it out!"

Ig's soft chuckle had them all looking his way. Star glared at him. "What?"

"I'm merely agreeing with Sunny. And I will freely admit I may have complained a time or two about your apparent lack of feelings for me."

"A time or two?" Laughing, Sunny stood and carried her dishes to the sink. "More like daily, but then Ig had to listen to me bemoan the fact that I had no mate, and no chance of finding one because all the good ones were taken."

She glanced at Fen and smiled at the twinkle in his amber eyes. "How wrong I was."

There was no talk of any of them heading for separate rooms once the kitchen was cleaned and the food put away. Instead they shifted and took a slow run to the hot springs where they bathed in the mineral-laden pool, and then, when their bodies were clean and minds totally relaxed, they trotted slowly back to the cabin.

The night was clear and cold, and there were no threats on

the gentle breeze. Nothing to interfere with this chance to be together, all of them as mates, for the very first time.

Igmutaka shifted first and opened the door. Star trotted inside, still in her wolven body. Sunny paused on the top step and shifted at the same time as Fen. They clasped hands, reaching for one another so automatically, Sunny'd not even had to look to grasp his hand in hers.

There was no question of Star and Ig going to their downstairs bedroom. As if they thought with one mind, all of them headed up the stairs.

Holding tightly to Fen's hand, Sunny couldn't stop smiling. Nor could she forget how far she'd come since that day so many years ago when she'd discovered she was not what she'd always believed. She was not a cripple. Not a foster child without family or friends.

She was Chanku. A shapeshifter of uncommon strength. A beautiful young woman on the verge of adulthood, capable of loving. Of being loved. She'd known then that she would never be alone, that she would always have the pack. And maybe, one day, a mate.

Now she had even more. Not just one mate but three, and together there was nothing that could stop them. Nothing.

Fen had known this time was coming, had known when he and Ig found that amazing link and discovered a bond beyond anything either of them had expected that the time would come when they would have sex, all of them together as mates.

No. Not just sex. They would make love, because it was love he felt—love more powerful than anything he could recall. There was no rhyme or reason behind it. One didn't fall in love in a matter of hours or a few short days.

No. Love took time to grow, didn't it? Time to grow strong and true, except the love he felt for Sunny, for Igmutaka and

Star, stunned him with the strength behind it. With the sense that this was the most important relationship he would ever know. Stronger than the mate bond with Sunny. Stronger than the bond with Igmutaka. This was a bond linking the four of them tighter than anything found between two. It was beyond his understanding, and yet he believed.

He trusted.

There were no rules to cover what they had. No way to describe the intricate, intimate feelings imprinting themselves on his mind or coursing through his body—feelings that made his heart race and his skin shiver with the promise of forever.

They reached the top of the stairs, and Star shifted. Standing tall and beautifully naked, she held one hand out to Ig and the other to Fen. Still holding tightly to Sunny, he grasped Star's hand as well.

Sunny took Igmutaka's, and they stood together, hands linked, minds and hearts open.

Igmutaka took the first step. With a kiss for Star and a smile for Sunny, he moved toward Fen and cupped his broad shoulders with both hands. "You are not what I imagined," he said. His lips slowly curved into a sexy smile. "But you are exactly what I need. The one I want beside me, sharing the love I feel for Mikaela Star and the love you feel for Sunny Daye."

Fen grabbed Ig's shoulders, and his soft chuckle made Sunny smile. "Honestly, Ig? I never imagined any of this. Not you. Not Star, and certainly not Sunny. I never imagined love finding me, or me finding love. Never knew enough to dream of what this kind of love would feel like. Now that I know, I will never, ever give it up. Not you, not Star, and certainly not Sunny."

He glanced at her, and she realized his thoughts were guarded, as were Igmutaka's. Wanting more, she pressed against his barriers and felt them dissolve with her first touch.

He opened to her. Through him she touched Star as well.

Fen grinned and she tried the same with Igmutaka. She'd never been able to breach his walls, not when he wanted to hold her out. Now, with the slightest touch, he opened to her.

She felt Star and Fen, both of them so totally linked with Igmutaka that it was as if she touched not three mates but one.

"I wondered when you would join us." Ig grinned at her. "You've always had such strong natural barriers, but I knew they would eventually come down."

"I didn't know." She should have been embarrassed, but there was no condemnation in Ig's words. Not in Fen's smile or Star's broad grin. "I'm still getting used to one mate. Three is way out of my comfort zone, but I'll learn."

"I know exactly how to expand that comfort zone of yours." Ig grabbed her hand and dragged her to the closest mattress. Laughing, she tumbled over him when he tugged. Fen and Star were right there beside her. She shot a grin at Star and winked at Fen. Then she turned to Igmutaka and held out her arms.

Star found herself staring into eyes of dark amber instead of green, and a coil of heat tightened her womb. Fen studied her with an intensity that should have been unnerving, except there was so much more than mere lust in his eyes that she couldn't help but respond.

She ran her fingers over his broad chest and circled one taut, male nipple. He sucked in his breath when she pinched him lightly between thumb and forefinger, grabbed her by the waist, and slowly lowered her to the mattress.

Igmutaka and Sunny lay on the mattress beside them, and Ig was sliding his huge cock between Sunny's thighs. She'd never imagined how erotic it would be, to watch her mate make love to another woman.

A woman she loved. A ripple of need charged through Star—Fen's need. She turned her focus to the man kneeling between her thighs. Fen was huge and yet so perfectly proportioned that he didn't seem all that big—not until he knelt between her legs and stroked his erection in one massive fist.

Igmutaka was large—Fenris Ahlberg was even bigger. Everywhere. Fascinated by the thick cock bowing in a graceful curve toward his belly, she reached out and ran her fingertips along his full velvety length.

The veins twisting along his shaft fascinated her—he was thicker than Igmutaka, who was practically legendary among the rest of the pack, and easily as long if not longer. Her inner muscles clenched as she traced the silky skin across his broad tip and swept her fingertip through the milky bead of fluid.

His muscles clenched, and he growled. She glanced at the couple beside them just as Ig slipped his full length deep inside Sunny. "Does that make you jealous?" she whispered.

He shook his head. "Gods, no. It makes me hot. Too damned hot. I want to last with you, and already I feel like coming."

"No. You do not feel like coming." Laughing softly, Star curled her body forward and licked across his soft glans. His penis jerked in her hand, and she squeezed. "Control, dear Fen."

"You're trying to kill me, aren't you?"

"Never. I want you around for a long, long time." Then she wrapped her lips around the thick crown and sucked him deep inside her mouth. He didn't push—no, he let her take the lead and swallow as much of him as she could. She'd always loved oral sex, and since she'd discovered she could swallow Igmutaka's full length, she figured she could take Fen's cock as well.

She could and she did.

He practically whimpered when she slipped almost free, caught the flared crown with her lips, and then took him deep once again. Twice more she sucked him down, her cheeks hollowing with each powerful draw. He growled and reached for her, gently pulled himself free of her mouth, turned her beneath his big body, and knelt with his knees at either side of her shoulders.

"I want my chance to taste, Star."

His voice sounded so soft, that Finnish accent so sexy, that all her inner muscles clenched in need. She grabbed his sac in her right hand and wrapped the fingers on her left hand around his cock. Then she pulled his thick length down and caught him with her mouth. She held him there, with her lips just behind the broad flare of his glans, and teased the tiny opening at the center with the tip of her tongue. His taste was rich and salty-sweet, and she licked him again. And then again. Gently squeezing his balls, she stroked his cock and kept up the teasing licks with her tongue.

His breath rasped in and out of his chest, and she sensed his resolve not to come no matter what she tried, that nothing she did could force him over the edge until she had found her own release. He leaned forward and speared her deep with his tongue. Her body clenched and all her inner muscles jerked as he changed his angle and licked long, smooth strokes from her clit to her anus. She tried to concentrate on his beautiful cock, but it wasn't easy.

He was just too good.

His lips found her clit, and she arched against his mouth, whimpering, squeezing his shaft and balls tighter than she'd intended. He groaned, but it was a sound of pleasure, not pain, so she kept squeezing, rolling the hard orbs between her fingers, nipping and sucking the broad head of his cock, squeezing along his full length, all while sliding her other hand up and down that fat, heavy shaft.

Sunny joined them, and then Igmutaka rolled close and took control. Of the four of them, Star knew he'd had the most experience with groups of lovers, and she practically laughed around her mouthful of Fen. She had a feeling that tonight, no matter how tired they might be, she'd be making up for any experience she might be lacking.

Ig quickly had Sunny on her back with Star between her thighs. Sunny whimpered when Star dipped her head and immediately began feasting between her legs. She was quickly lost in the flavors and textures of Sunny—her friend for most of her life, and now her bonded mate.

With her butt in the air and her mouth buried between Sunny's thighs, Star sensed movement behind her. She turned a bit and glanced out of the corner of her eye.

Fen knelt behind her with that huge cock of his wrapped in his right fist. She felt the broad glans brush her labia, and then he leaned forward. Slowly, smoothly, he slid all the way inside. She groaned and lifted her mouth away from Sunny for a few agonizingly sweet moments as Fen filled her.

He paused when his sac rested against her labia, and she felt her muscles ripple along his full length. Then he slowly, carefully, began to thrust.

This was absolutely surreal. And arousing. Gods be damned, but Ig could have spent hours merely watching the women. Both so beautiful, each one totally unique. Fair Sunny lying on her back with her long blond hair spread beneath her shoulders and flowing across the mattress, with Mikaela Star kneeling between Sunny's bent knees, her dark, curly hair tangling over Sunny's pale belly, the deep bronze color of Star's slim back an exclamation point of color against Sunny's fairness. Both women were close in height—his mate maybe a couple inches taller than Sunny—but they were built the same, both of them gorgeous in their own way, and their similarities outweighed their differences.

He watched as Fen slipped his huge cock deep inside Mikaela Star's pussy. She was his mate—after so many years, his—and yet it was such a beautiful sight, watching as Fen slowly, carefully filled her that it affected Igmutaka on a spiritual level. He was so tightly connected to Fen that he felt as if he was the one pressing forward, experiencing the taut ripple of muscles over his cock. Ig wrapped his hand around his own thick erection and began to slowly stroke himself. Up, down, and back up again, rolling his palm over the tip, adding another layer to the sensations.

It seemed to take forever before Fen stopped pressing forward and he paused, straightening his back and seating himself even deeper. Watching them, his fingers still tightly clasped around his own shaft, Ig chuckled—he'd sighed at the same time Fen and Mikaela Star sighed.

Fen held very still. Curious, Ig opened to his thoughts, and this time he laughed out loud. Fen was softly cursing in Finnish, but Ig understood him perfectly—he was telling himself not to come, to hang on, to think of anything but how good this felt.

Ig sympathized. He wasn't even involved in their ménage and yet he was ready to blow his load all over the place.

Fen turned and met his gaze, and the corner of his lips curved into a smile. "Ig? Behind me. You top, okay?"

For all the times he'd done exactly that with other men, Ig's mouth still went dry, but he nodded. This wasn't just anyone—it was Fen, and Igmutaka wasn't really sure how either of them would feel about it when he took a position superior to the man.

As much as they loved one another, they still had so much to learn about each other, and without any words between them, Igmutaka realized he had quickly accepted Fen's more dominant role.

All of them were new to this intense polyamorous bond, a relationship unlike anything any of them had experienced. Each of them wanting to learn more, to discover more, and yet afraid of hurting what they were so carefully building. But Fen had asked. It had been his idea, and it was exactly what Ig wanted.

Then he made himself think of anything but how good this was going to feel. Of how hot he already was, because if he let himself imagine what was coming, he'd be lucky to last ten seconds.

The tube of lubricant was still lying on the floor where he and Fen had left it, but at least there was some left. Ig put a generous amount in his palm and then scooped up enough with his fingers to spread it down the crease between Fen's firm cheeks. He paused a moment, admiring, and almost laughed out loud.

Years ago, before the first time he'd done this with Adam Wolf after first gaining his human form, he'd never noticed another man's ass. Even after sex with Adam and then so many other male members of the pack, he'd not focused on the physical beauty of other men. He'd seen them all as potential sexual partners but never as mates, never as objects of beauty.

Now he found himself checking out the lean, muscular curves of Fen's butt like he was some sort of connoisseur, and he had to admit, he liked what he saw. He ran one hand over Fen's taut flank, loving the way his touch made Fen tremble.

Ig settled himself on his knees between Fen's thighs and stroked his erection with the stuff left in his palm with one hand while working that tight opening in Fen's ass with his other.

He watched carefully as Fen stroked slowly and deeply into Mikaela Star, finding his own rhythm through theirs. As soon as he felt it, felt the thrumming rhythm of their loving, felt the beat of their hearts in his heart, Ig knew he was ready. He took a deep, calming breath, pushed against Fen's tight ring of muscle, and carefully pressed forward.

It was fascinating to watch, the way that puckered opening slowly spread for his huge cock, how the broad head of his glans reshaped to fit through the taut ring of muscle. He felt pressure around his glans as he breached the opening, the slight give of muscle before he finally slid inside.

Watching as objectively as he could, Ig realized each of them made an equal adjustment to allow one very large penis through a correspondingly small opening and on into an extremely tight space.

A tight, hot, wet, slick muscular space that rippled along his full length, and damn but it was worth it. He sighed and Fen groaned. Ig paused, giving Fen a chance to adjust to the pain of entry, to turn that pain into pleasure. Holding perfectly still, he stroked Fen's flanks as if he were gentling a stallion.

After a moment, Fen's head fell forward and he began to move inside Mikaela Star once again. Ig followed, slowly, carefully, until he felt the soft brush of his balls against Fen's butt. Together, they found their rhythm once again.

And Sunny—dear, wonderful Sunny—opened her thoughts as Igmutaka completed the link, connecting all of them in this singular act shared so intimately by each. Sprawled beneath all of them, lost in pleasure, she whimpered softly and lifted her hips to bring her pussy closer to Star's mouth.

With lips and tongue, teeth and fingers, Star took Sunny closer to that amazing precipice. A precipice shared.

Sunny's arousal was Fen's. It was Star's and Igmutaka's. He was caught in their shared experience. Caught in an overwhelming, beautiful, mystical, and arousing connection of desire, of need and fulfillment, of love unlike anything he'd ever known in all his long life.

Caught up in the moment, he leaned over Fen's back, stretched his arm beyond Mikaela Star's slim shoulders, and caught Sunny's hand. He tugged her fingers, pulled them close enough to kiss her palm just once, intending to make their connection even more profound.

Images exploded in his mind. Sensations flared, a visual flash of light and heat, of sensations shared. He was Fen, filling Mikaela Star with each powerful stroke, taking that huge cock of Igmutaka's deep inside, loving the burn and stretch, the pleasure edged with pain, and feeling connected as he never had before.

He was Mikaela Star, so in love with her spirit guide after so many years of wanting him, loving the way it felt with Fen's big body covering hers while Igmutaka stroked deep inside Fen, filling her with sensation.

He was Sunny Daye, and yet he tasted Sunny's flavors through the connection with Mikaela Star, just as he experienced the purity of Sunny's love, her powerful sense of being one soul, one single being who was part of this amazing connection, this singular sexual experience where each of them shared and felt and loved together. Not alone. Never again alone.

Ig reached out, pushing the mating bond to Fen, to Sunny, and to his beloved Mikaela Star, catching the link as it came back to him from each of them. The big loft glowed with the power of their bond, with the sense that their connection was growing stronger with this night's loving.

The climax, when it hit, was a tsunami rolling over all of them, a wave of power beyond anything Igmutaka had experienced.

And when it ended, when they lay there with limbs trembling and lungs struggling to draw enough air, it took a few moments for Ig to realize they weren't in the cabin anymore.

The mattresses were gone; the log walls nowhere to be seen. At least Ig and Star and . . . *Oh, crap.* He had a moment of panic, but thank the goddess Sunny was here, too. Fen clasped her hand in his, holding on for dear life, gasping for each breath as his initial panic subsided.

Finally, he raised his head and gazed around.

They lay in a field of emerald green with an impossibly blue sky overhead. Trees surrounded them, but the colors were too bright, the growth too perfect. It felt oddly familiar, but not. He nudged Ig, whispering, "Where the fuck are we?"

Ig shook his head and blinked. Gazed around and blinked again. "I think we're on the astral. But how?"

Sunny slowly sat up and shoved her hair out of her eyes. "Definitely the astral." She grinned at Ig and Fen. "Damn, you guys must really be good. I mean, Ig's made me see stars on occasion, but actually leave the planet?" Laughing, she grabbed Star's shoulder. "Star? Wake up."

"Huh?" Star sat up and shook her head. "What's going on?"

"I think we orgasmed ourselves right onto the astral plane."

"No, we didn't. Did we?" Eyes wide, she glanced around. "But why? How?" She focused on Igmutaka. "What's going on? Eve's got to be behind it. Do you see her?"

Fen stood and slowly turned, looking for Eve, for anyone who might explain what had happened. Then he saw it—a silvery shimmer beneath a huge tree not twenty feet away. "Over there, I think."

Ig, Star, and Sunny stood as well, and together they watched as the shimmer took form and shape, and within moments, the beautiful woman Fen had seen at Anton's home was standing there in a long white gown, smiling at the four of them.

Fen couldn't help himself. He leaned over and whispered in Sunny's ear. "Toto? It appears we're not in Kansas anymore."

17

He'd seen her only the one time, but there was no mistaking the goddess Eve. Fen fought a powerful urge to fall to his knees, but since the others remained standing, he managed to stay on his feet.

"Welcome." Smiling, Eve moved closer, and her form was entirely solid on this plane. Not the translucent figure Fen had seen at Anton's. She reached for Fen's hand and Ig's. "You have no idea what you have accomplished, but the Mother wants you to know she is pleased and very appreciative."

"But why?" Fen glanced at Ig and then back at Eve. "What's going on?"

"Sit, and let me explain. Sunny and Star, you too. I've missed you so much." She waved a hand, and there was a picnic blanket at their feet with a large hamper of food.

Though they'd just eaten a huge dinner, Fen realized he was hungry again. Confused, not really sure what was expected, he took a seat beside Sunny. Ig and Star sat across from them, and Eve sat gracefully between the two men.

"Please. Eat, and I'll explain what I can." She waved her hand, and glasses of wine appeared. She snatched one for herself, grabbing it out of the air. Fen tried not to stare, but it was impossible. This had been a day to beat all others.

Eve took a sip and then set the glass aside. "The Mother is all powerful, but she doesn't know all the answers. Creatures with free will have a habit of making choices that sometimes make no sense at all to any of us on the astral, but it is not our place to run your lives, merely to help where we are able.

"Anyway, with that in mind, the Mother does, on occasion, get visions with glimpses of a possible future. The future really can't be determined until it happens, but then it's the present, right?" She shrugged and gazed at all of them, but Fen decided she really wasn't expecting an answer.

Smiling, Eve continued. "Anyway, she had one that was absolutely terrifying, foretelling the end of your world. An ending caused by nuclear annihilation in a pointless little war started by a small group of terrorists. The men that you helped capture were the seeds of that group. They had to be stopped so the plan would not only never be carried out but never be conceived. Your actions, and those of the FBI agent you helped, have cut a thread that had the potential to unravel entirely, to destroy everything we know and love."

"But you couldn't tell us anything?" Ig leaned forward, and he was obviously pissed. "You couldn't let us know what we were facing?"

Eve shook her head. "No, because we didn't know. All the Mother was sure of is that those men needed to be stopped. And Fen needed to be found." She smiled at Fen, and something inside him cracked open and began to blossom.

"The jade wolf." He touched his amulet and then stared at her. "And Ig's jade puma. They're connected, but how?"

She nodded and closed her eyes, and he sensed that the goddess was drawing from memories even she hadn't recalled. Not until now.

"After the first Chanku arrived on this world, after they began to disperse and their powers slowly faded, they realized there was a need for spirit guides who would help their people adjust to their new lives. They infused the carved jade with the same powers that you take from the grasses in Tibet. During that time, Liana, who was the goddess, lost track of her people, but it appears that there were at least two spirit guides created."

Ig glanced at Fen. "But he's not ancient; not like I am."

"In a way he is, Igmutaka. When Fen was born, his mother drew on her wolven side and refused to turn him over to the ancients to be trained as a guide. She hid him. He grew up as a wolf, grew old, and eventually died. And was reborn, more than once, but each time, he was hidden away."

She smiled at Fen, and there was a sense of life, of warmth in her smile that filled him. There was knowledge in that smile as well, and he would save it, store it away to look at later. Later, when he wasn't sitting in an impossible place with a woman who couldn't possibly exist.

"Over and over, you have returned, Fen," she said. "But your fate was always to be hidden from the destiny originally intended for you. The jade wolf appeared with each reincarnation, and that is your link to the spirit world. The Mother had no idea where you were, and I had no idea I should even be looking. Until now."

She rested her hand on Fen's shoulder and stared into his eyes. "What happened to your mother was both her destiny and yours. Your father was merely the instrument, but you are needed now, in this modern world, more than you were ever needed in the past. Even so, I am sorry for your pain, for your mother's loss."

As Eve's words washed over him, Fen tried to remember a life before this one, but there was nothing.

"No." Eve shook her head. "You would not recall those past lives, though it should explain your affinity for Igmutaka. You are both of the Berserker line, chosen because you are strong and powerful and command respect by virtue of your inborn qualities of leadership."

"But I thought Berserkers were killers." Fen glanced at Igmutaka, who merely shrugged.

"No, not because of the breed. Originally, in a time long past on a world that no longer exists, Berserkers were created to protect, to be powerful warriors loyal to their Chanku brothers. The name originally meant 'protector,' but there are always those who will try to corrupt power. With your amazing intelligence, strength, and size, you can become a vicious enemy, but it is your choice, not your destiny.

"This is not a foretelling. It is merely what the Mother and I have talked of between ourselves, that you and Igmutaka will be valuable assets to the Chanku population as they are faced with many problems in the coming years. Humans resent Chanku, and they will continue to search for ways to rid the world of your kind, or to exploit you. But you will persevere. Chanku are a strong and resilient race. You have the Mother and me on your side. And you have so much love."

She gazed at all of them before smiling broadly. "Eat. Loving each other as you do burns a lot of calories."

Sunny yawned and sat up. The bedding was tumbled in every direction, and she was pleasantly sore from the night's activity. Star slept soundly beside her, but Ig and Fen were gone.

From the tantalizing smell of coffee and bacon, she knew exactly where to find them. She left Star sleeping, grabbed a robe against the morning chill, and headed down the stairs.

Ig was in the kitchen frying bacon, and Fen sat at the counter drinking coffee. She slipped up behind him and kissed his shoulder. Some of the love bites she'd left on his neck a couple nights ago showed in the morning light. She thought about leaving a new one, but he turned and gave her such a sexy grin, all she could think about was not melting in a puddle at his feet.

"G'morning, sleepyhead." He kissed her and she yawned.

"Did we really end up on the astral last night?"

"We did. Did we really come back here and make love half the night?"

"We did, which is probably why I'm a bit stiff and sore this morning. In a good way."

"Where's Star?"

"Here."

Sunny turned and broke out in the giggles. Star's hair stood up in all directions. She'd put on a pair of Fen's boxer shorts and an old T-shirt that looked like something her dad might have left behind. It reached almost to the hem of the shorts and had definitely seen better days. "I need coffee," she said, heading straight for the pot.

A minute later she handed a mug to Sunny and took a seat across from Fen. "Is anyone going to explain what happened last night?"

Fen nodded sagely. "We saved the world, had a picnic with a goddess and maybe even the Mother of all, and came back here and screwed the night away. Nothing exciting."

Star growled. "I thought it was a bad dream."

Ig walked over and gave Star a kiss, and then went back to the bacon he was cooking. Sunny had never seen him looking so domestic with his hair tied back in a long tail; faded, baggy sweats hanging from his lean hips; and an apron tied loosely around his waist.

"Not a bad dream, unfortunately. Anton contacted me early

this morning. The chopper's fixed and they're back in San Francisco but planning to head home to Montana later this afternoon. He confirmed a lot of what Eve said. The guys we stopped were part of a terror cell that's been operating in the U.S. for years. They're naturally born U.S. citizens, so they can't be deported, but no one has been able to catch them at anything they could be locked up for until now."

"But we've stopped them?" Sunny snuggled beside Fen. "I'm good with that. We can't do everything."

"We did enough, for now."

Fen leaned close and kissed her. She loved the way his lips felt on hers. Loved him. She kissed him back.

"But I think it means we'll have to be vigilant," he said. "It means watching out for more than merely our own interests." He kissed her again. "Have I told you this morning that I love you? A lot."

She smiled against his lips. "You can tell me again."

He laughed, then he reached across the counter and looped his fingers behind Star's neck and pulled her close for a kiss. "And I love you, too. And that big lug burning the bacon. But I sure hope you're up for a truly crazy future, because it appears Ig and I have some sort of weird destiny between us."

"What?" Sunny grabbed his arm. "I didn't hear that. What are you talking about?"

Fen glanced at Igmutaka. "Do you want to do the honors?"

Ig shrugged. "Sure. Fen and I both dreamed a deeper conversation with the Mother. Because of our extra abilities."

"Abilities connected with those jade pendants we've got," Fen added.

"We may be called on, on occasion, to deal with issues that aren't really issues, yet." Ig lifted the pieces of bacon out of the pan as he talked and laid them on folded paper towels to drain. "The Mother doesn't know everything, like Eve said, but she gets feelings. Sort of like Anton's premonitions but on a grander scale."

"But Ig and I agree, and we've told Eve." Fen glanced at Igmutaka and they both looked grim. "We will do nothing without your approval." He focused on Sunny. "You and Star have to be all in on this, or we'll tell the Mother no, that we can't serve her in that capacity. This mating, the four of us, means that all of us are part of any decision."

Sunny glanced at Star and they both started laughing. "You're kidding, right?" She leaned close and kissed Fen, and then shot a loving smile at Igmutaka. His glance went from her to Star and back again. He was frowning.

Shaking her head at the cluelessness of the males in her life, Sunny had to bite back a laugh. "Don't you get it, guys? We are one person. The four of us are mated. Me and Ig and Star as well as you, Fen. What is important to one of us is important to all of us."

Star nodded and reached across the counter to grab Sunny's hand. "I've heard my parents joke about Anton and Stefan's ongoing argument over destiny versus random happenings, and I think we've all, including Stefan, come down on the same side as Anton. There are things we are fated to do. Eve called this your destiny, Fen. That makes it our destiny. All of us, together."

He stood and wrapped his arms around Sunny. She felt his love, his acceptance of the changes in their lives, and his excitement for whatever was to come.

He kissed the top of her head and then rested his chin in her hair. "Ig? Why don't you get in touch with Anton. See if they can swing by and pick us up on the way back to Montana. Is that okay with you, sweetheart?"

Oh yeah. Definitely okay. "I'm ready."

So am I, sweetheart. So am I. "I figure destiny will find us, no matter where we are."

"S'okay," she said. "As long as we're together."

"I like the sound of that." Fen sat on the stool and pulled Sunny into his lap. He gazed at Star and then shot a smile at Igmutaka. "Together. The four of us. Works for me."

Turn the page for a special excerpt
from the first book in
Kate Douglas's new Spirit Wild series

DARK WOLF

An Aphrodisia trade paperback on sale now!

1

Crickets chirped. An owl hooted. A dusting of starlight shimmered faintly against granite peaks, but here at the forest's edge, all was dark. Shivering slightly in the cool night air, Sebastian Xenakis stood beneath the gnarled oak, just one more shadow among many. With great humility and as much confidence as he could muster while standing naked in the darkness, he raised his arms, drew on the magic coursing through his veins, and once more called on the spirit within the tree, one he affectionately thought of as *the lady*, humbly asking for her strength.

Nothing.

"Damn it all." He exhaled, accepting the rush of air for what it was—a huge blast of frustration at the serendipitous nature of his magic. He stared at the massive tree towering overhead and methodically emptied his mind of all thoughts, all distractions. He put aside anger and frustration, fears and hopes, leaving room for nothing but *here* and *now*. Focusing everything within, he opened his heart to possibilities, and waited.

A few long, frustrating minutes later, he felt her warmth envelop him. An unexpected frisson raced across his bare shoulders, along his arms. It caressed his naked buttocks and swirled over his belly, lifting the dark line of body hair that trailed from navel to groin. Then it slithered along his thighs, circled his calves, and tickled across his bare feet. His cock, flush with hot blood, swelled high and hard against his belly, giving homage to the gift of power.

Then, sliding away as soft as a whisper, the intimate sense of touch, of sentient communion, bled off into the damp loam and returned to its source through thickly tangled roots. Sebastian sighed, a shuddering acceptance of sensual pleasure, the gift of contact with such a powerful force.

The lady of the oak.

His erection remained, strong evidence of her touch, the visceral connection he'd made with a spirit ancient beyond recorded memory. His body thrummed with her life force, with her power, until Sebastian felt each and every one of her thick and twisted branches spreading far and wide, until he bowed beneath the age and innate wisdom of the ancient tree. This mother oak must have stood here, a silent sentinel of the forest since long before the dawn of modern history. A few heavy branches had fallen over time, but he knew her roots were strong, her branches healthy. As if challenging time itself, the graceful beauty and symmetry of the tree remained.

He remembered the first time he saw the oak, recalled the sense of life, the sure knowledge of the tree's spiritual power. It was on that day he'd learned his father wielded the kind of power Sebastian had quickly grown to crave.

Standing just beyond the reach of the great branches, unsure of his relationship with a man he barely knew, Sebastian had watched Aldo Xenakis call lightning out of a clear, star-filled sky—call it and control it with the deft hands of a master.

He'd been seduced so easily, so quickly by that flashy show of fire and magic. Of power. Immeasurable power. So thoroughly seduced he knew he might never break free of its siren call.

Might never break free of the man he'd consciously sought, despite his mother's warning. Now it was much too late. His die had been cast, commitments made, and he was almost glad his mother was dead.

Glad she couldn't see what he'd become.

Sebastian quickly shoved thoughts of his moral weakness, his failures—and his father—aside. There was no need to mar the beauty of this night. He took a deep breath and then, almost as an afterthought, cleared his mind of all obstructions and drew more power to him. Pulled it from the earth, from the sky, from the water of a nearby stream, from the mountain itself. The fire must come from within, but he called on that as well and felt the power build.

Then he buffered the swirling energy with the strength of the oak until it was entirely under his control. Until he was the one holding the power.

Unlike his father, unwilling to display or even acknowledge such arrogance, Sebastian turned and bowed his head toward the oak, giving the tree's spirit his grateful thanks for her help. Then, spreading his fingers wide, he consciously breathed deeply and opened himself to the energy flowing into him from all directions. A brilliant glow surrounded him, but it wasn't lightning that lit the dark night.

It was power. Raw power he'd pulled from the earth, from the air and water. From the spirit in the tree and the fire burning in his soul.

Within seconds, the light blinked out. Gone as if it had never existed at all.

As was the man. In his place, a wolf darker than night raised its head and sniffed the air. Then it turned away and raced into the forest.

* * *

"Lily? Have you seen this morning's news?"

Lily Cheval fumbled with the phone and squinted at the bedside clock in the early morning darkness. Blue numbers blurred into focus. Her best buddy looked at her out of the screen on her phone. "Alex, it's six fifteen in the morning. On a Sunday. What can possibly be important enough to . . ."

"There's been another one, Lil. Just inside the entrance to the park this time."

Lily bit back a growl and sat up. The last body, discovered less than a week ago, had been found along the highway leading into Glacier National Park in Montana. Much too close to the Chanku pack's main residence. The one before that had been on the outskirts of Kalispell. "What have you got?"

Alex sighed and wiped a hand across his eyes. Poor Alex. How he'd ever ended up as the pack's liaison to the Flathead County sheriff's department was beyond understanding. He might be brilliant and charismatic—not to mention drop-dead gorgeous—but he was not cut out to deal with, much less deliver, bad news, especially early on a Sunday morning.

She wondered if he'd even made it to bed the night before. His eyes looked bloodshot, and Alex did love his social life on a Saturday night.

Even in Kalispell.

"Same as the last seven," he said, pulling her back into the conversation. "Young woman, beaten, brutally raped. Throat torn out. Just like the others, probably killed somewhere else and dumped. A park ranger found her body beside the road."

"Shit. I hope you've got an alibi." She hated having to ask, but with public sentiment the way it had been heading . . .

"I was with Jennifer last night. I got the call on the way home this morning."

Jennifer. Poor choice of woman, but at least she could account for Alex's time when the attack occurred. Frustrated,

Lily dug her fingers into her tangled hair and tugged. Anything to help focus her thoughts. "Let me know what you find out. Check with the pack. See if they've got any new leads. I'm stuck in San Francisco until after the reception, but I'll try and get up there by the weekend."

"Okay. Sorry to wake you, but I just wanted to warn you. Be careful. Whoever's behind this, they've hit the Bay Area just as hard. I'll find out what I can. Thanks, Lil."

Quietly Lily set the phone back in the charger and leaned against the headboard. Another young woman dead. Another murder with all the signs of a wild animal attack—except for the rape.

Just like the other seven.

Eight young women, dead by a combination of man and beast. Five in or near Glacier National Park. Three in the San Francisco Bay Area.

And where were the largest populations of Chanku shapeshifters?

"Glacier National Park and the San Francisco Bay Area. Shit." A chilling sense of premonition shuddered along Lily's spine. If they didn't find the one behind this, and find him soon, someone was going to be hunting Chanku.

The sharp click of Lily's heels echoed against the pale gray walls of Cheval International, one of the more profitable branches of Chanku Global Industries. She walked quickly toward her office, wishing she could ignore the tension headache pounding in sharp counterpoint to her footsteps.

Her father insisted headaches were purely psychosomatic—according to Anton Cheval, Chanku shapeshifters were impervious to human frailties. "Tell that to my head," she muttered, timing the steady throbbing between her eyes against the click of her heels.

Damn. She did not need a headache. Not on a Monday, not with a full day of meetings ahead, including lunch with the mayor and a one-on-one with the head of security.

Resentment of the long-lived Chanku shapeshifters had been simmering for years, but the recent series of attacks against young women had brought that simmer to a boil. It didn't help that a local celebrity had taken a very public stance against the Chanku, blaming them for everything from the current downturn in the economy to the vicious rapes and murders.

Aldo Xenakis had been a thorn in Lily's side ever since she'd assumed leadership of Cheval International. Recently, his verbal attacks had taken on a frighteningly personal slant.

It didn't help that he owned a massive amount of land that abutted her father's vast holdings in Montana. It was bad enough he was stirring up resentment here in California, but Montana was home. Having longtime friends and neighbors turn against them hurt Lily and the rest of the pack on a much more personal level. They'd worked hard at being good neighbors, at integrating themselves into the community.

Now this.

"Good morning, Ms. Cheval."

"G'morning, Jean." Lily paused in front of her assistant's desk. "Have you got today's calendar?"

Jean nodded. Gray haired, round-faced, and very human, she'd been Lily's assistant since Lily'd been named CEO of the company seven years earlier. And, while Jean continued to age, Lily still looked as youthful and fresh as the day she'd walked out of UC Berkeley with her MBA.

One more reason for humans to resent shapeshifters, though she'd never noticed any resentment at all from Jean. Considering the good pay and generous benefit packages all CGI employees—including all Cheval International hires—received, she didn't expect it to become an issue.

Lily glanced over the daily calendar Jean handed to her. The morning wasn't too busy, but . . . "Why have you got a question mark by my lunch date with the mayor?"

Jean shook her head. "Her office called a few minutes ago. When the mayor's schedule went out to the media yesterday, they forgot to black out your lunch appointment. Reporters know when and where you're meeting, and the mayor said she'd understand if you decide to cancel."

The pounding between her eyes got worse. Goddess, but it had been too long since she'd shifted and run. Right now, Lily really wanted to chase down something furry and kill it. "Not necessary," she said, rubbing her temple. "We really need to talk. Maybe I'll wear a disguise."

Jean grinned as she gave her an appraising look. "Don't think that would help. You're hard to miss."

Lily raised her eyebrows and glanced at Jean. "Thank you. I think." She grabbed the mail Jean handed to her and headed toward her office, but paused at the door. "I'm expecting a call from Alex Aragat. Be sure and put him through even if I'm on something else."

"Okay." The phone rang, but before answering it, Jean added, "You'll find a list of the calls you need to return on your desk. Uhm, more than a few from your father." Lily just shook her head when Jean laughed and said, "He wanted to remind you not to forget the reception Thursday night."

"I wish," Lily muttered, but she turned and smiled at Jean. "I won't. And even if I wanted to, dear old Dad would make sure I got there on time."

Lily shut the office door as Jean took her call. She glanced at the clock over the bookcase. Seven thirty, which meant that with any luck, she'd have time to get her desk cleared before lunch. Her head was still pounding like a damned jackhammer, but she flopped down in the comfortable chair behind her desk and read through Jean's messages. All were carefully organized by importance. The stack from her father—and damn, but how many times had the man called?—was set off to one side.

Obviously, he was already awake. Might as well check in with the boss first. The phone rang as she reached for it. She glanced at the caller ID, sighed, and flipped on the video.

"Hello, Dad. I was just getting ready to call you."

"How's your headache?"

She frowned at his smug image. "How do you know I've got a headache?"

"Because I've been trying to mindspeak all morning and I know you're blocking me."

"Oh." No wonder her head hurt. She'd developed the habit of keeping her shields high and tight since she was just a child, but that never kept her father from trying. He'd rarely managed to give her a headache, though. "Well, if you knew you were giving me a headache, why'd you keep pushing?"

No answer. Typical. She was convinced he only heard what he wanted to hear.

"You've talked to Alex."

Not a question. He'd know, of course. Anton Cheval knew everything. "Yes. He called first thing yesterday morning, but he didn't have any details. I expect to hear more today. Have you learned anything else?"

"How well do you know Aldo Xenakis?"

"Not well at all," she said, used to her father's non sequiturs. Amazing . . . her headache was gone. She almost laughed. Dear old Dad had been the cause all along. "Why do you ask?"

"His son will be attending the reception Thursday night. I want you to meet him."

"He has a son? Since when? I thought Xenakis lived alone."

"The younger Xenakis has stayed in the background. From what I've learned, he didn't even know Aldo was his father until a couple of years ago. When the boy's mother died, he traced Aldo through her private papers."

"Interesting. Why do you think the son's important?"

"He's been staying at his father's home up here for the past month. You know where the house is. It's a few miles from our place, though our properties share the southern boundary. Tinker thought he smelled an unfamiliar wolf near the edge of our holdings night before last. He traced the scent to a ridge on the Xenakis property. The wolf scent disappeared, but he picked up the trail of a man and followed it to the house. The only one there was a young man who appeared to be Xenakis's son."

"He's Chanku?" Now that would be interesting, considering how xenophobic the father was.

"We don't know. The elder Xenakis has powerful magic. If the son inherited his father's gift, he could be shifting by magical means, not natural. I want you to get close enough, see if you sense anything."

"Do you think he's our murderer?"

"I don't know, Lily. But the women have been killed near Kalispell and in the San Francisco Bay Area. Xenakis has homes in both places, and his son spends time at both locations. I've got Alex looking into his schedule now, checking flight records, that sort of thing. Be very careful."

"One question. What's his name? How will I know him?"

"Sebastian. I don't know what surname he used before, but he's taken his father's name. Look for Sebastian Xenakis. Tinker says he's tall with dark hair. And really odd eyes. Teal blue, according to Tink. Not amber like most of us. And, Lily?"

"Yes?"

"I love you, sweetheart, but I have a bad feeling about this. Be very careful. We don't know a thing about this guy, but he's got my sense of premonition in high gear. No specific danger, just a strong feeling he'll have some kind of effect on our family."

Lily stared at the handset long after her father had ended the call. The pack might tease Anton Cheval about his premonitions, but invariably he'd been proven correct. She flipped on her computer and typed in Sebastian Xenakis's name.

It never hurt to be fully informed about the enemy.

"Lily. So glad you agreed to meet even after my office bungled this so badly."

"Well, hopefully the media haven't bugged the dining room." Lily smiled at the mayor and shook her hand. "It's good to see you, Jill." Then she nodded toward the group of reporters gathered just outside the restaurant. "I was hoping they were here for you, not me. It's been awhile since I've run a gauntlet like that."

Mayor Jill Bradley shook her head as she reached for the menu. "It's the killings, Lily. We're doing everything we can to keep a lid on things, but . . ."

"I know." Sighing, Lily reached for her own menu. "I heard from Alex Aragat, our pack's law enforcement liaison in Montana. People are scared, and I can't blame them. My father's got every available resource working on this from our angle."

Jill shook her head. "My gut feeling is that it's not a Chanku killing these girls. I think someone's trying to raise public anger against shifters."

Lily had to agree. "Dad feels the same way, but until this guy is stopped . . ."

"Or they. DNA is inconclusive, but I've been told it points to more than one perp. Wolves, definitely, but possibly more than one human committing the rapes."

Crap. "They've narrowed it down to wolves?"

"Yes. We're keeping a lid on that info." Jill spread her hands in a helpless gesture. "Your people are catching enough flak as it is."

"No kidding. Is it a single male? If a woman had consensual sex before the attack, it could explain more than one."

Jill nodded. "There's one consistent set, a few variables. That's the conclusion. For now."

The waitress reached their table before Lily could respond. Jill set her menu down to place her order; Lily closed hers and studied the mayor. Jill Bradley had held her post for almost five years now, and her popularity had yet to wane. She'd become a good friend and a powerful ally, a woman Lily would have liked and admired even if she hadn't been the mayor.

It never hurt to have friends in high places. Smart friends. The fact that she had already considered what Lily figured was happening was a good sign. She glanced up and realized the waitress was waiting patiently for her order.

"Hamburger. Rare." Lily smiled at the waitress, waiting for the admonition that rare beef wasn't safe. Instead, she got a saucy wink. "You got it. Be back in a minute with your wine."

"Did we order wine?"

Jill laughed. "It's on me. I figured you could use a glass about now. I know I sure can. Let's discuss the reception and your father's generous donation. The other topic is too frustrating when we don't have any answers."

"I agree. I think we're being set up, but I'm not sure it's more than one person."

Jill's dark brows drew down. "You'll let me know if you learn anything to substantiate that, won't you?"

"Of course. I mentioned Alex Aragat, our pack liaison with law enforcement in Kalispell. He's working on a couple of things, but at this point it's all supposition."

The waitress reached the table and opened a bottle of wine. She poured a taste for the mayor, who sipped and quickly agreed.

"I'll have your meals in a few minutes. Enjoy." Smiling, the young woman moved on to another table.

Lily tipped her glass in a toast to her friend. "Here's to the new wing at the museum. I saw it this weekend. It's turned out beautifully."

"Thanks to your father's generosity."

Lily dipped her head, acknowledging the mayor's comment. Anton Cheval, via Chanku Global Industries and its subsidiary, Cheval International, had become a generous benefactor over the years, and Jill Bradley's status as mayor had benefited greatly from his many gifts to the city during her administration.

"Consorting with the local fauna, Mayor Bradley?"

Lily fought the urge to spin around and glare. Instead, she sat perfectly still, outwardly calm and relaxed, though she raised one eyebrow at the mayor. Jill set her wine on the table and glowered at the man beyond Lily's shoulder.

"There's no call for such rude behavior, Aldo. You're interrupting a private lunch."

Lily slowly turned in her chair, at a disadvantage to the tall, elegant man standing much too close behind her for comfort. The hairs along her spine rose and she bit back a growl. She'd never met Aldo Xenakis in person, but the man was on the news often enough. Lately he'd made a point of baiting Chanku shapeshifters, and Lily Cheval in particular. She recognized him immediately.

Shoving her chair back, she stood while privately enjoying the satisfaction of watching him back up when he realized she met him at eye level. "Ah, Mr. Xenakis. I'd say it's a pleasure, but we both know differently." She smiled, showing a lot of teeth, and held out her hand. He stared at it a moment. Lily didn't waver. Reluctantly, he shook hands.

The frisson of awareness left her wanting to wash her hands. There was something wrong about Xenakis. Something she couldn't place. Oddly enough, it wasn't her Chanku sense that left her skin crawling.

No. It was her magic, something as much a part of her as her

Chanku heritage. Her innate power recoiled almost violently at the man's brief touch.

Lily surreptitiously wiped her palm against her slim skirt. She noticed that Jill wasn't the least bit welcoming. "Was there something you wanted, Aldo? Ms. Cheval and I are enjoying a private lunch while we discuss business."

She placed her emphasis firmly on *private.*

"No." He stepped back and nodded. "I merely saw a beautiful woman sitting here and took a chance to say hello." He kept his gaze planted firmly on Jill and blatantly ignored Lily.

Lily remained standing, purposefully invading his space until the waitress arrived with their meals. Aldo stepped out of her way and then left without another word. Lily turned, sat, and raised her eyebrow again as she glanced at Jill.

Jill shook her head. The moment the waitress was gone, she took a sip of her wine. "I do not like that man. Something about him . . ."

Lily nodded. "Makes your skin crawl?"

"Exactly. Why? He's handsome enough. Well mannered."

"Rich and powerful." Lily laughed. "I bet he's asked you out."

"He did, and like a fool, I accepted. I couldn't wait for the evening to end."

"Did he make a pass?"

Jill shook her head. "Nothing so obvious, but he makes me very uncomfortable. Just a feeling I wasn't safe with him."

Lily took a bite of her blood-rare hamburger and swallowed. "You sure you're not Chanku? You've always got good intuition."

"No. Not a drop. I was tested. Took the nutrients for two weeks. Not even a hint of the need to howl." She shrugged and turned her attention to her salad.

Lily used her French fry as a pointer. "I'm sorry. I think you could have given the guys in my pack a run for their money."

Jill sipped her wine. "I still can. I just have to do it on two legs."

They both laughed, but at the same time, the fact she'd tried the nutrients meant Jill had hoped she was Chanku. Lily was sorry for her, for the fact that her friend had wanted something badly enough to go for it, yet failed.

It was something Jill had to accept she could never have. Lily wondered what that would be like, to want something that was totally impossible, something forever out of reach.

They concentrated on their food for a bit. Then Jill set her fork down. "You know, Lily. I think the world of you, and I really love your folks. You're good people. All of you, your mom and dad especially. They give generously whenever there's a need, and they've done a lot for this city, even though they don't live here. I don't want to see these killings hurt any of you, but if we can't find the killer, I don't know how we're going to keep the anger under control. I worry about your safety."

Lily glanced toward the crowd of reporters waiting at the front door. The questions they'd thrown at her as she walked into the restaurant had been pointed and ugly. In their minds, shapeshifters were committing rapes and murders, and she was just as guilty as the ones actually doing the deed.

The sudden jackhammer inside her head had her gasping.

"Lily? Are you all right?"

Jill reached across the table and took her hand.

Lily pressed fingers to her skull. "Just a minute."

Her father's voice filled her mind.

There's been another killing, Lily. A woman's body was found about ten minutes ago in Golden Gate Park, not far from the garden your mother designed many years ago. If you're in a public place, you might want to find somewhere private to finish your lunch with the mayor.

"Shit." Lily took one more quick bite of her burger and tossed back the last of her wine, taking a moment to consider the consequences of her father's words. She focused on Jill, one of the few people aware that the Chanku were telepathic. "My father just contacted me. There's been another murder. The body was found about . . ."

The mayor's cell phone rang. She answered the call, but her gaze was glued to Lily. With a soft curse, she asked a couple of brief questions and then ended the call. "That was the chief of police. I'm needed back at City Hall." She stood up. "I'm sorry, Lily. I'll do what I can."

"I know. Thank you. Go ahead. I'll get lunch."

Jill was reaching for her handbag. "That's not . . ."

"Go. Call me later."

"I will." She slipped the strap to her purse over her shoulder and gave Lily a quick hug. "Later. And thank you."

Lily watched her walk away. A pleasant-looking woman in her early fifties, Jill Bradley looked like someone's mom, not like the head of one of the nation's largest, most diverse cities.

She walked as if she didn't have a care in the world, passing through the throng of reporters with a quick smile and a friendly greeting to the ones she knew.

Lily wished she had that kind of grace under fire. She handed her card to the waitress, signed the tab when it came after adding a sizeable tip for that perfectly prepared, almost raw burger, and walked toward the back of the restaurant.

There was no way she was going to try and get through the reporters. Nope. She'd take the coward's exit, through the kitchen and out the back.

And the first thing she'd do when she got back to the office was call Alex. The last murder had been in Montana, but this latest had happened barely a mile from her office.

She wondered where Sebastian Xenakis had been last night.